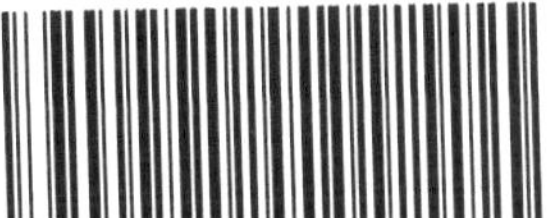

THE BIRTH OF LOS ANGELES 1767-1826

And the Genocide of the Tongva

Los Angeles County – The names of Native American Tongva villages and the current names:

Haapchivet = Chilao Flats above Tujunga.
Povuu'nga = Long Beach
Hu-Mali-wu = Malibu.
Topaa'nga = Topanga Canyon
Pemuu'nga = Catalina Island.
Tah-ur's villages = Banning and Rialto
Shevaanga = San Gabriel/Alhambra.
Yaanga (Yangna) = Downtown Los Angeles
Pasekeenga = Altadena.
Kaweenga = Hollywood/Universal City
Ashuukshanga = Azusa.
Pemookanga = Walnut/Pomona

Dedication: To all People of The Land, of All Continents, in their struggles against empires, to regain their identities, culture and to have proper compensation.

To my fourth grade classmate in 1951, Socorro, who shouted at our teacher "We are Not Extinct!" when the teacher said that the languageless, root digging Tongva/Gabrielino Tribe had died out and were replaced by 'civilization.'.

They are rebuilding. Their web sites are listed.

See EPILOG – Pg 477

CHAPTERS

PREFACE - THE CROWN

1534

VENIZIA, ITALIA

Lorenzo di Fiorenza. in commoner's clothing, made it his habit to sit in the central section of Cathredral San Marco with a clutch of advisors around him, watching the pairings of the powerful .

He rejoiced in the ecstatic quadraphonic waves of brass chiming from the four corners of the Cathedral playing one of his favorite Gabrieli canzonas. The trumpets and the lower horns imitated and echoed from four directions in heavenly conversation.

The material conversations, both before and after Mass, with important men of the secular and the sacred worlds were commonplace here, and in this setting, many turned to Lorenzo to resolve problems of the City States.

The choir was beginning it's entrance when a hurried set of hand signals to his right side pointed to a clandestine contact who often carried important information. He was an insider privy to dealings between the Vatican and the royal emissaries of the Spanish Court.

The man's demeanor indicated urgency. 'How can you interrupt me in this place!' Lorenzo thought with a dual annoyance as he watched the man shuffling in the aisle. 'How can you interrupt Gabrieli?' was the first annoyance, and, 'How can you keep our relationship from not being observed when you make a show of approaching me in a public place like this?'

The danger of the man appearing like this resonated deeply. It had to be of great importance for him to risk exposure. It seemed appropriate to leave.

He turned to Rudolfo at his right elbow and whispered. "Tell Carlo," the seated aide on the right aisle, "to greet him as an old friend and to walk him into San Marco. I'll turn right on leaving. They can follow me to the pottery vendor."

He left between movements with only Rudolfo accompanying him. He smiled and made 'I'll be back soon' symbols to the ones who caught his eye, noticing whether anyone was watching carefully or was following him out.

In the pottery store the furtively excited man described the details of an agreement with the Vatican to accompany a massive Spanish plan to colonize and control the entire 'New World' under the leadership of the Jesuit Order. The plan would be implemented within weeks. Ships were readied to sail from both Spain and Portugal.

Lorenzo leaned back against the side of the inner doorway feeling a bit dizzied and overwhelmed by the scope of the plan. 'How will this effect Florence? The independent City States? Venice? The control of Rome over us?'

"Can you get me more specific information?" He asked.

"Within the week. At your residence, Sire?" Knowing that he would be well paid for this personalized service.

"Yes, quickly. It will be worthwhile for you." seeing that this will bring a new stage to a greater Italy and Italian/Spanish relations, surely a step toward unification. All through the Vatican's control! 'New times indeed!' Seeing his world change in an instant

1542

FIRST CONTACT - LAND OF THE TONGVA

Condors and Golden Eagle Spirits circled the edge of a white spotted emerald sea, gliding over a shoreline of wide flat sand and a rock and brush sprinkled basin. A smoky haze rose from the fires of two hundred villages spread far inland on flat green; mountain and hilly plain stretching to an endless arid desert.

Agitated humans walked and ran, alone or in groups, to the coastline. They'd known their own six man longboats that paddled always between the coastal villages and the four islands, an hour's glide out to sea, but the view was different today.

They saw moving island/boats with human on them with brightly colored sheets of blood and grasslike material floating above the boats. Tribal runners came from the southern lands of the Kumaayay and beyond, spreading news of The Sea Visitors.

Runners left the coastal village of Puvung-na spreading to the north and northeast telling about the wonders at the beaches. People came in clumps to the coast to stare at the huge moving islands.

The Visitors came close to land, in the lands of the Tongva, and the watchers knew that the moving islands were boats made by humans. Creatures stood on the boats behind sides that looked like colored wood. Wood from huge trees. 'Where are trees that were that big?' The Creatures on the high points had shiny round heads. Humans? Those on the flat parts were also human-like with arm movements. Shouts were heard. Human!

The sheets above the boats were dizzyingly bright.

"How did they do that? What is that made from?" were common questions.

"It is some kind of fine weaving. A finer weave than the islanders of Pimu and the northern Chumash were making. From what?"

<<< 0 >>>

Captain Juan Cabrillo, his beard turning gray, was in pain from growing infections. The view from the ship showed a densely populated place that felt like a perfect place for a settlement. After weeks of mapping these new holdings of the Empire on the western coast of the Americas, there had been nothing like this. He turned to the lanky young Jesuit priest on the rail to his left.

"Look at that plain! It's the largest concentration of villages we've seen. Look at that smoke hanging in the air! Like Toledo's forges! There must be thousands of Indians here! What do you think? We should stop and plant the flag and Cross here."

The Father was pleased. He saw only curiosity from the natives. No display of weapons or shouting. It could be a docile flock. "This looks like an ideal spot"

Juan and the Jesuit entered a small boat and were lowered into the bay and rowed ashore by eight armed sailors. With the priest and four sailors, Juan waded onto the slope of the sand. The natives, 'Indians' ran toward him, stopping a stones throw from the newcomers, watching the visitors pound a long staff with the bright red and yellow flag of Spain into the sand and hoist and implant a seven foot tall crucifix.

Juan shouted in Portuguese to all sides. He repeated the statement in Spanish.

"In the name of the Empire of Spain, I claim this land for God and His Majesty King Philip the Second and the One True Church under Pope Paul the Third." Juan scooped up a handful of sand, chuckling at the name he'd chosen. "I name this land of those receiving the blessings of the Empire 'The Bay of the Smokes'" Juan and the priest walked backwards, blessing the crowds on the beach. They waved, looking back to shore as the choppy surf carried them back to their ship.

"What did he say? What are those?" The actions made no sense. "Why did they put the Four Directions sign on the beach? He talked to air as though he could be understood. Why did he do that?"

"We don't exist to them. Just like rabbits or crows."

They admired the fine finish of the wood of the crucifix and the intricately detailed silk, the colors of the delicate banner. It provoked weeks of arguments about its meaning. The precious left-behinds slowly shredded, collapsed and disappeared over the years and became a distant memory through the generations and grew into a frequently altered legend of The Sea Visitors

1767

LORETO MEXICO

Captains Fernando Rivera y Moncada and Gaspar de Portola received the orders they'd been anticipating through the year. Dozens of well-armed troops knew that a major action was about to begin. They didn't know against whom. It could have been the local Indians, although there had been no troubles with them in the past few years. The order, when it was given, was a surprise to many of them, but to those who received regular news from Europe it was not totally unexpected. There had been tension for years.

It was the Jesuits. It was the way, coordinated with Pope Clement XIII, that they stole the riches, won by the Crown, to divert it to the Papacy.

All across Europe, coordinated at the same time, in the Spanish Empire and all it's holdings in the Americas, in France, in the two Sicilies and Parma, all Jesuits were to be rounded up with only the clothes on their backs and marched to harbors where large boats were waiting to take them on a long sea voyage to Italy.

The Jesuits of all nations faced a crowded trip with poor nutrition and with many deaths from scurvy, to be dumped at Civitavecchia in Italy "As a gift to the Pope," They were forbidden to write or speak in criticism of the expulsion or risk large fines and denial of support to the Papacy from the controlling Bourbon Empire.

Rivera y Moncada and de Portola carried out their leadership of the raids with precision and were well rewarded with promotions and new orders for the prime incursion and settlement of Alta California with the new Franciscan Order. Franciscans promised more obedience to the Crown and were moved immediately into the vacant Jesuit holdings. The soldiers doubted that they would adhere to their loyalty to the Crown. They, like all from the Vatican, would probably try to divert hidden riches to the Papacy as the Jesuits had done.

Padre Junipero Serra now led the order in the Californias and was committed to building a string of Missions up the Alta California coast, statedly under the Crown's control.

The plan had the approval of the Bourbon King of Spain, Carlos lll, who did not speak Spanish, but spoke French.

The Habsburg King of England, who did not speak English, but spoke German, strongly opposed the plan as an act of war. They both wanted exclusive control of The New World, through the ships of Spain, or the ships of England.

CHAPTER 1

1769 – ALTA CALIFORNIA

Governor General Gaspar de Portola had itchy blinking eyes, constantly wiping at dust and swatting buzzing insects. He rode at the head of a weary force of sixty-four Spanish soldiers, fourteen priests and one hundred twenty animals marching north from Presidio San Diego, with much farther to go.

They'd sweated through days of desert heat, bouncing tumbleweeds, cacti, scratchy brush and stinging nettles, walking now beside a small and calm river.

Low hills rolled on the right. Flat plains spread endlessly to the left. Fifty horses and seventy mules had survived out of one hundred eighty military animals that had left Sonora two months earlier and then from Presidio San Diego last week.

Six 'Soldados de Cuero,' leather armored soldiers, plus four trained native herders were riding long shifts to round up strays. The rest of the men walked their horses. The Padres stayed in a tight group at the rear reading bibles aloud, or reading through traditional sacred books and scrolls.

De Portola rode a tall tobacco colored horse with Ensign engineer Miguel Costanso and Lieutenant Pedro Fages beside him. It had been just over a year since he, and all of the commanders of the Americas and Europe had rounded up the Jesuits, striped them of belongings and shipped them, penniless, to Italy. He was unaware of what fate would befall them, but he didn't care. They had chosen their fate. The eagerly awaiting Franciscans were his new 'companions' now.

The enemy of The Crown, Pope Clement Xlll, protector the Jesuits and the theft of the monies of the Empire, had died on the morning of the critical meeting with the representatives of King Carlos lll. It was assumed that he was poisoned. 'Such is life,' Gaspar thought. 'They were foolish to steal from us.'

Men left bright markers on the trail to create the road between Sonora and the capital of the new territory of Alta California. "El

Camino Real," The King's Highway, to open the territory for commerce and governance.

The Padres at the rear gazed ahead at a mountain range with a great brown haze ahead. Father Juan Crespi had a good feeling about the view. The valley at the base of the mountains would be an ideal place to build a Mission as per Father Junipero Serra's instructions. The smoke hanging in the air indicated a population of heathen converts to create agriculture and to build a beautiful Mission. He froze with an odd sensation.

A young lieutenant walked beside Gaspar. "There are new plants up here that have tiny nettles that make painful sores." Stopping with a shocked expression. Gaspar felt a rocking motion from his horse that felt like staggering. "Please God, not another dying horse!"

"Terramoto!" The lieutenant screamed, struggling to stand. Men shouted all around them as the dust rose. Screeching horses bucked and bolted as Gaspar's mount tilted to the side with wild fear in his bulging eyes. Gaspar pushed off the saddle to avoid being crushed by the falling horse. The pounding of the earth struck him like fists through his armor. As he landed on his back. "Sweet Jesus," he mumbled, preparing to meet God at last.

Corporal Ochoa was walking beside his horse as the quake hit. "Dios!" he cried. The frightened horse's chest pushed him to the ground and the full weight of a hoof crushed his left shoulder. His screams were lost in the shouting from every side.

Father Crespi's instinct was to kneel and genuflect to the enormous power of The Lord, but the quake didn't allow him the comfort of kneeling. Flung to the gravel, he tried to support himself on frail arms and assumed a fetal position with the other fallen men, and praying that the panicked horses would not trample him. Then he prayed for an undefined forgiveness. The shaking eased and stopped.

Soldiers squinted through the dust. In the front, de Portola shouted repeatedly to assemble in ranks. "Forget the horses for now! Come to order and count off! Men of the Church, over there!" None were missing. Two had broken legs. Ochoa's arm dangled loose from the socket. The men made nervous jokes and struck heroic stances. Several had lost bladder control. One pointed left and shouted.

"The river!" It was full of gentle water on their left side. A calm, soothing place to let the horses drink and to wet cloths to wipe the grime off of their sunbaked faces. The river was gone!

"I have to write this down!" Costanso shouted, sitting on a sand pile at the trailside, searching through his leather pouch for writing materials. The knot of gathered Priests debated the meaning of the event. The shaking of the earth. The disappearance of the river. There had to be a purpose to it. It was the will of God. It had to be within the Divine plan.

A shout went up from the forward ranks. "Look!"

Bubbling, dancing water flowed across the desert to their right. A Miracle! The river changed course. The horses that had moved from the group were still within the river's new boundaries. Herders ran to gather the horses one by one.

Gaspar walked to Father Crespi, brushing clouds of dust from his brown robes.

"Father Juan. Are you and your brothers well?" Crespi raised his eyes to the heavens. "Yes, and in awe of the ways of The Lord." They walked to the edge of the new river with their aides. Crespi knelt as the Franciscans joined him to either side and spoke blessings to the river. He rose and made the sign of the cross while setting both feet in the water.

"I name this The River of the Sweetest Name of Jesus of the Earthquakes." Turning to Gaspar. "Let us pray that it keeps its sweet temperament." Gaspar allowed a private smile at making this violent event of nature into a convoluted complement to Him and The Son.

He motioned to Fages who shouted. "Tellez! Leon! Machado! Bring the squads to order! Report losses and injuries!" Gaspar watched the spooked horses gathered, the mules lined up and the spilled provisions re-packed. He knew the fear of being left behind with no presidio in reach. They had to feel stronger together and hold the camaraderie necessary to be a tight unit until civilization could be found. They called off numbers. Five men couldn't walk unassisted. Gaspar climbed onto a sandy three foot rise and shouted in his loudest voice.

"Before we mount up and continue. We will look at what happened. The earthquake threw us to the ground and frightened us. We can admit it! Some of us may have soiled their pants." A few of the frightened soldiers laughed and pointed. "Then the miracle of the river. First it was here. Now it is there! A Mystery! Many things have changed around us, but one thing did not change. Ask yourselves what that is before I tell you" He gave a count of six.

"The thing that has not changed is that we are the strongest fighting force in these territories! We march under the Cross of our Savior...and the flag of King Carlos lll ruler of Spain and the Territories of the New World" The men mustered a mild cheer as he continued. "This earthquake is not the work of our Lord. It is the work of Satan...We have survived it! All those without damage will watch over and assist the injured. Fray Crespi will now bless this spot and we will continue."

"We will mark and dedicate this area to the blessed Santa Ana" Crespi began.

TONGVA LANDS

(TO BECOME THE LOS ANGELES BASIN)

Translucent Golden Eagle and Condor Spirits flew under the Sun in and out of clouds over the great curve of Mother Earth.

Naahanpar ran his increasingly demanding daily path through brush and grasses, rocky slopes and riverbeds challenging him to be the strongest of his village. He always felt the great Spirits in the sky above him and his Ancestors below him pressing him on.

The Bird-Spirits swept down and inland over the tans and greens of a dry grassland plain bordered to the north by snow-topped purple mountains running West to East, flanked on the South by hills flowing East to an endless desert. The Tongva populated plain had spreading columns of smoke from the fires of villages that had lived stable lives for a thousand years.

The Flying-Spirits were Eternal. Linked to the land and Tongva spirituality. The temporal nature of the land existed in a tableau From the Birth to Forever.

Changes in the shoreline from earthquakes and tsunami, flooding and raising the beaches to become the villages of Mali-wu and Topanga, time and shape-shifting to luxury dwellings of Hollywood elite and hillside hideaways of artists and recluses. Swept aside by fires and floods, only to be rebuilt for more dramatic cycles. An island arose from the sea, occupied as the Island of Pemuu'nga for centuries, to be cleared of it's people and renamed Santa Catalina Island.

The Spirits floated East into the flatlands, rising and clearing the cliffs that became Santa Monica, it's burned native villages shifting to cattle herds to bean fields to tract homes with office buildings. They swooped inland over Kaweenga village, becoming Hollywood, growing high and shrinking with waves of ambitions, rising onward and eastward over the ancient central village of 'Yaanga, seeing the Spanish invasion, eviction, birth of downtown Los Angeles, Mexican, U.S., and overseas owners. Wild growth out and up, sea to desert, mountains to southern hills, choked with smoke, shaken, fallen, to be gloriously built again.

They turned sharp left, climbing over the oak trees of the flat village of Shevaanga, to become San Gabriel, and reach the top of a great mountain watching over it's domain, then to curve West over rounded peaks, back toward the sea. Far below, nestled in a deep gorge, lay the peaceful and unassailable, two thousand year old village of Haapchivit, to later become Chileo Flats.

The Golden Eagle and Condor Spirits returned again to sea to retrace their endless vigil.

DURANGO – NEW SPAIN (MEXICO)

Jose Antonio Basilio Rosas grinned into his wife Maria's pained but ecstatic eyes as their fifth child was born to them in eight years. The joy they felt was an extension of their love of the land

and their lives on it. Another boy would make their work and lives easier.

He was pure Indio. Tarajumara from the central interior, but his work, as a stonemason, was in even more demand in the North Western territories of Sinaloa and the opening lands.

He looked into Maria's face and the wailing boy's thrashing as the Curandera cleaned and wrapped him in a soft wool baby blanket.

"The wonders you bring are the true miracles. I love you so much! Our little Jose Alejandro will be a strong, strong boy!" Knowing that in four months, a trip for the family to investigate Sinaloa was in their future and it would be good.

TONGVA LANDS – SHEVAANGA

Naahanpar strode into Shevaanga as the Sun was four fingers high above the eastern flatland in the gap of of the foothills south of the purple mountain range. The ocean and Pemuu'nga Island was on the Western horizon.

Shevaanga lay in the plain east of Yaanga, the central and largest village. An extended arm to the horizon with the four fingers held horizontally translated to one hour's time in travel of the sun. 'Two hands away' meant a two hour's walk.

Shevaanga's two hundred fifty villagers had stability. Their summer fires and winter floods were blunted by centuries of brush clearance and drainage channel digging. Her industry was based on plentiful oak trees and of leaching out the bitter flavors from acorns to make finely ground meal for cooking.

Sevaanga-vik, Chief of Shevaanga, showed pleasure and anger more than most. He intervened in disputes, family problems and coached children who woudn't respect their elders. His height of 5'6" was tall. 140 pounds made him a winner in tests of strength. His dark, round face was a weathered map of lines from hard travel and laboring in the desert sun.

He looked from his stool in front of the chief's Greathouse across a smooth dirt central clearing of the village as his wife,

'Atooshe', skipped across to him, kicking rocks with a strut, wearing a wide grin on her plump face.

"You can do the rest tomorrow," To the woman and son sanding and polishing his toenails. Their father had died and Sevaanga-vik gave them food every week. "Thank you, thank you," backing away gratefully and greeting 'Atooshe.'

The respect that he had for his wife was legend. She came from a leading family of the village. She'd bonded to the old shaman, Pul Tah'ah'har as a child. She'd learned the herbs and cures for infections and illnesses. She had the affinity. Everyone saw it. She had never stopped learning. She organized women into workgroups for large acorn meal production, herb gathering and processing and grew the village's trade more than it had ever been.

When Pul Tah'ah'har' became sick and was dying there was no other choice. The Pul, or Shamanic, Caste was the province of men, but the usually conservative and traditional Elders agreed. 'Atooshe' became Pula 'Atooshe', the village Shamanka, Spiritual Leader and Medicine Woman. She became the second most powerful person after Sevaanga-vik.

"What are you so happy about?" He asked.

"Little Poonu' was sick from bad rabbit. I made her spit up yesterday. She had my teas all night. She's better now. They gave us these," putting two rabbit hats on his lap.

The more they worked together, the more their liking grew until lust intervened. Frequent touches consumed them until they announced their marriage partnership. Her short, dark, firmly packed roundness and cheery attitude easily drew people close to her. When a boy, Hachaaynar, was born to them, continuance of their line promised stability and prosperity to Shevaanga.

Nahaanpar waved as he passed the Greathouse to his dying mothers hut. Nothing worked. They tried their best. She was slipping away.

<<< 0 >>>

Young Hachaaynar stood in a field, blazing with colors, of anise and manzanita practicing speed and aim with his throwing sticks, freezing, pretending that a tumbleweed over his left shoulder was a rabbit, whirling and sidearming the stick through the center of the plant. He didn't think that other nine year olds could do it that well.

Two runners came up a trail from the Southern Lands into the village. He ran to the Greathouse. The runners were sitting on mats talking excitedly with mother and father telling a story with great meaning. There would be a passing of the legendary Sea Visitors. The strange hairy men out of departed ancestor's remembered stories.

"Will we see them?"

"Yes, my darling."

Soon, a third runner arrived saying it would be a full moon before the strange creatures would be close enough to see. They were still deep in the Kumeyaay lands to the South.

'Atooshe' packed to return to her Pula hut, back to work. A person of Pul caste could not live in her own village, even with her own husband. 'Atooshe' had to live out of sight of the village to commune with Spirit and for troubled people to visit her in privacy.

North of Shevaanga, her round kitcha hut structure was typical of houses of the village. It was made of many thin trunks of young green saplings, smoothed of branches, and driven in a circle deep into the ground, then the branches were bent, lashed together at the tops and covered with layers of woven flattened reeds with a round hole at the top to evacuate the smoke from a small central fire in a ring of stones.

They hugged and promised to go together if the Sea Visitors ever arrived. Hachaaynar walked with mother to the outskirts of the village. He turned excitedly. The hoop and spear playing field wasn't deserted. His friends are practicing and the two top players, Nahaanpar and Three Hawks were playing again each other in the center of the field.

"Look! It's Nahaanpar!" Pointing to his teacher and body sprinting like a mountain lion to the rolling hoop, throwing his spear through the center at top speed, whooping loudly, leaping and rolling on the grass at scoring his point. Three Hawk's hoop was thrown by his teammate. Digging his toes into the starting sand he raced to catch up, closing enough to get a good angle, bringing the spear back, calculating the amount to lead the hoop and the drop of the distance. He grunted like a bear with the effort of the throw and grined with a howl as the spear went through as cleanly as Nahaanpar's. Nahaanpar had to start from farther back and try a greater distance.

Hachaaynar sat on a patch of grass not daring to yell or show that he favored his teacher. Three Hawks jumped and pranced as Nahaanpar dropped behind his teammate for the pursuit. His speed and precision was breathtaking to Hachaaynar. He squinted to take in every motion and detail. He giggled with pleasure at the beautifully made point, but then Three Hawks topped him.

Back and forth. Each point seemed impossible to make. Villagers lined the sides. Two walnut dice games begin under nearby oaks. Four of Hachaaynar's friends flopped down beside him.

"Want to play when these guys finish?"

"Sure." But hoping Nahaanpar would take him hunting later and show him how to aim better while running.

CIUDAD DE MEXICO – NEW SPAIN

The Manila Galleons had carried his Parents to New Spain fifty years ago where their names were changed to Rodriguez. Their skills as metal-smiths brought them solidity and a good home.

Firearms had always attracted Antonio Miranda Rodriguez. He liked the sound and the precise workings of their action. He experimented with the composition and mix of the explosive powder. It was more than a simple interest that he held. It was more an obsession with how to improve the tools of the soldiers.

His friends called him 'Kuya' and 'Tonyo' but most people called him 'Chino' because of his Asian features and compact stature. 'Filipino' and 'Chino' were interchangeable to them.

Maria Margarita was pregnant. They had only been married for two years and this was earlier than he 1had expected, 'but life is life,' he shrugged. It would be good to have a family of his own.

There were many glowing stories of the opportunities in the lands to the North. He would continue to ask. 'What was the harm?'

VILLAGE OF HAAPCHIVET
TONGVA / SERRANO LANDS

Ferns, brambles and holly filled the spaces between the taller willows and mountain pines. Travelers learned not to look down, but to concentrate on the spaces in front of them. A bear or mountain lion might demand the same space. When people traveled in groups, the animals retreated.

Nine hands after leaving the flatlands the trail leveled off. Giant boulders flanked the sides of the well-worn footpath. In a gateway of rocky walls a smoky clearing opened, full of life. Travelers entered a village with the scent of sage and smoke from spiced cooking deer and rabbit meats.

Children chased with cattail darts playing tag between the round kitcha huts. Some of the huts had sharp points and were mud packed in the Serrano style. Haapchivet blended two tribes. The Serrano lived with the Tongva. Two languages were spoken. Intermarriage was common. Most of the Serrano nation was far to the East.

Haapchi-vik, the chief of Haapchivet, was Tongva. His wife, Kethu, was Serrano from long lines of leaders in this village that had survived in peace for a thousand years. No one would dare attack it because of its natural walled access.

Haapchi-vik and Kethu had two children. The boy, 'Aachvet, was an impulsive eleven year old and angry at being catered to and allowed to win games when he could have been easily defeated. He felt patronized. His parents didn't understand him yet. His sister did.

Tooypor was nine years old. Her reputation as a brilliant learner and fascinating speaker spread beyond the village. Children begged her to play and to listen to stories she'd improvise. She asked perceptive questions to travelers and traders. She spoke about trade and products as would be expected from a chief or negotiator but not from a child. Runners from other villages would wave and chat with her. They'd ask Haapchi-vik about her wellbeing. She loved 'Aachvet and talked him through his frustration.

The village's Pul Tuwaru lived in a cave with low ceilings near the mountain's peak. The cave's soot covered walls that had pictograph markings of histories from ancient times. He walked stooped, with a limp. He wore less than the cool weather demanded. His bony ribs provoked jokes. His rasping voice matched his turtle-like deeply creased features, but the respect he commanded touched every villager.

Kethu and Haapchi-vik sat for the evening meal. Achvet and Tooypor prepared the eating area. Pul Tuwaru entered, out of protocol, as only he could. "Haapchi-vik Pahr," using the term of esteem, and preparing a meeting of more than passing importance, he sat on a thick mat by the fire.

"Ask the children to leave." Haapchi-vik pointed and the two walked through the village without question.

"I have been watching your daughter. Everyone mentions her. Usually something she's told them about themselves."

"I'll tell her not to be disrespectful. She shouldn't annoy people." Haapchi-vik looked to Kethu. "Did you know about this?" Tuwaru interrupted. "It's not a bad thing. They come to me to confirm what she says. I do. Always." watching their skeptical expressions.

"I want to make her my apprentice. She is young, but she learns quickly, but first, there is a Pul in the flatlands I want her to study herbs and medicines with."

"Away from home?" Kethu shook her head.

"Not any Pul. A Pula. She is young and the most talented with medicines. We communicate through runners nearly every day. She sends us the willow bark potions that helps to stop the fevers. Her skill will bring our village forward and your daughter will be the one to do it."

"She's a child." Kethu looked to Haapchi-vik, frowning in concentration.

"She's a very special child." Tuwaru said.

Haapchi-vik gestured South. "We don't get as much trade from the flatlands as we used to. We see more from the other side." Pointing North. "They don't have as much good stuff, like the flatlands." Squatting at Tuwaru's side.

"Do you promise she'll return and not become part of their village? That she'll return to see us two times a moon? Always a Haapchivitam?"

" I'll have Pula 'Atooshe' swear to never have little Tooypor become a part of any village but ours. She is a good teacher."

"If you have her swear and she knows that we will come with weapons and fighting men if our daughter is not honored, I will allow this."

Kethu knew that when he took a position, he would never be swayed. She nodded. "It will be done.

NYARIT – NEW SPAIN

Manuel Camero, only seventeen years, knew how to run Monte games and how to get the prettiest local girls to slip behind the stables or of their parent's houses walls to play sex games with him. Always with the understanding that it wasn't really sex if his man thing didn't go in their female thing where the babies came out. All of the other games weren't what the Priest called 'Sin.' A few agreed. By now, all of the parents knew him and warned their girls to stay away from him.

'It was stupid! They all were stupid! This place was stupid!' The Capital of New Spain sounded great! Thousands of people with money, and girls!

'Soon', he thought, 'very soon, I'll be out of this place and having a great time where the living is good!'

SHEVAANGA

'Atooshe''s Pula hut sat amid herbs, rabbits and running springs. Runners carried messages with conditions for the arrival of the apprentice. 'Atooshe' had heard about Haapchi-vik's daughter for over a year. She'd watched the skinny girl last year at a wedding between a man and woman from their villages. In the smoke of sage wands and chants and dancing, the she was poised for a child of her age and observing groups of people at the gathering with a keen eye.

'Atooshe' watched as Tooypor moved to the powerful people of the villages. She avoided making eye contact. She probably understood the issues of the moment. The other children were playing but Tooypor was learning.

Tooypor at nine was fluent in the dialects of both villages as well as the Serrano tongue of her mother. The children saw her as somehow faultless and idolized her. 'Why would children venerate another child?' She wondered. The guide arrived with Tooypor. She had grown taller. It would be easier to climb and reach the vines and herbs in rocky places.

She had a narrow face and a straight nose with penetrating, polished obsidian eyes with flecks of green in them and long black hair that she tied into a loose knot that hung below the middle of her back on a slim and wiry body that had walked and run many hilly miles.

"I've heard good things about you. You have a reputation."

She smiled with downcast eyes and replied. "Pula 'Atooshe''pahr." I'm happy that I have a chance to learn. Reputation is just talk. The only reputation I want is to be your best pupil"

"You know how to say things to please people." Preparing a distance under flattery. "Do you know all of the stories?"

“Pul Tuwaru has been teaching me the origins, the winds and directions, the times and the Moons and part of the journeys and lessons of Chinigchnich. I have much to learn.” ‘Atooshe’ surveyed her posture and downcast eyes. It seemed part genuine and partly exaggerated humility. There was deep pride and a sense of entitlement in this daughter of a powerful chief.

“Do you dream? What do you dream about? What do you think about when you’re alone?” Seeing the girl’s brow knot and her eyes go to distant focus.

Tooypor spoke slowly about the things that she hadn’t anyone. Even Aachvet. “I dream.” Averting her eyes. “When I dream, sometimes, I am in a place that is more real than, than the place where I wake up. I may be in our Greathouse, or in the woods, but I’m pulled into the Earth, or..floating up in the sky, where..I ..see everything. I understand what my mother and father feel. What hurts them and what would help them. I go into places where the animals and birds, the plants, they speak to me. They speak..,but,..not in words.” Looking up at ‘Atooshe‘s face. “I can‘t tell people about these things, but, sometimes, I‘ll talk to animals.” She giggled. “Sometimes they stand still and listen. Am I wrong? No one else talks about this.”

“We will talk more my Tooypor.” ’Atooshe’ hugged her. Tooypor hugged her back strongly, ’Almost bearlike.’ She thought. ’A stronger girl than her appearance suggests.’ “You will stay here tonight. We will leave as the sun rises for your first lessons in the medicines and of gathering the right ones for preparation. I’ll tell the guide to meet you here when the sun is three hands high.”

Tooypor woke three times before dawn hoping 'Atooshe' would wake making preparations, but it was fully dark. She closed her eyes becoming a lizard flitting from bush to bush, to understand each plant, living the lizard’s quick and tiny life until drifting into sleep.

CHAPTER 2

SONORA - NEW SPAIN

Private Jose Vincente Feliz was expecting Maria Ygnacia Feliz to deliver their forth child in September.

“I don’t want to have to leave before the baby is out of you and safe. If Anza’s expedition calls me before it’s time, I don’t know if they’ll accept it as a reason to stay.”

“Before the baby is out?” She teased, “Is it going to the Cantina?”

He loved her and wanted as many as they could sire so that the brothers and sisters would be close in age and become like friends to eachother. The other motivation was that they would be able to provide for Maria and him after, he hoped, early retirement and a calm period on a ranch or farm. Other soldiers did it, quite successfully, and some had earned large grants of land from the Crown.

‘I can always dream.’

SHEVAANGA

After dawn a Golden Eagle swept west along the hills of the western coast and rose above the beaches, showing Pemuu'nga Island out to sea. It froze mid-climb appearing to fall backwards in a swift banking turn to the left, accelerating east over the basin, diving through the smoke of two hundred campfires and brushfires, through the haze in the still air. The Eagle gained speed toward a sprawling village, closing in on a large playing field. Men and women, boys and girls, playing games of stick throwing, stick and ball, field hockey and dice games.

Nahaanpar aimed on the run. He saw the coyote sized hoop rolling parallel to him with two opposing players gaining on it. One of their spears narrowly missed the hoop to the rear as it hit an irregularity and bounced a foot in the air.

He calculated how much to lead it and predicted a second bounce. The closer player threw at the same time, missing, just under the second hop, while Nahaanpar's short spear whistled through the center. His friends cheered.

He solved problems for them of hunting and predicting the movements of the prey. He explained the reasons. He never called them stupid. He always complemented them on their games, after he'd beaten them.

He walked into the woods after the game and lined up his spears at the base of his feet and took the one he'd made a dirt scratch on. It seemed out of balance. Barely noticeable but it curved slightly. It was a successful throw but not a perfect throw. He carefully cut branches to find a replacement that wouldn't curve.

On the brambly path to his dying mother's kitcha three giggling girls ran by and slapped his butt, skipping up the trail. It happened often. They weren't his age. Their families didn't have stature. The chief's son, Hachaaynar, ran up chattering about how great he'd been.

"When can you take me hunting for rabbit? I've been practicing with throwing sticks. I can hit rabbits on the run just like that," swinging his arm sideways.

"How about tomorrow morning. I'll come to the Greathouse after I bathe." Watching the delighted boy run home.

SAN DIEGO BAY

Sergeant Pedro Fages stepped off the ship San Carlos and immediately threw up his hands and swore at the hills and the sky.

"How can the idiot cartographers put us 320 kilometers off course on a 100 kilometer trip? Damn their souls to Hell!" turning to his friend, Corporal Cruz, who was also furious as well as the other soldiers at being kept on a disease infested boat for so long with no medication and only confusion from the captain and crew. Cruz could only mumble in a low voice.

“So much scurvy and fevers. I’m afraid that I’ve picked up something also. We have a harbor and a Presidio de San Diego to build.” Motioning to the soldiers dragging themselves into formation before him and continuing as though nothing had happened.

“We will rest in this pleasant cove until morning. We will split provisions with the soldiers up the beach who have camped here and send for more supplies from the South.

SHEVAANGA

'Atooshe' and Tooypor crisscrossed the flats above Shevaanga gathering herbs and bark from the gifts of the Earth. Condors, Eagles, Hawks and Crow flew overhead. The fields hissed and whooshed with wind, insect and animal life under the rustling grasses. Rabbits chased and played. Frogs and lizards explored from the streambeds beside the gravel path. They skirted games of teens playing with throwing stick.

'Atooshe' brought her to a circle of seated women striping yucca fibers, separating sage leaves, grinding and leeching acorns.

Tooypor had seen women doing work in her village. She’d never been concerned with what they did. She’d rarely listen to their conversations.

She asked. “Do you work with them or do you only direct them?” Knowing Father wouldn’t want her to do repetitious tasks.

'Atooshe' laughed at her over-protected helper. “How do you think bitter acorn becomes sweet meal? What do you think a Pula actually does? How does the mugwort become paste? How does sage and anise become the powder that protects villages when the frosts come? How does willow bark become the tea and poultice that eases pains and fevers? Do I do it all? No, little one. It’s them. If I had to it I’d never have time to commune with Spirit.”

“They do the same thing every day?” With a scrunch of the face bordering on a pout. In the moment she spoke, she felt shame at missing such an obvious thing. The feeling deepened seeing her teacher's look. 'I'm so stupid! Now she disrespects me.'

"We are instructed by the Spirit to take Mother Earth's offerings and use them wisely. We, the Pulum, learn to prepare them correctly. We can't do it all. Our potions are prepared by these women." 'Atooshe' watched Tooypor inspect each woman and her tasks and said. "Your Pul Tuwaru does the same in your village."

They smiled as 'Atooshe' walked her around the inside of the circle. Tooypor's face lit up at being recognized as Pula 'Atooshe''s companion. Her eyes grew bright.

"A-ah-heh," She stepped from person to person and lowered her head."Tooypor of Haapchivet" 'Atooshe' said.

Greetings flowed into Tooypor's heart that she belonged here, even though she was 'stupid' sometimes. She would spend more time with the women of Haapchivet if father would permit it, even if he didn't. Why would he if it helped? She still felt foolish. It would not go away easily. She saw something basic she had missed. She knew that crafts were repetitious but saw the work of the Pul and Pula as solitary occupations of wisdom and plucking out cures. She saw that no one could be left out. She looked at each face to memorize them.

The sun was five hands high as 'Atooshe' led Tooypor up the foothills. They climbed a smooth flowered hillside with a rainbow's mix of brilliant colors leading to a gravelly ascent to the Great Eagle Rock.

A soft rumble started far away and grew louder. Then it became slammingly loud as the ground shook more strongly with each step. It became hard to stand. She put her fingertips to the ground to keep her balance. New sounds came from up the hill. 'Ahtooshe' shouted "That way!" pushing Tooypor to a dip in the ground.

A clatter of rocks rolled down the slope to the side of them. Sand and rock slipped downwards. Rabbit sized and then coyote sized boulders high on the hill rumbled toward them. A great bump knocked them off of their feet.

‘Atooshe' grabbed Tooypor’s arm and pulled her into to a hollow dip. They scrambled on all fours, dodging small bouncing rocks to reach a safer low spot and lie flat. A log hit Tooypor‘s hip. She yelped and they both rolled into a deeper depression in the ground.

They squinted into eachothers eyes, unsuccessfully looking for fear on the other’s face. They lay still with the bouncing earth slowly calming. They stung from many stone hits. As the shaking stopped they were again surprised by each other’s grins.

They had survived.

“There is anger in the air.” 'Atooshe' said, holding Tooypor’s steady hand. “I’ll ask the spirits. Shevaanga can withstand it, but your village has rocks all around. “

Tooypor‘s voice was firm. “There are stories in Haapchivit’s past that tell of these things. We are not harmed by shaking. Our rocks will not move.” Feeling privileged to experience this with her teacher beside her.

'Atooshe' worried about the runner from Haapchivit. “This is a sign of change. When you get home, ask Pul Tuwaru to meet with me at my hut tomorrow.

JALISCO – NEW SPAIN

Jose Vanegas remained single in spite of the many desirable women who he knew as co-workers in the wool mills. Several had clerical abilities and were able to help him in inventorying the uniforms for the military. He was easy to like. He was helpful to those above him as well as those below him in the growing factory.

Not many pure Indios like himself had knowledge of the basic mathematics and language of large-scale trade but he continued to study and learn in his time at home. There was a world of opportunity for him and the right choices would make him a wealthy man. There were programs to help him advance in the world.

He knew the life in Jalisco wasn't the best, but he could learn and become ready to build a family when the time was right. The world was changing. He would be ready.

NAYARIT – NEW SPAIN

Jose Fernando de Velasco y Lara had come from Cadiz, Spain to live and explore the posibilities of New Spain and it's territories.

He was always good at farming, so when he found a rich area of land in the Baja California area with a good administration of friendly Spaniards, a capitol of the territory, he grabbed it as fast as he could.

A devout Catholic, he met Maria Antonia Campos at Mass on three occassions before asking her to dine, and shortly, asking her to marry. She led him to her parent's house immediately.

They traveled to Sinaloa in a grand carriage, with an elegant wedding, and returned to the farm together.

SHEVAANGA

Tooypor, 'Atooshe', Tuwaru and their four guards took thne trail down to Shevaanga. Three runners and groups of children passed them on the rocky path.

Tooypor knew that Father and the Elders would move slowly. If 'Aachvet was coming, he'd be jealous because she seemed more powerful with two powerful Pul.

The village came in sight, filled with young and old from all Four Directions. Different clothing and dialects crowded the lanes. Groups gathered and moved about looking for runners/guides from their area.

Runners, Chiefs and Pul gathered their people. Six separate groups gravitated to the Southern edge of Shevaanga. They knew that The Visitors were traveling toward them. Advance scouts reported the movements. The groups went to sit along the rises overlooking the gravel washes the Visitors would have to pass through.

'Atooshe' joined with the Shevaavetam but Pul Tuwaru told Tooypor to stay close to him and the group from Haapchivet.

On the embankment, Tooypor squinted at the moving shapes to the East. The Visitors were traveling slower than the runners. A runner from Haapchivet came up the hill pointing. “They will pass here!” Throwing a rock toward a flat gully that once was a streambed. Tooypor imagined them with fish scales and gills.

Dust hung in the chilly air to the east. Hundreds, young and old, sat, stood and milled on the sandy, rocky and grassy rises. Young bored children played tag and hide-it games. Teens played catch and accuracy throwing games until there were shouts that they were in sight.

The animals were the first things recognizable, and then the bright weavings held high on poles. Men rode on the animals. The animals let them! The hat on the one in front reflected the sun with the look of fish scales!

Her heart was pounding. She looked at Tuwaru, 'Aachvet and Father, the elders and children. All were leaning forward in silence. What kind of animals act as servants to humans? if they were humans!

As the procession came closer she saw leather straps around the first animal’s nose. There were friendly dogs in her village but no big dog would ever let anyone ride on it’s back. There were seats on the animals. One walking with a man holding it had a seat on it’s back.

The walking men were humans. Some had no hair on their heads. They walked together and wore brown weavings like bear colors. The others had bright reds, browns and light sand colors shining bright through the dirt and dust coating.

Their clothing was a weaving of some kind. It moved so softly. She wanted to touch the shining hat and sit upon the animal. Everything was different.

She understood what the runner had said when he came to find her and Pul Tuwaru. It was like a legend. The Earth shaking, the animals, the Sea Visitors. The people from far villages all gathered together. It was a time of change to be told from generation to generation.

As they passed, a bald man in bear colors called in a loud voice, "Bless you!.....Bless you!" and "...The Lord!" Strange sounds. The man in the front shouted, holding his arms high and moving them, "...subjects of...Crown of Spain...Juan Carlos..." and more strange words.

Tooypor saw people from the eastern villages following to see where they would go. She hoped it was to the ocean to see the floating clouds.

As the column passed, two young men ran to the path to look at animal droppings. One touched one and yelled, "It's very soft! And hot. It's steaming! They eat plants, not meat." His friend laughed, jumping up and down pointing at him but Tooypor didn't laugh. She admired his courage in finding out. She turned to Pul Tuwaru.

"It was smart to look at the animal's dropping, wasn't it?" hoping that he agreed.

Tuwaru grined. "His friend was foolish to mock him. We now know something about the animals. They are more like deer than bear. Now we learn something about the men. They are indeed men."

'Atooshe' waited for Tuwaru and Tooypor to catch up. There were more than two hundred people following.

"They are only men." Tuwaru said as they approached 'Atooshe'.

"Yes, and sickly ones among them. Large sores on hands and faces."

"Then we have something to trade." Pul Tuwaru included Tooypor in his glance. "They show weakness to infections. That's 'Atooshe''s area. Her medicines will heal the sores."

"The weavings are what I want." 'Atooshe' declared. "I don't know what kind of dyes they use to make it that bright. Did any of their words sound like any language you've heard?"

“None. Different than any. They act like we would understand.” Pul Tuwaru’s brow was furrowed. “Why would they think that? They didn’t ask us to answer. Who would talk without caring who understands? Not wise!”

Some visitors on foot moved to the sides and handed small sparkling things to the nearest women and children. They smiled and said more word sounds. Tooypor wondered why such grand creatures wouldn’t think of a simple thing like listening and talking to find an understanding. Every tribe and village did that.

A handsome older boy ran to 'Atooshe' and spoke animatedly. He seemed to be a respected friend.

“The hats reflect like water but have no wavering motion!” He said excitedly. “I’ve seen obsidian polished to that reflectiveness but it would be too heavy and fragile for a hat unless they are strong as bears, it must be a lighter material near the heaviness of thin wood. What do you think it is?” Looking eagerly to her. “Look at this!” Handing her a round clear stone that looked like ice.

“I think I know a way to get close to them.” Turning to Tooypor. “I’ll be training this very talented girl in the skills of the Pulum. Tooypor, this is Nahaanpar of our village. He has great skills also.” Tooypor thought, He is very good looking.'

People split to the sides to avoid animal droppings. Tooypor breathed as she passed, ’Yes the scent is different from animals of the woods and deserts.’

Villagers followed. The procession turned to the North a short distance from Shevaanga and gathered around the bald men in the brown robes.

<<< 0 >>>

Fray Crespi called for Gaspar to stop.

“This looks like the right location.” The Franciscan Fathers moved to join him. “We may come to an agreement here. What do you think of this place?”

"Fray Juan, I will be direct. There are some large villages nearby. I see your reasoning in being close to a good workforce but it depends on how warlike they are. I don't see many carrying weapons. Most are curious. That's good, but the location should be on higher ground. More defensible and better drainage."

Crespi stepped away, looking in all directions. "I love these mountains. The soil looks more fertile here. This will do. I'll walk two score meters West of that oak tree, a square of twenty-four meters on flat ground. That will be the heart of Mission San Gabriel Archangel." He looked at the Brothers in his command and moved to stand next to Gaspar's horse.

"Brothers Cambon and Somera will stay to start the foundations and gather materials. Gaspar will have to provide soldiers for the actual labor."

"I can leave two horses and six men."

Crespi lit up. "That is most generous, General. That will be a good start. Bless you for your generosity."

"How will you communicate? This is an isolated outpost on an unmapped spot. I'll leave one more man and horse for you to report your progress every five days to keep the highway in use. The civilian Pueblo will be very close when we find the right spot"

'Atooshe' watched the brown clad men walk to an oak tree and move to the west, pacing and placing rocks in certain spots. Those with animals took branches and larger stones into the space. Others uprooted plants and threw them to the side. They shuffled around to smooth the surface and kicked or threw the smaller rocks out of the now square space. She wondered if they were doing a magic to honor the four winds, but she saw a pattern rising, "They are making a greathouse. A place for Chiefs and elders to meet." She said to Tuwaru.

'Atooshe' saw the time to make contact. She leaned to Tuwaru, took his hands and whispered. "Now it's time" She rushed to the Shevaanga group and pulled her husband aside. On receiving Sevaanga-vik's agreement, 'Atooshe' filled a large tightly woven basket and gathered acorn meal from all who had more than a day's supply.

Tooypor watched the villagers fill the basket. 'Atooshe' made strangers become helpers. None of the chiefs would ask for help like that and get it. They would have meeting after meeting with elders, or threaten for what they wanted. 'Atooshe' included people. She didn't intimidate them. 'Atooshe' put the strap of the basket on her forehead. Tooypor walked to a high spot to watch. 'Atooshe' saw who the leaders were. If she wore a smile and kept her eyes on them, she would not be turned away.

The bearded one with the fish-scale and the old brown-robed bald man stood near the center of the square. The men stared at the small brown woman with high pointed bare breasts walking toward them and turned to each other. Crespi whispered. "Dear God!" at the sight of a temptress.

She aimed her smile at Portola and Crespi. They stood mesmerized by the barely clothed woman with the waist-length, straight and silky, black hair. She looked like an erotic dream in this hot and windy landscape. Crespi saw her as sent from the Devil himself. They were aware of the scores of Indians watching from all sides.

"She will be trouble for us, Gaspar." Crespi intoned, while shuffling from foot to foot, feeling uncomfortable under the woman's gaze.

"Yes, she could be." Replied Gaspar, stepping forward to greet her, raising his palm for her to stop. He turned to Crespi. "If many women here are like this one, I fear for my troops. We are outnumbered."

Portola raised his hand and turned to his troops to speak in a loud voice.

"There will be no leering or improper sounds." Glaring for emphasis. "We are guests and we are surrounded. We will bow our heads politely. We will not talk, laugh or stare at her, no matter how difficult that may be. Understood?" The men looked at 'Atooshe' and then looked at the ground. "I will now accept her gift."

She watched the man speaking and the reactions of his tribesmen. He turned back toward her. His eyes showed worry or fear, as did the bald man. She reached behind for the straps of the basket and swung it to the ground, ducking her head out of the strap. Renewing a wide smile of welcome. The frightened bald man made down, up and side to side motions with his hand that looked like he was invoking the four directions and spoke in the strange language as though he expected her to understand.

'Atooshe''s smile became real as she spoke aloud. “What are you saying? What language is that?” Almost breaking into laughter as she asked, “Why would you think I would understand?” Knowing that nothing she could say would have an effect. She reached in the dry acorn meal and lifted a pinch and put it in her mouth with overacted pleasure.

The men approached the basket. Each took a small pinch and tasted it. In spite of smiles and nods it was obvious that it was no pleasure. 'Atooshe' nodded and touched each man’s sleeve. She turned to shout to the sand dune where Tuwaru and Tooypor stood.

“They are very strange!” She turned back with her warm smile and motioned to include the troops in sharing the acorn meal.

Tooypor and Pul Tuwaru held hands, amazed that 'Atooshe' would walk to the very center without fear. She saw that more people would frighten the visitors and was impressed by the Pula’s wisdom. She looked back at Sevaanga-vik’s tight face, watching his bold wife’s actions. The man with the fish scale hat called and two men walked forward to carry the basket to his circle of similarly dressed men. It appeared to Tooypor that they were pretending to eat but dropped most of the meal on the ground.

“Are they really eating?” Tooypor asked with a twitch of the nose.

“Very good, little one.” Tuwaru nodded in appreciation. “They do not like our food.”

'Atooshe' walked up the hill with a look of conquest. Something was hanging from her neck. As she approached, she jiggled her prize and rolled her eyes. “Oh, dear Mother Earth!” she chuckled,

“We may have much to learn from them but they are so lacking in wisdom.”

Tooypor saw the shining beads of the fish scale material. At the bottom was a shining representation of the four directions. The sign that they carried with their long, straight sticks and the fine weavings.

“I am too tired to follow them.” Pul Tuwaru said squatting on his heels.

“I don’t want to follow either.” 'Atooshe' sat disappointed and bored from her brief contact, playing with the crossed trinket. “What is this made from?” holding it up and rotating it close to her nose. “It’s like finely worked obsidian but heavier. Strange stuff!”

Hachaaynar ran from his father’s group and flopped down and squinted at the cross on 'Atooshe'’s neck. “What is it?” He asked. Sevaanga-vik and Nahaanpar sat beside her examining the trinket as the visitors, and the dozens following them, continued toward Yaanga and Kaweenga.

Nahaanpar kept examining the crossed object, rotating it, rubbing it and holding it a hands width from his eyes looking for any flaws or irregularities in it’s surfaces. “This is magical.”

“Will they float into the sea?” Tooypor asked Pul Tuwaru. “Will they go to Pemuu'nga and join Chinigchnich?”

Tuwaru looked depressed. “No...Whatever they are, these are not gods!.

<<< 0 >>>

As he rode north Commander de Portola re-read the dispatch that was delivered from Loreto. He was still unsure as to how to react publicly, but settled for a wry smile.

On the morning of the climactic meeting to settle the conflict over the Jesuits between King Carlos lll and their corrupt defender, Pope Clement Xlll, The Pope suddenly died. An unidentified officer had written in the margin, “ He was poisoned. God be Praised.” Gaspar did not find that unlikely.

CHAPTER 3

1771 - SINALOA – NEW SPAIN

Pablo Rodrigues was born in Sinaloa. He was proud to be Opata Indio and was devoted to the church. Between his work times as an independent day laborer he would do volunteer cleanup and repair to all of the local churches. He kept up with all the news of Portola and Rivera's travels through the gossip spread from the military, through their wives and the churchmen. It sounded like exciting times to the North. He kept up and thought.....'just maybe.'

MISSION SAN GABRIEL

Fathers Juan Crespi and Pedro Benito Cambon walked the Mission perimeter frequently seeing the foundations becoming uneven after moderate autumn rains. They remembered mocking looks and laughter from the native men and the gestures from one of the neophytes from San Diego who had learned a few Spanish words.

“Agua!” The man repeated, making rolling motions with his hands, motioning to the higher ground to the North. The meaning was clear. In a heavy rain, water would course through the lower ground to the Mission.

“We chose too hastily.” Crespi muttered looking toward the mountains. “We were swayed by so many heathens. It looked right. It looked like their largest village was nearby. Not only the curious, but a good workforce.”
Juan had walked the grounds many so times. He mapped the floes of the groundwater and noted the sandiness of their spot and contrasted it to the loamy soil to the North. It was a poor choice. The storms of the coming months would have them in endless repairs.

“Is it time to cut our losses?” Pedro asked. “We need men to build trenches and rock piles to divert the floods until Spring.

Then we'll build foundations near their Seeba village with Seeba labor. There's no hope of building a base here. They laugh at us. We'll never have control here.

"Yes, we move North in Spring."

<<< 0 >>>

Tooypor chased 'Aachvet and Hachaaynar, through the spiny brush on the slopes above the plains. A swirling, slow moving wall of gray hovered over them. Ponu' and Charaana caught up with the three. Pudgy Na-amah ambled far behind.

Flashes of lightning glowed behind the Eastern clouds. Tooypor held her breath and counted until a faint thunder sound was heard. She looked up at a tree to check direction of the clouds, moving from the East towards them.

"It's becoming dangerous! We need to get home fast. It's easier to go to Shevaanga. 'Aachvet and I are needed at home. Hachaaynar, you lead them."

Hachaaynar nodded and gave a quick hug before slapping arms and guiding the younger ones on their paths home. Hachaaynar felt slightly angery when Tooypor made decisions and expected everyone to do as she said. He liked her courage, like a boy, and her looks, like a girl, but he didn't like her pushiness. He ran faster as he thought about it. The others tried to keep him in sight as the rains increased. Na-amah fought off tears trying to see the two girls ahead. Ponu stopped Charaana and shouted ahead for Hachaaynar.

"We will wait for Na-amah." Ponu said. "Hachaaynar only cares for himself. We won't forget the weaker ones." Charaana slapped Ponu's arm and nodded, pleased that Ponu felt the same way she did. "We will stick together."

Hachaaynar soon saw that he'd outrun them, angry for letting his feelings show.

Tooypor made him feel irresponsible. He retraced steps. He heard sounds ahead and called out.

“Ah-hey-ey!” until he heard giggling. Mud clods started falling around him from the mist.

“Were you going to leave us behind?” Charaana sloshed mud at him. Ponu came from the side.

“We will wait for Na-amah.” Shouting until the pudgy boy appeared in the mist.

“We’ll never leave you, but you have to become faster!” She scolded. “You won’t survive if you stay slow. Promise you will keep up. Try to become fierce like a cougar. Round little squirrels are only good for food. Are you food?”

“No,” he scrunched up his face, angry at being criticized in front of Hachaaynar.

Tooypor and 'Aachvet leapt from rock to rock up Haapchivet’s trail on a shortcut they'd known from years of crisscrossing the rugged terrain. They kept to raised areas. Water ran down in rivulets. Soon the boulders thinned and wet vegetation and soil comforted their feet. They joined the trail. A family with four children clambered up the trail a hundred paces ahead of them. Their clothes were Yavit from Yaanga.

'Aachvet and Tooypor closed the gap. The muddy trail started slipping away as the last boy stepped into the sliding ooze. An older brother reached out but slipped on his stomach and lost his grip. The boy screamed and fell toward a raging mudfloe.

Tooypor instantly felt and pictured the surfaces, motion and trees and bolted down the hill, half leaping, half sliding on her heels, crouched like a mountain lion, plotting her course like a hawk. She grabbed the boy by his arm and threw herself and the boy down on their hips and crashed feet first against the trunk of an oak tree.

She held him, tears making amber paths down his muddy frightened face.
‘Oh, Wiote!’ She lay with her eyes closed, trying to sort in her adrenalized numbness how much damage she had sustained. ’Why did I do that?’

They lay still as voices called from above. “We are safe! Go to the village! We will come later.” She shouted loudly and clearly with her eyes closed, hoping not to repeat herself.

'Aachvet looked at his crazy little sister. Who would take a chance like that and do it perfectly? He looked to the stunned family, staring from the path‘s edge.

“Come now! It isn’t safe here. They will come when the rain stops,” pulling and pushing the woman, man and three boys ahead.

Tooypor had the child straddling her shoulders entering a sea of laughing faces of Haapchivetam. She was proud of how quickly she understood the motion of the child and the mud, the spacing of the tree and the time it took to tie the elements together. She saw it in an instant. No one else she knew could have. No one would see the instant reason and method. She smiled. Even 'Atooshe' was too old and heavy to make it all come together like that. She knew ‘Aachvet had told father the whole story. They’d be proud of her. She smiled and waved to everyone, knowing that’s what a heroic person does. Her father, mother and 'Aachvet stood in the path with puzzled looks.

“Your brother says you risked your life for this boy who is not of our village. I am glad you aren’t hurt, but it seems unwise.” Haapchi-vik turned to his son. “You need to control the little Pula more.”

'Aachvet felt a moment of pride.

“I can control the rainstorm, maybe, but no-one can control thıs little storm.” Sharing a grin that spread through the family.

Tooypor couldn’t let the fullness of her vision pass without making her reasons clear. It came in the instant of deciding to jump.

“It is important that the family is not from our village. They now owe us loyalty and a favor. We may need their help in the future. We should feed them now.”

Haapchi-vik, Mother Tah-ur and 'Aachvet looked at each other. ‘What a strange way for a girl to think.’ Was in each of their minds.

“Yes. We will feed them now.” Father said

AFTER SIX MONTHS

Nahaanpar calculatingly married a woman from the family of the leading trader of acorn meal. They had planned to raise children and were building a large house when she quickly passed to the creator after infection and fever. His dreams now were of the amazing materials of the invaders. Shevaanga’s women took long looks when he was near. Men challenged him as the best player at field hoop and spear games. His hunting was the most productive. His persuasiveness increased the villages trade. It came easily. He was guard and companion to Hachaaynar.

He was fascinated. 'Atooshe' had approached the strangers and offered them acorn meal. It was funny. She mocked them and they didn’t realize it. The brilliant colors and the material of the shining hats haunted his thoughts. He compared things his people made to the wonder of it. The square corners of the polished souvenir stayed with him every day. What did it mean?

“How do they do that?” The shining material and ringing crystal sounds. The bells that make loud sounds. At the same pitch! The brilliant colors with sharp definition from one to the other. A blood color against a deep green. A stripe of wildflower yellow against clear ocean blue. All more vivid than ocean, flowers or blood.

“How?”

He walked the sandy flat desert east of Shevaanga. Smoke rose from the fires where the beards were building the square longhouse and sheds.

“Why do they make them square? Why from mud? On low places, in spaces where no animals but lizards and snakes live. Why do they talk without caring if anyone understands them?’

He had to look close. He’d seen Kumeyaay from the south working with them. How do they communicate? He knew some Kumeyaay language. He thought about the words and signs that he knew, walking closer to the beards’ village. He threaded through tumbleweeds and scurrying reptiles on the approach to their structure. Two men pulled planks from a fallen mud covered wall as Nahaanpar approached.

“Auka,” Hoping they understood.

A dark squat man said something like “Maam a maaj” that he couldn’t understand. They stared until the taller man pointed toward Shevaanga. Nahaanpar touched his chest and pointed. “Shevaanga,” with a nod and smile.

The short man pointed at the far end of the plank and bent to lift his end. The tall man moved to the middle and motioned to Nahaanpar to help. It was a chance to learn. The plank was amazing! The corners were even and the surface was smooth. It was soft from being in water and mud but the feel of it and the precision of the sides was astonishing. It was made from a big tree that had been worked by hands of great patience.

They carried the plank past the main longhouse and placed it on a pile in a square bin made of logs. It had round circles on each side to help it roll. The circles were made of heavy wooden planks, cut to fit together with round edges and bound together with the a material, like the hats, that was hard as obsidian. Nahaanpar picked up a rock and chipped against the hard material to the amusement of the men. He asked "Mayith?," not knowing the full "What is this?"

The tall man took a stone to the door and reached up to a bell and struck it. He went to a wooden trough and lifted a handle with a flat shining end and tapped it with the rock. He then said something Shoshonean that was understood from tribe to tribe and village to village.

" Magic. It's magic."

<<< 0 >>>

Tooypor walked to 'Atooshe''s hut after another quake that made collapses in the Haapchivet trail. The hut was gone! Things she knew on the path looked out of place. One of the old trees, a familiar marker to her, lay on it's side away from the trail. A stream where they'd bathed had a large rock that diverted the water to each side, splitting the stream. Parts of the hut lay in the stream.

"Pula!...Pula!," More frightened with each call. Maybe she'd stayed in Shevaanga waiting for Hachaaynar. She turned, sorting the possibilities. "I should know this!"

Tooypor's heart pounded, lifting sheets of tule and handfuls of soaked herbs, throwing them aside, expecting to see a foot or hand of her mentor. She collapsed, sobbing to the waving rustling trees. She hated this feeling! With a jerk, she threw herself upright and strode to the trail and with her arms held to the sky. She shouted to fight off her agony.

"Spirit! Give me strength I need! I'm true to the path! Give me strength! Give me 'Atooshe'!"

Tooypor ran the path through the foothills to Shevaanga. Each new gully and displaced plant caught her eye. Each sound had an echo of the Pula's voice until she passed the trees on the long sloping plain to Shevaanga. In the distance, she saw the dot of the camp of the beards. 'Why did they stay away? What do they want?'

She called on all the spirits to have 'Atooshe' be there at her village for her. In Shevaanga.

CHAPTER 4
NAHAANPAR'S BAPTISM

Nahaanpar looked at the white painted walls and carefully made and colored statues in the wide room. Two brightly clothed beards and two shiny-headed men in the brown robes stared at him. At his side the two Kumeyaay workers stood. Behind him were four young Tongva from the eastern villages. They also came to learn about the visitors and their new ways.

They were given jobs to do in construction and maintenance of the camp that the beards called "Miss-un."

Nahaanpar repeated words. "Miss-un," "Es-pan-yuh," "Yay-zu," "Nee-fight," and saw the brown robe men approve of his progress. He picked up more words from the Kumeyaay and with practice, he said them well. He knelt with three Asuks-gna villagers after the Kumeyaay showed him what to do. He looked at the dusty leather sandals of the brown robed man as he spoke on and on with strange sounds and an occasionally splashed water. He wondered about the bruised young Pimo-gna woman leaning with quiet tears against the back wall.

The bald men had the four "Nee-fights" rise. With solemn nodding the older bald man put a chain of beads and symbol of the four directions around each of their necks and spoke, repeating something many times. When the man called Fray Cambon reached Nahaanpar he repeated the strange words and touched Nahaanpar's chest, saying three times. "You...Ni-koh-lahs---ho-say. ....You.. Ni-koh-lahs---ho-say....You...Ni-koh-lahs---ho-say"

He Smiled and pointed until Nahaanpar repeated "Ni-koh-lahs-ho-say."

"Nicolas Jose...very good. Nicolas Jose.

<<< 0 >>>

Hatchaynars heart beat fast. His arms and face tingled hearing Tooypor’s voice. She asked a child outside the longhouse. “Sevaanga-vik? Pula 'Atooshe'?,” Pushing the hanging doorstrips aside, she thrust into the large room and was grabbed in a bear hug by 'Atooshe' laughing and swinging her wildly.

“Tooypor, my sweetest one. You’re safe! We all worry about you!”

Hachaaynar filled with emotions he couldn’t control. Again, with her!
The tingling, the fear, as though a dangerous animal had jumped from a bush, the dryness in his mouth and worse of all, a feeling in his loincloth that scared him and made him walk away when they were together. He didn’t want to be laughed at when she was around.

“Tooypor! I’m so happy that you’re safe! I was scared!” Feeling like a worm under her gaze and the surprised looks of the villagers and his family. He was much too loud! Everyone was staring!

Sevaanga-vik looked to his wife with a twinkle in his eye. She wiggled her eyebrows up and down. They tried not to laugh, knowing the children might understand that they were being watched, that the accidental contacts were not just by chance. It would be good if they liked each other.

An alliance of Shevaanga and Haapchivet with it’s weaponry of fine bows, arrows, obsidian and hard stones, large deer and stone grinders would help trade with the outlying tribes of the Mojave, Tataviam and even Chumash through the intermarriage. It would increase the influence of Tooypor’s family through family ties of Sevaanga-vik to leading families of Yaanga, Asuks-gna and Pimo-gna. Strong reasons for a union of the children.

In her happiness at seeing her teacher safe and accepting her, even loving her, Tooypor was surprised by Hachaaynar's loud outburst. The room was quiet other than 'Atooshe''s motherly cooing. He sounded so stiff trying to get her attention. She remembered his poutiness as the rains began. She looked over 'Atooshe''s shoulder at him. He looked confused.

Hachaaynar walked out of the doorway, picked up a stone and threw it as far as he could, hating his stupidity.

“Why do I feel this way? How can I be this stupid? I can’t act this way! I am a man! All the elders know I’m strong and brave enough to become chief when my father says I can. Why does she do this to me?,” picking up and throwing more stones.

“I’m a man! I’m twelve winters old!”

SINALOA – NEW SPAIN

Private Roque Jacinto de Cota took his sac of venison home from the mercado to his wife Juana Maria Verdugo de Cota. He'd missed the assignment to accompany either de Portola or Rivera y Moncada to the Alta areas but knew that as soon as there were new settlements, they both would make homes there.

The rumors of large land grants were more than simple rumors. He knew.

SHEVAANGA (1772)

Tooypor and 'Atooshe' cleared a rocky spot in the woods. They made it level with the villagers help and gathered herb baskets. They took the good poles and panels from 'Atooshe''s second hut and arranged them as darkness closed in. Tooypor sat exhausted beside the fire

“In two moons you will have your rite of womanhood.” Looking into the shining eyes. “Along with your mother, I would like to be your Spirit Guide.

Tooypor wished for this from her first day as 'Atooshe''s apprentice. Her year of twelve springtimes weighed on her every time the sun rose. She would no longer be a child and would have many advantages of adulthood. She would be of equal stature with 'Aachvet, who would have his passage to manhood in the next spring.

The pricks and dyes on 'Aachvet's cheeks and arms would mark him as chief-to-be. He was already taller than father, easy to anger and arrive at false conclusions.

Tooypor could deflect him and turn his thoughts to solutions with results. She held 'Atooshe''s hand. "I am glad you consider me worthy. I will always be true to the way of the Pulum." She bowed her forehead to the back of 'Atooshe's hand. "I will be proud if you will be my Spirit Guide."

'Atooshe' smiled. 'This pup has talent to become a Pula among Pul. "I have felt the animal spirit that will guide and attach to you."

Tooypor was afraid it would be a creature she disrespected. 'Atooshe' was surprised by the look of confusion on her face. She needed reassurance about her strengths. She'd seen weaknesses, but this wasn't the time. After the jolt from the earthquake and Hachaaynar's foolishness, the girl needed words of strength.

"You felt sadness and rage at the strength of the shaking. You shed tears at the sight of my hut and the thought that I'd perished." Tooypor nodded. "You refused to stay and mourn," The Pula continued. "You stood to find the truth and shed no more tears." 'Atooshe' took both of Tooypor's hands and held her gaze.

"There is one animal among the strong that has the ability to shed tears. It has a warm heart and loyalty to protect it's kind. It has the strength and speed to defeat its enemies. It has the patience and depth to commune with Spirit. It dreams and holds true hopes. Even Cougar knows to avoid a fight with Bear unless he's cornered. Your visions will confirm it. The spirit of Bear is your guide and spirit."

Tooypor felt the affinity.

As night became cloudless black, Tooypor watched the hundreds of stars watching them and a steady stream of meteors crossing from right to left. She wondered what her visions would be in the fasting and Datura ceremonies. Whether Bear would become her Spirit Guide.

Nicolas Jose set out to learn two Spanish words a day. He found himself averaging four. The men with the hats of the element "Steel" or "Leather" were "Soldiers" and would only order him to do hard work. They would laugh or shout harsh sounding words.

He asked the tall Kumeyaay, Juan Bautista. Juan told him that they were bad words. It was hard to explain them. Some of the bad things didn't make sense and some seemed natural. The way they said it was what made it bad. No one did those bad things to their mothers and sometime a whole village took care of the children.

A father could be anyone, but a mother is the real creator. She could not be disrespected for successfully bearing a child.

He understood Spanish orders better than the older Kumeyaay did. He was told to lead other Tongva in digging and rock removal. There were seven Tongva from his village who had also come to the Mission out of curiosity.

The young woman who had watched him "Baptized" told him a soldier carried her there on his horse and had hurt her. She was afraid to run because her village was past Yaanga and it was open space in between. He didn't know what to tell her.

Two more soldiers came from “San Diego.” The only work they did was to sit and watch him. Three times a day they’d ride their animals in a long circle around the flatlands, then return and sit, watching.

It was not the time of discovery he’d hoped for. Each day was becoming like the one before. He’d learned a few more words. He learned that the brown robed ones spoke a different language to each other than they did to the soldiers.

They gave him body coverings of fine woven material, “cloth.” He liked it, but not enough to stay. He lay awake through the night thinking about this craziness in his life. ‘I have to return. Tonight!

As morning broke, he made his return to Shevaanga. He left the tan woven shirt and pants folded on the straw sleeping mat with the clumsy sandals. He looked out the doorway and ran feeling a joyous sense of release and finality.

He threw himself to the ground and rolled to the side of a patch of manzanita at the sound of a pursuing animal.

He barely breathed. He was relieved to know that “horses” had no sense of smell and that the area was unfamiliar to the soldiers.

<<< 0 >>>

Corporal Rufino Rodriquez found nothing worthwhile in his posting to this Mission San Gabriel Archangel, a fly infested dump of an outpost for the holier than thou Franciscans in a miserable desert.

He woke in his bunkroom hearing feet on the gravel. It was a relief to see an Indian run across the crude clearing that was being built to form an elegant patio ‘someday.’

Rodriguez’ musket was loaded at his bedside but his boots weren’t on. His horse was unsaddled and there was no one to assist him. He wasn't raised to do servant's work but the thrill of a chase made it quick and painless.

"Hah!," he shouted in the ear of Marta, his fifth horse of the year.

"Hah!" digging with his spurs, eyes darting over the brush-spotted little dunes and gullies. "Hah!," with excitement at being able to send a rebel savage to Hell.
He rode with little moon and no tracks to follow in the sand. No beauty. No women. No escapee. No sign of a man. The occasional fleeing coyote was not worth the noise of a shot and reloading on the run.

After an hour of crossing wasteland he felt exposed to eyes from the savage's village. He was alone and was too far. He listened for sounds and turned back cursing this worthless place.

"Marta" was the name he gave to even numbered horses. He kept a journal. He was literate, unlike the barely literate three soldiers at the Mission. He knew that he would get promotions while the others would be stuck forever.

"Jasmin" was the name for odd numbered horses. When one died or became lame it was replaced with the next even numbered one.

Marta and Jasmin were the first prostitutes he had lured to the back of empty warehouses in Barcelona when he was a teenager. He rode them mercilessly. When they came to, he started again, pushing their faces into the dirt and yanking back on their hair. He left them in comas. He didn't think that they had died. He thought that they might still remember him for his strength and endurance. He never saw them again.

He treated horses more gently now but many weren't up to the task. Marta was treated well. There were few horses to replace her.

His family had been nobility of Catalonia, cousins of the Marquis. Landed, with plentiful orchards and a home close to the castle during the brief Catalan independence. He was proud of his family's history, but he kept a constant fury at their downfall close to his heart.

Barcelona was besieged, attacked and sacked by the Bourbons and Madrid and left in ruins. His grand-parents and young father were evicted from the estate and made servants. The rape of Catalonia went on through his childhood. His only escape from poverty and dishonor was to join the Expeditionary Forces.

Rufino traveled to this Hellhole. He listened to the accents of the officers. Mostly Catalonians like himself. It would be a short time until he had commission to something worthy.

Nicolas Jose saw Rodriguez on his horse as he crawled along breaks in the brush. He stuck to the sandy parts and crouched to sprint through the muddy channels that ran low along the dunes. He lay still as Rodriguez' horse passed within a quarter mile. He recognized Rodriguez as the man who smiled like a crazy person when he said the bad words and as the one who had slapped the young Yaanga woman in front of him.

Nicolas Jose felt ashamed for not stopping Rodriquez. He'd be flogged or worse if he raised his hand or spoke, but now it would be different. Now he was coming back to Shevaanga to stay.

The closer to the village the stronger the feeling came upon him. "I am Nahaanpar, son of Tookoopar. Guard of Hachaaynar. I'm coming home." He smelled the deer, rabbit and sage. He hungered for acorn meal and honey. He ran the final 200 yards with joy.

<<< 0 >>>

Padres Chambon and Somera came to the office room of Sergeant Verdugo with a question that was bothering them and occupying their thoughts.
It had been a long while since any communication had been received from the Most Holy Padre Junipero Serra. His location was unknown to them and Padre Crespi hadn't informed them

about future plans for churches for the civilian Pueblo de la Reina de Los Angeles.

It would only be sensible if there were plans for more than a simple church for a growing town as they had heard rumored. As it grows as large as they were anticipating, a Cathedral would be most appropriate.

"Sergeant Verdugo" Somera began, "We haven't heard from the Diocese in Loreto. Do you know anything about the planned civilian settlement near the Yaan Indian place?," seeing only a shrug. "There has to be something."

"It is all a mystery to us" He answered. "The plans for advancement up the coast other than the Presidios to grow in the area of Santa Barbara and Monterey are all we are informed of. There will be other communities, San Jose will be one."

"With Franciscan Catholic churches of course."

"Of course." Amused by their obvious insecurity.

"You will please share any information with us?"

"Of course. We are partners in this new land of Spain."

"Of course." Taking an unsatisfied leave of the Sergeant's office.

THE ROYAL PALACE – MADRID SPAIN

King Carlos lll listened with great interest to the reports from New Spain. The expansion was going as planned. The Natives who had been under the control of the Jesuits were generally peaceful when the Franciscans took over the Missions.

The large Pueblos of the Southern Holdings were on the way to becoming Cities of the Empire that could hold off the British and Portuguese.

The plans for the Northern extension of New Spain were before him with General Galvez and Marquis Teodoro de la Croix presenting the paperwork. Galvez had aids pin large maps to an Arabic patterned tapestry on the wall

“The British navy is still formidable in the Northern Seas but they are more ineffectual on the Western coasts and the upper Californias. In the Californias, the settled parts and the new Northern Pueblos and Presidios should hold off any Russian incursions but we need to settle heavily farther to the North as they travel, mainly with footsoldiers, from the frozen areas. ”

King Carlos looked from face to face nodding and reading the charts.

“You know, when I was a child, they had this huge expanse shown as an island.”
The men remembered the Californias described as islands.

“We’ve seen those maps. I think the British may still believe that.” The handsome and lean De la Croix quiped.

“Portola’s reports look good about a Pueblo of the Queen of the Angels near the new Franciscan Mission, How soon can that be established?” The King asked with a furrowed brow, calculating the time to head off foreign claims.

“It could happen within four or five years depending on how quickly the Franciscans develop an active workforce, first in planting and harvesting for the troops, then for herding. We have the plans for cattle and sheep in place.”

“Can it be earlier than that?”

“It all depends on how well the Mission civilizes the pagans. There are Catalonian soldiers to oversee their efforts and to insure that they don’t steal as the Jesuits had.”

King Carlos lll replied that it was all satisfactory, in French.

SHEVAANGA

Nahaanpar became short tempered. Separated from the rituals, hunting and flirting. Boredom came back. He found the stone metates, the grinding and leaching of acorns primitive. The throwing sticks and arrows seemed a waste of time compared to what he'd seen. There were ways of doing things that took less time and produced more tule to weave or food to grow.

"Why would we want their kind of food?" Sevaanga-vik asked. "We have a good life here. Why make lines in the ground and disturb the natural order. Plants live their life as they are meant to."

'Atooshe' said. "Do you see the way they live? They way they talk without caring if they're understood, make their greathouses, treat animals and plants the same way. It's only to control. They want everything to follow their orders. They don't respect things. The Earth, The Moon, The Sun, The Sky, Rain, Plants and Animals don't have reality to them. They are only things to give orders to, and disrespect."

He listened to her and remembered. He had been with Lopez, the fattest soldier, when they saw a small deer near an embankment. Lopez rode toward it. The deer ran. Lopez headed it off. With the loudest noise Nahaanpar had ever heard, Lopez pointed at the deer and the deer fell, blood spurting from its neck. What Spirit could control that? Doubts and wonder haunted him.

In the morning he ran to the North with two old friends. They climbed the foothills into the oaks, leaping from flat spot to flat spot, holding bows clenched out to their sides with four arrows each, laughing and insulting each other's prowess.

They'd done it many times. Today it felt ineffective. They'd find deer. They would ignore rabbits. They might encounter coyotes or a mountain lion. He might bring down two animals for food or protection of the village but he would always remember Lopez and the power of his stick.

Rodriguez would have pointed the stick and downed him as easily as the deer. How could he explain what he'd seen? How he'd carved the meat of the deer and found rips in its flesh and blood pouring from its heart.

Who would believe the power that he saw? It was the power of....He hadn't a word it. The power of a cougar driven mad. The power of lightning for a living man to throw. There was no happiness in the hunt. The laughter was for nothing. The effort was useless. Nahaanpar waved them away and turned down the hill to Shevaanga.

He saw 'Atooshe' and a young girl gathering medicines in a field of rippling greenery. They were under patches of shadow from billowing clouds floating in a clear sky. 'How beautiful this was after the barren earth around the Mission.'
It was an uncomfortable balance. Quiet comfort and predictability against wild moments of new discovery. Even with it's danger and ugliness he felt excitement at learning at the Mission that he would never have here at home. The steel and horses. The firesticks and bell sounds. The languages and ways of doing things with wood, wax and cloth. 'There must be a way of doing both without being hunted down.'

'To be Nahaanpar in my village and to be Nicolas Jose, learning their languages and helping them understand my people. How can I do both?'

<<< 0 >>>

Tooypor shivered through the first light of the morning. The flaps of the door quaked with gusts of wind that whispered and shouted to her through the night.

Visions poured like the sweat on her brow and ran through her body under the soft and damp fur covers. In a sudden eruption, she vomited the Datura mixture and screamed and laughed alternately. She didn't sob in sadness. She sobbed for joy of her senses overpowering her mind.

Bands of light from the play of smoke and crackling embers brought designs of nature symbols. She saw animal movements in the flickering shadows that lunged at her or swept her into their worlds. She ran with rabbits and was crushed and ingested by cougar, merged into his blood and saw through his eyes in the night, sure-footedly thrusting up the oaktree trunks, leaping from branch to branch until the flash of the full moon made her narrow her eyes.

She felt herself moving, thrashing in the covers. She consciously opened her eyes wide. The moon crashed upon her and shattered her into specks of flickering tears and raindrops in a lake. Her mouth was dry and she called out for water.

'Atooshe' and mother were at her side, low and out of view, ready to help and guide her path if she needed it. Pul Tuwaru sat in the dark corner to hear her mutterings and confirm her animal spirit.

Tooypor gloried in the feel of water on her mouth, running down her neck, splashing on her hair, coating the fur on her face and body. The skins wrapped tightly around her became a part of her. She felt the pride, the fear, the focus, the rage and the power of Bear coursing through her. She knew the dedication of path and single mindedness of Bear's pursuit of stability, continuity and balance in life. It's devotion to family and simplicity. She felt infused with solidity that carried a new kind of emotion. She sobbed with joy and again vomited, but held the new solid emotion through it all.

She had soared above her lands, through the clouds around Haapchivet and above white and gray fields of bubbling mist with the highest peaks rising through it. She dived through the clouds scanning the desert and forest villages. She crawled through the grasses with the bugs and lizards and burrowed into the Earth. She flipped and swam through alternating icy turbulence and then to warm calm waters. She rode connected in a swarm of wasps to their glowing hive of wondrous beauty.

She became the dew-filled flower that sprang to life and called to the bees and then withered with the season. She froze in the windy chill and crawled to her hibernation in the nearby cave.

She shivered in the skin wrappings and covered her glistening brow with her hands.

She had returned to that solid, unshakable form that would stand with her in the hardest times and remind her of her life-tasks.

In this clearing of the dreams, she squinted through her fingers and raised her head from the scented and bundled sage and rabbit skin pillow.

In the new light of her emerging adulthood, Mother Kethu and 'Atooshe' hugged and comforted her, listening and supporting her rapid and unintelligible chatter. Pul Tuwaru smiled. It was as he thought. The completeness of the journey, and the Bear.

<<< 0 >>>

While Tooypor received the passage to womanhood, Haapchi-vik prepared the celebration. Men made circles of logs and lit fires for roast deer and acorn cakes. Women gathered flowers and put embering pots of herbs around the outer circle.

Kethu and 'Atooshe' led Tooypor to the high spring and bathed her. She was full of chatter from the night's visions. She laughed and giggled. She told them of places she'd been and forms she'd worn. The Bear vision was confirmed. It was the right one.

"I'll be steady and thoughtful. I can't be as impulsive as I've been"

She no longer shivered, walking through the deep forest trail with the sounds of crows and rustling branches. Tooypor felt sheltered by her mentor's and her mother's love.

"This is the very best time to be alive in the most beautiful place, with the smartest, strongest, wisest, except 'Aachvet, people on Mother Earth." Smiling ecstatically into the misty morning sun.

The preparations for her passage were made in Haapchi-vik's greathouse, the largest structure, other than the ceremonial Vanquech. Nettles and dyes were laid out. Coagulants and disinfectants were in tar-coated fine reed bowls at the bench in front of the door.

People smiled, slapping their chests as she approached. Children were proud of the girl who had protected and taught them when grown-ups were too busy. Old women swayed and chanted. Men, young and old, stood in doorways.

Entering Haapchi-vik's greathouse. Tooypor sat on stacked Tule mats. Kethu and 'Atooshe' gathered materials for tattoos to mark her as a grown member of the village and a woman of great power. She closed her eyes and tilted her head back as Kethu's shadow crossed.

She imagined bird's wings as 'Atooshe' rubbed a poultice of sage and mugwort across her cheeks as a mild disinfectant and anesthetic. Kethu made marks with charcoal on her forehead, cheeks and chin. She wore a smile as mother's nettles stung and moved across her brow.

"Don't smile!" Mother warned. "The lines will come out crooked," as Tooypor giggled. "You can't put straight lines on a smiling face." Tooypor was glad her forehead was done first. After many pricks and applications of the dyes on her face she felt 'Atooshe' and Mama's hands shift to her right arm.

She saw Father, 'Aachvet, Pul Tuwaru and Ponu and Sa'a'ri beaming at her. The stinging was intense. She made a sour face, but she couldn't prevent a grin from taking over.

"Good! It's good!" Ponu enthused, holding up five fingers to the right and then five to the left, touching each cheek, motioning to the forehead, holding out four fingers of each hand, making a "V" shape, then four on each side of the chin.

'Atooshe' drew charcoal bear claws on each of her biceps. Mama pricked the design into her skin, 'Atooshe' started the back of the arm. "Holly leaves." She said. "For your endurance and connection to Mother Earth. Holly is the plant that came out of the designs of the smoke. It chose you."

Hatchaynar was afraid that he wouldn't be invited to Tooypor's rite of passage. His outburst had shamed him. He felt that people considered him childish. He watched faces to see if he was looked down upon. After bathing at the Three Tree Spring, he entered the village and passed the Holy Vanquech sweat lodge. Father and Nahaanpar were squatting and talking. He hoped it wasn't about him.

Nahaanpar had been gone half a moon and had become moody. Not the man Hachaaynar had grown with as his protector.

Sevaanga-vik spoke carefully. Nahaanpar had spent time with the beards but couldn't or wouldn't explain what they wanted and why others from the village didn't return. He spoke of "metal" and "horses," but not why they were here.

"Four of our youths are missing. They were taken by soldiers. Can you return to the beards' camp? Bring back Ha'achnaap? Others?" Watching Nahaanpar's fretted brow and diverted eyes.

The request fit his desires but the other side of it was impossible. The Spanish wouldn't allow people to leave. How could he return without being shot or flogged? The part about returning to Shevaanga was easy. It was home, but it was a big risk to approach the Spanish when Rodriguez or even Lopez was on patrol.

“I want to return to their camp and learn what I can of their ways. I might be killed if I approach alone. I need a reason to reappear. I don’t know how, yet. ”

“Can I trust you to escort Hachaaynar to Haapchivet? Are you still a Person of the Earth?”

Nahaanpar raised his eyes to Sevaanga-vik’s. “I can always be trusted.” Unsure of the truth of that and if he could keep Nahaanpar’s life from Nicolas Jose’

CHAPTER 5

Nahaanpar kept with Hachaaynar up the mountain trails to Haapchivet. Sevaanga-vik and his party of elders had dropped far behind. Nahaanpar had visited the mountain village often as a runner carrying messages and dentalium bead value strings for trade negotiations.

Hachaaynar came with a chance to gain stature in Tooypor's eyes. He promised himself that Eagle was his guide and not Squirrel. Energy pulsed through his chest and legs. He would run faster up the trail if Nahaanpar could keep up.

Nahaanpar wondered why the boy seemed so eager, but also distant from him as if he had sensed the change in Nahaanpar's direction. Did his father tell the boy to watch him? What was this trek to Haapchivet? Who is this girl they are so interested in? Was it the one that 'Atooshe' had with her? She wasn't a Shevaanga child. He became winded after three hours of climbing. He couldn't do much more of this, he thought sadly. 'The mountains are for younger people.'

"We need to stop for a while." He called up.

"No. We are nearly there. You can rest later."

He knew the words were coming and saw his sense of his place in the world was changing. The Spanish give him orders and he follows. The boy gives him orders and he follows. He had followed orders before, but as a leader and a free man who could argue back if an order did not make sense. He could have answered Hachaaynar back and told him was tired but not without worrying it would come back as a weakness or failure. He felt fear to contradict the young chief-to-be. It would come back to Sevaanga-vik. He would be less.

"Yes, Hachaaynar. We'll be there soon." Pushing himself forward to keep up with the excited youth.

<<< 0 >>>

Frey Cambon sat on a patio chair squinting toward the reddish setting sun. He enjoyed the open courtyard, watching Lopez and Rodriguez ride herd on the field laborers building the new fences to divide agriculture from the soon arriving cattle and goatherds. Not the best of men but reliable enough to keep the rebellious ones on order. Lopez was somewhat lax and Rodriguez tended to be easily angered. A good enough pair for now. Better ones will come.

One rider with an extra mule to leave for the Mission passed through with a note saying that more soldiers would arrive with provisions and tents for the engineers and crews to start El Pueblo de Nuestra Senora la Reina de Los Angeles.

“You can be sure that the secular Crown will alot far more to its commerce from the funds of the Holy See than will ever filter down to us.”

Somera had heard this often both from Cambon and at every meeting of Padres and could only nod. “How true.”

Somera always felt a wee bit annoyed at his pleasure when the neck openings of the overly large tunics slipped down the arms of the skinniest of the young neophytes and they didn’t seem to care. ‘Very little modesty among savages’ he repeated often while enjoying the soft budding curves and graceful stooping and giggling. He forced himself to more spiritual thoughts. He’d trusted the man he’d baptized as Nicolas Jose. The man had fled. Why?

Lopez’s horse stopped at the edge of a dune. In the sand, covered with insects and scabs, lay a woman’s body in a Mission shift. She must have been there a week. He caught the smell before he saw her. He didn’t see an obvious cause of death but anything could happen here. He called Rodriguez and pointed to the corpse.

Rodriguez rode up and shrugged. “One less to feed.” They rode to Cambon.

“That shorthaired woman. The one who wove the mats. She’s dead over there.”

Rodriguez motioned. “We can bury her there, no?”

“That wouldn’t be right.” Cambon fretted at one more gone. “Bring her in for a Christian burial.”

Lopez brought rough cloth from a shed and hooked a drag sled to his horse, dreading the sickness he knew would come at lifting the rotten flesh onto the sled.

He saw Rodriguez grinning at him and knew somehow Rodriguez would get out of doing the hideous work. As he formed the thought...

“One man can do that, but I saw a stray, maybe two or three, sheep, moving toward the hills.” Pointing the opposite direction from the dead Indian.

“Both of you do your work.” Cambon said waving them in their respective directions.

Lopez glared after Rodriguez’ cloud of dust.

<<>< 0 >>>

An overflowing crowd of people stood on the peripheries of Haapchivet. Elder tule cloaked Chumash women chatted in clusters, next to Mojave hunters in fur-tailed dangling bonnets along with shivering and overactive Tongva boys from the coast, milling and jumping around, unused to the altitude’s morning chill.

Nahaanpar stayed at the boy's side. They threaded their way into the inner circles. They saw Serrano families from the East. Some wore mountain dress and some desert Serrano who'd walked here for three days were wearing layers of their finest weavings.

Sevaanga-vik arrived after two hands and saw the two approaching him through the crowd. He affectionately watched Hachaaynar's scanning of faces looking for a glimpse of his Tooypor. Sevaanga-vik smiled at the transparency of his son's actions.

In traditional ways it was inappropriate for a male to act cub-like toward a female, but in this case it was forgivable. The power of a merger plus the intelligence and beauty of his girl would make a strong man out of Hachaaynar.

"Father, this is huge!" Motioning to the hundreds around the central clearing. "There have never been so many coming to a Womanhood ceremony!" Whirling in wonder. "So many villages! It's like a trade fair."

"Many know her." Sevaanga-vik nodded.

'Love her family's power.' Nahaanpar thought to himself, looking at the food preparation and aromatic embrings around the crowd. He saw racks of spears that were longer and heavier than those of Shevaanga and Yaanga. The men were broader and more muscular from the climbing required by the altitude. More of the women were willowy. Less acorn meal and more activity. More meat of large animals. Not as many rabbits. 'Atooshe' moved toward them.

"She is almost ready." She grinned excitedly. "Start clearing the center and a path from the house so that Charaana and I can bring her." Scurrying back to the greathouse.

Nahaanpar was sure the girl was the same he'd seen 'Atooshe' tutoring in the bright fields. The freedom of that moment stayed with him. He wondered if anyone could see the pain of his split desires. He felt bad about glances from strangers and acquaintances. He didn't feel peace. He looked forward to the dance to come. He could raise his thoughts to his ancestors for guidance.

He watched Sevaanga-vik and Haapchi-vik move toward each other with self-satisfaction. last year he would have felt happy for their achievement in joining. Now it felt shrouded.

Hachaaynar moved to his friends and kept his eyes toward Haapchi-vik's house until the door covers parted.

Tooypor was carried out on 'Atooshe', Kethu and Charaana's shoulders. Three
village girls stayed close behind to support her if Kethu faltered.

The crowd hooted rhythmically and parted, pointing to the tattoos and shouting "Pula Tooypor! Pula Tooypor!" She blushed with an attempt to hide her pride but her laughter broke through.

Hachaaynar watched as she beamed and giggled with all the adulation. As he heard 'Pula! Pula!' over and over and remembered he could never live under the same roof with her.

Nahaanpar saw it was the slight and wiry girl that he had seen in the field. Her face was thinner than average with large intense eyes that seemed to have green in them. How strange he thought at first, but he'd seen green eyes among the tribes of the seacoast and northern deserts. This was her first day of not being a child. He had never seen such a fuss made over someone so young.

Tooypor gave up all attempts to control her laughter as her body rocked and more hands held her up to let Kethu step aside. The smiles and shouts raining upon her were as intense as the datura dreams when she soared with the Golden Eagles.

The vision seized her. Her expression changed as she rode the shoulders of the women she loved. She whispered to the sky, "You are my eternal stream. I flow with you to the sea and come back with the rain to feed Mother Earth, forever," hardly aware of the words but inadequate to the flood of feeling that ran through her.

She felt all creatures of all ages flowing in a circle through the Earth, Sky, Waters and Earth again as waves of blue dust. A big blue river that flowed up from the earth through her feet and her hands and surged up into the eternal river in the night sky. Her tears of joy flowed.

Nahaanpar and Hachaaynar saw the serious turn to her expression as her mouth moved with the words. They both thought she was uncomfortable with the way she was being carried. They relaxed as her ecstatic smile returned. She raised her arms and whooped like a coyote and made an Eagle squeal as she was lowered. She whirled and stamped as sticks were clacked and shakers shaken. The long dance began.

Hachaaynar passed jumpy clumps of Haapchivet teens toward his family and Shevaanga villagers. He kept from moving close to Tooypor. He fell into a chant to Chinigchnich and the Path and slowly lost his outside thoughts.

Nahaanpar closed his eyes, welcoming the sounds as a way to lose his outsider's thoughts and reconnect with the ways. He visualized his ancestors' faces looking on him and his situation. He flowed into the group's trance of repetition of movement and the rhythm of words and sticks. He focused on childhood memories and images of his grandmother and her stories of the old days. He felt shame at his departure from their ways but felt their forgiveness and love. As long hours and exhaustion brought dizziness to him, nothing existed other than the rhythm and the words that he intoned in a deep rasp. He no longer felt divided.

'Atooshe' couldn't stop watching Tooypor's joyous dance. They circled and hollered, pumping their elbows and stomping with abandon. Tooypor's eyes were closed in a world far from human struggle, where weight and measures, distance and time didn't exist other than fleeting flecks in the world of light.

They took peeks at each other as people tired around them and the clearing thinned. Their noses wrinkled and cheeks began to hurt from constant smiles of pleasure. As dawn approached, they wrapped in furs and collapsed by the central fire. They slept with dreams of family and abundance.

Four soldiers on four horses leading four mules with a separate mule and a well-behaved horse for Padre Crespi arrived during the night. Crespi went straight to a cot and covered himself heavily before waking at dawn.

Padres Crespi, Cambon and Samora stood in the flickering candlelight of the drafty chapel. Four seated new soldiers felt the danger of the words. Rodriguez and Cordero were the only ones to welcome the chance of action in the remote villages. Lopez and Andres preferred staying with guard duty and not being exposed to entering villages, surrounded or picked off in unfamiliar terrain.

"Can we expect reinforcements from San Diego before going into heathen territory?" Lopez asked, looking from face to face.

Crespi nodded seriously.

"This will not happen overnight. It will be more than a week but less than a month before we make our first aggressive contact to recruit native laborers and converts to the True Faith. Other soldiers will not be sent. I've asked " He felt uncertainness in all but Rodriguez, stretching back and looking sternly at Lopez.

"One blast in the chest of one of their big men and they'll be lining up to be baptized and do the work." Rodriguez said softly.

Cambon spoke. "It will take more than gunfire to fill our neophyte force. The main problems we face for stable control will be language and religion. We can deal with the questions of the True Faith and their superstitions only when we can explain the truth and necessity of Christianity to them. That will take language."

"The best neophytes that we have cannot explain our simplest requests to their own villagers let alone the neighboring ones. There must be ten languages within three hours ride! We need to spend the week teaching the smartest ones from the nearest villages enough of our language to make our requests clear. "Crespi added. "I have made a list of the phrases that we want understood." Unfolding a small parchment.

Rodriguez' thought was "Raise your skirt and touch your toes" as Crespi continued.
"We are friends.....We have gifts for you...Come to our home......Help us.. We will help you." He paused. "There is more but that will do for now."

Cordero asked "Padre, I know what those mean, but how do I tell these stupid people what friend is, or a gift?"

Cambon handed a cup to Lopez and said slowly, "A gift...for you." Pointing from one to the other. "Gift.......you." Passing Crespi's paper. "A Gift....for You...then you will repeat it to them ten times." Motioning around to the walls of the room. "Home! Or House!. My House! Come!" Bringing his palms in to his chest. "Come!..I.. Invite!..Come!..You" Pointing. "You Come! I Gift!" Putting an arm on Crespi's shoulder. "We!...Friends!" Both hands on Rodriguez' stiff shoulders. "We!...Friend!" Surprised at the flinch and panicked expression. "I'm not sure how to communicate 'Help' yet, but we have to help with their simpler tasks and say 'help' enough so that they will say their word for it. We repeat over and over until they understand us and can say it in their own language."

Frey Samora watched the soldiers move from dread at recruiting to confusion at the task of communication.

"It will take a new way of acting toward them." Cambon continued. "Most are slow to learn except simple orders, but the one or two who are quick and eager, those we will treat with respect and constant attention."

"We'll give them extra food and larger quarters. If they have problems with another Indian, we'll support our man. We will speak with them like they were one of our own."

Samora saw that Rodriguez smirked and watched his outstretched boots wiggling back and forth in utter boredom. He had never noticed much about the soldiers. The meanings of the Bible occupied most of his thoughts. Rodriguez looked up, catching Samora's eye, lowering his eyes back to the floor with an amused snort.

Crespi's eyes took in the faces. "This will be more difficult because of the languages that have nothing in common with ours. Other than the necessary sacred words of the Mass for their baptism, we will only deal with common Spanish. We lost the best one from their Seeba village but we have two good learners from the Asusa village. We will take turns through the day winning them over and seeing how much they can learn."

Cambon added. "We will treat them as friends. Agreed?" The soldiers nodded.

<<< 0 >>>

Nahaanpar woke. It had been light for a while. He rarely woke after the first glow from the west. The hill and wall of trees made it darker than the dawns of the flatlands. He raised the aromatic fur covers from his face and rose to his feet with deerskin wrapped tightly to him. The encampment had lumps under covers in all directions. Most were motionless. Some stirred. Clumps of children played quietly. Some walked to the center of the village preparing for their long walk home. He stretched, feeling invigorated by the cold blast and threw the fur aside..

"Aaaaaheh!" Jumping up and springing on the balls of his feet, remembering that Hachaaynar had slipped out of sight and later waved, walking with his father to the Haapchi-vik main house.

Nahaanpar was no longer needed except to return with the Chief's family. A group from Asuks-gna were passing herb and playing dice for each others clothing. He joined. He stopped feeling the cold.

People were leaving. Most had never traveled for a Womanhood ceremony before. It meant important contacts. Products became known and remembered by special listers under Pul Tuwaru. Traders from the islands, deserts and the mountains beyond would see the variety and make deals.

Haapchi-vik, Sevaanga-vik, Charaana, Kethu, Hachaaynar and 'Aachvet slept in the GreatHouse. The two lumps of bearskin in the far corner moved.
'Atooshe' peeked from the opening of her skin into the other fur blanket. Tooypor's hair was over her face and blended in with the black bear's fur. The tip of her nose was just visible. 'Atooshe' tickled it and waited. Three times she repeated the touch until the nose twitched and a hand came up to rub it. 'Atooshe' reached but her hand was yanked mid-way and her finger bitten by laughing Tooypor. Their noses were inches apart as their eyes locked.

"Good morning, Pula Tooypor," her finger still between Tooypor's teeth.

"Good morning, Pula 'Atooshe''pahr, I'm not Pula yet." Releasing the finger. "That is many seasons away."

"Not many," Rolling on her back, looking up at the clay-packed weaving of the ceiling. "Your talent is recognized." Reaching her hand back to hold Tooypor's.

"Were you surprised by how many people came to honor you?"

"Yes! They didn't all come for me. They came for father. I've never seen most of them and they wouldn't know me if they saw me tomorrow."

"They'll recognize your marks. They mark you as powerful."

Tooypor giggled. “Did you see Hachaaynar? He stayed far and looked away when I smiled. I can’t tell sometimes if he respects me or dislikes me,”

“Oh, little bear-cub. He respects you. He doesn’t dislike you one little poppy seed’s worth.” She squeezed the hand. “He may like you a whole poppy field’s worth.”

“He acts funny. Different from two seasons ago.”

“He is changing. Becoming a man but not there yet. Boys are funny when they are becoming men. They take foolish chances, get angry easily when they don’t get their way. Hachaaynar will make a good man. He won’t get angry easily and he thinks things through carefully.” She squeezed the hand again. “He asks about you often. More than anyone else. I think he thinks about you very, very often..with respect.”

Tooypor smiled with her face in the covers, knowing that the feelings in Hachaaynar were good ones. With all his clumsiness, he was a good man.

<<< 0 >>>

Nahaanpar walked lost in thoughts behind Hachaaynar and the Shevaanga family through the foothills loaded with gifts wrapped in skins given by Haapchi-vik and traders from the high desert tribes. How could he return to the Mission, keeping faith with his ancestors and Sevaanga-vik? Sevaanga-vik had something in mind.

He watched Haychaynar with affection, picking up rocks and lobbing them with great accuracy, kicking sticks and helping some of the older villagers carry their loads.

“I’ll take those.” Following Hachaaynar by lifting half the skins from an elder’s shoulders.

Sevaanga-vik looked back and made a sign of approval. He saw his son was sharing the load. The event had gone well. He felt solidity from Nahaanpar that he hadn't felt when the journey began. He spoke quietly in 'Atooshe''s ear.

"This has been a big step forward for all of us. See how Hachaaynar seems more manly." She smiled approval, glancing back at her son. "I see a relaxing in Nahaanpar too. This trip put at him home again. I have plans for him."

"He has changed, husband. Be careful."

<<< 0 >>>

Rodriguez shuffled from foot to foot, watching Lopez baby talk to an idiot Asuks-gna man who followed like a puppy. "Teach him this!" he shouted, rubbing his crotch and gyrating his hips.

The Indian imitated him to howls of laughter from the soldiers. "Have him do it for Cambon!". Rodriguez said. "The Frey might invite him to live with him."

Lopez stopped cold. "You don't say things about the Fathers! You can joke, but not blaspheme!"

"They aren't Saints! Do you see the way he looks at the girls? Somera too." He poked Lopez' chest. "Blasphemy is about the Lord and his son Jesus Christ and the Blessed Virgin. Drooling goats in robes may feed and house us but they are servants of the Crown like us and servants of the Holy See, The Lord may guide the Pope, but not these payasos. We keep the savages from having them for dinner. That's our only obligation to them. "

Lopez turned the Indian toward Rodriguez and said slowly. "Sold-ier. Stupid Cataloon Sold-ier...Sold-ier."

Rodriguez put his hand back to the codpiece.

"Big sold-ier! Him, little soldier." walking away.

Lopez led the Indian to the fence. "Fence," pointing and tapping on the fence until the Indian said "Na-angang. fence." They smiled and nodded. “House” was more difficult. A wall became “fence.” When farther away the house became “land” or “hill.” After many times the “house” remained “house.”

The older gnarled Indian was named Miguel de Gabriel. Many were named for the Saint of the Mission. He’d been banished from Asuks-gna for stealing twice. If he returned he’d be killed. The soldiers mocked him and thought him less than human. They spoke to dogs better than they did to him. He pretended to not know what they meant after he understood. “House” meant any structure, whether a square mud building with rooms like the padre’s place, or a lean-to for wood or tools. “Man” meant humans. “Horse” was their large animal and “dog” was anything that barked or howled except Coyote.

He saw that Lopez was slow and patient. Good-hearted for a Spaniard. Padres greeted ‘Miguel’ before the others from Asuks-gna. Only the young man, who was kidnapped from Yaanga, was treated like Miguel, given extra food and taught the strange language. What the bad man Rodriguez said had to be an insult about his penis.

Private Cordero walked his Yaanga man through the mounds and gullies. “Rock...Rock...Sand...Sand.” and “Bush, Tree... ..Bush, Tree.” The man was impossible, thought Cordero.

“No, idiot! Not bush! There’s no bush there. That’s a rock!” Picking up the rock and starting over. “Rock!” Then picking up sand in the other hand, restraining himself from making the fool eat it. “Sand!”

Tooypor threw herself into study of plants, trees and rocks with added fervor. She left for 'Atooshe''s hut at dawn. She brought the strong and lanky daughter of a Serrano Pula with her. Tah-ur, from an eastern desert village a day beyond Asuks-gna. She knew more about mountain lions and snakes than Tooypor and was a faster runner. She came to learn about the Haapchivet plants.

They exchanged words from their similar, but distinct, dialects. The mixed Serrano and Tongva was comfortable for Tooypor.

“I’m not sure I’m ready for twin apprentices today.” 'Atooshe' said, “But you two seem joined at the hip!” heading into the forest. “Keep up with me!” The three sharing fast twittering exchanges punctuated with laughter.

Tah-ur had learned the skills from her father and was working up the courage to
become his successor. “But I can’t be. There is too much opposition from elders and council.”

Tooypor spoke. “You are more learned than I am about the far villages and the animals and the eastern legends. Other than Pula 'Atooshe' and Pul Turaru, you’re so smart! The smartest!”

After three days of adventuring, Tooypor knew she had a sister. They hugged, promising to stay in contact through messengers, forever.

SINALOA – NEW SPAIN

It was a good day in town for Antonio Mesa, a Negro campesino selling his small allowance of the bean crop that he’d harvested for the French family who owned so much of the land on the outskirts of town.

It was a good year for his sales. He felt that he could now propose to the beautiful mulatta who worked as a nanny in the family’s home.

When Ana Gertrudis saw him enter the field and walk straight to the porch with a big smile, she that knew it would be something important for her, and she had guessed correctly.

“Ana Gertrudis, I have come to you to ask for your hand in marriage. I can now afford a small home of our own, and,…. I love you. Please accept my proposal of marriage.”

At nineteen years, she felt that she was becoming too old for a man to want her for
marriage, except for Antonio. He was special.

"I will, Antonio. Oh yes. I will."

SHEVAANGA

Nahaanpar fixed thatch on a woman's curved, sloping windward walls, listening to her complaints about the neighbor's children. He stocked her bins with acorn and wood. He'd joined hoop games and threw curved sticks with rabbit hunting parties, and waited for this moment. He entered and sat at Shevaanga-vik's request.

"You know what I want you to do. Are you able?"

"I've thought of it day and night. I could never approach during daytime. Soldiers would recognize me and use their firesticks. I need the protection of the brown robes. The brown-robes treat me with respect, for their kind."

"How can you get past their warriors to the brown-robes?"

"I have two ways that might work. The most direct is to go when there is no moon before dawn. I would climb through a square hole into the big room they call a chap-el. I would cover myself with their fabric and hide behind their big cross-man until the brown-robe arrives and crawl to his feet. They like it when we crawl."

Cross-legged, Sevaanga-vik absentmindedly picked at his polished toenail with fretted brow. "That might be good, but I see three danger places. You approach alone in the dark night when the cougar, coyotes and even bear are out hunting. You may carry bow and arrow, but you can't take them near their camp. If they find them later, you will be under suspicion." He holds out two fingers. "I've seen the square openings. They are high. It will make noise when you climb in and you won't know if warriors sleep inside." With three fingers extended, he continued. "If you can hide inside until the brown-robe arrives, you do not know if he will accept you, fight you, or call the soldiers."

Nahaanpar saw problems in each. "It isn't without risk." Waiting for a better suggestion from Sevaanga-vik.

"What is your second plan?" Focused on Nahaanpar's downcast eyes.

"If someone from the village could approach during the day, perhaps an old person with a gift or basket, and tell whoever their new translator is, that Nicolas Jose wants to come back to Padre Cambon, the most fair brown-robe....."

"Better!" exclaimed Sevaanga-vik. "They won't kill or kidnap an old woman with a basket. What is their word for brown-robe?"

"Paw-dre...Padre."

"Good! We will teach her to say 'padre' and to repeat it until they take her to...which 'padre?'"

"Cam-bone...Cambon"

"Good. We teach her to say Padre Chambon until she is there with a translator." He nodded vigorously. "I know the woman. An acorn grinder, frail looking, old and ugly. None of them would force themselves on her, but she is strong for travel and she is a smart one."

He pursed his lips. "I still don't know what they want. They try to make plants grow where plants won't grow."

"They want to make us obey their Hay-soos the cross-man and turn us away from Chinigchnich. They want people to work for them."

Sevaanga-vik shook his head. "They want us to understand their language but they don't try to learn ours. If they want a bridge to reach us, why don't they just come over, play some games and eat with us and trade. Does it mean nothing we have has value?"

Nahaanpar knew the truth of that. It was as Sevaanga-vik said. The Spanish thought that only their way had value. That the Tongva only lived for acorns and dug for roots. "What they hold to their hearts are complicated things that others make for them. They have their things sent to them from...I don't know where. They think their cross-man and the brown-robes make things happen. Make everything in the world happen. That we are only good for working for them"

"Why would they think that?."

"The brown-robes speak a different language from the soldiers. They say it is the language of their god. The soldiers are their slaves and will kill anything that their god says to kill."

"We need to either make a bridge of trade....or fight them." Sevaanga-vik said sadly

."You have told me of the firesticks. Can we drive them away?"

Nahaanpar shook his head. "I need to find out."

CHAPTER 6

NICOLAS JOSE'S RETURN

Private Andres rode his western rounds making a comic song about a girl from his home in Sonora. She kept losing her goats and was so tired from chasing them she'd fall asleep as her parents, the priest and he, her fiancée, were talking with her. Her snores and their pleading made up the repeated chorus. He kept papers in his leather pouch about the populist changes in Europe against the Crowns of Spain and France.

He was the only full blooded Mexican Indio soldier who'd learned to read well enough to follow the new messages of freedom sweeping the world. He kept his knowledge hidden from the Spanish soldiers. He received pouches from Sonora with news about Europe. The worlds across the oceans excited his mind. Freedom would come to Mexico one day and he swore he would help to bring it.

He saw movement on the footpath the Seeba Indians used to travel east. Trotting forward, he saw a short old woman carrying a large basket. Most Indians walked past with nervous looks, trying to ignore the soldiers. This one flapped her free hand at him and repeated "Padre. Padre!" He signaled her to follow and slowly walked her to the mission, humming parts of his song. He saw the tiny spots of Lopez and Rodriguez on their horses to the south.

Padres Jose Cambon and Angel Somera were in the chapel.

"Padre Cambon. Padre Cambon" She pronounced clearly, looking from one to the other.

"Yes. I Cambon." Tapping his chest, wondering how she would know of him.

"Padre Cambon." Not remembering what she was supposed to say. "Padre Cambon." She repeated, slowly turning 360 degrees, looking at the room and it's wonders.

He stooped to look in her eyes and hold her attention. His palm to his chest, he again said "I Cambon!"

Part came back to her. "Nee..las...Ho...say." Looking intensely, proud of her words. "Neelas Hosay!"

"What language is this?" He asked Somera. "It sounds like Spanish or Latin."

"Jose." Somera said. "Possibly the neophyte who ran away, Nicolas Jose."

Her eyes widened. "Nee-ko-las Ho-say! Nee-ko-las Ho-say!" Setting down her basket and tapping her arms on her sides. "Neekolas Hosay!"

The priests exchanged quizzical looks as Cambon continued. "What about Nicolas Jose?"

"Nicolas Jose." She said, trying to remember the other words.

The three stood motionless until she suddenly started pointing at the two of them and then to herself and said the word. "Trans-late-tor....Trans-late-tor." Both understood her request. Somera raised his eyebrows and took on a half-smile. "Our translators are horrible. I doubt if they can shed much light on what she has to say."
"Andres." Said Cambon. "Have Cordero and Lopez bring their prize neophyte translators here immediately." Andres clicked his heels and bowed his head before rushing out the door.

Rodriguez saw unusual activity. First Andres rode to the west and brought a walker to the Mission. Later, he rode to Lopez and then to Cordero and brought them to the Mission. What was going on? Why was he left out? Long after the soldiers entered the Mission and no-one came to bring him in, he spurred his horse homeward.

Was it against him? Were they sending him away in dishonor? Had they somehow found out about that foolish little runaway woman he'd taught the wrath of God to? He'd laughed at Lopez throwing up when he found her.

"What the hell is going on?" Feeling fire in his neck as the horse picked it's way through the rough terrain in the six kilometers between his position and the Mission.
"What the hell are those bastards up to?"

Cambon, Somera and the three soldiers watched the Indians chattering, pointing and gesturing. After many exchanges the Yaanga man came to Cambon.

"Nicolas Jose..want..come back." He fidgeted trying to find the words. "He...." He acted out a gesture of ducking and covering his head. Then he covered his face with panicky looks.

"Afraid?" Offered Somera, making similar gestures.

Cambon raised his hand and spoke. "Nicolas Jose wants to return but is afraid to. That makes some sense...What else.... Why is he afraid?" The woman repeated something several times to the Yaanga man and he said. "He come..." Pointing to Cambon. "Gna here!...You."

Cambon nodded with vigor, understanding the meeting. "Good! Nicolas Jose wants to return to the Mission, but is afraid and wants to talk with me about his receiving forgiveness for running away. Very good! He was the best we'd had. He will be an asset. Should we take him back? "

"Absolutely! We can't have Indians out there afraid of us and telling stories that will scare others. Why on earth is he afraid of us?"

Lopez spoke up. "He was frightened of the musket when I shot a deer, and, he also seemed afraid of Rodriguez.."

"He'll have nothing to be afraid of. He'll get used to gunfire, but if we work with him on language, he will outshine all of our others in a week! That is a smart Indian. We need him."

He turned to the Indians. "Nicolas..come here... Nicolas," Pointing toward Seeba village, "Here!" Pointing at the ground, ushering the woman to the door and pointing first at her. "You......to Seeba.....Nicolas Jose....Here!" He made signs for the Yaanga man to go with her. All eight went into the courtyard to bid her goodby as Rodriguez approached.

"What's the big meeting?" Keeping as neutral a voice as he could.

Cambon smiled warmly. "Do you remember that Nicolas Jose who ran away?"

"Yes, what did he do?" Regretting missing sending him to hell.

"He is coming back. We are glad to have him return. He is a smart lad." Patting Rodriguez on the shoulder to Rodriguez' intense discomfort. "We will train him to bring many of his people to the True Faith and be a leader."

"He is insolent and untrustworthy."

"He is the closest to a leader of all the ones here. We need to be good to him and make him feel special." Looking directly at Rodriguez. "I want you to be good to him. It will repay our investment many times over."

The old woman and young Yaanga man walked quickly to Shevaanga to arrive before nightfall, they looked back often.

"I think they understood what you wanted, but they don't understand one word of our language." The boy said. "We have to act it out and even then, you can't be sure."

"Was that the Rodriguez man who rode up at the end?"

"Yes, he is very dangerous. He beats people, especially young women. He acts afraid of women like you. Did you see his expression when the brown-robe touched him?"

"He is the one Nahaanpar said would use the firestick. Do you think Nahaanpar will be safe?"

"I was going to use this trip to escape back to Yaanga, but I'll go back with you and Nahaanpar. I will make you both safer, but I'll go back home soon." He picked up rocks to throw and aimed at targets as he walked. "I was kidnapped by Cordero nine moons ago. I have friends at the Mission now. The invaders give me more than the others." He grunted at a long throw that hit a far-off cactus. "I can help my friends now."

The old woman patted his arm. "Nahaanpar will help you all. He will find a way to make them go away."

1772 -SINALOA – NEW SPAIN

"Jose! Jose!" Father yelled from the field. "Bring me water!"

Jose Moreno was turning twelve next week and was aching from the morning's picking, bundling and carrying the corn crops. He limped to the vat and filled leather drinking bags for father and himself.
He knew that he didn't want to do this forever. 'What else can I do? '

MISSION SAN GABRIEL

Nicolas Jose strode through the neatly laid out rows of squash stepping between half grown plants in the new vegetable plots, stretching his arms in the morning sunlight.

Juana FourToes smiled shyly as he slapped her butt on passing. “Good girl.” He smiled paternally as she faked surprise. He did it when people weren’t watching.

She knew that he liked it when she seemed mildly offended. If she showed anger he’d stop giving her pouches of wine to ‘make up.’ It was an acceptable trade. He wanted sexual favors once a month or less. He spread his attentions thin, which was fine with Juana.

He passed the newly walled courtyard to the side door of the remodeled chapel.
“Greetings, Blessed Fathers.” to Frey Cambon and the new Padre Mugartegui, as he crossed the back of the room to act as witness to his fifth baptism.

The tribal couple kneeling on the floor were strangers. From their look they could have been Kumeyaay or from the southern costal Tongva. They looked scared and pathetic in their woven native clothes. Soon they’d be dressed in proper Mission clothes. .

Becoming more fluent in Spanish and a smattering of the Padre’s Latin. He could tell the difference between Rodriguez’ rough Catalan and Cordero’s lisping Castellan dialects.

He had the respect of the soldiers, the comfort of his own room and bed, the pleasures of the ample sacramental wine and, his chest filled with pride at the thought, the special company of any woman who struck his fancy. The smart ones sought him out. The ones who denied him their intimacy and treated him hatefully had some bad food and hard labor ahead of them.

He understood the differences in needs and fears of the Spanish soldiers and learned to work with each one. What they wanted and the ways to conceal their 'carnal nature' from the Padres and, of course, The Lord. The soldiers couldn't be seen socially with lowly Indian women.

Lopez was easy. He liked plump, mature women. The young, flirty ones seemed 'too much like a daughter' and it embarrassed him when they seemed attentive. There were many ripe fruits to pick. Leading them to a meeting with him behind the Bird Face Oak was well rewarded.

Cordero liked young, slim girls like Juana FourToes. He took more risks, behind the stables or on the kitchen table where discovery was a possibility. He laughed that one day a Padre would walk in and the expression on his face would make the whole thing worthwhile. He could always "confess and get absolution for being seduced by a godless temptress." He was generous with the wine.

Andres was the hardest to understand. A Mexican Indian who didn't seem interested in women. Only 'a girlfriend back home,' never seeming to think about anything else, but he said.

"When my five years are up I'm going home. I'll be in Sonora at full pay, back with Mexicans. No more Spanish. No more hypocrite Padres." Andres never drank wine or said bad words. It was hard to trust a man who acted better than the soldiers he dealt with.

Rodriguez kept him frightened. He scared the other soldiers. Even the Padres were careful not to set his anger in motion. Nicolas Jose stopped supplying him with women after some had complained of being badly hurt, a few had run away, and then one had been found a kilometer from the Mission, partially eaten by coyotes.

Nicolas Jose knew he'd sent her to Rodriguez three nights before. He felt Rodriguez' hard eyes upon him for weeks after that. There were times in the fields when he would see Rodriguez at a distance trying to charm a pretty neophyte to meet him somewhere.

No matter how much he disliked the more prideful women who treated him like a puppet of the Spaniards, he would never send one to Rodriguez.

LORETO – NEW SPAIN

It was a time of celebration for Corporal Vargas. His abilities in calligraphy as a scribe in documenting the history of the building of New Spain had been recognized.
He now was promoted after service with Anza, Portola and Rivera and was told that he might be assigned to Presidio San Diego and the proposed settlement to the far North adjacent to the new Mission San Gabriel Archangel, the Pueblo of the Queen of the Angels.

“What a beautiful name.” Aloud. ‘That’s where I will retire. By the sea. With the Angels,….and a fishing boat, …..and big, big family.

<<< 0 >>>

Hills, passes and flatlands passed. Step by step. Tooypor felt fresh energy evey day with ‘Ahtooshe.’ Through the villages of Yaanga, Kaweenga, Jautıvıt and Guaspet, to the coastal villages of Topan-gna and Mali-wu. They crossed friendly Chumash lands and traded for shell, fishbone and dentalium products of the Islands. Runners kept in touch from their villages.

Occasionally a runner from Tah-ur would catch up after a long chase through many villages. He would bring gossip from the Apuimabit desert and Tah-ur’s adventures.
From the far west they walked past the trails to Haapchivet and Shevaanga and trekked east and north avoiding, the encampment of the Spanish, to Ashuukshanga and Cucamog-na before traveling into the Serrano village of Guachama where Tah-ur came with a large party to meet them.

The three embraced like sisters trading stories all through the day and night. 'Atooshe' became a teenager in listening to their enthusiasm and giggling., but there were also stories of young people who had left, disappeared or were kidnapped in plain sight by soldiers or the expelled tribesman who collected bounties to bring children and youths to the Mission.

Two moons after leaving Shevaanga they returned west along the base of the mountain range to skirt the northern boundaries of the land now claimed by the Mission.

Tribesmen who'd run away said the land was claimed for "The Crown." They tried to explain what that meant. It seemed to be 'A bright metal hat on some creature's head.'

"What an enormous head this creature must have to need all this space for his hat!" Tooypor said, knowing the phrase must have a meaning other than the one the runaway used.

Armed runners with spear and bow greeted them three kilometers before the village. Approaching Shevaanga they saw guards along the perimeter with bow and arrow at the ready. Sevaanga-vik and Hachaaynar stood to welcome them home.

"We are proud of your successes. Traders from many villages came because of your travels." Sevaanga-vik puffed up.

Hachaaynar took Tooypor's hands and said "I'm proud of you and glad you are safe."

Tooypor squeezed his hand. "I am pleased to see you. It is good to be in our territories again."

"Will you stay until our union?"

"Father wants to bring me to you. I will return to Haapchivet after resting, My whole family wants to carry me here for the ceremony. I wouldn't let them carry me all the way! I wouldn't trust them not to trip. I'll walk on my own until we are close. Then they can carry me."

They walked away from the village. He shuffled. They both threw rocks at targets.

“I feel like I have fluttering wings when I think about being alone with you, like…., a man and woman.”

She knew this was about the thing that no-one would talk to her about. She wasn’t afraid of bears or trails on high cliffs, but she was afraid to ask her mother or 'Atooshe' about what a woman and a man did that made them different from the ones around them. She couldn’t talk to the village girls about it. They thought she knew everything and she would lose respect if she showed ignorance.

“I shouldn’t say this,” He continued, “but I feel I can really talk to you. That you understand about everything. ...A man is supposed to know things, but,...I don’t know what to do. When we’re alone.”

“Neither do I.” Relieved at not being alone in this mystery. “No-one has told me.” Laughing with him. “I feel so stupid because everyone thinks I know everything!”

“Me too! They know I’m going to be chief, so the boys brag to me, but I didn’t know what they mean. ‘I’ve had so and so,’ or ‘she did this to my penis’. No-one ever did anything to my penis.”

Tooypor felt out of her depth but intensely curious. “I’m going to ask Kethu and 'Atooshe' to teach me all about it. If they tell me they won’t, I’ll pick up handfuls of medicines and throw them out the door until one of them sits down and explains it to me. You should do the same.”

“I will. They must tell me everything before our union,” They hugged like happy cubs and returned to the elders.

SINALOA – NEW SPAIN

Jose Antonio Navarro expected more business for his tailoring shop. Other tailors had better contacts with the army and had first call for military work. He had the leftovers and torn parts from cavalrymen's accidents that they wanted hidden from the senior officers.

He made smocks for pregnant women, grandmothers, yard and fieldwork and aprons for cooking. He wasn't in the best part of town and they couldn't afford to move toward the center. After nine years of marriage two sons were theirs in the last three years and Maria Regina Gloria's stomach was growing large again. It would be a while until the boys could help and expand the business.

He listened carefully to each soldier's rumors and upcoming posting, looking for a better place to locate. There had to be something better than this.

MISSION SAN GABRIEL

After two successful forays to Asusa village to replace the dwindling neophyte population, Crespi, Cambon and Somera agreed that it was time to test the nearest and larger Seeba village.

"We've had a hundred neophytes in August and lost forty to the disease. We need whole families from Seeba. If the children can be brought in, the rest will follow. We must silence any talk of sickness other than that their Gods are cruel to them and our God can save them. Nicolas Jose can tell them that."

Somera fretted. "Do you think Nicolas Jose is ready? Our Seeba Indians keep away from him. He never associates with them and, as far as I can tell, never gives them favoritism. They ignore each other."

“I’ve noticed the same thing.” Said Cambon. “He favors the women from other tribes. Too much, I’d say. ”

Crespi pursed his thin lips. “You’re implying fornication, I take it.”
“More than implication. It’s obvious he abuses his authority.” Cambon knew it was time to air out questions about ‘his man.’

“He does a good job in keeping the lazy ones and the rebellious ones from damaging the morale of the majority. He uses carrot and stick, but also deprivation. That’s good leadership. At least, he is the best Indian leader that we have available at this time. There are three or four who are becoming useful in communicating simple orders, but Nicolas Jose can control the Indians from the Tongva villages best in his way of coaxing and manipulating their productivity.”

“But.” He continued before Crespi could make a pronouncement. “He has most of the flaws that savages have. He is new to The Church and, of course, European values and virtues. I feel that he will learn, but first, he will serve us by recruiting from the village he has known from birth.”

Somera, hesitant to speak before Crespi had set out his statement, knew the importance of building the diminishing work force and saw his chance to add a point for Cambon’s position.

“Nicolas Jose has told me that he knows personally, the chief, the medicine woman and the leading families of Seeba.”

“I’m worried about giving him too much influence.” Crespi cautioned. “If he is given to sinful behavior and feels he has license to continue, he will create more problems than he solves. He needs stern talking to and discipline before being entrusted with being spokesman in even the most limited sense for our order.”

Cambon assented. “He will submit to our discipline. I will make it clear that he must repent of licentious behavior if he wants to continue his position and advance, as we desire him to. He will understand that our needs come first. I suggest that he pick a stable woman neophyte and marry."

"Yes, good. Good." Crespi stood and paced, hands clasped behind his back. "That will set a good example. Yes, he must marry. It will give him stability and a clear set of standards to abide by. He'll do it this week before we can take him to Seeba. He'll be baptized again with a clearer understanding of what that means."

Somera asked. "Shall we pick the best woman for him?" The three discussed candidates for an hour before deciding that Nicolas Jose should participate in the discussion.

"He hasn't been truly baptized with instruction." Cambon added.

"I think it's more than time. That will be a duty of Padre Mugartegui, unless you would prefer to?"

"He needs more duties. I approve."

<<< 0 >>>

Nicolas Jose watched his crew work in fertilization and composting, cleaning out the horse stables and inner goat grazing areas. They put sackcloth tarps on drag-boards and pulled the excrement across to deep pits to mix with leaves and waste plant material to fertilize the soil. There was never enough crop. The Padres expected miracles from the sandy, wind-whipped and parched Earth. They had no interest in the edible growths and flavorings that Nicolas Jose and his crews knew were all around them.

"They know what they want. We have to make their vision take life." He said when questioned by neophytes.

"It is a coyote's vision." A crewman would say. "Not a vision from the Earth."

Nicolas Jose also questioned their vision and what it would mean if their plans came to nothing. He learned how metal was made and the differences between lead, brass and steel. He had never seen a forge, but he'd seen lead melted and cast, steel heated and bent and heard the curses when the metal was too thick or the hammers too fragile. He'd seen cloth tear and watched the fine and course threads used to extend and repair the material.

There was no more mystery. The people he controlled and those who controlled him weren't his friends. He couldn't count on knowing them next year, or having their loyalty next week. They were replaceable without a second thought or remembrance.

'I am too,' waking at dawn and reaching for the leather bag of wine in the bedding. 'I am four kilometers from my home and I haven't seen my friends in two years. Even Sevaanga-vik, whom I promised to report to, has forgotten me. He probably thinks that I am a traitor. I know I'm not a traitor but I don't know what I am. I'm just trying to make do. He weighed the advantages in the Mission against his life with his people and the feeling that came over him when he was alone, looking out on the landscape he had known as a boy.

"I've lost my ancestors." He mumbled, squirting a long stream of the potion into his mouth. He had an urge to dance and quietly chant for enough time to feel their presence. He knew he couldn't do it in his room with its thin board walls. He thought about going in a ravine in the afternoon where he'd be out of sight and dance in the shade of a huge oak tree. He'd do the old ceremony by himself until he felt the guidance from Spirit and family. He'd be recognized as part of the Earth Continuum.

"By myself." He mumbled aloud. The dance would not help him. It would take a group, connected in spirit, for Spirit to intervene and heal the wounds of heart and flesh. "I'm alone." He whispered to his lost family and the spirits of the Earth. "I am alone."

He heard the coyotes whining and crying in the night. It was a sound he'd always liked. Now it felt like their sadness and their need for companions was more human than many of the disconnected people around him. 'Only thinking of the work of the day. Like me.'

The sound of roosters woke him. Chickens were the newest priority and the soldiers hid away the biggest roosters to train them to have cockfights behind the stable.
Juana Fourtoes waved to Nicolas Jose seeing him stride past the tile makers at the Mission wall. Behind them Rodriguez was barking orders at Miguel del Valle and his mixing crew.

"Hello, Juana." He said as he passed closer. His eyes looked sad. He didn't have his usual bounce.

"Hello, Nicolas Jose. Are you well?"

"Food that didn't set well." Making a sour face. "How is your work?" Seeing her slenderness and full-lipped mouth.

"I am pleased the squash are taking hold. I think this year will be better, but you...need to rest if you can. Too many are becoming sick from the bad cough and black tongue."

He walked away from her with a frown. Padre Cambon watched from his patio chair in the shade. It was time to prepare him for the task to come.

"Here! Come here!" He shouted.

Nicolas Jose sat at the stone bench.

"Good morning Blessed Father. The construction is going well. I look forward to the big chapel. The others do too."

"Yes, but it's going more slowly than we'd like." Wondering about his statement's meaning. Did it mean that he was actually more committed to expansion of the Church? Was it servility? How solid was this man to be entrusted with the most important contact attempted? Could he convince his countrymen to come to the Mission and stay.

"Our work is progressing more slowly because we have less helpers this month than we had two months ago."

"I have seen some sick but many are at their quarters with sick children. They will be back to work soon. They will pray. They will become better."

"I am glad that you have faith in prayer."

"Yes, Padre. Prayer will save them."

"Nicolas Jose, we, the Fathers of the Mission, have been watching you and your progress. We have questions."

Hearing this gave Nicolas Jose a chill at the possibility of expulsion. Had they spoken to soldiers?

"Yes, Padre," with downcast eyes.

"Nicolas Jose, you are a good man. You've helped us to spread the word of the Lord and you've been the best of your kind in communicating our desires to the tribes. In that, we have great confidence in you." He paused, seeing there was something he dreaded as well as hopes for praise.

"We've discussed giving you more responsibilities and benefits but there are questions about your unmarried status and your relations with neophyte women. Do you understand my words? "

"Yes, Padre." Expecting worse. Many of the words Cambon used were strange to him, but he would say 'yes, Padre' and Padre would be pleased.
"We feel that you should marry and live a stable life with one woman within the Church."

Nicolas Jose's eyes raised to the Padre's face and showed relief. "You want me to marry a woman here in the Mission?" Thinking immediately of Juana Fourtoes. It was not because of his arrangements with the soldiers. He had nothing to fear. Juana returned to his thoughts often and, although he'd sent her to Cordero in the past, he held off on sending her to soldiers again. The idea of marriage was at a good time.

"Is there a woman that you would want to marry?"

"Yes, Padre. How do I do that?" He'd witnessed marriages. He stood still while Padre Crespi spoke in the Priest's Latin language and Nicolas Jose made a stroke on the paper material where he was told his name appeared. The Kumeyaay couple spoke some words he didn't understand. He saw them later eating together, but working apart in the fields.

"How do I marry?"

Cambon laughed. "You marry one woman and one only. You make your house with her," Nicolas Jose bobbed his head to show understanding, "You do not lay down with another. Do you understand?"

"Yes, I understand. One woman. I will live in one room and one bed for two. No other woman."

"Good. It is grave sin to be with or to covet another."

"That is bad. I am good. I will marry one woman. Juana with the four toes on her foot. She is a good woman."

Cambon knew who he meant. A thin young girl with a quiet demeanor who would make little trouble for him.

"A good choice, Nicolas Jose. She seems a virtuous child. Very good." Grasping Nicolas Jose's hand. "You will go to her and make the arrangement. We will conduct the service in the chapel on the morning after tomorrow."

He couldn't object and continue to remain a favorite of the Padres. If he shared his room he'd have less cleaning. His clothes and bedding would be her responsibility. She would get them the best food.

“I will talk to her, Padre. She will be my wife.” He walked past the chapel to the field where the squash was being fertilized. She was stooping at the plants.

“Juana.” A rasp in his voice.

She wiped perspiration from her eyes, fearing he’d send her to a soldier. “What is wrong?” Seeing his fixed stare.

“Juana.” From two feet away. “I will marry you. You will be my wife.” Before she could think of a response other than disbelief. “Padre Cambon told me. You will be my wife.”

He was the most powerful non-Spaniard in the Mission. He was not ugly and he didn’t hurt her like some others did. “Yes. I am now your wife.”

<<< 0 >>>

Juana bathed in the chilly stream with seven young women in a group. They watched for Rodriguez or Cordero. They were afraid. it could put one who complained at risk. Being labeled a temptress or prostitute was close to a death sentence. It happened twice that they knew about. Being a group helped them.

A woman from Pimo-gna ran from Rodriguez and reached the chapel. She tried to tell Somera but Somera didn’t understand her. Rodriguez caught up and said she’d been prostituting to other neophytes in the fields and demanded that she be expelled. She was never seen again.

A young girl of 12 years was raped many times and ate enough Jimson leaves to try to kill herself. Her mother brought her to Crespi. He also didn’t not understand what they were saying. A soldier and two Tongva overseers called her possessed by the Devil. She died during exorcism.

It was hard for Juana to tell about Nicolas Jose's proposal. He was powerful and the favorite of the Spanish. She knew some of them had sex with him. They talked freely about their experiences except the ones that had been arranged with soldiers. No-one said Nicolas Jose treated them badly.

If she said he chose her, her friends would be envious. They would feel that she would get out of hard jobs and not be a good friend. They'd turn on her. Juana waded between the round rocks on the sandy bottom to stand close to a tall young woman from the Serrano northern hills.

"Sara." She whispered twice until Sara came close. "If I tell you something that weighs on me, will you talk to me and not tell the others?"

"Yes, you can trust me, but why me? You know your own people more than me."
If I talked to someone from my group, they might laugh at me and spread it all around. I need a distant eye. Could you do that?"

"It is important, no?" Looking at Juana with compassion. "A baby?"

Juana's brow knotted, knowing that a baby might soon follow. "No, not a baby, but..." She touched Sara's hand. "You know Nicolas Jose, the overseer?"

"Oh, yes." A frown on her face. "Did he hurt you?"

"No, no. I've been.., in his arms." Seeing the recognition in Sara's face. "You too?"
Sara nodded. "Only twice."

"Probably everyone our age. That isn't important to me. It's more important that we are truthful. He's asked me to be his wife, married by the Padres to him." Sara started to laugh. "He more told me than asked me. He said the Padres told him to marry. Tomorrow."

"Tomorrow! How can it be that fast?"

"I don't know. I can't say no without being expelled or harder work. I can't do any more without getting sick."

"You should be happy." Sara said. "You'll have protection. Better food. He isn't a bad man. He just speaks for them. Gives their orders"

Juana showed the face of her fear. "He is their speaker. Will I be seen as a traitor? You see? That is why I can't talk to my villagers." looking back if she was overheard. "I am afraid no-one will be my friend."

"If you are Nicolas Jose's woman, you will be seen in two ways. Some of your friends will become closer because you can give them advantages. You will have some power. Others will hate you from jealousy. A few will see you as trying to become Spanish." She squeezed Juana's hand. "I will see you as you are. A good woman."

"I am afraid. I don't want to be hated. No-one has ever hated me." She looked back at the women. "I'm afraid. How can I tell them?"

"The same way you told me. Tell them you are afraid that if you say no, harm may come to you. They'll understand." Sara tousled Juana's hair. "They are your people. Have some courage."

Juana moved back to the group with Sara at her side.

"Juana has some news for us." Sara blurted.

Margarita Six and Yavit Raquel and three more moved closer. The stream bubbled around their legs.

"Something has happened. I am afraid of it, either way it goes." She began. "Nicolas Jose told me that the Padres want him to marry. Tomorrow. He came to me and told me he wants to marry me." She continued quickly before their shocked expressions became words.

"If I say no, I could be expelled. If I accept.."

"You will be part of selling us to the soldiers!" Yavit Raquel pushed her jaw forward as two others, who had been similarly used, gave grunts of agreement.

"What else can she do?" Margarita scowled. "If she says no, she'll be sent to Rodriguez! What would you do? Pushing Raquel's shoulder with her palm. "I'll tell you why she should do it. It's good for us! If He is married, he can't mess with us without being an adulterer to the Padres. That's a word they take seriously." She poked with her finger as Raquel batted her hand away. "And if she's married," Margarita continued, "She can talk to him about our conditions. The stooping and planting for too long, the stupid food! I need acorn! And now it's banned!"
"And if he beats her?" Raquel pushed back. "She'll just be his quiet little slave."

Sara could take no more. "We never hear of Nicolas Jose beating anyone. He talks for them, but he isn't like them. Support Juana. It could make life better for us."
Canachin in the back added. "If he beats her, I'll bet he gets hemlock in his dinner!" They laughed. Juana felt less afraid.

CHAPTER 7

CIUDAD DE MEXICO – IMPERIAL MESSAGE

Returning to New Spain after a long absence, General Jose de Galvez brought continuance of his plans to civilize the New World as the official emissary of the Royal Bourbon Courts in Paris and Madrid. His plans for reform and expansion would be implemented without question.

King Carlos lll was impressed by the carefully drawn and presented plans. It stood out because of the enormous benefits of constantly growing chains of settlements and labor up the Western coast of the Americas securing the Crown's control in perpetuum.

De Galvez sat in a comfortable chair to the side of the room sipping wine while the King read page after page without comment. After nearly an hour he spoke.

"This is perfection. Every aspect keeps the Franciscans and pagans under military control without it being obvious. I love it. Do you have the personnel?

"Yes, your Majesty. It's in motion."

UPPER ALTA CALIFORNIA

Captain Fernando Rivera y Moncada's expedition had traveled arduously through semi-passable links to connect portions of the King's Highway.

The area before them was more beautiful than any they had seen in The New World. The gigantic trees and rocky reddish cliffs over fine white sand beaches promised everything they could desire except a useable harbor for large ships.

His leather-clad cavalrymen were protecting Lieutenant Pedro Fages and his Catalonian volunteers to build the foundations for the sites of new Missions, civilian settlements, Presidios and to find an accessible harbor to build the new Capital.

Father Junipero Serra and Father Juan Crespi led their column of Christianized Baja California Indians to create more Missions to the North.

Engineer Miguel Costanzo, always on the watch for new earthquakes to write about, documented the travels with enthusiasm.

The view from the last hill was undeniable.

“This is the Capital!” Rivera exclaimed. “This is the hill and the harbor of our King.” Seeing the smiles of assent all around him.

“This is Monterey.”

Fages’ men with Serra and Crespi’s Baja Indios set to work marking off spaces, digging the trenches and setting the first stones for the new Mission and a Presidio as well as suggested sites for a harbor, cannon placements and a new Pueblo de Monterey.

SHEVAANGA

Hachaaynar and Tooypor’s marriage brought five hundred guests to Shevaanga in the early springtime. Groups from five nearby villages and four distant ones carried baskets and rolled mats heavy with gifts. They made nine encampments in the grounds around the village.

Sevaanga-vik and 'Atooshe' were in place in front of the greathouse on straw-filled cushions covered with deep brown bear skins. 'Atooshe' spent the night at home for the first time in four moons. They coupled in the dark, under the warm covers like they had in their youth for three times. They felt the same about each other through their separation. She hoped a baby would come their way this time. It would be fine either way.

Hachaaynar and his friends waited with father and mother as the sun poked over the bald mountain to the east.

“We will play the walnut game on the mat until she comes.”

Hachaaynar fidgeted. They rolled the marked nuts over the fine woven grass to win drilled abalone shell circlets. There were no quarrels. His friends knew it was to keep him from getting nervous.

'Atooshe' and Sevaanga-vik greeted visiting Pulum and apprentices who brought gifts and flattery. The excitement of the morning slowed for Hachaaynar and 'Atooshe'. The sun rose toward its peak.

“She should be here by now.” Hachaaynar stared into the foothills.

‘Atooshe‘ patted his arm. “I’ll send runners up the trail. Tooypor didn’t want to be carried until they reached the flatlands.” She said, motioning to two lean Shevaanga men.

Hachaaynar said.“I’ll follow them.”

“No.” Father said. “You must stay and not show concern. You are a man now.”

Hachaaynar replied. “I am a man. I respect her villagers to protect her, but there are landslides that can block the trail.” He sighed. Appearances mattered.

“I’ll stay.”

'Atooshe' took pride in her son’s answer. In the past he would have been tongue-tied and walked away in a huff. She turned her head to catch the eye of Sevaanga-vik and was overjoyed to see his face crinkled up with lines in his eyes and a smile that was he trying to suppress.

She whapped him hard on the arm. “Our son is a man!”

Tooypor woke before dawn in a dream of flying down through the foothills and circling Shevaanga ever lower until her wings enclosed the village and people climbed into her feathers. She was lifting again in the air as a commotion outside the hut grew louder. A child was wailing. Something was being dragged along the trail downhill. A far away dog was yelping.

The importance of the day overtook her dreams. She felt a necessity to relieve herself quickly in one of the nests of leaves at the corner of the greathouse before running up to the warm water spring to bathe and toss the nest to the forest below.

“Ahhhh-yahhah!.” She shouted, bursting out of the door and running to the right to the main trail.

Groups of men and women were trudging up the trail but Tooypor was too excited to stay behind. The villagers shouted they were going to Shevaanga with her. A few early bathers came down the trail and grinned at her speeding up the trail.

Tooypor knew that her parents were up all night organizing the journey. Presents had come for three days.

She bathed with girlfriends, elders and trusted boys, she sang a joyous morning song in a strong clear voice and was joined. The air above the spring was charged with anticipation of the great day at Shevaanga. She saw no jealousy in the eyes of Ponu or Charaana. She regretted that Tah-ur wasn’t here to start the day with her.

Haapchi-vik wrestled one of five tightly bundled packs of three inch wide straight branches that were honed to a smooth finish by the Chumash. They were a man’s height and five to a pack. Four bundles were carried by two men each. Men stood by to help Haapchi-vik but he insisted on handling his load alone.

“I may be old, but.. this one will give extra strength to my daughter’s Pula hut.”

'Aachvet sorted rabbit pelts from the Mojave and was close enough to hear his father’s grunts. “Father, let them help!” But when father had a notion, nothing could turn him from it. “Father, it will be a long day. Rest for the journey.”

“Do your work!” Came back with a groan of effort.
'Aachvet put perfect pelts in a pile to take to Shevaanga and threw the larger group with imperfections to the sewing women to make cloaks for the children.

He heard shouts. “'Aachvet!” “Your Father has fallen!”
He ran up the slope. Four men lifted Father to carry him home.

“Father!” Seeing rolled eyes and labored breathing. He’d had little sleep, worrying over Tooypor’s union. No detail was left to chance. Every preparation for the trip to Shevaanga was scrutinized, checked and rechecked.

Haapchi-vik heard 'Aachvet’s voice panting for breath. He couldn’t walk. A boulder had landed on his chest and he thought it strange that he couldn’t see it coming. He squinted down his nose expecting to see blood but there was none.

“'Aachvet, my son.” Calling to the voice behind him. “Come to me.”

'Aachvet put his hand on the matted black hair with streaks of gray and white strands. The head was wet and cool to the touch. they rarely touched.

“I’m here. Tooypor is bathing. I’ll send Ha’ama’ar to bring her. She and Pul Tuwaru will make you well. I told you to let someone help you but you are so stubborn! But if you were not stubborn, you would not be chief!”

“You will be chief.” Haapchi-vik rasped.

“When I am older.” He clumsily rubbed the brow. “That will be many seasons. We will not let you go.”

They lay him on the mats of the greathouse. Pul Tuwaru rushed in and put his hand on brow, temples, sides of the neck and wrists. Tuwaru mumbled close to the chiefs ear but the only words 'Aachvet understood were “Old friend.”

“What is it? Why did he fall?”

Tuwaru pursed his lips putting the wrist between his palms. “Wildness of blood. He let it rage. He must rest and be joyous at the union. He must be still.” He tapped on Haapchi-vik’s chest. “You will see your daughter and you will be happy for her. You will let Kethu lead the procession and you will lie here counting the sticks in your roof. I’ll ask you how many when we return”

Haapchi-vik’s eyes were darty and anxious. Both men, holy man and son knelt by his face, 'Aachvet held his temples and promised that everything for the marriage was in place.

“There will be no problems. I’ll wait with you and your attendants until the travelers are down the hill. Then I’ll leave and catch up with sister. I’ll send runners to report to you. Stay here. Sing the songs. We will hear them.”

Haapchi-vik closed his eyes and wondered where his energy went. Not enough to fight them about going. The boulder was just above his chest. He could feel it when he tried to move. It could fall at any moment. Who could have done that? He slipped down a dark hole and was calm.

Tooypor was about to leave the spring with reed cloak in hand when a runner called and splashed through the stream.

“Your father fell while carrying wood.” He said.

Tooypor gasped. “How could I have not seen it?”

“He was carried home by 'Aachvet and Pul Tuwaru.”

“I’m coming,” throwing on the cloak and sprinting down the trail, leaving the runner behind. Bathers approaching the spring called to her. Their words were lost.

“Father!” Rushing in the dark room. Seeing his eyes closed. ‘Aachvet and Tuwaru sat on the mat beside him. She felt confused with no sense of what had happened to him. “Father.” kneeling, putting her ear near his mouth and nose.

‘Aachvet whispered. “He became in a rage over the preparations. Trying to do too much. He is resting now.”

Tuwaru put a hand on her shoulder. “It will be best if he rests today and does not accompany you.”

Tooypor ran her hands over her father, much as Tuwaru did and sat upright. “I didn’t see this.”

“Nor did I.” Brother whispered.

Tooypor watched the motions of her father’s chest, her eyes focused far beyond. It didn’t matter that 'Aachvet didn’t see. She had an obligation to feel great change, especially a change to her father. She’d failed by being concerned with her own happiness. She wished 'Atooshe' could explain this. Why was she so focused on happiness that she couldn’t see pain and tragedy standing beside her?

“I should stay with father,” realizing Tuwaru and 'Atooshe' knew how to care for him better than anyone else. She saw how selfish it would it seem if she stayed. “I should not stay with father. I will return here with Hachaaynar and ‘Ahtooshe‘. You will stay?” to Tuwaru, imploringly, once again a twelve year old.

"I won't let him fade in my care but you must complete your union for us all. It will strengthen his heart. It will make the village strong."

Nothing felt right anymore. To leave father behind? Or stay with him? Feeling unworthy of accolades. Not sensing his frailty. She clung to 'Aachvet, nearly squeezing his wind out. "What should I do?"

"You will go with mother. You will join with Hachaaynar and leave the care of father to Pul Tuwaru and Spirit. Chinigchnich feels us all. You have your task. You will go." He looked into her eyes. "You will go and be the strong, independent spirit of the bear. Father will be here for us when we return. I'll join you there."

She hugged 'Aachvet tight. He was no longer a child. He had father's confidence and voice. "How do you feel father's recovery? I did not sense any of this!"

She held her breath. 'Has Bear deserted me?.'

"You were too busy with the preparations. I was near him. I saw his panic growing. You had people distracting you. See. You are imperfect. I've always known that, but now you see it too. I hope you'll remember"

Pul Tuwaru added. "You are growing. There are reasons for this. I will be the one to guide him to uprightness and his old ways. He became too excited. There is no perfect, even you, our child. This has made your brother grow. Let it help you to grow. You are a talented young person. Not without human flaws. Go to Shevaanga"

The words of Tuwaru and her brother didn't help that her talent, her sense of the world past the immediate, was slipping away. The more she was admired and felt loved, the more she felt distance from the true path around her and the changes that she could effect. Concentration on little things and the big things sometimes canceled each other out. The simpler life was, the clearer the messages. Understanding the important things would mean saying ‘no’ to many choices. She vowed to ask ‘Ahtooshe’ how she makes her life more simple.

“I‘ve been foolish” She whispered, pulling the door covering aside. One hundred thirty people stood outside the greathouse when Tooypor and 'Aachvet emerged. 'Aachvet spoke in a clear and strong voice after whispering to Kethu.

“Haapchi-vik became ill and collapsed. He will join us in Shevaanga. We will go as planned but with Kethu and Tooypor in the lead. Walk slowly and with safety in your steps and we will be there before nightfall.”

<<< 0 >>>

By mid-day Hachaaynar had caught three runners on the trail angling across a long grassy up-slope overlooking the entire plain of the Tongva territory under a cloudless blue sky and springtime sun.

They looked back at Shevaanga in the plain and Pimog-na to the far left, with the camp of the Spanish intruders between the two villages. Beyond the Spaniards, a long blue shadowed line of hills curved to the south and west, bordering the lands of the Kumeyaay. To the far right the endless ocean sparkled in the west. Fires from Yaanga and Cahuen-gna made their haze across the flat plain.

The lead runner stopped and shouted back. “They come! The Japchivtam come now!.”

Up the trail through breaks in the oak and pine, Haychaynar saw movement and human shapes. ‘They’re coming! Tooypor is coming!’

“I’ll go back, Mahnayar, come with me.” Shouting to the runner nearest him as if nothing had been of concern, loping into Shevaanga he held his arms up. “They are coming. All is well.”

Rushing to sit, gathering his breath next to Sevaanga-vik and 'Atooshe.

“They are many and moving slowly. They will be here in four or five finger's time.”

'Atooshe' clapped his arm in relief. She had a feeling about the lateness. Haapchi-vik was a prompt man.

Sevaanga-vik nodded. “That trail has rock slides”

Hachaaynar felt butterflies racing through his blood. .

Tooypor wouldn't allow herself to be carried in the hills. They waited until Shevaanga was in plain view. She motioned to four women who were assigned separate from her guards to look out for her. “You can carry me now.” She was lifted on their shoulders. Three older women came close to back them up if one faltered.

“Stay close behind me.” Kethu cautioned. “Charaana and I will be side by side in front of my daughter.”

The group grew to over two hundred by the time they entered Shevaanga. Some from the north and west had camped on the outskirts to enter with the Haapchivetam. 'Atooshe' and Hachaaynar heard the approach and poked Sevaanga-vik out of a nap.

“How long was I asleep?”

'Atooshe' patted on his back. “Only a short time. They are here now.”

Hachaynar said. “I'm excited,” rememberinghis mother's instructions about what a good man and a good woman do in the night. He hoped Tooypor's knowledge would help. A flock of children jumped and walked backwards ahead of the marriage party.

Hachaaynar and Tooypor's eyes met. He stood with father and mother smiling at the people bringing Tooypor.

Tooypor couldn't stop thinking of the pains of her father, but seeing Atooshe' and Hachaaynar beaming joy at her made her eyes tear up with giddy happiness.

"Hiiiiaaaaaahhhhhaiiii!" She screamed as the hundreds around her, 'Atooshe', Hachaaynar, Sevaanga-vik, the children, young and old took up cries of exaltation and pleasure.

"We will join!" Shouted Hachaaynar.

"We will join" Giggled Tooypor, eyes locked on Hachaaynar, lowered by eight hands to stand next to Kethu.

"We will join." Mouthed 'Atooshe' to Kethu as she extended her arms, walking toward her.

'Atooshe' saw Kethu's expression and Haapchi-vik missing. Tooypor hugged her.

"Father collapsed this morning. Pul Tuwaru is with him and 'Aachvet just left him. They tell me not to worry."

"And you didn't stay." 'Atooshe' weighed her responses. "You came anyway. I am proud of you."

Tooypor couldn't think of much to be proud of.

"You put the needs of the villages above your own wants. That is always the right decision." Turning to Kethu. "I'll come with you to be with Haapchi-vik. I wish all strength to you."

"I didn't see it!" Trying to show a bright face.

"Like my mudslide." 'Atooshe' with a twist to her eyebrow. "We don't always see the obvious."

Hachaaynar hugged Kethu and said he would come to Haapchivet. Sevaanga-vik had the villagers walk to the Three Tree Spring where the pledges would be made. Old and young formed groups and followed. Emissaries from outlying tribes stayed close. To the rear, raucous teens got in fights and shouted insults. Some were sick from playing with datura and forbidden herbs. They sat at the side of the trail, retching and groaning.

Bands of woven fragrant flowers were draped on Tooypor's shoulders. Bundles of fine weaponry were presented to Hachaaynar.

Kethu and 'Atooshe' waved the embering sage sticks and intoned the words to the dance that went long into the clear star-filled night.

Tooypor and Hachaaynar left in the middle of the night with people mumbling the dance words. Most were staggering with fatigue and collapsing from too much good times. It was an hour's walk to 'Atooshe''s loaned Pula hut.

They compared their friends‘ comments. If anyone was jealous or angry, they didn't see it. A half moon lit the trail. They pushed through the reed door and flopped down on the mat and wrapped up in the blankets. As they saw the glints of each others eyes, they broke into giggles at their stomachs touching.

“Shouldn't we be naked?” Bumping her tummy in and out.

He laughed and shivered. “They say we have to, but I'm too cold to move now. 'Ahtooshe' told me how it's done. I want to when we are warmer. I feel a little tingly though. ”

She bit on his nose. “I can feel you getting tingly a little. Mother told me all about the things to do. There are a lot of things people do, you know. Not all at once. At different times.”

"I've always wondered about your waist. It's so little, and you don't have much stomach." His hands were stiffly against his own sides until she took a hand and put it on her waist and slid it down across her stomach. He giggled. "You're so smooth! Like a little child's tummy, but strong too."

She turned on her back. She guided his hand down her belly, feeling him react. "I say you are very tingly!" She said, brushing the back of her hand across the tingly part.

Soon all sense of cold had dissipated and laughter and sounds of exploration led to loud and pleasurable exclamations. They had a long night of talk about how it felt to do these things and what all of it meant and how hard it would be to live apart in their separate worlds of responsibilities.

Haapchi-vik lay before 'Aachvet, 'Atooshe' and Pul Tuwaru on a bearskin covered finely woven mat when Tooypor and Hachaaynar entered and bent down at his feet.

"You look well!" She squealed. "They took good care of you! I felt like a bad daughter for leaving you. I hope you understand. I had to."

"Are you a bear or a chipmunk?" Father asked. "You never need to apologize to me. It is your time to walk into the world. It will be my time to leave, but not now. It is my time to watch everyone else do things. That is good."

He gave a sly look to Kethu, standing in the shadows in the far corner. "I think that our brilliant daughter has been doing things. She seems quite happy about it." bowing his head to the blushing Tooypor.

"We don't want to live separately, but we will. It is my duty. I will live the Pula life."

Hachaaynar added. "I will visit her often. To be sure she is safe. My father will assign a guard to watch over her hut."

Haapchi-vik nodded. "I will assign a guard as well. Our villages will exchange runners often, It will bring us closer. We could make a relay village in the foothills near the Eagle rock to speed the runners."

Tooypor chirped. "That's between 'Atooshe''s and my huts. Can we have our own runners for our messages? It can save time."

"Yes, I agree to that. Hachaaynar?"

"My mother will want that. Father will say yes."

Pul Tuwaru put a hand on the shoulders of Haapchi-vik and the new son. "The first day or our alliance has made my vision clear. We have started a path to bring more villages together than have ever gathered before. Iitaxam! One people. And Tooypor will see this happen. One people. Iitaxam!

1772 - SINALOA – NEW SPAIN

The family of Jose Rojas was now in constant struggle with him and against the land, which was becoming harder to have useable crops sprout that were saleable, There was less demand for his masonry skills to support his family. This place was far less pleasing to him than the comfort of his native Durango. The urge to leave was taking a new form with him.

There were rumors of expansion to the North where stonemasons would be appreciated, but with five children and a sixth on the way, there might be a chance of subsidies for all of the family. There would be no subsidies in Durango. He was sure of that.

He heard rumors constantly. But this was a recurring one. Maybe with support and more work for all, it would keep the kids from fighting.

MISSION SAN GABRIEL

Nicolas Jose rode a horse beyond the Mission grounds for the first time. Walking closely beside Lopez, always ready to grab the reins if anything unexpected happened. Rodriguez' mount led the two Padres and four trusted eastern village neophytes on foot. Four other mounted soldiers stayed fifty meters back.

The honor of riding a horse was a badge that no other neophyte had earned. To be mounted on a horse like the Spanish made him a leader and envied by all those who accepted the newcomers as the new dominant tribe, not as'the invaders.'

He felt pride and discomfort on the horse. He could walk easily and trot a little as long as the trail was smooth, but otherwise, he had no control over the animal other than trying to hang on and to not let his panic show.

If the horse galloped he would shout for help and hope Lopez could halt the horse. He was afraid to pull hard on the reigns and expected the horse to turn and attack him if he did.

Lopez gave him the gentlest and most predictable horse. He prepared the words as they wanted and understood the goal of bringing fifty men plus women and children to build the Mission, and of course to become good Catholic subjects.

Sevaanga-vik would regard him as a traitor. No explanation of 'I couldn't get away. I was always watched' would do. He would be seen as an agent of the Spanish no matter what he said. The only way he could have more credibility would be by presenting the Spanish plan as harshly as possible, then mitigating the demands to appear a compromiser. He would ask for one hundred. He would get twenty. They all would feel that he had done his best.

Crespi and Somera lectured him about speaking patiently and presenting the request for the workers as the best option. Better food and more frequent meals. Food stored against shortage and clothing to warm them in the winter. A healthy environment against the spreading sicknesses. The sicknesses the Padres said were punishments for not accepting the One True God. He knew anything said against Chinigchnich would fall on deaf ears. The 'One True God' wouldn't make sense to the offspring of 'Mother Earth' and 'Father Sun.'

They were the people of the Spirits of all things here and gone. Stories about a man born and risen in a far land who could walk on water and bring forgiveness to them sounded like a hollow echo of their own stories.

He knew the right words; some in Spanish, some in Latin, to please the Padres, but it was all about Land and power for the Spanish Empire. The soldiers told him stories about Spain and Mexico. About gold and treasures and thousands killed by the might of their armies. Andres told him about Peru and the fall of the mighty Incas. He'd seen and heard what firesticks did and knew that Shevaanga had no idea of the finality of that sound.

The party crested the final mound. The low round roofs of the village and the grasses of the playing fields that Nicolas Jose grew on came into view. He smelled the herbs and cooking fires and saw the teens at play, learning to hunt, to be fast and strong. Learning accuracy with rabbit sticks. They ran toward the central clearing.

Rodriguez squinted at the village, trying to locate the women he dreamed about. Stroking the stock of his musket and imagining the possibility of an attack once they were within the savages camp and surrounded. He scanned the outlying shrubs for hiding places and ambush. He saw that nearly a kilometer to all sides of the village had been cleared of brush and the ground smoothed. He couldn't understand why they would do that. They had no defenses against attack. Didn't they have enemies?

Lopez rode to the left behind Nicolas Jose, watching how he behaved with the horse, ready to keep the horse from bolting. It would turn to disaster if Nicolas Jose couldn't accomplish the goal. The Mission would fall apart.

Crespi turned to Somera saying. “Quite an odd feeling, isn’t it? Walking into the lions mouth like this.”

Somera’s eyes were straight forward, with a thousand chilly fingertips running up his spine. “We are in the hands of The Lord. He will guide us....I pray.”

“I rather enjoy the sensation.” Crespi chuckled. “Feeling the emotions that the martyrs must have felt.”

“If martyrdom comes, I am ready.” Somera intoned bravely, though they knew there were a total of twelve loaded muskets plus sidearms to back them up in the unlikely event of open attack.

Sevaanga-vik, 'Atooshe' and Hachaaynar stood with twelve guards flanking them as the invaders raised dust on the trail. They saw Nahaanpar in the group riding on an animal’s back. It was painful for Hachaaynar, knowing that on the travels to Tooypor’s village, all the while he was watching over him, Nahaanpar was becoming the Spaniard’s dog-man.

“He is in the center, between the two soldiers. Looking like the leader.”

“Like the guide.” His father said. “Never a leader. One of their animals. Just enough freedom to move as they want him to.”
A young neophyte stood at the side of 'Atooshe'. He had carried the message that the Mission would send a party of friendship to Shevaanga.

“Tongva man is Nicolas Jose. Top Christian Tongva man.”

“Nicolas Jose.” 'Atooshe' repeated loudly. “Was he Nicolas Jose when he last came to us?”

“He was quiet going to Haapchivet. Like something was bothering him. He acted tired and kept to himself.” Hachaaynar squinted at the approaching figures. “He wasn’t like the one who had guarded me.”

Sevaanga-vik was silent as they approached, angry and curious about the man he'd trusted. Now returning with the invaders as one of them.

Nicolas Jose recognized the three of the Leading family. Hatcaynar grew two inches and looked fit. 'Atooshe' and Sevaanga-vik seemed unchanged. The village looked larger from horseback. Two hundred men, women and children stood behind Sevaanga-vik.

"Aaheh-pahr." Nicolas Jose made a gesture of respect to Sevaanga-vik.

"Now you've come after many seasons with the beards. Why?"

"They've come to extend help to you and ask for the help of the village." He lowered his head. "I know you must suspect my reasons. I've always thought of you during my absence and tried to prevent bad things from happening to Shevaanga."

Sevaanga-vik asked the predictable question.
"What kind of 'bad things' could you have prevented?"

Nicolas Jose created a menace and stood aside from it. "The expansion of the Mission grounds into your area. The Soldiers want to make it theirs. They'll expand to the east instead. They may move as far as Ashuukshanga to raise their plants, but I told them that my village had to be spared."

"Why do you say 'your village.' You've abandoned it. How is this your village?"

Crespi walked forward. "What is he saying?"

Nicolas Jose didn't reply.

"I keep your village in my heart but I have to bring their request to you. It isn't my idea, but there is a chance that it will not be as hard as their first offer. "

Hatcaynar felt like pulling the traitor from his horse and let the villagers deal with him. There are only eleven of them. Why should they make terms? His stiffness was read by 'Atooshe' who pulled on his hand.

Nicolas Jose continued. “They are moving their Mission village again. It be will farther to the north, nearer the foothills and a small distance closer to Shevaanga.”

“Closer to us?” Sevaanga-vik gripped his spear tighter as Rodriguez raised his musket. Crespi put out his hand to tell him to back off.

“But up there, by the foothills.” Nicolas Jose pointed. “It won’t be much closer. They need one hundred men to help them move.” He opened the fingers of his two hands ten times. “One hundred men to help them move and build. Then they’ll leave the village alone.” Sevaanga-vik couldn’t suppress a laugh as he motioned to Lopez and Rodriguez. “You say these men might leave our village alone?” Walking close to Nicolas Jose’s horse. “ I will call you Nahaanpar for the last time.”

Rodriguez leveled his musket as Sevaanga-vik continued. Nicolas Jose edged forward to block Sevaanga-vik from direct line of fire.

“You must leave these invaders. You think they give you power, but they steal your power. They make you their dog.”

“What is he saying?” Crespi became shrill. “Tell him why we came. Tell him now!”

Nicolas Jose put his palm up. “Wait! We must clear our past. We must talk.” Turning to Rodriguez. “No one will attack you. You are safe.” And back to Crespi. “If I can not get him to understand why I came to the Mission, none of them will come to the Mission. Please let us talk. Tell the soldiers it is peaceful. Sevaanga-vik, was my teacher and respected elder.”

To Sevaanga-vik, quietly . "No. I am not their dog. I am learning from them. I can help you exist with them as two friends with different skills, who help each other become stronger."

"What do you want? What are you asking? One hundred is most of our men. What will they give us?"

"Digging sticks for planting. Made of me-tal, Stronger and harder than any stone." Pulling a brass bell from his saddlebag. "This!" Handing it down with a clang. "This is me-tal! Look how smooth. The way it sounds. The digging sticks will help keep supplies under the ground. Make rows of squash like they do."

'Atooshe' stroked the small bell in her husband's hand. They both rang it two times. "We hear sounds like this from near the Mission and on their horses." She picked up a small stone and chipped at it, looking at the small marks. "It is stronger than the stone." He drew a shiny metal crucifix on a chain from his bag and handed it to her. "The four directions."

Hachaaynar watched his parents become entranced with the distractions, thinking 'Are they that stupid?'

Sevaanga-vik looked up at Nicolas Jose. "Why should we care about things like these? I wouldn't give up my men for these. If the invaders want our help, how will they help us? We don't need me-tal. We don't need anything from them." He looked into the horses eyes. They were so calm, like a dog after it was well fed. He thought he'd feel fear, standing close to such a huge animal, but it seemed at peace. He wondered what riding one would feel like. How much travel time it would save.

Nicolas Jose wanted to reconnect as he'd planned. "Sevaanga-vik. I will tell their chief that you have many questions. He is the hairless one to my right side."

Sevaanga-vik's eyes met Crespi's. Nicolas Jose saw an opportunity. He turned in his saddle.

"Father. It won't be easy. The chief says the hunting time is now. They need all men. He doesn't want gifts. They want nothing. This will be a long talk."

Crespi turned to Somera. "Not as clean as I'd hoped." He shrugged and looked up at Nicolas Jose. "Tell him that we want their friendship. It is cold. We have blankets. We have shelter for the children. We can protect them from enemies."

Nicolas Jose thought, 'they have no enemies other than us' and spoke surely to Crespi.

"Give me blankets to bring. This will take more trips, but you will get their co-operation." If there was a good chance of results, it could be everything he wanted if the Padres would approve, if Sevaanga-vik would accept his visits.

Rodriguez was bored. He didn't feel the Indians would attack. They seemed as bored as he was. The only interesting part was the ample bosomed thing standing beside the chief. It made sense that a chief would possess the prize wench of the tribe. His eyes met hers and he slowly rotated the barrel of his musket skyward in a way that communicated his thoughts vividly.

'Atoosho' understood the erection gesture and was so repulsed by the disrespect that only the negotiation kept her from plucking his eyes out. She saw Hachaaynar and her husband were only watching Nicolas Jose. She kept her eyes on them although she felt the Spaniard's leering like a persistent hornet's buzz.

Nicolas Jose continued. "Seeing you now in this village, after the way I was living, makes me know how far from my ancestors I've wandered. I want them to know me again. I want you, if you will, to let me sit with you again as Nahaanpar." There was stirring behind him from Tongva neophytes who could hear him speak. Speaking of ancestors' spirits was not of The Church. He turned back in Tongva to the neophytes behind the Padres.

"The village from which I came needs clear talk. This takes time to make real understanding between us," and to Crespi in

Spanish. "I must travel between Mission and here. If they agree, will you?"

'This is crazy.' Rodriguez thought. 'He escapes once, comes back and they let him. He fucks all the women and rules the henhouse. Now he wants to do it with the chief's wench and they'll let him.'

"Will they give us the men after the hunt?" Crespi asked with resignation.

"What is he saying to you?"

Nahaanpar knew the neophytes would tell the Padres if he made a pledge to Sevaanga-vik. He'd phrase it well and let his expressions carry the content. He moved his eyes from far right to far left.

"They want me to trade or negotiate with you." He leaned in with eyes intent. "I want to speak with you."

"You will. It can be." Sevaanga-vik pronounced, to the annoyance of 'Atooshe' and Hachaaynar.

Nahaanpar's hopes leapt. It was only a step from accomplishing what no other had done. To be the bridge between both worlds, He beamed to Crespi and Somera. "He agreed to talk about trade after the hunt. He wants me to come and explain what you want. It will take time but you will be glad. This is a wonderful opportunity! More than I'd expected. No anger. Only good trading. You'll see."

As the group parted, no one felt satisfaction other than Nicolas Jose. No help had been promised. A minor threat had been left behind. It may have seemed pointless, but to him, it opened a world of opportunity. To Rodriguez, it left a lingering fantasy.

CHAPTER 8

MONTEREY – THE CAPITOL

Rivera y Moncada, after founding the capitol of Monterey, received his appointment as Military Governor of Alta California and prepares for the transfer. 'It will be a wonderful home' he thought, knowing that his explorations would never stop. He stood before the mirror adjusting the medals on his perfectly tailored blue uniform with red trim and a cross sash with the yellow and red of Imperial Spain

He sends a note to the officers of his cavalry, renoun as the best and most skillful in the world, for the journey and plans to recruit families to settle the new area in the North of California. He emphisised the beauty and fertility of the land.

"Remind all of the prospective settlers of the safety of living next to the strongest Presidio in the Californias," hoping for a strong response from the Baja farmers.

"This will be the most beautiful place in the world," he had them repeat.

SHEVAANGA

Tooypor listened as Hachaaynar told about the visit of the Spaniards and the appearance of Nahaanpar on a Spanish horse, as one of them.

"The tall man who looked like he had lost something important. Always walking around the edges of things."

"I respected him. He treated me like I was a grown up."

"How long since you'd seen him?"

“Right after your ceremony.” Hachaaynar wore sadness. “He stayed around my father, and then, just disappeared. My father told me ”He is doing something important. Don’t worry. He will be back.” Stroking her hair.

“Do you think he will come back to us?”

“What you said. ‘Losing something important.’ When he spoke to father, it was the same way. Like he wanted to find his ancestors. What could be more important than that, but he‘s speaking for the invaders.”

“Do you want him to come back to us?”

“He was a guide to me.” Burying his brow in the nape of her neck. “I don‘t trust him.”

“I missed you this week.” Hugging his head to her.

“I’ve learned good things from Pul Tuwaru. I’ve started a record rock on the south face of The Ancient Woman Cliffs.” Rubbing his muscular back. “It tells of the alliance of our villages and the powers of Pula 'Atooshe' and Pul Tuwaru.”

“You’ve kept busy.” Nipping at her ear. “Do you have a feeling about this Spanish visit and Nahanpar’s return?”

She grabbed his shoulders, rolling him on his back, looking him from above. Her hair framing his face.

“Yes. He is ashamed of things that he has done. The Spanish want to swallow up Shevaanga like a mountain lion does. From a hunger. They don’t understand their hunger, but it never ceases.” Kissing his temples and mouth.

“How can they do that?” Feeling the week of separation slip away.

“I don’t understand that yet, but I will.” Pinning him down. “Now shut up.”

LORETO – NEW SPAIN

Jose Navarro wrestled with his sons as daughter Mariana laughed at his clumsiness when he slipped on the newly waxed floor, bringing little Jose with a thump on top of him.

Tailoring business was good and there was plenty of work repairing rips in the uniforms and making occasional dress clothing for the ladies. Even for an elegant wedding for the administrators, or a simple one for his neighbors.
Life was good and finally promised stability.

PEMOOKANGA

Tah-ur and two runners traveled west following the foothill trail to a place between the tall bald mountain and the distant pass at Pasakeg-na. To their left was the drying grassy plain that held the Mission and Shevaanga.

They saw a small bunch of children playing chase a kilometer down the gentle slope. A horseman was another kilometer beyond.

Corporal Cordero saw an opportunity to increase the Mission recruits as three children became detached. He knew he couldn't carry three, but two could fit on the horse for an eight kilometer ride. Two were girls of about ten or eleven. The boy looked older. Good for strenuous work, he thought. He moved to the north between them and the larger group, then turned on them. They ran. One of the girls was heavy and ran slowly. He decided to eliminate her first, coming up quickly, seeing her wide and panicky eyes as she twisted her neck back, kicking her in the head. She fell motionless in the sand. He smiled at his accuracy.

The boy and slim girl were running but had nowhere to go in the sandy plain. No big rocks. No hiding places.

He charged at the slim girl and aimed his boot at her back-turned face with less force than the first girl. Not to crush, but to knock her unconscious. He saw a spurt of blood as her nose split and she tumbled on the ground. He caught the panicked boy and brought him down with a solid kick to the back of the head.

"I'm good at this!" Congratulating himself as he dismounted and lashed the hands and feet of the boy and with great effort, hoisted and tied him over the back of the horse. He'd practiced kicks on cactus' many times, but this was better.

He reached the girl. She was groggy and bleeding from the nose and upper lip. He saw the motionless plump girl sprawled near a tumbleweed. In the distance three figures were running toward him.

"You don't have enough time, idiots." He mumbled as he pulled on the girls arm and dragged her to the horse. She was light. He threw her up over the barely conscious boy. Cordero climbed on, threading rope around their limbs and his waist and rode calmly to the Mission while listening to their whimpers, feeling that this was a good day. He rode west breaking into a canter,

Tah-ur and her runners realized they could never catch him. She reached the girl lying still and saw her neck was broken. The three made a chant over her but had no way to make a fire. Six other children reached them, crying and shouting about the bearded soldier.

"Which village are you from?" She asked.

"Pimog-na village. The boy is from Ashuukshanga village." Through anger and tears. "Invader took them to the Mission. Will they eat them?"

Tah-ur couldn't answer. She didn't know why a man would kill one child for no reason and then take two who might be dead also, on a animal to his village. Human People don't do things like that. She knew they ate strange animals that they brought in great herds from far away, but did they eat children?

"Can you bring them back?" Two girls pleaded, looking up at the three strong adults.

"We can't bring them back."

<<< 0 >>>

No-one saw Cordero arrive. He brought the children to the stables and tied the boy to the wall with rags stuffed in his mouth. He and neophyte Simon washed off the naked girl and raped her before preparing her to be trained by the work crew neophytes.

They dressed them in cotton shifts. Simon threatened them with the loss of their families if they complained. He said the other children would say things to trick them into talking. They'd be reported to the Grand Punisher who hides under the chapel and kills bad children.

A trusted neophyte led the children to the pasture to dig a trench and observed if they would become worthy subjects of the Church and The Crown.

Cordero passed Somera walking through the chapel arch and spoke. "We have two new converts from the eastern villages. Soon they will flock to us like birds in the springtime."

Somera passed the message to Fray Crespi, who included the prediction in his weekly dispatch to the Blessed Father Junipero Serra in Sonora, who in turn added to his missive to Pope Clement XIV, "There is real progress in converting the Indian population at Mission San Gabriel Archangel. Many new converts"

<<< 0 <<<

Nicolas Jose and two Kumeyaay neophytes left the Mission carrying twelve blankets from Mexican Missions to Shevaanga. The Padres gave him blessing to negotiate labor for Mission construction. He was authorized to move up, after the first session, to a trade for a small number of sheep, goats or pigs, but not cattle or horses. He could only include an animal after first gaining a minimum of five men for twenty blankets.

Cambon had coached him. It was worth a delay if a large block could be obtained rather than the sullen and infrequent dribbles from the eastern villages. It was a dangerous game but the rewards were immense.

Approaching the village on foot was more comfortable than riding on the horse. It felt powerful to ride above the others, but not the power of a man among men, face to face. It was a power that made him feel less a Human and more a False God. He knew how pleasing it felt to accept being a False God, but it was unworthy of a true Human. Iitaxum.

Men on the trail recognized him and his carriers. Hachaaynar was in the sage and willow processing area watching Tooypor help the women with the bark treatments that helped her father recover.

“The Nicolas Jose person is back,” He told her.

“We will go when I finish.”

'Atooshe' burned to tell Nahaanpar about the rude Spaniard who was with him, angry that Sevaanga-vik and Hachaaynar hadn’t noticed.

“You have to make him aware of the rudeness!”

“You ask him, wife! We will talk about the invaders intentions and of trade. How he views someone else’s lust is not my problem.”

“It isn’t Lust! It’s disrespect! It’s an attack on me and you, but you are being too selfish to see it.”

“It isn’t selfish to want to know more. I understand why Nahaanpar went to find 0out how they live. Look at him! On a great animal! My anger went away because of the magic that he carried." He pointed at the Four Directions metal cross on the chain on her waist. "You must feel magic from that! Why else would you wear it with Mother Earth amulets!"

"It's pretty. It reflects light. It isn't magic," She glared at him. "Of all things to be impressed with! Their me-tal and animals shouldn't blind us to their purpose.' She yelled. "They have no magic! They only have me-tal and weavings, not magic or the goodness of the Earth. Trickery! Don't be a fool!"

Sevaanga-vik looked at her with sadness. "I see that you are hurt. I didn't see what you saw, and it hurt you that I didn't see. I will think about it from your eyes."

"That is a beginning." She said as Nahaanpar was escorted through the door.

Nahaanpar had tucked the crucifix inside the neck of his shift and looked hangdog as the carriers set the blankets on the floor. He had them return to tell Cambon it was a safe trip.

Sevaanga-vik motioned. "We will sit." Including 'Atooshe'.

She watched Nahaanpar's face as she would a snake, wary of every twitch, looking for evil intent. Ready to burst into rage if her husband were entranced by any of the promises or shiny gifts that the snake brought or promised.

"Ava'aha, Tumia'r Sevaanga-vik. Ava'aha Pula 'Atooshe'-pahr. I did not come for men or blankets or what the Spanish want. I came to open myself up to you and to try to connect to what I have been and what I've left behind."

He saw 'Atooshe''s cold expression. He closed his eyes and bowed his head. "Please let me finish. I have to wash myself of the wrongs I have done."

Sitting cross-legged, side by side, Sevaanga-vik put his hand on 'Atooshe''s knee, and said. "It has been many seasons. Blankets don't interest me as much as what has become of our friendship." He felt stiffness from his wife to deal with the Spaniard who insulted her. "There are many things to speak of. Let us start with your absence. Speak."

He saw that 'Atooshe' directed more anger at him than Sevaangavik. He wondered if stories of his relationships with women at the Mission, or of the soldiers, had gotten back to her. He didn't want to tell, but if he had to, he'd cut into the serpent's bite and spit out the venom.

"I've wanted things, I've done things..." He bit at his lip and bumped on his thigh. "The Padres. The brown robe ones, talk about 'Sin'.....Sin is like mistakes. Bad things of wanting and doing bad things." He nodded slowly. "What you said about my ancestors' house. I kept the life I had grown with...away from my thoughts. I didn't think about my lost father and mother! That is sin. When I told you I would return and tell you what the Spanish were intending. It is sin that I did not. I am pulled in two directions and can't be Nahaanpar when I am there. I am Nicolas Jose when I am with them and I thought I had become that person...until I came home."

'Atooshe' could not stop herself. "This is no longer your home."

"Wife, you will leave!" He'd never told her that in a council meeting. This was different. He had to know how this change had come with this man he had trusted since childhood. He needed to know why some from every village had at first, seemed curious and then were never seen again.

'Atooshe''s face burned from the rebuke. She wouldn't take an order like that from any living creature, chief or not, he was a living creature and one with his share of flaws.

"I will stay!" Twisting her body. "I will hear out Nahaanpar's account without speaking until you have come to a determination about his position in Shevaanga." Emphasizing each word with a pointed finger. "Then I will speak."

“You will stay….. Quietly.” Their faces softened and there was peace.

“I did abandon my home, my ancestors, my trust, my sense of who I am, and I’m afraid.” He looked imploringly to 'Atooshe'. “I made a life at the Mission. I could have escaped, but I probably would have been killed if I had tried....I made a life there. I am married to an Ashuukshanga woman. Joined by them in their way.” He saw them exchanging looks. “I have learned more of their language than any other has. That is why they put me on their animal. So that I would talk their wants to you and tell them what you said.”

He sat straighter. “I did not tell them what you said. I made a story about you wanting to negotiate a trade so that I could return more times. It was to see you. To talk with you about the things that I promised ten seasons ago.”

Sevaanga-vik asked. “The first thing that I want to know is; why are you afraid? Are you afraid of me and vengeance of our people? For leaving us?”

“I am afraid that when I return to my home there. When I am Nicolas Jose. I won’t be allowed to return here. I’ll be lost to my life.” Seeing a look of incomprehension. “My life there teaches me things I can‘t explain. It‘s complicated and makes me feel asleep when I‘m away from what I can learn, but inside me, it makes me feel empty. Like parts of me disappear.” The fear was more than of place. It wasn’t from the outside. It was within. He felt it as a force that he couldn’t let go of. It possessed him. He shut it out of his mind before he could speak, but felt it as strongly as a broken leg or a poison in the bowels.

Sevaanga-vik turned to his wife. “Do you understand what he is saying?”

“Yes.” 'Atooshe' said simply. “He wants to live in both places. To wear their clothes and to wear our clothes.”

He raised his eyebrows and asked Nicolas Jose. “Is that what you want?”

He was glad that it could be reduced to such simplicity. “Yes, if you would allow.”

Sevaanga-vik continued. “I want to learn about their intentions. I want to understand how to make them go somewhere else.” Like speaking to the Nahaanpar of three years ago. “I would like to learn about their me-tal...”

“Metal.”

“Their metal, and I know the women want to know how to make the soft weavings.” Getting a backhanded slap on the arm from ‘Ahtooshe’.

“We want them to leave.” 'Atooshe' hissed softly.

Nahaanpar touched the cold metal of the crucifix that dangled beneath his shirt. “They will not leave,”

“They are on our land.” She continued. “There are only ten Spanish and nearly three hundred in this village. ”
“There are villages all around them.” Sevaanga-vik caught some of her spark. “I know they have horse animals, but they shouldn’t call land their own! They shouldn’t ask for our men to help them.”

Nahaanpar spoke with a voice that he felt they could hear was not his own. Was it obvious to them?

“They have sixty neophytes from southern and eastern villages who will fight for them. The six soldiers have heavy leather protection from arrows. They have things called firesticks. Sticks that make a loud thunder sound and make a bear fall dead at thirty paces away! Have you heard a loud sound like a big tree crashing down or a clap of thunder? I have seen a person killed by that sound!”

“I have heard those thunder sounds.” 'Atooshe''s brow fretted. “In the foothills above the Mission’s animal field. It sounded like two big sticks striking in a cave, but the biggest sticks! Do they kill Humans there?”

“It would be coyote or cougar there, but that is the sound. I tell you that they can do bad things to the village even though they are only six men. Their long metal knives, they say ‘swords,’ can kill many men who have clubs and wooden spears. The swords cut spears like reeds. They think nothing can hurt them. The soldiers think their hard leather makes them gods. The brown robes think that their god protects them whether they are alive or dead.” He looked deeply into the ground between them, through the woven mats, into the core of the earth itself and said.

“What is coming is horrible.”

'Atooshe' responded in a monotone. “What is coming is horrible. I have seen that too.”

“If they attack us, it will be horrible for the invaders!” Sevaanga-vik mustered a stony grim face with outjutting jaw.

<<< 0 >>>

Hachaaynar watched Tooypor lead eight women in scraping and inspecting piles of willow bark powder.

“I need to go in.” He told Tooypor.

“I will come.” Promising the village women she would return. They passed the two neophytes and two guards.

“Sit and join us.” Father said. “Nahaanpar is telling us about life in the Mission and the Spanish plans for our village and people.”

“Ava’aha, Nahaanpar” Hachaaynar mumbled sullenly.

“Ava’aha.” Tooypor recognized him from her womanhood ceremony and as the man from the Sea Visitors Atooshe' had pointed out years ago crossing the fields.

“Do you speak our language?” assuming she spoke Serrano dialect.

“I understand and speak many languages.” Offended that this Spanish collaborator would make assumptions about her. “I assume you speak Spanish.”

“And our language of Shevaanga. I have learned the language of the invaders, but I am not of them.”

Hachaaynar asked. “You ride their animal and lead them to us? You do their bidding. How are you not of them?”

He watched the pair sit. “It will take time for you to understand me, but I want the best for our village. I want them to understand that they, especially the beards, have to stop hurting our people. That they have to stay in their own area.”

‘Their own area’ rang heavily as Tooypor watched his downcast eyes darting from one person to another, looking for signs of their approval. She decided he wasn’t one to trust. He seemed like the ones at trade fairs who’d put less in the basket than you’d traded for.

Sevaanga-vik looked to Hachaaynar. “He’s been telling us about firesticks. The loud sounds from their fields. Bad weapons. Ma’hi.”

“Why would he tell us these things?”

“To warn us.”

“No!” He answered his father standing on his own. “It is to frighten us to help them. The help leads to control. They offer to help us, then take our land.”

"How could eight men take our land?"

'Atooshe' could wait no more. Her husband seemed too entranced by Nahaanpar.

"When they came, we thought they were going to the Great Sea. The Sea Visitors, but they stayed. They made their village near ours. They moved closer. Now they are moving even closer. Some of us have gone to them to live like their dogs. Now they want more. They send him to frighten us with their big war magic. How could eight men do that?" She paused rhetorically. "With our fear. With fascination with their shiny things. We should refuse all contact!"

Hachaaynar was proud. He'd worried about her and her Four Directions necklace. She was more solid than father.

Tooypor hadn't seen people making decisions about the Spaniards before this. Pul Tuwaru hadn't seen an invader since the day when they first arrived. Haapchivet was unapproachable by their animals, but 'Atooshe''s was directly threatened.
The "Pieme,' northern desert and coastal Tongva and Serrano, had little contact with them but Tah-ur had sent a message about them murdering children. She kept silence. It wasn't a time to speak but to listen to her teacher and her second father, Sevaanga-vik.

"How can you say you are of us?" 'Atooshe' continued. "You haven't been expelled, but I say you should be." Turning to look each person in the eye. "You've left us for ten seasons, doing their work and living their lifeways. You came here for them, not for us." To her husband. "Tumia'r. Chief. Take a choice!"

Sevaanga-vik squirmed at being put to a test for the third time. She could be so pushy! In front of the kids, too! He spoke firmly.

"He will return to their camp. He will not speak of our doubts or arguments. He will learn exactly what they intend to do if we won't provide help to them. He will try to bring to us a firestick and a long metal knife. Also other metal that can be used for knives or arrowheads." He tapped 'Atooshe' on the knee. "If, he can pass these tests, he is one of us. If he fails, he should never return."

'Atooshe' and Hachaaynar found it acceptable. Tooypor was glad that her teacher and the chief had found common ground. It was fair to put Nahaanpar to a test.

"I can do those tasks." Not seeing a closed door. "I am not sure about the firestick. It is too large to hide in our clothing. Give me this chance."

They agreed. They held reservations, but allowed the test. As Nahaanpar left, he gave a sheepish smile to Tooypor.She watched him carefully as he led the neophytes up the trail to the Mission. There was something very weak in him but an odd strength as well. 'A puzzle,' she thought.

1773 MISSION SAN GABRIEL

Fathers Somera and Cambon climbed the ladder. Evenly cut lumber was laid on the roof for a second floor of the Mission. They watched workers nailing and placing the pegs the way Corporal Andres had instructed them to.

Work went slowly. Cloudbursts made for days devoted to Bible study. Fray Crespi left for San Diego for instruction in administration of Church Property and the role of soldiers and new civilians in the Mission System. It was rumored that Fray Junipero Serra was coming for an inspection.

"The dispatch promised four more soldiers, but Lord, please make them better than these." Somera mumbled, adding. "Except for Corporal Andres, of course." In case he was overheard by the wind.

Cambon smiled, looking over the Spring landscape. Grayish strokes of snow remained on the purple high peaks to the north-east. Young greenery poked through the soil. Rows of new corn and squash were showing promise. To the north-west he saw fifty sheep and goats that had survived the winter. He turned to the south-west where the Indian village could be seen from this new height.

“Two hundred cattle will be too many for us, don’t you think?” Pointing toward the village. “They would be better kept and fed in that area.”

“Straight south would be better. We need to put up fences so they don’t steal the herds.Once they taste steak and ribs, they’ll lose their appetite for acorns. Have you eaten them?”

Somera made a face. “Crespi said he had to smile and pretend he liked it. Two hundred cattle and four more soldiers! Where can we put them all?”

GUADALAJARA – NEW SPAIN

“When will I receive permission from these Godless idiots,” He shouted to the walls. “They are all liars and thieves!” Knowing that the polite chat and banter was simply pure posing for him and that Rivera, Fages, de Portola and that ridiculously named “Knight of the Cross” de la Croix were only after whatever his established Missions could give them in crops and money. ‘They’ll steal our Neophytes.’ He thought, pacing. ‘Everything I build’ correcting himself, ‘that We build,….. will be taken from us, just as they took all of the True Church’s wealth from the Jesuits!’

He repeated his vow to never ride on a horse or be driven in a carriage like the Godless ones. Christ never rode. Even with my leg that carries the pains of mortality. “I will walk!” He said with a voice of steel. “There are Missions to build and good works to complete. I will walk!”

EASTERN TONGVA LANDS

Tooypor and two Haapchivet runners led 'Atooshe' with Shevaanga guards east through the foothill trails above Ashuukshanga to meet Tah-ur at the Three Warm Springs near

Kuukamong-na. They hugged and sat on flat stones by the side of the spring, dangling feet in warm water, mixing cattail pollen and honey to eat. Tah-ur described the kidnapping and killing of the girl by the soldier. She described a body she'd seen traveling in the lands of the Kumeyaay. There were small holes in the chest that had gone through the man's shield. She'd heard the loud sound that 'Ahtoose' described and found a coyote with a hole in it's side.
"They aren't staying close to their Mission. They go everywhere and make trouble. Why won't my husband understand that?"

Tooypor remembered how the 'Sea Creatures' had seemed a joke to her.

<<< 0 >>>

Corporals Alvarado and Verdugo took turns loping right or left of the herd heading North from San Diego. They'd drop to the rear when the wind was behind them and blew the choking dust forward. Sergeant Olivera held point position in all conditions. The forth soldier became ill and died in the saddle outside San Diego.

The four mestizo cattle drivers were told not to fraternize or speak to soldiers except to point out hazards in the route and to warn of observers seen in the distance.

Driver Julio felt tracked for over an hour. He noticed a shape to the far right side that seemed to reappear yesterday but he hadn't been sure enough of it to mention. Now he was sure. It wasn't an animal. It kept a distance to just keep the herd in view. He rode around the back of the herd to Corporal Verdugo.

"Capitan." Knowing Spaniards liked being flattered.

"Um." Verdugo grunted.

"A man is following us. Maybe two days. Maybe more. Across the herd to the right. Below that crotch on the second hill."

"Come with me to the right side. I will stay on your left." dropping behind and swinging to the right side of the herd. Verdugo stayed even with the drivers flank and kept watch on the cactus spotted desert to the east.

"I see him. Good work!" Keeping vision fixed on the moving spot over a kilometer away. "Ride forward and tell Olivera what we have. I won't pursue until he waves. Understand?"

"Yes, Capitan." Galloping eagerly to the point.

Verdugo eased to the right, parallel to the cattle drive and galloped straight at the observer and then a little behind the path to discourage the prey from returning to a hiding place that had been revealed. As he closed ground he could see that it was an Indian. As he came in musket range, he recognized the clothing as Ippi-Tapai from outside San Diego Presidio.

Within ten yards, he squeezed off the shot and the back of the man's head burst in a cloud of red mist. Verdugo brought the snorting horse to a halt short of the body and turned back without a further glance.

"An Ippi-Tapai followed us all the way into Kumeyaay territory. Do they have communication here among the tribals? I thought they don't communicate."

"Are you sure he is dead?" Olvera asked.

"No one was ever more dead."

"He could have followed us for three days. Keep a close watch to both sides and tell the driver he'll have all the wine he wants at the Mission."

CHAPTER 9

BLACK TONGUE

Cambon prepared for Serra's visit. He hadn't dealt with recruitment and Nicolas Jose's report for three days. Then he received a message that Serra wasn't coming this year, but only that more soldiers and cattle would arrive.

Nicolas Jose clung to Juana at night loving her scent and treasuring her passionate kisses and the mighty grasp of her thighs. In the quiet aftertimes he visualized a long and quiet life with many children in Shevaanga.

He watched her face in the dim room through changed eyes. He'd seen her face as a flawed one with too long a chin and eyes too serious. He now saw a deep and timeless beauty that could endure through old age. 'What a lucky man I've become.' He thought, finally seeing the chance to bring his life together
In the mild spring days he did overseer duties as regularly as he ever had but without the push of ambition. He waved to soldiers when they waved to him and made greetings. He praised the fieldworkers and animal tenders when he saw they did their job well. He corrected the ones who were slacking. He couldn't or wouldn't bring up the voice or glare to intimidate them to obedience.

He caught looks from the women he'd regularly taken sex with and avoided eye contact. He knew requests would come from a soldier to make arrangements with a woman in a field or behind a building. This time he would refuse.

For three days he was in a dream of being in a place with no walls. A place of waiting for the gift of wholeness and his true name. Between jumping and landing. Only in the night, with Juana, was he sure of the moment and was where he belonged.

On the fourth morning, Cambon was in his chair on the patio when Nicolas Jose passed. The Padre waved him over.

“Good morning, Nicolas Jose. Come tell me about your negotiation with the Seeba people. Sit, please.”

“Yes, Blessed Father.” Noticing the deep red color in the teacup and knowing it would be wrong to ask for one of the newly baked corn pastries on the plate.

“I present the blankets to the chief. He is gracious to you, with thank you,” bobbing and smiling with servility. “I talk with him long. He is a very stubborn man. Like cow.”

Cambon smiled. “Like a bull. A cow is a woman. A bull is a man.”

“A bull!” He replied with a pleased expression. “He is stubborn like a bull!”

“And what did you find there?” Reminding himself to interview the neophytes who’d accompanied him.

Nicolas Jose bit at his lip. “They won’t give men. If I can give animal,..it’s possible they trade for man. They like blanket. Would trade acorn meal, no more.”

Cambon made a face and observed his cringing and smiling emissary. The man used to swagger with an attitude that he could do anything. No longer. Why? He now spoke with language usage far below his abilities. Why?

“You seemed sure that we would succeed. Was there a reason this has changed?”

“Stubborn man. Just stubborn man. He want animals but, not to give men.”

“We need men, not acorns. Did you tell him about the Lord Jesus Christ and the Blessed Mother Mary?” Focusing on the Indian’s averted eyes. “Did you tell them about God Almighty and the blessings they’ll receive by becoming part of the family of God?”

“Yes, Padre.” Thinking that those stories would have him killed before any more was said. He knew the words, Latin and Spanish. He’d witnessed marriages and baptisms and repeated and kneeled at all the right places. But a woman having a baby without knowing the father? And it was God? But no one has ever seen him? And his blood is what the soldiers get drunk on? They don’t try to reach Spirit when they drink the blood. They only fight and say bad words?

“Yes. You are right.” Nicolas Jose nodded gravely to the Padre. “I must tell him about God and His Son! Not let chief make me stop. I will talk more about Jesus Christ.”

“I’ll give you one more chance to convince them without soldiers at your side,” becoming an experiment to see who this Nicolas Jose was. “I’ll send one goat with you.”

Nicolas Jose left the patio feeling angry at being pressured to please the Padre and of losing the chance to return to Shevaanga. He saw three boys with twig boats they’d made, floating them in a horse trough by the stables. He smacked one on the ear. “Why aren’t you working?” Motioning to the fields. “Where are you assigned?” Annoyed at their hesitation. He slapped the head of the next one. “Aren’t you brickmakers?”

“They’re drying.” The tallest one said. “They don’t have any more molds!”

“Ask Jose Tree-man to show you how to make molds! We need more bricks for the new buildings!” He glared. “Move!” They scurried away. He wondered what angered him.

He felt disrespect when Maria of the east corn turned away hurriedly as he approached. She wanted extra favors when he’d accept her private pleasures. Now that he was taken, she turned away.

"Why aren't you working?" He asked loudly. "The corn needs to be extended to the east. You aren't helping out your friends. What good are you?"

She looked back in confusion. He knew she'd been with fever last month. She'd been assigned to cleaning the rooms of the Spanish. She'd fallen down in the fields coughing, blood on her teeth and blisters on her lips and mouth.

"You knew what good I was when you mounted me! You know why I'm not in the fields!" Her shrieking becoming a hoarse cough as she turned from him holding her hands to her mouth. He remembered! with a curse at himself for forgetting.

"Forgive me Maria, for my bad acts and what I just said." He put a hand on her shoulder. She twitched it off as though he were an insect. She wouldn't turn her face to him. She walked toward the front gate holding her mouth and coughing.

He knew she wasn't going toward anything. Anywhere away from him. She walked ten paces, turning toward her quarters, looking briefly at him. Her hand stained red. Her eyes black pools of pain.

He felt sorrow for the way he'd treated her. If she died now, no one would blame him. He could go on as he was. He'd feel it was he who'd caused her death.

He stopped as though struck. "I am Nicolas Jose." His goals were Nicolas Jose's. He needed to have the youths, women and neophytes do their work to build the Mission. He wanted Juana to bare children. The children would be their joys and helpers as they grew old. He looked at the sandals on his feet and his clean white cotton pants and shirt. It was comfortable in the spring breeze.

"I am Nicolas Jose." Remembering the promises of Nahaanpar to Sevaanga-vik and 'Atooshe'. Feeling the fear that he couldn't speak then. The words stung and made him feel aches in his head. It felt like truth. 'Day after tomorrow I will be Nahaanpar,' He thought. ‘But I am Nicolas Jose. I feel and remember Nahaanpar when I am there. I want to be him. I hate him! When I am there, I hate me!.’ He bit into his now sore lip. “I can’t live this way!” He whispered, ‘I don’t know who I am!’

Tooypor and her guards ran through the Ashuukshanga foothills wearing only loincloths in the warm early sunlight with brilliant lupines, purple sage and poppies covering the slopes. Tiny animals scurried in every direction. Intoxicating pine fragrance and swarms of butterflies rose before them.

Tah-ur waited, lying with her feet submerged in the flow at the warm spring, wearing an imp’s smile. “I thought you would be faster than that. I was about to go home.”

Tooypor was unsure if it was play or disrespect. She was becoming sensitive to disrespect. She found dissension and jealousy aimed at her in many villages and tribes.

“Maybe I should leave if you are not willing to wait for me.” Jutting her jaw.

Tah-ur grinned and stuck her head out like a turtle. “What spirit jumped into you? Silly bunny-rabbit.” Splashing water at her. “I would never leave you.”

Tooypor felt silly at angering so easily. “I’ll race you home and the loser will feed the winners for six days.”

“You’ll prepare meals for both Hachaaynar and me?” Tah-ur flicked more water. “You are a good host.”

“We will laugh at you trying to hunt in our mountains.” Sitting and splashing back at her. “Falling down crevices and screaming and begging us to pull you out.”

They sat to continue the conversations that pulled them together, no matter how far apart.

“Our tale of creation and Nakomah and the messenger Haleheya, and your tale of creation and Quo-ar and the messenger Chinigchnich. The question is, ‘Are we both of the same creation, or of different creators?” Tooypor settled in to continue the thought they had started at their last meeting.

“My father says the same. I say the same.” Tah-ur said. Tooypor nodded in agreement. She felt that the creation was of all things to exist together. “But the majority of the council and elders say that Quo-ar was a low creation and that Chinigchnich was an animal demon.”

“You are still playing with my mind!” Tooypor hunched back and scowled, never expecting that.

“Most of them believe that. The Mojave too. I’ve met girls who went to your village and to Hachaaynar’s for your union. They joke about Chinigchnich walking across the water from Pemuu'nga. They say it is a Pemuu'nga and Yavit trick to make the shell and fish products from the ocean more valuable against the crafts from the desert. They said that your Haapchivet and Shevaanga promote that myth to get their trade cheap. A lot of them think like that, even while complementing you on your herbs and cures. Like the fool who told me about it.”

“What did you say?”

“I didn’t say anything. I punched her in the nose.”

Tooypor burst into laughter looking at Tah-ur’s expressionless face. “Is that true?”

Tah-ur smiled in her catlike way and patted Tooypor’s knee. “I did. That’s exactly the way it happened. Some of the girls are afraid of me because I run with people from different tribes and villages, just like you.” She brought her hand down lightly on the knee. “They are afraid to look at the horizon. They are frightened to look at other people as the same as themselves. They have been to the hills and mountains, but think in their flat ways. We both have the seven turtles rising out of the water. So do they."

Tooypor nodded and raised one finger. "It is after the First Men that the problems arise. Wewyoot is dying and Quo-ar is making the humans walk and think, but they are confused and disunited. They gain respect from Mother Earth and notions of behavior from the animal spirits, patience and planning from the moon and stars, but not knowledge."

Tah-ur sorted sand in her palm as she listened. "Our Pul have traveled far to the east where the Creator Nakoma had no messenger, but through the animal spirits, he gave all humans wisdom. I don't see it, I mean, from any creator. Wisdom wasn't spread around much. Look around"

"That is where Chinigchnich brought all of that in the three stages. As Saor, before he learned to dance. Then as Quaguar where he began to dance well and bring continuity to life, and finally becoming Tobet, dancing up into the stars in the eagle robes and leaving the codes of living well with the humans and spirits." Tooypor stretched back and kicked at the warm water. "It's the dancing together and commemorating the lessons that bring the wisdom. Not just hearing it and forgetting it. The ones you speak of, and we have plenty in Haapchivet and Shevaanga, have given up on community, the big us. Iitaxum! They lost contact with Spirit and only look at the ground at their feet. Not like you. Not like us. When they have pain and can't talk to those around them, they become separated. When they want something and can't have it, they get separated. The rituals can bring them contact and happiness. It makes a village a family."

"But..when my happy village sees Haleheya and Nakomah as low Animal Spirits…or these Brownrobes call us all devils and Maria-people, something is wrong! With the way that people see!"

Tah-ur broke open a packet of cattail pollen and mixed it in her palm with juice from aloe leaf. Tooypor took a smear and smiled as they shared it.

Tah-ur stared into the mixture and said. "Our creator, Nakomah, through his messengers, brought the animal spirits more peace and wisdom than the human spirits because their dominions were more clear. The long view of the birds and protection of the trees. The deep hiding places of the fish and the speed and coats of the four legged ones. Humans were naked and slow and didn't move together as well as birds or have the tools to hunt like the bear and cats. We are only as much as we help each other to be stronger. It's harder in the desert."

"It isn't easy in Haapchivet, but we hold tight to the traditions. Shevaanga is a much kinder place to live, except for the Spanish invaders being near."

"They are few, but no-one brings us together to make them leave." Tah-ur smiled, catching a glance from one of Tooypor's guards. She knew they were attractive and that people turned their eyes to them, together or apart, but there was no reason to fear disrespect, especially from trusted ones from their villages.

"Perhaps you will drive them out."

"Perhaps we will together, with Hachaaynar and the other villages."

"You know, they have a messenger also, who walked over the water."

"Isn't the woman in the robe the messenger?"

"She is the messenger's mother. Maria. That's why they call many of the girls they enslave 'Marias.' The Ashuukshanga girl dead in the four oaks spring was a stolen Maria."

"The messenger who walks on water, what is he called?"

“Cristo.” Tah-ur answered. “Yayzoo Cristo.”

“I couldn’t imagine why they’d have a messenger woman when they don’t have use for women except to enslave and kill them.

Nakomah respects women, doesn’t he?”

“Except when they steal or are liars. Then they’re banished just like men, ‘though lonely men sometimes take them in to feed.”

“It’s like that in Haapchivet, but I’ve never seen one actually banished. There are some from Shevaanga that were cast out and went to Yaanga to find mates and trade at the fairs.”

“What does Chinigchnich do with women who become banished?”

“The same as the men. They can’t participate in village activities. They can’t eat village food, they can’t go in the sacred places but they can participate in the sacred dance so that they can remain in contact with their ancestors. They can chant at that time and try to show that they adhere to the path.” She rubbed aloe on her ankle and soles. “If they do that three times without doing bad things, they are welcomed back, but people watch them to make sure they are true.”

“What if they still steal and lie?”

“They are killed. Usually with arrows.”

Tah-ur said. “It’s the same in the desert.” Rubbing the aloe on her feet and legs. “Do you believe our creators were the same?”

“They couldn’t be different. We see things the same. Our lives are connected to the same spirit. It’s all different words for the same thing. Don’t you feel that?”

“Yes,” answered Tah-ur. “We are one.”

LORETO – NEW SPAIN

Soldiers fanned out into the outlying areas of town. Others were sent to Sinaloa to recruit fifty families to accompany Governor Rivera y Moncada's party to Monterey. It wasn't as easy as they had expected,

The opportunity to start a new life on one of the most beautiful bays in the world with a parcel of land, tools, a horse and two sheep, two cows and a bull plus $90 dollars* for a commitment of two years wasn't attractive to many people, although that was much more than they could earn in a year .

"What more can these people want?" Catalan corporal Chavez moaned to his squad. "I've seen it. It's paradise on earth! "

"I have six more undecideds to visit tomorrow" Lugo spoke to the group. "The Mestizos, Indios and Negros are the most likely to seize the chance. Keep working on the chance to earn land grants and becoming the new elite in a new land. We can raise the numbers before the time to leave comes."

"We don't need to resort to threats." Chavez added. "Yet."

SINALOA – NEW SPAIN

Ramon Perez carried his wagonload of corn from his weevil-infested farm outside the town by thirty kilometers. He'd rinsed it and rolled the stalks and still the damage was apparent to any buyer.

His depression was exceeded by his wife's anger at him and the foresight of the neighboring farm to do daily searches and kills using a fluid that they wouldn't describe or share. She knew that it was planned to make them fail and take over their land.

Ramon brought the wagon into the market stall knowing that he would return with nothing. He worried whether the three soldiers standing by the gate would give him trouble.

"Hey, Ramon." The Concho Indio like him said. "We have an offer for you that I think you will like."

Ramon stepped down from the wagon and the three men laid out the benefits that he and his wife would receive if they were willing to be among the first families of Monterey.

"This is from Governor General Rivera himself" The Conch soldier said.

Ramon rode home after dumping the infected corn with the news for Clara.

MISSION SAN GABRIEL

Nicolas Jose followed Corporal Andres to the Padres office expecting a whipping or banishment for his failures.

"We've had enough of this." Cambon stood with Somera watching from across the small room. "You've been to Seeba four times and have brought us nothing."

Mugartegui said. "This has been a failure. I'll make notes for Baja before I return. You need much better translators"

Nicolas Jose kept a lowered head, watching a chipped nail poking through the broken netting of his sandal.

Somera hissed. "How could you bring them a lamb and a pig and have nothing offered in return?"

He mumbled. "The chief is a stubborn man. I try. I ask for help. He say no Seeba person will help." Still looking down with furrowed brow. "I promise blankets and more animals. Seeba people just look at animals and laugh at noises from them. They don't eat them. They watch them eat and laugh."

"I don't think that you'll make more progress from another visit." Cambon gazed out the small chest-high window toward the new grazing land. "We'll handle it some other way," turning with a brushing motion from his hand. "You may go."

They watched the Indian shuffle out the door. Somera said what had been on his mind for weeks.

"We need to handle the conversion like the Franciscan model for Mexico. Through the children. Andres, Lopez, Rodriguez and Cordero and the new ones will go out every day and bring in children, young strays and put them in classes. Teach them to pray and fit in to life here. Soon the parents will come. They are docile people here. We have nothing to fear from sticks and stones. Serra sees it that way and Crespi has seen the successes in Loreto and Sonora"

Cambon thought similarly. "We have enough overseers for control of children. Yes, I agree."

<<< 0 >>>

Nicolas Jose felt shamed and confused. When he was in Shevaanga he couldn't repeat messages of the Spanish to make demands to trade men for animals no-one wanted. A horse would create interest but pigs and sheep made no sense. No man would help the invaders.

He ambled toward his small room. He looked at the growth of the Mission yard, fields and buildings and felt some pride in the part he'd played in their progress until Nahaanpar's eyes told him it was stolen and that he was an instrument of the theft.

He knew how to make his tribesmen and the ones from the sea and deserts work for him. It was a bitter task as long as Nahaanpar was looking through his eyes. He could no longer shut the eyes out. He tried but nothing worked.

He entered his room expecting it to be empty and found Juana curled on the mat with sweat making points of light on her shoulder and forehead.

"Why are you here? What's wrong?" Squatting beside her. "Fever?" Placing his hand on the curve of her neck, "You are hot! With sweat! I'll get you covers."

"Don't. Just stay with me." She held his hand against the side of her throat.

"I'll stay. How long have you been here?"

"Six or seven fingers of the sun. I was dizzy. I had to lie down." She put his hand on her cheek. "You aren't angry?"

The tenderness that he felt was unexpected. She worked hard. She loved hard and comforted him in the right ways at the right times. She had strong friendship with the other women and was never angry at their jealousies and faults. The only one who truly accepted him.

"I've been feeling angry, but it's never you. You are why I control it and feel foolish when it spills out. To not hurt you or disappoint you." He stroked her brow. "Do you want to sleep?"

She nodded, closing her eyes and putting the back of his hand to her lips. "I feel so weak. I have seen others become sick like this and I'm afraid."

His eyes had become accustomed to the half light. "Open your mouth and put your tongue out.....more." Squinting close and wishing there was more light. He crawled the five feet to the door and opened it to daylight, returning to see the tongue. "It's darker. Do you cough?"

"In the fields. They told me to leave and rest."

He'd seen others fade like this and shared her fear. The tongue that darkens and blisters. The cough that becomes ever stronger until blood comes up and each cough brings more choking and blood until convulsing into coma and death. They all had seen it.

"You should sleep now. I'll go back to work and tell your crew that no-one should visit."

She nuzzled his hand. He left with a storm in his chest, He had to do his work.

CHAPTER 10

KIDNAPPED

Rodriguez was bored and deep in flights of sexual fantasy patrolling the northwestern grounds above Shevaanga to the base of the foothills. It was a long day and would be dark in an hour.

'Atooshe' and Tooypor saw him descending the trail from the Pula hut. He was a far spot against the yellow flowered fields but they knew it was the 'crazy one' who had killed the Asusk-gna girl and kidnapped others.

When he saw the two distant people, he turned his horse to the east on an angle so that they would not be afraid to continue southward. He had a feeling they were women.

They entered the long flatland trail to Shevaanga. He turned quickly northward to cut off their return to the hills and to come up from behind if they continued south. He would be able to disable the uglier one and carry the better one to a place out of view to put to use. He might find her worth keeping in the stable a while.

"He is coming after us!" 'Atooshe' shouted, breaking into a run with Tooypor at her heels.

"I don't think we can make it before..."

"I'll go straight home. You turn back to the hut."

"No! I won't leave.."

"Go! Now! The guards are there. Get them!"

"I can.."

"No! Don't disobey me! Run! Fast!"

Tooypor saw the horse gaining quickly. She turned right, angling toward the mountain trails. She hoped the rider would pursue her. She saw a substantial tree ahead to use as a shield while she used larger rocks to topple the rider or hit the horse's nose or eyes. She turned. The rider had turned toward 'Atooshe' and was closing fast.

'Atooshe' realized she was the target and searched for a form of defense. Sand to the eyes of the horse and man was a delayer but was weak. Stones thrown upward would have little effect and no usable branches were near. Only twigs from the light brush.

She eased left up an uneven rocky rise and stooped to gather three jagged stones that could dizzy most animals or knock a man unconscious. She was well practiced in accuracy and had a slight height advantage. 'Better here than on flat ground.'

She turned, Rodriguez recognized the snooty bitch from the Seeba village. The chief's woman. He saw that she had picked up stones and taken higher ground. He slowed to a stop, enjoying the sight of her hard breathing and sweat covered body.

"Jasmin." He whispered to his horses ear. "We are going to have fun today. Come on!" Edging the horse forward at a walk and bringing his shield forward over the horses ears, drawing his saber back.

Tooypor was frozen. She couldn't run from 'Atooshe' while she was in peril. The soldier was only feet from 'Atooshe' and Tooypor was over a kilometer away from them. She ran back to fight the Spaniard. There was no other choice. She sprang forward, leaping through lupines, poppies, sagebrush and large rocks, up and down small rises, losing sight as the horse crested the hillock where 'Atooshe' stood.

'Atooshe' hurled a fist sized rock at the horses nose as the Spaniard lowered the shield enough to deflect the stone, missing his own head, with the shield glancing the horses face. The horse snorted angrily as Rodriguez spurred him up the rise the last thirty feet. She threw again at the soldier's crazed, grinning face, wildly looking for a way to escape.

Rodriguez slapped the stone away with his shield, liking the way her breasts moved when she threw. 'It will only be moments now, my little doll. Only moments,' as the horse covered the last yard and she stumbled backwards, losing her footing, landing sprawled, her shoulder and the back of her neck striking a lump of granite but not feeling pain in her need for flight. She scrambled to rise.

Tooypor ran hard. She couldn't see the mound until she reached a higher point but only saw the place where they'd been until a horse and rider showed through the brush.

"'Atooshe'!" She screamed running through fire in her veins and mind, cutting her knee on a bush that wouldn't give way. "'Atooshe'! I'm coming!"

Rodriguez was above her as she got her footing. He edged the horses chest into 'Atooshe'. She staggered back two steps to his right. He leaned over toward her and with a sweep of his right arm, brought the handguard of his saber down on her forehead. He felt regret at seeing blood on her face, blunting one of the aesthetic aspects of his seduction fantasy. She was standing but her eyes were unfocused from the blow. He swung his left leg over and slid from the saddle next to her. He drove his left fist deep in her stomach, grabbing her hair to keep her from falling.

"Thanks be to………"

Tooypor ran through the moonless dark thundering against her lack of foresight. 'Atooshe' also hadn't seen the danger. Gathering cuts to her lower legs and knees.

She burst into Sevaanga-vik's greathouse and fell to her knees. Sevaanga-vik was consulting with runners from Yaanga and rose in surprise.

"What, Child!?"

"'Atooshe' was captured by a soldier! The bad one on the horse who'd insulted her. She is gone!" She shouted, rocking from side to side, pulling at her hair. "He may kill her!"

"Where are they?" An aside to the men. "Spears! Arrows!" Squatting, steadying Tooypor's shoulders. "Where are they?" hunting her eyes.

She saw the fear in him. Tooypor's continence changed. Tears stopped. She became steady. She saw the situation as an all-sided picture that she could inspect, like the movement of the mudfloe or the trajectory of a large leaping wildcat. It was predictable.

"If you go after her, they will kill you. It is clear. He will expect you to come. I was wrong when I said he may kill her. He was hurting her but she won't be killed. If you attack without the whole village at your side they'll kill you. That is what the Invaders want. No leaders. After you, they'll go after Hachaaynar and my father. Only bring the whole village. In the daylight."

The men were struck by the change in the girl. Sevaanga-vik touched her face to understand where this adult and calm voice came from in this child wife of Hachaaynar. He churned for revenge no matter what the risk, but her calm eyes and the clarity of her vision made him hesitate.

"Tell me all. How did it happen?"

She closed her eyes a moment. "We were returning from the hut. As we entered the flats, a Spanish soldier was riding below. We thought he was leaving but he cut behind us. 'Atooshe' told me to run to the hut and get my guards. I thought we were safe and there was time." Her face contorted at the memory of deciding to go alone. "I wanted to stay with her but she said to go. She did it to protect me. I'm ashamed. I could have saved her."

Sevaanga-vik shook his head. "It isn't your fault. It's the invaders. You couldn't stop a soldier."

"You mustn't go without hundreds with you!"

Tooypor could't let her emotion for 'Atooshe' dilute the vision of Sevaanga-vik's need to survive. Rushing into the darkness would be foolish without the strength to overrun the invaders.

Hachaaynar rushed in. "Wife, what has happened?

"Your mother was captured by the Spanish."

"One man." Tooypor added. "The crazy one who may..." She was interrupted.

"We will leave in the morning!" Sevaanga-vik spoke, wanting to leave now but feeling it could be a trap. Nighttime could help if they were not expected. This had to be a planned entrapment.

"I'll gather the men." Hachaaynar kneeled by Tooypor. "Were you there? How did you escape?"

"'Atooshe' told me to run. I shouldn't have. I ran back when he turned to her, but I was too late. The horse was too fast." She wouldn't mention the loincloth on the ground. "I don't think she will be killed. She will be kept until we can free her. We must do it carefully. I have a vision that it can only be with the largest numbers. Only then will it succeed."

Sevaanga-vik listened like a drawn bow. "There are only six soldiers. Hachaaynar will gather ten good bowmen and we will leave as dawn approaches." He held up his hand to stop Tooypor's interruption.

"You will gather up villagers to follow us. We will go to the mound near the Mission and call to Nahaanpar, or whatever he is called, to meet and bring 'Atooshe' back to us. If they refuse, it will be war and we will kill them all. If they bring her, we will tell them to go back to their homelands."

Tooypor saw disaster with twelve men. She said. "Sevaanga-vik, please wait long enough..."

"You've said enough! You say you should have stayed. You did not. I've heard all you've said. You will stay and gather more people., Hachaaynar and I will bring back 'Atooshe'."

"But if it is a.."

"Enough! You'll do as I say!"

Hachaaynar saw his father would not relent.

Sevaanga-vik glared and paced to the door and back, occasionally glaring at Tooypor.

"Father, I'll pick the strongest and most skillful."

Tooypor knew it wasn't the place of a woman to contradict a chief or her husband publicly. She hoped she would gain

'Ahtooshe''s stature in time, but speaking up now would be angrily remembered. It would fail.

"Wife, you will gather the men and all those able to fight." Hachaaynar had never ordered her in that voice before. If they'd been away from Sevaanga-vik she'd have slapped him or kicked him where it hurt. She held her temper and looked at him as a stranger.

"I will bring the whole village."

Sevaanga-vik yelled. "Only fighters! Do you listen?"

Tooypor spent the night gathering villagers to assemble a force to release 'Atooshe'. Young men chanted and slapped shoulders. Older men clapped throwing sticks together. By the first eastern glow, she led more than one hundred villagers to the chiefs hut.

Six seated women looked up at the war party from the mats of the greathouse. "They have left."

Tooypor saw the empty spear rack and burned at Hachaaynar's disrespect in leaving without her.

"How long ago?"

"Less than two fingers ago."

"Are your husbands with them?"

"Yes. ten men and the chief."

"Hachaaynar?"

"Beside his father." The deeply lined woman said. Her husband was in the party. Tooypor knew she was afraid but each of the women would sit through a season to show that their men would return to them.

Tooypor shouted. “We must hurry!” Running up the trail with a hundred men and women behind her. In a short time a fearful noise made her stop.

Sevaanga-vik ran with Hachaaynar on his right and Kweeti, his best bowman, on his left. The others kept pace behind. It was barely light. The sun hadn’t cleared the blue mountain range to the north-east. The path ahead was blocked by rises and dips.

They crested a mound. A mounted soldier several hundred yards ahead saw them approach. The man rode quickly away, falling out of sight as they entered a depression of streambed.

“We can’t catch him. They will be warned!” Hachaaynar called out.

Sevaanga-vik felt the fire in him that had burned from the moment the girl had burst into his house. “Keep the pace!” As he increased his own.

They ran to a high point and saw two horsemen in the center of the trail holding the sticks that Nahanpar had warned them about.

Lopez reached Rodriguez in the next sector. Rodriguez was relieved there were only twelve of the natives on foot. Not enough to overcome them with spear and arrow. He knew what was on their minds. He looked forward to sending the cuckolded husband to Hell.

“We’ll hold here and let them come to us.” Checking his musket and pistol, hoping Lopez was up to the task,

“I’ll back you up. You take the first shot.”

Rodriguez’ eyes were bright with anticipation. He watched the group come within range and waited to have a sure shot. Frightened, Lopez raised his left arm holding his shield.

“Rufino! What are you waiting for?”

Rodriguez recognized the chief between the slim son and the muscular one on the left. 'Come a little closer my friend,' as the muscular one raised his bow on the run.

Lopez was surprised at the speed of the arrow coming at his head. He ducked and raised his shield in time to deflect it. "Jesus! Shoot!"

Hachaaynar brought the notch of the arrow to the sinew on the run and took aim.

A puff of smoke rose from the horseman's stick and a horrible noise burst in his ears. Pricks like nettles stung his forehead and arm.

Sevaanga-vik gasped and fell out of view. Hachaaynar saw a splash of red and turned to see father fall back, his chest torn open like a sliced animal.

Kweeti was on the other side of the chief. He froze in amazement at the sound and Sevaanga-vik's fall.

Pudgy Na-amah rushed past with an angry cry taking five strides. A second explosion sounded and the boy's head burst with a spray that left stinging spots on their bodies. Two men behind shouted as fragments stung them.

It was like nothing ever seen or described in legend. The horrible thunder in the hands of a human! The instant death! The spray of the precious fluid of life. The chief, so strong a leader, lying at their feet.

Four men turned and ran in fear. Hachaaynar dropped his bow and started to pick it up. Kweeti grabbed him by the shoulders and yanked him back up the trail.

"We can't leave Father!" Hachaaynar shouted.

"I'll bring my group for him. You must go to safety. You are chief. We can't lose you!" Dragging him off balance and telling the remaining fighters to help pull Hachaaynar.

"No! Bring father!" Screaming as the retreating men saw the two riders slowly moving forward doing rubbing motions to the firesticks.

Rodriguez wasn't confident enough to ride them all down. He was sure he'd made his point, but he had an idea that would put the fear of God in them for eternity.

Lopez saw madness in Rodriguez' smile. "Let's return and report this now."

Rufino moved his horse forward, keeping his eyes fixed on the retreating Indians. He'd reloaded and was feeling energized with more power than he'd ever experienced. He moved slowly so they wouldn't run in panic. He wanted them to have a clear view. He saw many Indians on the trail in the distance coming toward them, but it would be a quarter of an hour before they would arrive. 'Too bad,' he thought. 'You're going to miss the show.'

"Come back!" Lopez shouted. "There are too many!"

He looked down at the open-eyed, open-mouthed twitching corpse below. He dismounted, laying down his musket, grinning at the savages up the trail and drew his saber, lifting the head roughly by the hair, swinging the saber full force against the neck.

"Whore mother of Jesus!" Angered that the blow didn't sever the head and he needed another. The second slice separated the head. He held it up and to the side, not minding the blood splashing his trousers and boots.

"Aiiiiiiiii-Hi-hi hi!!!" He screamed with joy at his trophy, embarrassed that one blow would have looked much more competent and fearsome.

Lopez crossed himself and said. "Sweet Jesus. Forgive us and protect us." Seeing four Indians running back toward them. "Rufino! Go!"

Rufino sheaved the sword, picked up the musket and mounted, splashing blood on the saddle and flanks of Jasmin. "Aiiiiiiiii-hi-

hi-hi!!!" Turning and laughing while galloping past the panicked Lopez. "Look at those stupid bastards!"

"There will be Hell to pay for this!" Lopez yelled.

'That will be Then.' too pleased to consider Hell.

<<< 0 >>>

Tooypor ran faster at the second thunderstroke, furious they'd leave her when her plan gave safety.

She saw two horses raising dust away from a group of men to the sides of the trail. There were shapes in the center of the trail that the standing men were closing around. Some dropped to their knees on the trail. The shapes were two humans lying on the rocky trail.

Hachaaynar was on his knees before his father's headless corpse. He had never seen such evil. These Spiritless invaders were demons on their land, with blood, words and blankets they offered, pretending to be humans.

Mother and father were both taken in two days. He couldn't mourn or send them to the Ancestors without his father's head or his mother's body. He saw Kwetii''s feet next to him and vowed, "I'll walk to them and kill or die today." Wanting to die as much as live.

Kwetii' looked down at his friend, the new chief. He had fear but had to speak. "You are now Sevaanga-vik. you must survive. Daylight will betray us. Night will help us."

"We must get father's head. His body must be whole. I never should have turned back!"

Kwetii' turned at the shouts and running feet. "Tooypor." He stood back as she approached.

She saw the spattered and dusty tatoos on the chest and thighs looking over Hachaaynar's shoulders at the man she'd warned not to go with so little protection. Nothing she could say to him could ease his pain. It would be wrong to touch him until he was ready. She looked beyond Sevaanga-vik's headless body and saw one of the fighters in a pool of blood, the top of his head gone.

'How could this happen? Does the loud noise take heads off? How can spirits become whole?'

Kwetii' spoke quietly. "The invaders have weapons that can defeat us. He wants to attack. Try to stop him."

'He must see me as responsible for 'Atooshe''s kidnapping and father's death.' She chose not to speak until he had first spoken.

Hachaaynar knelt, eyes closed, feeling Tooypor's presence and wanting to die rather than face her. She was right. Only the full strength of the village would have made the invaders ride away. Then Father would have led all the villagers to the Mission. There would be too many arrows to....His thoughts went back to the sound and the spray of blood. How many firesticks were there? How many soldiers? Did the brownrobes have them too? He knew that he had to kill the one who had taken the head of his father.

He still wanted to run to his death or stab his heart with an arrow but he felt the eyes of people on him. They were now his people. He had to be leader. He turned, kneeling, to his wife. Her fear melted. She knew he saw it and felt his understanding.

"I won't lead an attack today." He nodded gravely.

She felt respect. She wanted to drop to her knees and hold him. To cry in each others arms and to wail like coyotes at the evil that had come. "That is good." She said, knowing they had to appear strong. No matter what they felt, they had to be solid replacements for Sevaanga-vik and 'Atooshe'.

Hachaaynar turned to the fighters and motioned to the young men who'd edged up to them. He spoke clearly and strongly. "Carry them behind us to home. We will plan the recovery of Sevaanga-vik's head and re-unite his body before the ceremony." Walking along the side of the trail with Tooypor past the murmuring throng of villagers.

Behind them a pack of teenagers argued for an attack now, saying they'd make a night raid with or without the cowardly Hachaaynar. "How can he turn his back?" "We need a chief who'll take action, not an herb picker."

Hachaaynar and Tooypor walked to the front of the crowd to lead his people home. Eyes forward.

"You are a good man." She said.

"You are a good woman." He replied.

They turned to each other for an instant, and without breaking step, tears gushed from their eyes. They turned forward, hoping no one saw what they were feeling. They walked with mountains on their shoulders. They'd just left twelve years of childhood behind.

MISSION SAN GABRIEL

Rodriguez argued to have the head posted on a stake at the Mission gate as an example of the foolishness of rebellion. Cordero and Machado supported him. Lopez and Andres said it was disgusting and would only create anger.

Rodriguez entered the dim office of Padre Somera with his two supporters at his side.

"I was attacked on the western trail by a pack of savages from Seeba village. They shot arrows at Lopez and me. We fired and killed two or more of them."

Somera rushed to the door. "Juan! Juan! Come quick." Sitting on his bench and signaling to wait until Father Cambon hurried in.

"Continue Corporal Rodriguez, please."

Rufino embellished with more arrows in the air and the wild eyed chief leaping up at his horse, knife in hand, but felled by the saber just in time.

"My sword cut through his neck. I'd taken hold of his hair and the body dropped away." He gesticulated with an expression of panic. "I held the head up in the air and the savages fled in terror."

Cambon gasped. "You killed a chief?" The priests looked at each other knowing a full attack would follow.

"I can make sure these godless creatures will not harm us." Rufino continued with an air of command, lifting the oiled and scarred blood-stained leather sack onto the dark wooden plank that served as a desk. "Here."

The priests gasped, guessing the contents, as Rodriguez undid the strap.

"No! I believe you. It is the head of the chief." Remembering the man who had refused his people to work for the Mission. The bullish man Nicolas Jose described as stubborn. Why would he attack? He'd never shown interest in us.'

"What provoked the attack?"

"Blessed Father. You know they're savages. They act on impulse. He was a hot head." Intending to enjoy his spoils when he could slip away to the shed. "I have spoken to the men. If we post this on a stake near the gate it will show the gentiles the cost of rebellion. They are a superstitious lot. They dare not risk the same fate."

Cambon and Somera found it repellant. They saw the soldiers were in accord with Rodriguez. They were their protectors and set policy for security. After questioning, Rodriguez was given clearance to stake the head outside the gate. When they were away from the Padres the three soldiers laughed and felt their first success.

Military Governor Rivera approved the choices of Padre Francisco Palou on selecting the site for the new Northern Mission and settlement, but the Presidio location had been wholly in his hands. It was partially to ease the constant pressures from Frey Junipero Serra.

The new specific locations chosen were thoroughly pleasing to all of them for all three purposes. The settler's areas were on the South side of the deep bay that wrapped around with usable shores on all sides. The inland arm swept around with islands in the center.

Fernando nodded. "What could be better? A harbor to rival any of Europe will be built right here!"

Frey Francisco agreed. "This is the base of a great settlement to grow across these gentle hills. I can see it now! It will grow easily and I can see where the Mission, maybe the first Cathedral, will be built. Right in that raised area between those hills in the center."

"That would be an inspiring center to those of the Faith." Trying not to sound patronizing as he was often accused.

Fernando looked toward the wide mouth of the bay and saw how canons placed on both shores and along the coast could sink any British or Russian attempt to enter Spanish lands.

"It all fits." Seeing the easy defensibility of the location. That higher hill overlooking the mouth of the bay was an ideal place for a Presidio that can be larger than the one for the Capitol.

"Wouldn't this make a better Capitol than Monterey?" Palou visualized Cadiz or Le Havre being built here.

"This we must name for the patron Saint of our order."

They agreed that this would be named "San Francisco."

SHEVAANGA

Tooypor explained her plan walking in Shevaanga. Hachaaynar would die if he followed his first instinct. Needing to kill or die was wrong. If he fell, the village wouldn't survive. Being chief meant more than commanding. It meant planning for survival.

They reached the great-house, Hachaaynar assigned Kwetii' and Kiukyoo to go with her to Haapchivet to recruit more people.

"I'll arrive before nightfall. We'll return with hundreds before the sun is two hands high." She spoke with solemnity. "Don't let them catch you up in an attack. It will be a disaster."

He watched the three go north swallowed in the dusty cloud of the returning villagers. He felt glares as he turned back and shouted.

"We'll wait until morning to carry out a plan to drive the invaders out of our land. We'll have help from Haapchivet"

Hachaaynar's head throbbed, besieged by loud angry men with demands to avenge his father's death with a frontal attack this night. One of father's older friends barked in his face.

"Tomorrow will be too late! They'll be ready for us."

"If you won't fight, we will!" From a chorus of youths.

"Avenge your father!" Yelled a shrill woman.

The decision was solid. He called Maachhar and five trusted runners to come forward. He threw mats by the Vik's chair, folded them for height and rose to speak.

"An attack now is what they expect. They kidnapped my mother to provoke a war party and their scouts had weapons that stopped us on the trail." On saying it, he realized it didn't make sense for the Spanish to stop them with only two scouts.

"Pula Tooypor has a vision that my mother is alive. She is bringing a large party from Haapchivet to build a force that can overcome the invaders' weapons."

The murmuring from the impatient men rose as he said. "We will repair and gather our weapons for the morning's assault."

One of Sevaanga-vik's close friends, a craggy round man with long, grey hair, shook his fist and turned to the dozens crowding into the great-house.

"Calling this child, Tooypor, a Pula, makes the word less! She was only being trained and this boy is not a chief!. He doesn't know when to attack!"

The air buzzed with danger. A young voice was soon echoed by others outside the doorway. "He is not chief! He is not chief!" and, "We need a chief!"

Hachaynar saw that he had to take control. He stepped on the Vik bench.

"I am appointed by ancestors and will avenge my father. We will avenge my father and rescue Pula 'Ahtooshe', my mother." He could hardly be heard over the shouts.

Ma'achar was three years older than Hachaaynar. Strong and aggressive. As accurate with a bow and throwing stick as Kwetii'. He'd taught Hachaaynar arts of fighting and tracking. He waved to his teammates to come close as he leapt to the bench beside Hachaaynar. He shouted.

"He is now Sevaanga-vik! There is no other! If you say otherwise, you must leave! You must pack your homes and leave Shevaanga!" Pulling a club from his waistband and raising it over his head. His friends felt the wave of power and did the same.

"Sevaanga-vik! Seeba-ik" spread from the supporters in the front and continued with the protestors pushed out the door. People chose sides. The majority was now with Hachaaynar but a third were silent.

Forty teenagers and men who'd called for the attack and shouted for a new chief, marched across the village to regroup.

Three Hawks, a stocky leader of the hunting teams, took control, shouting from a high spot.

"The frightened child will let them kill and kidnap us until we have no land and no people. I'll end their terror right now! We have enough fighters here to kill them all!"

He knew the invader's animals and long shiny knives were useless against forty men with arrows and long spears. "Who has courage? Who is strong?"

"A'aha!" Rang through the crowd. "Apusterot! Hu-u-rka!""Who will join me? "

The loud cry of. "No'oma'! I will!" Was heard through the walls.

Men at the Greathouse door looked out and signaled they couldn't see anyone.

"What do you think?" Maachar asked.

Hachaaynar found it made sense considering the thinking of those who had left.

"Hearing them shout 'I will' doesn't mean they'll attack me, at least not on this day. They want to attack the Spanish. I do as well, but I want to be sure of victory." Motioning to the outside. "They are willing to lose their lives without being sure of victory."

"How can that ever be sure?" A stooped and crippled elder who had been close to the old Sevaanga-vik asked.

"Before I lost Mother and Father, I thought like those out there. I know how easily the good and strong perish. Father was standing beside me. Tooypor was right. We should never have left without the whole village. The invaders would have fled. Father would be alive. Now that the invaders are prepared, we need all of us together, and Haapchivet as well.

MISSION SAN DIEGO

Father Jaume walked the Mission grounds, pleased that the landscaping was so beautifully executed and that the recently Christianized pagans followed directions so well from the Baja Indians who shared their language. The number of pagans baptized was increasing weekly. Several had married and seemed to abide by the rules of marriage.

Father Serra, the founder, had made two inspections and had left with compliments on the work Jaume had done to reach out to the savages and bring them into the faith.

Now that the Presidio was an official entity and expanding the Mission's security was now assured.

Father Jaume walked back through the arches with thoughts of which new crops would fill out the needs of the soldiers as well as the neophytes.

It looked good.

HAAPCHIVET

Tooypor and the two runners reached Haapchivet at nightfall. They forced the pace with muscles aching to beat the moonless dark across the rocky trail.

"You are a fast woman." Kiukyu said as they entered the aroma filled village at cooking time.

She burst into the greathouse during a council meeting of elders. Father and Pul Tuwaru looked at her sternly. Elders said "Get out" in low voices at the inappropriateness.

"It's about Sevaanga-vik" They leaned forward. Haapchi-vik frowned. "Is it true? A Shevaanga runner met one of ours and told him the chief was killed. We were about to send people to find the truth.You must leave." Her father said with a frown for his daughter's breach of protocol.

"There's more to tell." Frustration welling from the long run and the vision of disaster if this wasn't handled with overwhelming numbers. "I must tell you what is happening. You need to hear."

"You must leave the council of elders." He repeated, to nods and grunts of agreement. "We'll send a delegation to find the truth and then decide our path. You wait outside. If we have questions, we'll call you."

"You must hear me." She stood her ground unafraid. "His head was cut off! The invaders are keeping it!"

"You must leave!" Firmly. The old men picked up the message of the chief. "You must leave." The father added. "Wait outside. We'll call you later."

She would be banned from meetings if she pressed. She thought of the endurance of Bear. How the anger and need for justice and revenge had to be tempered with patience and tactical sense. Not to let the first thought to mind become the only thought in mind.

"I'll wait to be called." She said with a strong voice and backed to the door, head lowered. She saw Pul Tuwaru with a look of pride nodding with respect. She did the right thing, for the moment.

When she stepped out the doorway, 'Aachvet was standing with her runners.

"It is true Sevaanga-vik was killed by the invaders?"

"Yes. I came right after it happened." She led him to a patch of soft weeds beside the greathouse where they'd played and talked all through their lives. She pulled his hand to sit also. He knew it was a moment that would test him.

"'Atooshe' was taken by an invader. The same man who killed the chief. I don't think she was killed. I feel she is alive somewhere. We may save her, but that is why Sevaanga-vik and Hachaaynar went with ten fighters to the Mission. "

"Hatchanar was nearly killed. He was next to his father. He is in danger now in Shevaanga. We are all in danger now." She held his hands tightly, speaking as though he were now chief.

"I see this moment with the invaders with perfect clarity, like looking down into a valley. I see the results. I saw it before the fighters attacked without enough support from the village. I saw death and defeat." She brought her face close to his to lock him into her vision.

“I see death and defeat tonight and tomorrow, unless the council listens to me and approves my plan.”

'Aachvet’s eyes widened in disbelief. “Approves your plan? You can’t walk into a council and tell them things!”

“This is different from anything in the past!” Grabbing his forearms to keep him from moving. “Don’t stand!” With a shake. “You need to understand what I’m saying. You need to help them understand it. All our lives will depend on it. ”

He had seen her angry at times and seen her need to control people around her. She could order people and they would follow. Men and women, stronger than her. They would follow her, but, he’d never seen her like this. A fire in her eyes and a low rumble in her voice.

“You really are a bear!” Feeling the weight of Sevaanga-vik and Hachaaynar on him. “I will listen, my sister. Help me understand.”

She told about ‘Atooshe' and the run to Shevaanga, the chief’s reaction and Hachaaynar blaming her. Of their anger and need to attack. Then she told him her vision of what it would take to recover ‘Ahtooshe’ and her fear for those who’d leave too early. By the time she’d finished, 'Aachvet saw the foolishness, with hundreds of villagers ready to follow, of twelve men leaving them behind.

“I see the flaw.” Quite seriously. “It’s an easy trap to want to be the boldest spirit and to be the one remembered for a success. He respected Pula 'Atooshe' more than the village.”

Tooypor looked at him. ‘Where did he get that wisdom?’ and prepared to make a larger step, hoping he could take that step with her.

“Many of the strong ones in the village want to be the heroic one. They call Hachaaynar weak because he understands that the village is the river that can sweep the invaders away. Now that the invaders are prepared for an attack, it will take our village to bring enough strength to the flatlands. To make the river a flood.”

“I think it will take long talks to convince father!”

"Do you understand how important this is?"

"Yes! I have never heard a firestick, but if they used them to kill Sevaanga-vik, we must take them away."

"It's much more than that. I have to tell them about the head. There can be no ceremony without it. Shevaanga will be a sinkhole of bad spirits unless Sevaanga-vik is made whole to join the ancestors. We can't defeat them with an un-whole body. We have to bring Haapchivet to Shevaanga tonight. We must be there in the morning to have the strength!"

He asked more questions. She answered step by step until he said.

"I see the necessity of every step. It makes sense to me. If I remove a part, it no longer makes as much sense." He leaned back with his hands supporting him on the long grass, pausing for effect. "They'll never let you do it."

"Let us do it. I'll walk to the center now and I want you standing tall and speaking up strong beside me. It is all their lives we are speaking for." She put two fingers against his chest. "Do you have the courage for it?"

"Yes I do, sister." He grinned. "I am ready for this!"

<<< 0 >>>

Three Hawks was fit for hard night travel and known for his eyesight.

Thirty men followed Three Hawks with well made bows and tightly woven bands holding ten balanced and true arrows. They crouched as they ran slowly, looking ahead for any sign of a scout or horse.

They approached the rolling ups and downs of the trail past the point where Sevaanga-vik was killed. Three Hawks hunched low on the trail and signaled the attackers to stay low and keep to either side of the trail, until the Mission was in sight.

"Be ready for the fire stick and spread to either side before letting fly." He whispered. "Be sure to retrieve as many arrows as you can find after a kill. You will need every one."

They moved through the low brush at the sides of the trail past the dark spot that one of the original twelve said was the blood of the chief. They saw wisp of smoke from a Mission oven rising above the tops of the brush.

Corporal Andres lay behind a half buried log imagining hoards of local Indios rushing down the trail with horses and cannons, attacking like the Mongols or Saracens of the books. He disliked the thought of killing other Indios. His mind drifted away until he realized after squinting hard, that there was motion on the sides of the trail. He nudged the drowsy new mestizo man, Montez. "They're here. Run," dreading taking lives.

Montez hewed to the low ravines and drainage ditches. Cordero saw him approach and woke Rodriguez, Lopez and the three remaining reinforcements from San Diego. "They've almost reached the spurs." He whispered.

"Take positions." Rodriguez said in a calm, low voice to hide his excitement at being able to kill tonight. He resented the intrusion on his plans for the chiefs wife. She was the best looking woman in this Hellhole and it would be a shame for her to smother before he could pump out a little of his discontent in her. It would be the fault of these stupid little savages if she were dead before tomorrow night. He vowed with a small smile that none of them would be running home this time.

Three Hawks felt uneasy with a clear view of the path and walls of the enemy. Nothing seemed odd other than the lack of small animals that usually lurk near where humans gather food. He had an instinct for the scurrying and tiny calls.

New noises he heard made a surge of adrenalin. Loud enough cries to be heard by the invader scouts. Two men of his men flopped down on opposite sides of the trail holding their feet pulling at them or something on them.

He moved to the man nearest his left side. A young boy next to him dropped to his knees and rolled on his side with a second yelp, reaching around to the back of his shoulder. Three Hawks saw the whites of the boys wide eyes as he strained not to cry out more.

Three other men dropped with sounds of pain as he drew close to the boy. He did not see an arrow but there was something like a large spider on his shoulder.

“Stop!” A hoarse whisper from a man directly behind him, pointing to the ground in front of Three Hawk’s feet. He was watching the boy’s face and hadn’t looked down at the ground. He reached down.

There were dark pinecone sized spiny circles on the sand. The touch was smooth and cool feeling but each side had four sharp points with barbed ends so it couldn’t be removed when it stuck in flesh. There were two more arms pointed out so it could stick from any angle.

“All stop now!” he hissed, rising to signal in the dim moonlight for all to hold their positions.

Andres saw the dim shapes stop and heard barks of pain along with other sounds that were human. He felt there was a chance the Indians would be demoralized and turn back. It seemed there were less than he’d expected. He said a prayer that he wouldn’t have to fire.

He had three loaded muskets at his side, two side arms, a saber and five reloading kits in easy reach. He could fire them all in the time a group of men could clear the first marker, a large cactus ten meters ahead of their position, then the cactus marker for a quick retreat. By then Rodriguez and the five mounted soldiers would have charged the disoriented hoard and driven them deep into the desert.

He squinted at the attackers in the distant spotted desert, thankful that they weren’t advancing.

Three Hawks led twenty-one men removing the disabling traps, throwing them into a clump of tumbleweeds until they found no more. The nine fallen with the spider points in their flesh had crawled together to cut them from each other's feet and backs. Three Hawks ordered them to stay and provide arrow support if the Spanish charged.

Three Hawks advanced with the hunched down men along the right side of the trail toward Andres' muskets.

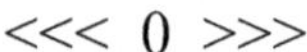

Padres Cambon and Somera had burst into his room at bedtime. Nicolas Jose, still in mourning, had finished coupling with a bony Pemookanga girl moments before and pulled the blanket over her head, concealing her identity but not the obvious. Cambon ordered him to command six trustees to keep neophytes locked in their quarters.

"There is serious danger tonight." Somera scowled. "All locked up. Now! No exceptions." As he left. "Her too!"

Rodriguez, Lopez, Cordero, Alvarado and Olivera heard two gunshots in quick succession and spurred their horses around the inner clump of olive trees toward the gate as Neophytes Miguel de Gabriel and Juan Bautista flung it back.

Sergeant Verdugo brought four neophytes carrying arms to positions along the wall facing to the south. He instructed them with hand signals to fight any intruders with their hands. He placed the muskets against the wall to pick one after the other. The neophytes hadn't fired a gun.

"If the savages reach this wall, I'm afraid no Christian will survive." He shouted to the Padres before locking them in the Chapel.

Five horsemen surged out the gate raising a cloud of dust over the staked head at the side of the trail,

Rufino felt these two days had been the most rewarding and exciting of his life. The musket and sidearm would serve him well but the saber would bring the greatest crunch of visceral satisfaction. He had no fear or thought of being injured or killed. Only the joy of killing a man he could call enemy.

Three Hawks stopped in his tracks at the power of the explosion ahead of him. A man four places to his left gasped and fell. Another loud bang and two more of his friends dropped back with sounds of surprise and pain. He saw a flash of light but nothing was distinct enough to aim at. He ran steadily with his bow up ahead of him and arrow threaded tight looking hard for a target to hit.

A third blast came from the spot he was focused on. A log across a dune that was thirty steps ahead. As he was aimed, drawing the string back, his left eye stung suddenly and his vision blurred, unable to see the log or the firestick. He slowed, feeling a sharp burning of his eye and a flood of tears blurring the sight of his hand wiping at his face. He heard another explosion and the cries of agony from the injured fighters, until the thundering galloping of animals became louder.

He dropped his bow and felt across the ground to find grass or a leaf to wipe the stinging from his face and saw blood on his hand. He heard more firesticks, thudding and moans as the animals grew louder.

He tried to see from his right eye, flooded in sympathy. He could make out vague movements in the grayness, and staggered across a small dune, keeping his footing with difficulty. He heard a horse's snort and a man's laugh above him and no more, as a sword sliced through his skull to the base of his neck.

Rufino looked from Lopez to Cordero at each side to see if they were having a good time of it. He never dreamed that defeating these people would be so easy.

If a man was facing him and aimed, Rufino leaned forward with the shield angled up. Jasmin had her breastplate pierced twice but from what Rufino could see, it was not deep or threatening to her.

After the arrow flew he fired the musket, keeping the side arm in reserve. The attacker was blown backwards with no hope of survival. The wounds were always fatal. He would then back away and reload. He hadn't needed the sidearm because the retreating Indians had spread out.

If the man was running from him, he'd either swing the saber wide to catch him a glancing blow and turn Jasmin around to ride up slowly in order to carefully place the final coup. If the man seemed unpredictable Rufino would run the horse directly into him and deliver the deathblow as the fool arose. He especially enjoyed surprising the comical blind man holding his eyes.

As the few remaining Indians were found and killed, Alvarado and Olivera returned to the area where they'd placed the barbed spiders and dispatched the crawling wounded with their sidearms. Rodriguez and Cordero were assigned to stay out until after dawn, looking for stragglers and wounded. They found none.

One man had burrowed into the sand, pulling a large tumbleweed over himself and waited until daybreak to crawl a circuitous route before turning to Shevaanga.

Nicolas Jose listened against the outside of the rough hewn barricaded wooden doors of the men's neophyte sleeping quarters near the chapel. He'd watched Alvarado bar the Padres inside.

Hearing the shots, he knew the soldiers were killing men from Shevaanga. Men he knew. He heard movement and voices from inside the walls. "Go to sleep!" He shouted, and heard them scrambling to bed. All the neophytes had seen the head of Sevaanga-vik on the stake outside the gate. They knew the villagers needed revenge.

He knew fear day and night. He failed to get cooperation from the village. He was hated in one place and tolerated in the other. He'd failed to keep Juana from being taken by black-tongue. He would have to go back to keeping the soldiers supplied with women if he were to advance or keep his position.

"Damn this life!" He mumbled through his teeth, using a Christian curse consciously, staring at the locked chapel. The fate he cursed was an immediate one. The battle raging outside the walls was secondary to the thing that would comfort him in this hateful night. Locked in the chapel with the Padres was the Blood of Christ. He knew the many swallows of that holy liquid would make the pain go away and he would be able to sleep.

"Damn Alvarado!" Blotting out the sound of gunfire, staring at the chapel door.

<<< 0 >>>

The sliver of the Moon moved six fingers in Ha'apchivit Tooypor and 'Aachvet listened to the raised voices in the greathouse. One faction wanted no part of Shevaanga's trouble. Haapchi-vik and Pul Tuwaru insisted on sending fast messengers before dawn to get the facts and pledge support. No mention of 'Atooshe''s kidnap. It was too much to take. She pressed her shoulders forward. It couldn't be ignored. She punched the side of 'Aachvet's arm and motioned with her chin.

"Are you ready?"
His expression changed to the impish adventurer that she knew. "We can move them off their mats. Let's do it."

"Are you scared?"
"Sure, but, that's nothing. I see it too." He gave a solemn nod. "I'm more scared to not do it." She held his hand approaching the door. They hesitated, and walked steadily into the open circle of men.

"You haven't been called." Her father pronounced.

She replied strongly. "I've been called by Spirit and the voice of the dead chief. I'm a witness to the capture of the Pula and death of the chief of our related village."

She turned to Pul Tuwaru, who was nodding and squinting like the hunched over eternal turtle-spirit, admiring her lack of fear.

"My husband, the chief, is in danger from the invaders, and also the foolish ones who want to attack without planning how to overcome the firesticks. I've heard the foolish ones. You have not! I've heard the firesticks and seen the deaths they have caused. I've seen the insult to tradition and ancestors by taking off the head of Sevaanga-vik. You have not!"

'Aachvet spoke up. "There's no time to waste with talk. They need our help. By tomorrow sunset it will be too late. We need every man who can fight to come with us before the sun rises."

"Every woman too." Tooypor added, causing frowns. Some elders wanted no women's involvement in village matters. That the chief's daughter was Pula was barely tolerable. "The women," She continued. "bring not only greater numbers for the enemy to fear but they can carry more weapons to us."

Pul Tuwaru was the one person with weight enough to tilt the decision toward the young intruders.

"I feel what brings these two to break tradition." Walking around them with his palm raised over their heads. "The part we know is that she saw the attack on, and kidnapping of, her teacher, 'Atooshe' of Shevaanga, and that after reporting this to Sevaanga-vik, he led a party to recover her and was killed. The runner had told us that and she had witnessed that. We can say that we know that. She knows that Sevaanga is in danger. Her husband is now chief and we are now linked as villages."

"I will continue." Spoke Haapchi-vik, rising and speaking to the ones he knew were the most inclined to keep from villages that needed aid. "If we were attacked, Sevaanga-vik would have come to defend us. Even though our home is hard to attack and easy to defend. He would bring his best to us." Placing a hand on his daughter's shoulder. "She is our emissary to them, and now, she is their emissary to Haapchivet. She comes out of urgency. It cannot wait."

Tooypor bowed her head and turned to the elders. "I would never commit a disrespect. I speak with full respect, but Spirits speak to me. I speak for Sevaanga-vik. He must be complete. We must have his ceremony." She crossed her wrists over her heart. "I ask for the young men and women to leave with me tonight. None of the council need go. We will not do anything foolish. Our path is to keep the others of Sevaanga from taking risks that will make them weaker."

After short arguments led and squelched by Haapchi-vik and Pul Tuwaru, the council agreed.

‘Aachvet and Tooypor rushed out to gather a cadre to bring eighty youths with light arms to the flatlands.

<<< 0 >>>

Hachaaynar and his six guards took turns trying to sleep, two fingers at a time, watching to the dim north-east, under the white sliver of a pale moon in the black twinkling sky, listening to the fighting in the night.

The sounds of firesticks made sleep impossible. Each knew the day would test every bit of their skill and energy and a rested mind and body would be more up to the task.

“I count twenty and two.” Pax’iwo whispered, hearing a sound like a distant cough. Men around him gave hand signals to confirm the total.

Hachaaynar opened his eyes. “Yes, twenty and two. They couldn’t have taken more than thirty fighters. The firesticks must miss sometimes.” His eyes closed again. “It doesn’t sound good. It couldn’t have been a surprise. It was what they wanted.”

Pax’iwo’s brother, Pak’ishar murmured “Tooypor was right.”

Hachaaynar kept his eyes closed but nodded slightly to himself.

‘Yes, she was right.’

CHAPTER 11

RECOVERY ATTEMPTS

'Aachvet and Tooypor led eighty of the most fit down the trail as the sun glowed behind the mountains to their left. In two hours the sky was bright. In another hour the sun had cleared the of Eagle Claw Peak and spread it's warmth over the Haapchivetam. The flatlands were now visible below.

Singing songs of the springtime about the opening of new life and ancient songs for strength in battle, they hid signs of their weariness and discomfort. There were twisted ankles and skinned shins but they kept together, sometimes holding a shoulder for balance or holding a limping one by the waist.

They wove through pine groves under the beak of the great Eagle Rock to the flat trails under the ancient semi-deserted site of Pasakeg-na and the transition from hill foliage to the sand and rock of the flat plain dotted with sagebrush, cactus, tumbleweeds and bright yellow fennel, merging into long waving grass patches and streams of mountain snow runoff.

Approaching Sevaanga, Tooypor saw no signs of the usual activity, but there were no children playing in the fields. No hunting or old people skinning pelts and grinding acorn meal. She listed fears and dismissed them one by one.

If there were a fight for succession of chief, whoever won would be on guard and have a scouting party to watch. If all the village fighters had left to attack the Mission, there would be rows of women at the mouth of the trail to the northeast to show their faith the men would return. There had been no mass attack.

If the invaders had attacked the village, there would be people in hiding or bodies on the grass or the trail. The beards hadn't attacked.

She saw three horses and riders far to the south approaching the Mission from the Kumeyaay area.

At the entrance of the village she saw the mass of people in the center. In the clearing through the rows of curved sided huts, villagers sat in a circle listening to Hachaaynar and two men at his side. As Tooypor and the Haapchivetam came into sight, cheers arose. People ran and tears flowed telling of the night.

Hachaaynar walked her through the throng and introduced her to Kut'amay, the single survivor of the night's attack. Barely older than she was, he spoke with downcast eyes telling of Three Hawk's promised victory over the invaders.

"I saw and heard all of my friends die."

"How many died?" She asked. "And how many Spaniards were there?"

He showed thirty for dead and five for Spaniards. She signed back to make sure of his count. "How could that be? You are all hunters. How could five invaders kill so many?"

Kut'amay described the barbed spiders, the death of Three Hawks and the confusion of the horses in the dark. He confirmed that firesticks seemed to never miss.

She felt doubt about the approach to the Mission until Hachaaynar gave her information that made her head swim with a vision as clear as a recent memory.

"Three I'itax'am had deserted the Mission yesterday morning. They told me that my fathers head is attached to a stick at the entrance of the mission. A disrespect that has many neophytes frightened. It's an insult that makes me crazy. I think about killing them at every moment, but until I saw you and the Haapchivetam, I knew it wouldn't be sure of success. Now it will be."

She took his wrist and turned, looking for unoccupied ground to lead him away from the villagers. She looked in his eyes and he knew it was urgent. She pulled him to a space between huts. His guards abided by his sign to stay.

"Over here." Pointing. "Sit with me." Leading him down with both hands and keeping hold of them while they sat face to face in the grass. She leaned in three hand widths from his nose and began.

"I know you have anger. I share it. I feel it all at the murder of Sevaanga-vik." Holding her palm up to keep him from interrupting. "I share it with the taking of 'Atooshe'. She isn't dead! We'll get her back. I can feel it!" She locked his eyes like a cougar. "I feel the anger at the loss of your fighters. They didn't think. I'd stop them if I'd stayed."

"You would have been killed. I was protected, but you are seen as Haapchivetam."

"I'd try to stop them as now I must stop you." Expecting the rage of dried tinder inside him. "Listen before you speak! Your life depends on it!"

He leapt. She pulled down on his wrists. He broke away from her grip with an outward twist and brought up his fist but withdrew it in shame. She'd raised her arm to block while keeping his eyes locked in hers. "Snake!" he hissed. She pulled on the gripped arm while blocking his free arm. "How can you say that!" still in rage.

"Listen and think! Take a breath and listen." Seeing the guards start to walk toward them. "You know that I don't speak without reason. I'd have traded places with 'Atooshe'. I'd sacrifice my life to save Sevaanga-vik." Yanking on his arm and motioning to the approaching guards. "Make them stop! Listen to the true vision to recover your father's head and save Sevaanga."

"You have saved us by bringing the Haapchivetam." He waved away the guards. "That was your help. Stopping us is crazy. Why are you changing?" Calming down for an answer.

"You told me the three neophytes had escaped and saw your father's head. Yes?" He nodded slowly.

"It is a trap. Bait to bring you to their front door. Even if you bring a hundred, two hundred fighters. They will kill you. They will lock up the neophytes and use the firesticks, traps and shiny metal sticks before the arrows and throwing sticks can kill them."

"So we let them to do what they want and leave my father's headless body without rest and to be lost to the Spirit and my ancestors? We are more than a hundred here. They are ten. How can I stop?"

"Because you will not recover the head if you attack. You will be killed along with most who go with you. I'm not a fearful person. I know you aren't guided by fear. Let me ask you three things." Her nose six inches from his. "Three neophytes yesterday morning. Why didn't the others help Three Hawks last night?

Two. When you go to the Mission, you expect neophytes to help you. Why would they to help you rather than to help them destroy you? They feed them. They have traitors like Nahaanpar Jose to point you out."

She saw he was either going to strike her or burst out in grief and collapse.

“Your father needs to be complete. Would an attack be stronger without his spirit with us? Shouldn’t he be complete first? I ask for a reason. You know I don’t speak to hear myself talk. There is a reason as clear as the one I saw before the first attack”

She pulled him down by the wrists and held his shoulders. “We can recover his head first. We can make them trip on their own strengths. We can get more neophytes to leave them and join us. It is a vision strong and clear. If you let me, it will succeed.”

It sounded like a delirium. He read the certainty in her face. “How could that happen?”

“Women.” She replied. “I will bring a hundred women with me. I will carry 'Atooshe''s basket with me in the daylight. We will be unarmed. We will point at the head. They will send their traitor and he will tell them that they must give it to us. The neophytes will see this or hear of it and return to their villages.”

He turned to the large contingent from Haapchivet. He saw the massed women. He added the Sevaanga women and the clarity of the crazy vision swept before his eyes. The monsters couldn’t attack unarmed women without the neophytes abandoning and escaping. They are monsters though. He weighed the choice.

“It can be more than a hundred.” He said.

<<< 0 >>>

'Atooshe' drifted in and out of consciousness as the light grew through the spaces in the shed’s walls and the heat increased. Her hands and feet were inside a Mission horses blanket that was tied at the feet, waist and neck, allowing only breath and a limited view through a slit. She had binding over her mouth. She tried to will herself back into sleep or death but the pain, thirst and memories persisted.

She thought this was the third day but it could have been the second. She'd never gone two days without bathing and as the heat rose, smell was her strongest sense.

"Please let me die before he returns." She asked Father Sun. She sweated into unconsciousness and woke to feel the throbbing wounds growing beyond her wildest imagination as the day refused to end.

MISSION SAN DIEGO

Father Jaume had seen signs of resentment and insubordination from the outside passing savages and some of the neophytes for months. Their anger seemed to be growing and the recent flogging of an instigator had seemed to fuel it rather than to set an example to discourage rebellion. He awoke with a soldier bursting through the door screaming.

"Up! Quick, Father!" Pulling him out of bed before he could change into robes that were more presentable than his night smock.

"Why are you doing this?"

"Where is a space you can be locked in?" The soldier had wild eyes and Jaume wondered whether he had offended the Presidio.

"What have I done?" As he spoke the words, he heard screaming in the courtyard. Not only one or two voices. It sounded like shouts from all directions.

"Hurry! We can't hold them off any more." Pulling on his arm to get him out the door. "Where is locked closet to hide you?"

"What is going on?" Beginning to feel fear.

Screams of pain echoed down the hallways and one distant shot was heard as the soldier pulled him to what appeared to be a closet door.

“Hundreds of savages are attacking the Mission. We never expected this here.”

Two more gun blasts came from the front doorway.

“Jesus!” The soldier gasped. “They’re here!” As running feet pattered on the approach hall. The soldier pulled on the door. It opened and was filled with bibles and statuary. “Damn!” he shouted as a group of Indians ran around the corner and before he could level his musket, an Indian fired a blast down the hall with pellets striking the soldier, disabling him, and wounding Father Jaume.

‘Indians with guns!’ he thought in panic as they pounced on him, stabbed and pounded him with statuary.

In the daylight a pair of heavily armed squads inventoried the smoldering Mission. They estimated that as many as one thousand Indians had attacked the Mission.

It was unexpected, but as far as could be determined it was purely regional, still, more soldiers would be added to Northern Mission duty.

1775 - SINALOA

With his fiftieth birthday approaching, Luis Manuel Quintero had grown strong from a lifetime of fieldwork. Corn, beans, hay for the horses, the new wheat plants and the attempts at growing rice.

He listened eagerly to the stories about de Portola’s and Rivera y Moncada’s explorations into the new Alta California and the chance to bring Maria Petra and the five boys to a place where they would have support and a new life on their own land.

SAN DIEGO – ALTA CALIFORNIA

Three soldiers left Presidio San Diego with two separate sets of orders from the Viceroy. Corporals Machado and Galvez were assigned to make order of the provisions and write dispatches to Headquarters in Sonora on how the Franciscans administered the Mission with an eye to future profitability to the Crown.

Afro-mulatto Corporal Jose Maria Pico had a hidden agenda to report to the Viceroy via courier with separate dispatches on the condition and controllability of the local Indians, to report on corruption among the soldiers and, if possible, to find compromising information on the Padres personalities, their sexual and monitary activities.

Pico, though of lowly rank, was at twenty two, a favorite of Fages, Bucarelli and the commercially minded administrators of the Crown. ‘A mind like a general’ was often said about him. He spoke all the Spanish dialects as well as passable French and the Arabic dialects of the Moors and Sephardic tongues of the Jews. Only Capitan Ortega knew of his other mission and why he had to watch the Indian convert, Nicolas Jose.

Rufino Rodriguez was exhausted from three hours of sleep spread over two anxious nights. The thought of visiting the shed and collecting the benefits of his pretty little prize was the thing that kept him energized.

The joy of sinking his saber into a savage’s skull or ripping his heart out with a close musket blast had its limits. The thought of her hot, sweaty and stinking body being driven across the sand by his thrusting and her moans of pain were what kept him awake and wishing for the end of these stupid attacks.

‘Why don’t they accept that this is our land and leave well enough alone? Or at least, would they please hold off for a few days so that I can keep the sow alive!’

He felt temporary relief seeing Lopez being sent to meet the three riders approaching on Camino Real from the South. It couldn’t be a better time for more guns to arrive and for some activity where he could slip away to the woman, if she were still living. He planned to drag her corpse behind the horse to a ravine if she were already gone. ‘What a shame that would be! Damn these savages!

<<< 0 >>>

Hachaaynar and Tooypor pulled aside the strongest and most influential men to present the plan. They expected resistance from the younger males. They were surprised. First from Pul Tuwaru, Haapchi-vik, 'Aachvet and all of ‘Aachvet‘s friends. The men saw logic in her tactic.

She brought in Mother Kethu, Charaana, Ponu and the elder Sevaanga women. The women were full of suggestions for the most impact to bring shame to the invaders. To assure their safety the full compliment of armed men would stay out of sight with scouts positioned to signal if the women were attacked.

They wanted to wear little in the mild spring weather to show no weapons. They wanted thick red ochre smeared over their faces, bodies and hair to withstand the sun of the day and wind of the night. By nightfall they were in accord to leave before dawn.

Sergeant Rivera stood tall, more carefully dressed than usual leaning against his doorway watching four riders enter the gate and dismount. Lopez gave an uncharacteristic salute. Olivera had requested better than average fighters who could read and had a basic knowledge of mathematics to plan the Mission’s beef production.

He expected a Moorish mix in one of them but was surprised by the African complexion of Pico. The man was known to be a favorite of Ortega and Captain Fages. Why a mulatto would carry such favor seemed a mystery. Father Serra had accused Fages of plotting against him, so a man of Fages’ trust would be a good ally when the Fathers became too impractical.

He saluted and brought them into his quarters.

“I hope your journey was uneventful. These past three days have been a trying time for us.”

Machado smiled. “Corporal Lopez gave us an account. We saw no signs of hostiles. We saw a cloud that could have been people or a herd of animals moving westward from afar, but no Indians near us.”

Lopez spoke. “I told them we won a great victory last night but it won’t be the end of it.”

“Did you see the fly covered head on the stake by the front gate?’ Olivera asked.

“I saw it and smelled it.” as the others made repulsed faces.

Olivera raised his brows. “Yes, it’s disgusting. I’m not sure that it was effective. One of the soldiers killed a chief who was trying to attack the Mission with only ten men! A fool?” Lowering his brows to a crooked frown. “The soldier convinced me that the head staked at the gate would frighten the locals into submission. Last night they attacked with forty and tonight we expect more. ”

“More than forty would be hard to overcome.” Pico spoke for the two watchful newcomers, wary at entering hostilities from the first day. “How many fighting men do you have?”

“With you three, nine soldiers of the Crown, three useless Padres, five unreliable trustees and ninety neophytes in lockdown.” Looking from one to the other. “Not the best balance, but we are well armed and have a vast store of ammunition. We’ve never lost a man”

Pico wasn’t sure of his riding companions let alone the personnel of this garrison in a daily battle for survival. It was supposed to be a short stay for him. He was to get the information needed and return to Loreto and lovely Maria Estaguia Gutierrez and take her hand for life. He didn’t want to be in a battle zone. A report of needs and relationships was all he wanted to bring back. Not wounds or death or to be the barer of sad news for relatives.

“We have a crisis that will take a head, so to speak, tonight or tomorrow.” Olivera continued. “So your timing is exquisite. We are informal here. As long as we observe the proper forms with the Blessed Padres and keep the Indians working without killing us or each other, we should all be well rewarded for our efforts.” He motioned them out the door and moved around them. “I’ll show you the grounds.”

They understood what he meant by ‘well rewarded.’ Land grants in northern Mexico and in the lower parts of Alta California had made ordinary and industrious soldiers men of considerable property. That promise made the risks of Missionduty tolerable.

“This is beautiful countryside,” red cheeked Corporal Machado spoke.

“Only in the springtime.” Olivera replied. “It will dry up to tinder as the summer comes and we will have wildfires and then floods and freezes through the winter. You are seeing it at it’s best.” The four rode out on a tour.

Rufino leaned against the south-western adobe wall watching a sullen trustee shoeing Jasmin as the newcomers rode with the sergeant out of the gate and turned east. He walked hurriedly through the courtyard, knowing there would be no reason for them to stop at the locked storage shed a kilometer to the north-east. He stood in the shade of a two year old olive tree that barely cleared his head. When the four riders reached the end of the squash field, they turned north beyond the shed. There were wisps of snow snuggled in the top cracks of the distant mountains as Rufino saw them recede enough to risk the shed.

He felt a jumble of expectations crossing the untilled ground to be used for future pig or sheep herds. He kept the shed between their line of vision wondering if the prize was alive or dead, with no feeling of desire. Only curiosity.

'Atoosho' was unsure of what the noises of the day or night meant. It was hard to distinguish anything beyond the burning and throbbing pain spreading through her body from her vagina, anus, aching, pounded kidneys and pain behind her eyes. No matter how much she wanted sleep and death, it wouldn’t take her.

She saw a shadow on the cracks of the door’s joints and the sound of the bar being slid. It made a chill shake her body. She felt more panic sweep her. She heard whimpering rise in her throat but couldn’t form a scream. She forgot about the rope tied across her mouth.

As a crack of light grew, she heard more than one distant voice call. “Rufino! Rufino! Come quick!”

“Puta Madre!” Rufino growled, sliding the bar back,, running back to where Somera and Cambon were standing and gesturing, pointing to the far side of the chapel.

Jasmin was on the ground, convulsing, twisting her head with froth on her lolling tongue and her eyes rolling wildly. On the ground was a woven bag with a mix of honey packed leaves of plants that Rufino had been instructed as poisonous. The nails and hammer lay on the ground and the sullen trustee was nowhere to be seen.

His instinct was to take a horse from the stable and chase down the traitor. Looking out at the gently rolling plain toward Sevaanga, he saw a thousand traps and a thousand tattooed faces that would be delighted to see him riding out alone. ‘No.’ He would stay and meet the new soldiers from San Diego and spend the day preparing for the inevitable night’s attack and find the Indian devil later.

His one solace was hearing the female’s moaning as he approached the shed. It brought back the excitement that was lacking earlier. ‘Let her stew a while longer,’ he thought. ‘So much more the pleasure when we meet.’ Knowing that through it all she would be thinking of him.

Olivera brought the three corporals back before the sun settled above the western hills.

Nine soldiers stood at the chapel walls. Cooks carried platters of porridge to the tables outside the sleeping quarters. Trustees brought ten neophytes at a time with their earthen bowls, ladling out to each and sending them back inside. The frightened, disoriented faces were haunting to the new men. “They outnumber us ten to one, but they slump like beaten puppies.” Galvez whispered to Pico.

Pico replied. “I’ve seen it in Dominica, Mexico and Alta California. If death seems the likely outcome to rebellion, you have the meek faces. God help us but that can change fast.”

The soldiers ate the same porridge as the neophytes. Sleep was assigned in three hour shifts.Rodriguez was in the forward position to the west, with the notched log and three loaded muskets. Cordero and Lopez were similarly armed and dug in thirty meters to the outside of the north- west and north-east walls, making a triangle protecting theMission.

Corporal Andres after firing into the darkness, was to be on point for the second shift but while lying on his bunk, a thought itched at him to continue writing his song to his Josephina before he died, but he'd thrown the oilcloth packet in with his winter gear as spring came. If he was going to die tonight he wanted the poem and notes about this place delivered to her so she'd know how much he loved her.

He wiggled into his boots and set out unarmed, waving to Lopez passing in the fading light. He'd brought flint and two candles. He knew he'd recognize the cattleman's knots on the bundle.

He wrestled with the tight bar jammed into the notches and heard animal sounds. He feared rats had eaten through the cloth. The bar came loose. The sounds were human. 'Female!' his lips moved. "Blessed Jesus!" As he knelt, flicking the flint to catch the oil on the wick.

She barely had strength to whimper but fear made her more alert than she'd been in two days. Her eyes were sharp as owl's in the dim light. It was an invader. A different one. Smaller and younger. "Please kill me!" She said as sparks appeared. 'Is he going to burn me? Wouldn't he drag me outside first?'

The candle caught. He saw it was an Indian woman with rope over her mouth and bruises on her cheeks and forehead. Black caked blood was on her lips and chin. He caught the stench of feces and urine and slid back to fresh air.

"That bastard Rodriguez." He said aloud, throat choked up, knowing damn well what he'd do to anyone who dishonored Josephina this way.

"I'm so sorry! I'm so sorry!." He couldn't see her in the darkness other than the reddish reflection from one eye. She could be anywhere between twelve and sixty years old. He drew his knife and slid in close to cut the rope. She couldn't scream. Her breath and sobs erupted."Damn Him!" He hissed.

'Atooshe' heard the anger hoping death would finally come. He had a shiny weapon in his hand. Tears came to her eyes. The pain was about to end. She felt the cold metal of the knife brushing against her throat, then the rope across her mouth loosened.

He cut the rope holding the blanket at her neck and loosened it, showing her neck and shoulders. Her panic and breathing increased as he cut the rope at her waist. ‘He is looking at me! He is going to rape me!’ “No! No! Please! Kill me!” She tried to say in her language.

He saw more welts and the stench of infection. He didn’t want the other soldiers to have access or know about her until the Padres had been told and could assure her safety.

“I am so sorry for this.” Seeing she was naked under the blanket and horribly mistreated. “I’ll bring you water and food.” Seeing nothing but fear in her eyes.

He took two trips back with water to drink and wash, a bowl of porridge and a container of honey. He wished he knew about medicine. He slid back and stood, latching the door.

She was angry that she couldn’t tell him to kill her. ‘He’ll come back with the other one to hurt me more,’ looking for a tool to drive into her neck or, increasingly, to dig under the sides and escape.

She tried to stand or crawl. She collapsed exhausted. Sounds came from outside the door. It opened slowly. The same soldier returned carrying two buckets of water and a sack of rags.

“I’ll be back.” He said, locking it again.

She dipped a rag in the water and wiped her hands. scooping the cup into the precious fluid, drinking through cracked lips and nearly choking on it. The effort of kneeling to reach in the bucket brought pain to her genitals and stomach. She fell on her side and felt darkness sweeping her into sleep again. Later there were footsteps near her head. She was still alive. The younger beard had brought food and more water. He left with strange words.

Andres closed the door and whispered. “Bless you.”

Rufino lay behind the notched log watching for motion from the west. It was hard not to fall asleep. He felt no attack would come this early. The crying wails of the coyotes told him no humans were in motion down the trail. He visualized the little trustee dying in a dozen painful ways. Disemboweled by the saber or knife. Dragged behind a horse on a rocky trail. Shot in the legs and arms and burned.

“Fed the same poison!” Hissing aloud with a fantasy of watching the puffy face distort and choke, spewing reddish foam from his ulcerated stomach. ‘Yes. That would be good.’ He’d never poisoned a person, but it would be fascinating to watch. Perhaps one of the other troublesome trustees. Perhaps Nicolas Jose if he still is too much of a servant to the Padres to send him women.

“No action” He said as Alvarado came to relieve him before midnight. Rufino thought about trying to get to the shed. He needed sleep.‘Daylight will make it more memorable.’

Tooypor, Hachaaynar, 'Aachvet and Pul Tuwaru brought elders and Pulum of both villages to the central clearing. They brought friends together in circles to explain the idea behind Tooypor’s tactic, then one group and another, person to person, until there was understanding to bring it under Hachaaynar’s leadership.

Haapchi-vik stood aside and watched his daughter with pride. She moved passionately from one person to another pressing for something never seen before. A move that seemed to excite the women with the strength they had as a group. There were laughs, shouts and stamping that he’d never heard with such verve.

Some men seemed confused by the joy the women brought, but the lesson of the night and the sudden loss of thirty of the strongest men had them feeling powerless and afraid. Only knowing they would all be armed and nearby to protect the women allowed pride a graceful way out.

Provisions of food for two days were distributed. All would bathe and coat themselves in red ochre to protect against sun and cold.

All would sleep and wake rested for a ceremony of strength to be led by Tooypor.

Sevaanga's love and confidence in her powers rained upon her. She knew her vision couldn't fail.

As she and Hachaaynar prepared to sleep together in the greathouse. a short, barrel-chested man with a Pemookanga dialect and a Mission shirt was brought in by Tukoopar.

"He said he just escaped the Mission and knows who killed Sevaanga-vik."

"I am Ku'tap. From the eastern villages. I explain."

" Why did you come here?" Hachaaynar asked, wondering why he had a smile.

"I have seen how," he searched for the word that communicated human evil that would be understood, "Evil they are. I couldn't stay, knowing what they do. I know which man killed your father. They had me work for him. I've learned to work with horses. I poisoned his horse and left."

"You are welcome here." Seeing another sign that the prisoners were ready to escape.

" Tukoopar. Give him a place to rest."

The neophytes were fed before dark and brought into lockdown. Nicolas Jose couldn't escape looks of hate and betrayal in the faces he'd grown to know. He'd had respect to get the work done. It would be harder now.

Rodriguez passed on the way to the point carrying an armful of muskets and sidearms, glaring at Nicolas Jose, swearing one day all the dirty Indians will roast in Hell's fire. Rodriguez spoke loudly and quickly, assuming he wasn't understood. He was. The daggers in his eyes weren't lost.

Nicolas Jose saw three new soldiers bedded down by the Padres against the southern wall. Sergeant Olivera led the Padres to the chapel and locked the door for their protection. He joined Verdugo to sleep against the wall. Corporal Andres was missing.

Nicolas Jose lay in his room wanting to get sleep and put the coming battle out of mind, but pain of the heart and mind came to him again and again. The more he tried to distract, the more it wouldn't leave. He relived his last talks with Sevaanga-vik, trying to reconcile his identities, seeing Hachaaynar and 'Atooshe''s contempt repeated over and over interspersed with the hate stares of the last two days.

He couldn't go back. He was hated in his new life. Only the lowest women would associate with him now. Those who'd come to him in the future would hate behind their smiles.

An hour after dark it was quiet. Soldiers slept. Conversations from the neophyte quarters were hushed and secretive. Distant coyotes promised no attack for hours.

He squinted up at the sound of footsteps. Corporal Andres approached the chapel's side door and tapped. He was persistent and kept tapping and scratching until there was an answer. He said.

"It's Corporal Andres. I must make a report to you." Waiting for a response. "Yes. It's important." Nicolas Jose tried to hear more. The door opened and Andres entered. No more conversation could be heard.

He thought of how many of his friends would die this night. How many teammates and hunting mates were killed last night? Thoughts came and went. No answers. No end to the circles of bad thoughts.

After an hour Corporal Andres crept out of the chapel and lay down to sleep next to Alvarado.

Finally sleep came

.

<<< 0 >>:>

Tooypor woke as the owl songs ended, signaling four fingers before dawn. Her dream took brilliant life as a bear towered over the Mission and tore apart a rabbit sized soldier and his horse. She gathered her power sticks, powders and her husband's sacred bundle with scrolls and marked bark symbols of the family's powers and alliances.

Hachaaynar woke and leapt to his feet anticipating a day to be known in legend. He hugged her. She hugged him back with more power than he had expected.

"You are a bear spirit!" Laughing with joy, returning the hug, pretending to cough and gasp.

Thirty people, ten men and twenty women, were outside. They walked to the clearing. More arrived. There were crisp sounds of boys calling people to come out and rattling of sticks against the sides of huts. No one was asleep by first light. The sky glowed in the east. Ninety women, girls and toddlers started up the trail with Tooypor and the elders at the head.

Hachaaynar and eighty armed men followed and took positions at the base of the last rise before the Mission. Four women shuttled water from the springs to the women in front.

Tukoopar and Kwetii' crept on their stomachs to the lip of the rise to signal if the Spanish began an attack. Tooypor told them to be certain it was a real attack or an attempt to scare them off.

The women marched with adrenaline energizing each vein as the dreaded structure grew closer. It was the most dangerous thing they'd ever done. Knowing many brave men had fallen on this trail. Knowing they were not only reuniting their chief, but saving the long identity of their village.

Tooypor stopped the march a hundred meters from the staked head and urged the women and children to spread wide, circling a quarter of the Mission walls, hoping it was too far for firesticks to reach.

<<< 0 >>>

After sunrise Rodriguez and Lopez saw a cloud of dust on the trail from Seeba village. Lopez called Nicolas Jose, slumped on the chapel steps drunk.

"Get up! Sound the alarm! Move your lazy ass!"

The Indian glared and clanged on the bell, Frey Somera was at the gate of the back wall hearing from Andres and fretting over the sick Indian woman in the shed.

"If she is as ill as you say, I can give her last rites. We'll give her a Christian burial when it's safe."

"It isn't ill!." Andres said, with more force than he'd ever used with a man of God. "She's been raped and beaten, must likely by Rodriguez. It would be a mortal sin to let her die and for Rodriguez to continue the things that he has done. He is the reason we are under attack. Insane to use that head! How savage Spaniards can be! Don't turn away!"

The shrugging Somera tried to walk back.

"Prayer won't solve this! Come with me now!" Andres hissed.

The warning bell clanged but Andres pulled the priest to the shed. "You can save this poor savages soul, but on this day we must save our own souls as well." As they reached the shed, shouts raised the resting soldiers and neophytes trustees to the south wall to see the advancing Indians.

Rodriguez was joined at the gate by Alvarado and Pico.

"Good God, that thing stinks!" Pico stared at the fly spotted head on the stake.

"I don't think that it did it's job as a charm to protect us." Verdugo sneered. "It seems to attract trouble."

Rodriguez felt the sting of Verdugo's attitude of superiority. 'How dare he break rank! I could smash his pointy Castilian nose and be within my rights,' but instead he said.

"If they seek trouble, these muskets will put them to rest. It is time to win the war and bring them into the system. They are beaten. Their chief was foolish. They have lost their bravest warriors. Even with one hundred warriors, we nine soldiers can defeat them in daylight. Splatter the ones following with the heads of their leaders and they will run like rabbits. That head is proof of our strength."

Somera held his sleeve to his nose. The odor of decay and elimination brought childhood memories of a 1757 siege near Mexico City where a months worth of rotting bodies made the whole town uninhabitable.

“We’re too late.” Backing out the door before his eyes grew accustomed to the dark.

'Atooshe' heard the door opening but was too weak to lift her head or open her eyes. She’d vomited the porridge but drank the unclean water. She used the cloths to wash as much as she could before the tenderness of her sores became unbearable.

“She’s breathing!” Andres fell to his knees and put a wet cloth to her brow. “She’s alive! Come back in!”

Somera inched back into the shed and saw the naked woman before Andres flipped the blanket over her torso. “Will she live?” Hoping for the negative.

“Not if we leave her here! We’ll get help to carry her to the chapel.”

“No! The neophyte quarters perhaps. A diseased gentile does not belong in the chapel! I must insist.”

“The neophyte quarters then. Take the feet!”

“My back is bad. I cannot carry.” Backing to the door. “Please. Get one of the soldiers. I must return now! Can’t you see that we are under attack?” Walking to the north wall. “Go to your post! Go back when it’s safe.” Striding away.

Andres leaned to her face. “I’m so very sorry. You must be a mother. Your children are probably attacking us now because of what we have done to you. I’m sorry to have caused this.” Washing her brow and chin, putting a fresh blanket under her head. “We aren’t all like this. I am Indio. In Mexico I have an India fiancée. You could be her mother. I’ll come back.” He filled a cup. “Drink. We will bring you to safety.”

She watched him leave. ‘Why are they doing this to me? Why can’t I die?’

<<< 0 >>

Tooypor led the women and children into position as the soldiers, Padres and trustees lined the south wall.

Cambon looked back. “Where is Somera?” He shouted, eyes fixed on the distant gathering. Too far to see faces but close enough to see that there were no men.

“He’s coming.” Cordero shouted as Somera ran from behind the chapel .

“Jesus, Joseph and Maria! There are so many of them!”

“They are women and children. Where are the men? What are they up too?”

Sergeant Olivera shook his head “There were thirty men in their attack. There are many more than that in their village. The men might be circling behind us. Lopez! Check to sides and back!” Squinting at the motions from the group. “Now look at what they are doing! They are pointing! At the gate!”

“No. At the head!” Cambon said with certainty.

Pico moved beside Olivera. “They are trying to make us feel shame over the death of their chief.”

Rodriguez said. “How could we feel shame for defending ourselves against crazy people shooting at us? The chief tried to kill Lopez and me on the trail.”

Olivera turned, shouting to Nicolas Jose, slouched on the chapel steps.

“Nicolas Jose! Go out and find the leader. Find out what is going on and what they want.”

Nicolas Jose put on a neutral expression, walking to the right as he exited the gate to avoid the stench, wishing he had taken more wine before this craziness begun.

He had to concentrate on each step to not stagger approaching the semi-circle. The thin girl was leading a chant or prayer. It was

Hachaaynar's wife, the girl from Haapchivet. She, like the others, were smeared with red dye. They planned to stay the night.

Tooypor recognized the traitor walking toward them. Women remembered him from his approaches with the Spanish and made whooping and coyote sounds. Tooypor did nothing to stop them except to yell. "Keep pointing!"

He knew it was to induce shame. The past two years weren't worth it. He looked from face to face at the jeering women, recognizing some of them and amazed at the growth of the eight and nine year olds he remembered. He lowered his eyes and walked toward Tooypor, hearing coughing that he knew was the black tongue sound,

"What do you want?" Ignoring the women standing nearby.

She pointed to the basket by her feet and at the head.

"We want Sevaanga-vik's head returned so that his united body can be buried in the proper way. We want Pula 'Atooshe' returned safely. We know that she was captured by the killer of Sevaanga-vik."

"No-one is at.." He started to say.

"We want the killer banished from your camp."

He studied her narrow upturned face. Her nose was relatively thin and her face had tight features that he considered more Serrano or Mojave than Tongva. He crossed his arms.

"Why do you act like this? Strutting in front of the elders and making demands. Only a chief's daughter who had never been told that she is foolish and only follows her whims can act this way."

She took a step toward him, saying. "You are a man who has betrayed his village and ancestors. These people know you. I know you. You are a man who helped kill Sevaanga-vik. You come from your masters to ask what we want. I've told you. Now go back and tell them," taking two steps back and signing goodbye.

"I need to know more."

"You've heard. Go tell them!"

He looked incredulously at this...brat. He could think of no other word. How could she, and these infants and hags, make demands of the Mission? These idiots will get themselves killed because of this Haapchivet child.

He glanced along his left side at some of the hooting women. His focus went to one in unison with her neighbors.

It was his mother! He grew dizzy from the vision and squinted his eyes straight ahead, praying for a great bottle of The Blood of Christ to stop the mirage. He looked back. She was gone. He swore to raid the chapel storeroom.

Corporal Andres joined the others at the south wall as Nicolas Jose walked back. He had a hard time looking away from Rodriguez, wondering what could make a man, one who bragged about his family and education, into a beast. He saw the women across the trail and knew Rodriguez would like to shoot them. What was the point of standing unprotected in front of a madman who decapitates men and does inhuman acts on women? He saw children in the ranks. What kind of madness is this? A tight group formed around him.

Nicolas Jose looked face to face, feeling his mother's eyes on his back. If he could have, he would have walked past them all and filled himself on the Blood of Christ until a better dream carried him away. His legs were about to buckle. He found a weak voice.

"They have brought a basket. They want the head so they can bury their chief."

Olivera felt weight lifted. He hated the obscene and filthy thing. This made an easy way to defuse a potential disaster, if that were all.

" We will allow them to remove the head. They must promise that their people will not attack us. Wonderful! Tell them that and bring me their answer." A smile lighting his patrician face for the first time in three days.

Nicolas Jose bit at his lip and watched his sandal paw an inch or two back and forth in the sand.

"They say the chief's wife was kidnapped by a soldier here. They want her returned."

Somera and Andres' eyes met. Olivera noticed their response and guessed there was truth to it.

Rodriguez stiffened as he spoke in a voice of certitude. "They make excuses to provoke us. We can drive them into the desert like rabbits. To hell with them."

Andres spoke up quickly. "There is a woman, a tribal woman tied up and beaten in the northeast storage shed. Father Somera and I just came from her. She is alive." Looking at Rodriguez.

"If she lives," Somera added in a low voice, "We can't return her to savagery. She'll be protected. She'll have a bed in the neophyte quarters and be baptized. There can be no other way for her."

Cambon held up both palms in a gesture of finality. "There will be no concessions to them other than the return of the head. We agree with Sergeant Olivera that we must. The woman will stay." Looking at Nicolas Jose. "Go now and tell them that."

Tooypor could see the twelve men's heads talking behind the wall. She saw tribespeople aligned with the invaders at the steps of the large building and groups of three and four near the flat buildings where their slaves slept.

Then Nahaanpar walked toward her.

"Keep pointing." She called as the chorus of hoots and coyote calls rose all around her. Her eyes burned into him as he shuffled the last few yards to her.

"What do your masters say?" knowing that the women would tear him apart if she told them to.

His eyes fixed on his mother's faces howling shame on him. He wished he could tell her spirit that he only wanted to learn new ways. To find out about metal and cloth and to improve their lives, not to lead them to slavery and death. That he wasn't a traitor.

"I told them. I argued for Sevaanga-vik's return and completion of his body. I explained the need for his ceremony. They'll return his head. If you want me to, I'll take the basket and bring his head back to you."

His eyes held tears. He wanted forgiveness. He knew that he'd receive no thanks for the disgusting task.

Tooypor felt the power of the moment. He had shame and the Spanish had agreed to the first demand.

"I want 'Atooshe' brought here now!"

He shook his head. "'Atooshe' isn't here. If she were, I would know." He looked at her pleadingly. "I will find out for certain, but they have no 'Atooshe' and they'll never banish Rodriguez."

She said. "What is that name? Repeat it."

He wished he had thought first. "Rodriguez. Corporal Rodriguez."

"Rod-ree gess. Yes? The man who killed Sevaanga-vik?"

"Yes. He's the man. Rodriguez." Feeling relief at not lying. Hoping he'd redeem himself in his ancestor's eyes. "They'll never send him away. They don't think that way. They'll protect him in the face of any demand. I know them."

She saw there was still a part of Nahaanpar within this Ho-say person. She softened her tone. "I haven't seen him. Can I see which one he is there?" Motioning with her chin and pursing her lips at the grouping.

He looked back and turned to her, moving his right hand. "He's the one on this side and third over." She looked beside his shoulder and nodded.

"Tall. Thin. A narrow beard. More narrow than the others standing by him?" He took another look.

“Yes, and thinner. Always either laughing or angry. Nothing in-between.”

She watched every muscle of Nicolas Jose’s face and his posture. He was trying to become a person. A confusing and confused person but maybe one who could become more than an enemy. A semi-chief in the invaders trust, but he was willing to point out the killer invader to her. He was willing to negotiate for the head.

“I feel you aren’t yet one of them. You haven’t grown a beard yet. Do you know all your ancestors are with us?

Nicolas Jose looked for forgiveness as the girl turned the full glare of the sun on him.

“Did you know about 'Atooshe''s capture?”

While not turning from his mother. “No. I never heard that until today.”

“Did you know about Sevaanga-vik’s killing?”

“Yes. When Rodriguez brought the head and bragged about it. He convinced the brown robes to put it outside the gate. I was afraid. Everyone was afraid. Many neophytes wanted to go back to their villages but the soldiers and trustees ...”

“Like you.”

“...locked them in their buildings. I did also. Yes. I did also.”

“Did you help the invaders in the fight at night?”

“No. I was told to stay on the steps.”

“And do what to help them?”

“Only to sit still and not move. They don’t trust us. I’ll try to find Pula 'Atooshe'.” Hoping he could still make a bridge to his village by arranging her return without causing a war. Appearing a hero to the Padres if the women were to withdraw with only the head. “It may take a couple of days, maybe more, but I’ll find out”

Tooypor was ahead of him and his delicate footwork. She felt that he wanted to please whoever he was with, even if the next person wanted the very opposite.

“It will be too dangerous for you to travel back and forth to give us the help you offer.” She said softly, “It will be better if an escapee relays your messages about Pula 'Atooshe', but there is another thing we need to know, and I am sure you will understand.”

He did, even before she asked for Rodriguez’ assignments. He would have no problem passing that along.

Sergeant Olivera wished he had a spyglass to see more clearly. “What could be taking so long? Is that small woman their leader?” He saw Nicolas Jose pick up a large straw basket and walk back with a much more confident gate than when he left. “They will accept the head and withdraw.” With an assured nod of the head.

“What of the woman that they claim. Will they insist?” Olivera asked, with Andres, Somera and Rodriguez hanging on the word.

“I told them there is no woman here. They will leave. I told the truth. I’ve seen no woman.” Seeing relief from the Spaniards. “I’ll return the head. I need a cloth to lift it.” Olivera motioned for one of the blankets by the wall. Andres watched Rodriguez, knowing he’d try to get to the shed first.

Nicolas Jose removed the head to keep as much of the flesh on the skull as could be saved in the blanket. He held his breath and brushed off some of the worms, but the smell of the sun-baked skin wasn’t as strong as the previous day. He carried the folded blanket to Tooypor in both hands. Her expression softened.

He bowed his head in respect. “You must carry it back carefully and keep the sides of the blanket up. I’ll try to find Pula 'Atooshe' and find out where Rodriguez will be and get a messenger to you.”

“Why would you do that yet stay with them”

"No-one likes Rodriguez, and I can help so that less people are hurt," more to himself than to her.

"We will withdraw now. It will look like a victory for you," with the beginning of a reassuring smile. "You will locate Pula 'Atooshe' but you will not take interest in her. You will keep away." Taking the blanket in her arm and keeping a dried sage branch pressed under her nose. "There will be a new neophyte who will whisper my name. When he comes, you will take him aside and tell him everything." She turned to each side and shouted. "We can go back now!"

Olivera was overjoyed. "He's proven his worth today! Look! They are leaving. Simple as that." Watching the reactions of Cordero, Lopez and Rodriguez as Nicolas Jose walked to them, pleased with himself, in a jumble of mad thoughts. The pleasure would be in the fate of Rodriguez.

Andres quickly chose Verdugo and Pico to come to Somera. "We must bring the woman into the chapel now!" As he hustled them to the side of the chapel before Rodriguez could react. Andres turned back and knew Rodriguez' one hope was undone by their action.

'Atooshe' drank as much of the stale, muddied water as she could, edging to a crack in the wooden slats to see where the distant familiar chanting sound was coming from. It was faint memory that wafted in and out of the shed in soft waves. Racking chills flowed through her spine and over her arms and scalp in the heat. The sounds seemed to tell her that death was finally near.

She recognized two chants that alternated. One was for strength and one was for a lost chief. She found it odd it would be for her. A woman doesn't receive that song, but she'd never heard the rite given for a Pula. Could that be right? Was she mourned as a chief?

She slept until she heard the door opened. Voices and footsteps made her open her eyes. With a bolt of fear she cringed at the thump of a Spanish boot a hand's length from her brow. They were speaking too loudly for normal speech. They sounded angry or surprised. There were voices speaking at once. They were arguing! 'Are they going to rape me or send me beyond.' She spoke as clearly as she could.

“Please kill me now.”

She hadn’t the strength to let out a shriek. A blanket was wrapped around her. Rough hands lifted her from around the backs of her knees and shoulders. She gasped for breath as she was lifted into the stabbing sunlight, her eyes shut tight but lanced by the brightness of the day. Each step jostled her body up and down and side to side sending new spasms to the muscles and joints of her legs, spine and neck.

“Please kill me now.” She repeated.

Rodriguez stood by the Mission wall and moved to the right just far enough to watch the four men enter the shed and emerge carrying the limp shape in a blanket. He hoped she’d died during the night but there was a chance she could die en route or that he or a bribed trustee could smother her before she could identify him. She has caused too many problems for the Mission.

“To the chapel. To your own room.” Andres glared at Somera, praying he had the guts to not duck out on the church’s responsibility for this.

Pico saw moral strength in the usually quiet Corporal Andres. Not many Corporals would speak to the Franciscans in that tone without the backing of higher-ups. He was willing to challenge authority on behalf of this woman. ‘Unusual.’

Verdugo stood to the side, noticing Rodriguez peeking from beyond the chapel, certain that he had something to do with this. Verdugo had categorized her shape as ‘attractive’ from the brief glimpse that he got. He hoped that her recovery would permit him some knowledge of her virtues, still in fantasy as they cleared a bench and laid her on her back.

“Are there curanderas here?” Andres looked around the room without expecting results from men who would consider faith in curanderas a renunciation of their Catholicism.

Pico responded immediately, turning to Somera. “Get a translator. Preferably a woman and not one from her Seeba village. ”

As Pico and the Padre left the room, Verdugo asked. "Do you think that this was done by Rufino?"

"I have no doubt that he did." Andres answered. "I've suspected him for months of crimes against the natives. Some of the women's and children's bodies in the outlying lands. If the chief attacked and these other hostilities happened because of her, then Rufino could have caused our deaths because of his..."

"Sickness of arrogance." Alvarado said.

"Well put." Added Olivera. "What do we do about him?"

Andres said that sending him to Presidio San Diego for trial might be a solution, but realized that a literate Catalan charged with sex crimes would be given the mildest of reprimands, if anything, and sent back to take revenge on his accusers.

"We make sure that one of us keeps guard over her, and of course, to keep Rufino out of here."

"She says the same thing over and over."

Verdugo hid his first and less kind response. "That she wants to go home?"

"Will you go to the Presidio?" Asked Olivera.

Andres sat and watched the woman's ashen face as she mumbled in what was beginning to sound like a chant. He'd heard similar repeating words from people in the last stages of black tongue and the Indian's disease.

Andres moved his lips and small sounds came out as the thought formed and his eyes moistened. "I will be steadfast and true for you as for my own Tarahumara love. I want you to live and recover your health. Please live....we aren't all evil. There will be a better day for all of us. Please survive." He took a cloth and poured water from Somera's pitcher and ran the cloth over her forehead, cheeks and neck.

Her eyes opened wide. She repeated the words loudly, startling him. He tried to repeat the words, hoping to understand.

'Ahtooshe' overcame her fright watching him trying to say. “Let me die! Please let me die!” ‘Why is he saying that!’ She thought, before understanding that he was trying to copy her. She was alive! She was in their camp! This was the one who came and untied her. He was the one who brought water and the horrible food. He was one of the ones who had carried her in such pain. ‘Why is he copying me? Is he mocking me before he kills me? Why are they doing this to me?’ Willing herself to close her eyes to shut the world out of her consciousness.

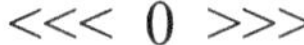

Hachaaynar felt relief after three days. A runner approached telling that Tooypor and the women were returning. She’d accomplished the impossible by returning father’s head from the invaders. She would have news of mother. Maybe that the invaders would finally leave and return the land to the Original People.

Then he saw Father. Dried peeling flesh on a shell of dark bone with sunken maggot filled purification in the sockets.

“How can we be sure this is father’s? Was this the one that the demons put at their gate?”

Tooypor took the blanket and wrapped it.

“Now it can be placed under the sand painting with his body and the ritual can be completed. We can do it tonight. His spirit will be united with the ancestors. He will join Quo-ar and Chingchnich and help guide you. This is only a step. Things don’t always happen at once. The meal isn’t good until it is ground, leached of bitterness and toxins, until it dries and is formed and combined in the right way. It takes stages just like this will take many stages”

Hachaaynar stood staring at the folded blanket at his feet with no comfort in this answer, barely hearing until the last sentence. “and they seemed relieved to give it up. Some things are unresolved. Their translator, the one who was Nahaanpar, says that there has been no word about ‘Atooshe’ as a prisoner or victim of the soldier.” She touched his arm. “We now have a contact inside. A very unreliable one but we can send a good person inside as a courier and the strange one will let the person return to us, I think it should be a woman, We will know when there is news about ‘Ahtooshe’. When and where the demon soldier will be riding alone.”

Hachaaynar’s focus came full center. “That will be good. I thank you. Father’s spirit will be with us. We will complete the ceremony tonight. I know who the contact should be.” He signaled Kwetii' to take the blanket.

“This will be a new start.”

<<< 0 >>>

Rodriguez and Lopez rode arcs on the southern perimeter of the grounds. They didn’t talk of the attacks. Lopez felt unsafe. They completed the six hour shift passing Cordero and the new man Galvez mounted at the gate.

“Anything?” Cordero asked.

“No sign of life.” Rodriguez grinned and dismounted. He saw Padre Somera, Sergeant Olivera and the prissy Corporal Andres approaching him.

“Gentlemen.” He said.

Olivera took the lead. “Rufino, you are under arrest. It is only a temporary measure. We’ll get to the bottom of the woman kept in the shed and the death of the chief of Seeba village.” Taking the musket, pistol and saber from him. Andres felt more satisfaction than he had expected. He saw Lopez roll his eyes heavenward as if to say ‘Thank God.’

CHAPTER 12

A PARTIAL VICTORY

All, from elders to infants, were gathered on the side of the village around a sand painting being made around the willow bark woven covering on the re-united body of Sevaanga-vik. Women of Sevaanga were aided by Tooypor, Charaana and Kethu. Their chant for Sevaanga-vik and the village's well-being was echoed through the crowd.

Hachaaynar returned with eight men carrying dry sage and willow branches to cover the painting, burn the body and let the smoke carry fathers spirit to watch over him.

The feeling surrounded him that he was chief. The rage of the first few days had made his role one of reflex and reaction. He saw it now as a constant mantle of long-time planning and empathy with and for the youngest to the oldest, for the weakest to the strongest, and, the most to least patient. He could bring disaster as easily as success.

He remembered mother and watched the sad faces of her friends. He was alone, except for Tooypor. He needed to ask her what she sensed after returning from the Mission. Whether mother was alive or dead.

After a long night of mourning, praising and dancing, Hachaaynar and Tooypor waved off the last of the villagers and left the cooling and steaming gravesite.

They ran their hands over each other's hair, face and body as though they'd never seen a human before. He found with her their long hidden tears and the cooing, moaning sounds of doves as they soothed the pain away. A tornado of spirits swept circles around the room. Their mouths locked with hunger for life and they fell to the fragrant woven mats to prod and paw and excite each other with the need in their bellies and loins to ignite a blaze and bring something new and wonderful into this place where so much pain had visited. They lay on their backs watching the stars through the circular vent hole.

She said. “I feel that 'Atooshe' is alive. I can feel her out there.”

“Will she return?”

“I don’t know. I don’t know. It is a strange feeling. I wish I knew more.” Before the first sleep in days took them.

<<< 0 >>>

Rufino spent the night cursing the idiot priest and Mexican. They couldn’t prove anything. Who gave them the right to assume a savage who couldn’t even speak was his responsibility? They only had Nicolas Jose’s word that the insurgents had said she was the chief’s wife. Only that the chief’s slut wife was missing! Who could prove it?

Before noon, Galvez and Cordero brought him to Sergeant Olivera’s office. Rodriguez sat.

“This is bad, Rufino.” Olivera began. “Pico gave me a dispatch that we’ll host a large party from Mexico under General Anza. They’ll stay a short time before continuing north. I can’t have scandals here.”

Rufino felt more at ease from the brotherly, even if Castellón, Spaniard‘s tone. If anyone here would understand this craziness, a true Spanish officer would. Rufino started to speak but was waved off.

“You’ve put me in a bad spot. I know this isn’t the first indiscretion. There have been grumblings from the trustees and from your comrades. Rapes and even deaths at your hands. This becomes a big problem for me and this Mission of the Franciscans.”

Heat rose in Rufino’s neck and head. This might be an enemy indeed.

“I have a dilemma. A court marshal at this time will take time from Mission business. We have no scribe. We can’t be sure the Seebas won’t resume hostilities.” He stood in front of Rufino. “We are short of fighting men and you are the best fighter here. Do you see why your...loins... Are a problem for us?”

“I didn’t do any...”

“Shut up! Nothing you will say will change this.” Olivera leaned in to Rufino’s quivering face. “You’ll have prison if I care to pursue this.” He leaned back. “I don’t.”

Rufino’s confusion had him shaking his head.

“I will return you to duty with a warning.” Olivera spoke slowly. “You will not go near the woman, The blessed Padres have taken her as a project. We will have her as a convert. We will win her over to convince the Seeba people that we are good and generous. You will keep far from her.”

“I will keep far from her.”

“You will keep your desires under control. If you do, I will transfer you to San Diego. If you can not act properly for three months, I will have you sent in chains. Do you understand me?”

“Yes, Sergeant Olivera. I will be no trouble.”

“Corporal Andres has made accusations. I will not accept them as charges because I need good soldiers for battle. You will be polite to Andres and not insult or resent Mexicans or Indians. We all will be watching you.”

“Yes, sir. I will obey.” Wondering if that were possible.

“You will stay far from all neophyte women, especially this one.” Waiting for Rodriguez to show recognition. “ You will ride away from groups of gentiles and report their movements to the gateman. You will not engage them. You will be watched and not supported. You will be kept in the cell for two days. I will then tell Cambon that you have repented. You will take confession. Say what you need to. It will pass if you control yourself. ”

“Yes, Sergeant Olivera.” Bowing obsequiously on his departure, returning to his cell, flanked by guards.

<<< 0 >>>

‘Atooshe’ woke. Two older women were whispering and bathing her. She opened her eyes. It was comforting and kind after so much pain. Their touch was as soft as butterfly wings. They spoke a Tongva dialect from the eastern deserts. As she moved to see them she felt undiminished aching in her groin and kidneys.

“Is this in the Mission?” Startling one to her right.

“You’ve slept a whole cycle of the sun. We’ve bathed you three times and now you speak.” With a sweet smile and a deep bow of the head.

“We were told that the Padres had saved you after the bad soldier hurt you. We will help make you well.” An old crinkly faced woman with a Pemookanga accent spoke as to an old friend.

'Atooshe' raised her head two inches, feeling her loins covered with thick material and saw the crushed willow bark and guessed that willow poultice was packed over her hurt areas.

“Are you Pula?” ‘Ahtooshe’ asked, doubting that the beards would have Pul among them.

“I worked with Pul Teh’ehgehi before he died in Pemookanga. I came to find my daughter. Now she has me stay for her and her baby. She works in the fields. She told me that soldier is a very bad person. Not like the Padres. They are good and spiritual. We will make you well if you sleep and dream good things.”

The darker, round woman asked in Tongva. “Are you the woman from Yaanga? Or from the islands?”

“I am from Sevaanga, only six fingers walking to the left of the sun.”

The round woman nodded gravely. “The village that attacked us. The one with the crazy chief.”

'Atooshe' jerked upright and fell back in agony. “Crazy? The chief, Sevaanga-vik, is my husband. He is not crazy. He is wonderful. He must have tried to find me.”

The women looked up, probing each others eyes and stepped away. The older one said. “You must heal now.”

“Where is he? What happened?”

“We do not know, beautiful lady. I will try to find out after you rest. You need sleep.”

The younger one kissed her brow. “You are so beautiful. You look like the painting of the Virgin Mary. We do not want you to suffer the pain of this world. We and the blessed Padres will make you well.”

“Take me to my husband. To my village.” Feeling the beginning of wanting to live. Wanting to become strong again.

“We will help you. Sleep and don’t worry.” The older woman said as they edged out the door and barred it.

<<< 0 >>>

Ta’her’que was a strong and barrel-like woman in her thirties and lifelong friend of 'Atooshe'. Hachaaynar thought of her first. He watched her carefully before suggesting her to Tooypor as the person to defect in the night to the Mission.

“She is old enough for him to recognize her. I know she can be trusted.” He whispered to her as they walked.

“I was thinking of Charaana.” Tooypor started, but saw that a Haapchivet woman could create a problem among so many flatlanders.

“Yes, Ta’her’que would be right.”

<<< 0 >>>

Nicolas Jose woke alone as he had for a month. There were things to attend to. He needed to get the field workers to form ranks and do Mission work the first thing every morning instead of standing around gossiping about attacks, the crazy soldier, the chief, the woman who they said was a chief's wife, dead or dying in the chapel office.

There was his promise to keep to the arrogant girl who led his mother's spirit to him and pressured him so much. He was glad she had. He hoped it was 'Ahtooshe' and she was alive. He hoped he could send the 'bastard' Rodriguez to his death. He took a word Rodriguez used to insult him and returned it. 'Yes, 'bastard.' A bad person'. The bastard who'd killed Sevaanga-vik.

Ta'her'que lay against the grassy berm with the field workers just in sight. Three weeding women moved to a stone's throw from her. No guards seemed to be close.

"A'a'he' " She called, poking her head up to get their attention. "A'a'he' " until the tall one slipped over to her. "Where are you from?" Ta'her'que asked.

The woman squeaked happily and looked back to her friends. She grinned widely. "Yaanga like you! Do you want to work with us?" Knowing she'd receive privileges if she brought a convert.

"Yes, but not like this. I have no clothes. Do you have a robe. Can you bring me one like yours?"

In a short time the tall one came back and dropped a robe on the ground from under hers.

"Will you show me what to do?"

"It is easy but hard on the back after a while." She pointed at the plants in the long field.

"They want only that kind. They don't want any of these kind." Leading her into the field. "When you see a start like this," Pointing at a thistle plant, "Pull it up and throw it in a pile between the rows. Keep the piles tight. Don't let them get spread out. After a while, a man with a big bag will come and pick up the piles. If they have too hard a time picking up sloppy piles, they will report you. That will be bad for you."

"What will happen if I do?"

“You are new so they will forgive you, but if you keep doing it, you might be whipped.”

“Whipped? With reeds?” Ta’her’que asked.

“Woven hides. Just make sure that your pile is straight and no one will whip you. If you do well they will give you new clothes and food everyday and use their magic to make you ready for the afterlife, their Heaven.” She smiled expansively and gripped Ta’her’que’s hands like treats for a a special child.

“The only way you can get into Heaven is by being good for them. They will teach you the lessons. That the ways of Chinigchnich, Quo-ar and Wyote will take you to a place where you burn in fire forever. Where after you die you are still alive, but on fire. A fire that never ends. There is much pain in this world, but through their Jesus Christ, there will be no pain in Heaven.”

Ta’her’que nodded solemnly.

On the second day Nicolas Jose recognized Ta’her’que walking with a woman he’d been intimate with. Her eyes were on him. She gave a small hand-signal of recognition. It was the moment he’d anticipated. He watched them walk to the southeastern squash fields and turn south where weeding was done. He went to neophyte Pedro to give him bagging duty. He told him he’d be observed today.

“I will be pleased if you watch me today. I do a good job. You will tell the Padres I’m a good worker.” Eager for favor. “One day I will be as good a worker as you, Senor.”

Nicolas Jose gave an obligatory smile and said “Bring two flasks of water from the well. It will be hot today.”

“Yes Senor. I go for you”

'Atooshe' felt her fever break in the night with two women taking turns washing her and piling on more poultice and blankets until she felt smothered in their weight. She was beyond fear. She accepted death. Their kind ways let her see them as helpers more than tormentors.

She had visions of animals on fire and villages flooding. She heard the women reading strange things. Then, in her language, the words for blessings and a young woman who'd never had sex and names Ma-ri-ya and Yay-zu over and over as a cold shaking attacked her body and a new vision came of being a doe fallen down a snowy slope, tumbling and lying dying in an avalanche. She drifted into darkness.

After two days of confinement with good wine and food, Rufino was released from his cell, warned to do and think about nothing but his duty of the day until he could be transferred out to Sonora or San Diego.

His first patrol assignment was the northeast sector. Far from Sevaanga. Nowhere near the chapel or the neophyte quarters. He was not to insult any soldier or speak about any of the incidents of the past month. Each hour added to his sense of impotence. He sulked at seeing the looks of Andres and the phony, hypocritical priests. Even his comrades Lopez and Cordero barely acknowledged him other than a little twitch of a head shake.

'Damn this place and these idiots.' Mixed with the damning the bitch who brought him this trouble. If she had died there wouldn't be all of this stupidity. He heard she was barely living and that some heathens, that even the priests described as 'witches,' were trying to save her.

"For what?" seeing the lazy Cambon sitting on his chair, reading a boring Latin text that no-one cared about. Pretending he didn't have a little priest of his own under his sanctimonious robes. "So they can fuck the sow themselves!"

<<< 0 >>>

The days passed slowly for Tooypor. She sat behind a large juniper bush on a rarely used trail. The morning sun beat in waves on the rocky rolling terrain near the gullies and shallow ravines where as a child she first saw "The Sea Creatures" making their first foolish attempt at a camp.

Tingling ran through her like fear, but somehow different. It was the like the burning and chilling blood when she raced down the mudfloe to save the boy, or stood face to face with a bear at the river. 'Now I am the bear!'

She was naked other than a loincloth and red mud dye with rendered deer fat smeared across her back, shoulders and chest to protect her from the Sun. She had charcoal marks on her face and shoulders to replicate the sacred symbols of her honored father-in-law, Sevaanga-vik.

She crouched for two hands until the agitated owl sounds told her the time had come. She rose and walked onto the trail toward the foothills.

She didn't look back. She walked slow and languorously, picking at shrubs and aware of the motion of her hips as she shuffled lazily. The trail rose and curved to the right, leveling toward two wispy Palo Verde at the top of a rise surrounded by spring sagebrush and small dying rodent-pecked shells of baby saguaro cacti.

Every sound was seized and sorted furiously in the bee-hive buzzing of her senses. The trail leveled out and the first clear sound of hoof beats came to her as she reached the Palo Verde. She fought against looking back. She turned to the right around the two trees and started to run down the other side of the rise.

The sound of the pounding hooves grew lighter as the horse ceased driving uphill and the crest flattened out. She couldn't slow down or turn. The sound became deafening. She felt she'd miscalculated. She stumbled and shrieked, rolling onto her back trying to rise. The horse and rider towered over her.

Rufino rode at ease on his own. His thoughts were far from the hypocrites in the Mission. Only Olivera seemed to know the realities of life for men of breeding. Olivera didn't belong here either. It would be wonderful to be back in a city after this hell. Even without a promotion he could be living well.

He resented this patrol of the northeast sector but standing at the gate would be too dangerous for him. Too many neophytes knew the story. Too many unknowns could approach the gate. He would be unarmed. This was the least demeaning. He rode this third day of freedom, musket ready, toward the tall, blue and gold mountains to the northeast.

After an hour of sweeps from the sheep herd area, he took the trail toward the northern boundary.

Even two hours after sunrise, he could see this would be a scorching day. Insects were thick, flitting from bush to bush. Lizards scurried for shelter at the vibrations of his new horse, Marta's, heavy tread. She wasn't as quick a horse as Jasmin, the one the groom killed, but she had heft and power.

He saw a coyote crouched in a far-off bush stalking rabbits in the yellow anise-scented floral carpet and red prickly pear blooms poking through as he approached the uneven lands before it became foothills.

The foliage became sparse and the trail rocky as it rose and dipped. Flocks of small birds flew by in agile, circling formations like the cavalry of the Mongols.

Then he looked up the trail and saw the girl.

He saw she was thin and shapely. She looked covered in blood, but the savages use red mud traveling in summer heat.

He moved to a canter to close the distance without alarming her and causing her to run to a log or cave to take the cover that Indians use in the wilds. Her shape was what he'd been missing around the squat women of the Mission.

"Oh yes! Let us see you from the front my little rabbit." He whispered, picking up the pace, spurring Marta forward as she rounded a pair of Palo Verde trees, dropping out of sight.

He leaned hard into a right turn as Marta crested the rise, closing the remaining yards to claim his trophy. The flapping loincloth fired his hormones instantly as she seemed to waver and stumble in panic, showing her full beauty as she fell.

He started a joyous shout of conquest as an arrow drove through his cheek, from right to left, blurring his vision. He tried to level his musket but a hail of throwing sticks crushed his hand and shattered his elbow. He whimpered as loudly as Marta, releasing the reins to try to pull the arrow loose from his face. Marta reared violently with a piercing shriek as she pawed the air, and Rufino fell backwards, kicking out of his stirrups.

Tooypor saw the horse and rider rear up above her. She scrambled backwards to the right of the trail, palms scraping nettles as the arrows found their mark and the bearded monster was thrown down in front of her. The man who'd taken 'Atooshe' and killed Sevaanga-vik with the firestick.

The plan had turned to fear in the last moments. Hachaaynar flew out of the low sagebrush landing with both knees on the chest of the Spaniard. He drove the long engraved chief's bone dagger through Rodriguez' left eyeball, pounding it with a stone, through his skull and deep into the sand of the trail. He breathlessly kept pounding until Kweeti' grabbed his hand and patted his shoulder.

"Don't break the dagger! You did it good!"

The eight Tongva men and one woman stood over the twitching man watching him kick slower, moving less and less moment by moment until there was no more motion.

"Do you want the animal?" Kwetii' asked.

"No. If it comes back, kill it." Hachaaynar said, picking up the firestick. "How does this work?" He asked after inspecting it.

"They touch this part." Kwetii' pointed at the trigger. "Do you want it? We have to be very careful with it." Moving Hachaaynar's arms so it was pointed away from them.

Hachaaynar pointed the barrel close to Rodriguez and experimented pulling on the trigger until it discharged, flying out of his hands. He fell backwards holding his ears. They held their ears while the painful ringing sound subsided, stepping forward in awe as Hachaaynar rose. They stood in a tight group over Rodriguez. The red flesh of the chest and face spread across the trail in the shape of an oakleaf.

Hachaaynar picked up the musket and aimed it toward the horse, a long stones throw away. He pulled the trigger but nothing happened. He dropped it on the sand and said. "I don't want their demon-sticks or any part of their lives. No beads. No animals. No bells and blankets." He held Tooypor's hand and hugged her tightly. "Now my father can rest."

The sound of a distant shot came back to the Mission. Pico brought the news into the office of Sergeant Olivera.

"It seems that every time we hear a gunshot, it comes from Rufino." Olivera said to the mulatto.

"What will be done about him?" Pico asked.

"We will send him to Presidio San Diego on his own." Shrugging dismissively. "Before General Anza arrives."

'Atooshe' woke from a less painful sleep to see Madre Josephina, the older one, weeping at her bedside.

"Why do you cry, Mother Josephina? Please tell me."

"I have been cruel to you, my new daughter." Shaking her stringy gray hair. "I deceived you and hid so much. I can't keep lying to you."

She told the story of what had been hidden. The killing of her husband and the attack. The deaths of many men of her village, but the story became one where the entire village had been wiped out. Nothing about Tooypor or the severed head.

"My son, Hachaaynar?" A lost eternity behind her tears.

"All of the males were killed." The old woman said. "Your son is dead."

'Atooshe' remembered the chants she'd heard in the shed for the death of a Chief. Her son was dead also.

When Josephina left, 'Atooshe' wept through the evening, night and early morning, drifting in and out of sleep. She remembered how she'd wished she'd died. She saw visions of the village, husband and son blown before a windstorm, swept into the far desert and buried in sand. She saw her death in the shed and many times of death under the watch of the two chanting women.

“I have died. All my life and history has been killed.” She said to Josephina in the early morning. She told of her dishonor and death. “I am dead.”

“But you have been reborn.” Josephina said ecstatically. “You have been placed in the hands of Jesus.”

'Atooshe'’s unfocused eyes looked beyond the rooms walls into a world lost forever, populated by dead parents, husbands, sons, daughters and never to be born babies.

She closed her eyes and repeated. “In the hands of Jesus.”

“Yes, my daughter. You are now in the hands of Jesus.”

QUEBEC, FRENCH CANADA - 1776

The news swept the World. Throughout the Bourbon Empire, in France, in Spain, in Italy, the Sicilies and in Canada there was rejoicing and celibration.

The Colonial Americas, the colonists, the Americans, had finally revolted against British rule. They were engaging the British and Hessian Redcoats with arms and they needed assistance from the Bourbon Empire. Sub rosa.

King Charles lll delighted in the event. The British had torn much of Canada away from France and here was a wonderful way to gain some of it back by helping these “Americans,” as they called themselves.

Many of the firearms from Canada could work their way, via the Indian tribes that had been aligned with the French, to the colonial rebels and further cripple British Empire forces that could be used against New Spain and other Bourbon holdings.

FIN - PART ONE

PART TWO
CHAPTER 13

1779 - SINALOA

The recruiting orders had finally arrived from Mexico. Viceroy Bucarelli, Governor de Neve and Commandant General de la Croix had signed and forwarded the papers to Loreto and Sinaloa.

Don Fernando Rivera y Moncada was now appointed as Lieutenant Governor of the Californias. He called Corporals from all of the neighboring areas to begin sending their men to scour the ranchos and shops for the first settler families to build the Town of the Lady of the Angels.

Rivera found it difficult to give exact inducements to the soldiers to offer the farmers and craftsmen. Governor de Neve hadn't spelled them out except in the most broad, even vague, terms.

"You will tell them all that they will receive farming land. A lot to build a house for a married couple with two children. They will be given at least one horse, two cows and sufficient tools to work with."

The first reports were dismal. Few considered leaving their land for an unknown region with unknown benefits and unknown support.

"How many soldiers will be there?"

"How many animals will the give us?"

"We have children. They can't travel hundreds of kilometers to a place we heard is full of wild people."

Only two recruits were signed up. There was no possibility to continue with settlers to Alta California without better inducements.

Rivera sent messangers to Crespi, Somera and Portola who became Governor of Puebla, to find special qualities about the Pueblo de Los Angeles to sell the idea to simple farmers.

MISSION SAN GABRIEL

Nicolas Jose sat high riding his tall chestnut horse up a gentle hill with a clear view of the Mission's two thousand sheep. He stretched his arms out and yawned loudly under a single oak on the crest of a rolling hill. 'Alcalde' would be his name. "Acalde Nicolas Jose" sounded good, like a Spanish title of nobility.

"Senor! Senor!" Three shepherds shouted from down the hill. The older one with a limp pointed. "Sheep sick there!" Three squatting Tongva peered into the shrubs. He cantered down the slope. They bowed in deference as to a Spaniard.

He kneeled. A young sheep was convulsing with foam at the lips. If he'd had a pistol, he'd dispatch it to show power like a Spaniard. He stood and ordered the shepherds to drag it to a gully for the coyotes to devour.

He rode back to check the women husking corn, the brick makers and horse wranglers, the tillers and planters and pickers of the ripe crops.

He handed his "Condor" to a smiling, obsequious groom in the Mission courtyard. "Thank you Senor Nicolas Jose." Leaving the boy with a nod of appreciation.

Maria Regina sat spinning prime wool for weaving. She had her own section of patio in front of her private room adjacent to the women's servant's quarters. She kept a clear distance from the Nicolas Jose of her village.

He made a tipping-the-hat motion and sneered 'good day' to 'Queen Maria' as he passed. The woman who considered herself above simple Indian laborers like him. The reincarnation of the Virgin Mary. The one who had been 'Atooshe'. The one the priests ordered fancy imported clothes for their Queen to resemble the painting of the Blessed Virgin.

He went to a flask of brandy behind a pitcher of wine in his room, thankful the last grape crop produced a potent blend. All his trustees now had ample portions. He'd made a stable and workable pecking order. If you do your work, you're left in peace. If you disobey orders, you're whipped or denied food. If ones under you obey your orders, you get wine. If the order givers under you do well, you get brandy.

The glow started spreading through him. He thought of the new girl, Juanita. She embodied everything he'd hoped for after a long series of hidden couplings that, other than the moment of ejaculation, left him bored and unsatisfied.

Juanita carried herself like a prideful doe. Her grace caught the eye of every man. Her refusal of his advances were done with tact. Her wit in conversation and her cleverness won admiration. His days became quicker anticipating seeing her. He rejected coercing her favors. She had to be respected and to become a true friend. She would make a worthy wife.

SINALOA

Jose Moreno listened carefully to the offer from the private, on his third visit. It sounded much better than the last time.

“I'll think about it. I'm getting married soon and it will be different with her, and we want children. That will make it harder.”

“There is extra compensation for children in families, in wedlock, to help grow the town. A young child or baby will be counted as a person. ”

“It's sounding better, but if you'll come back with details like how do we travel? What do we do for food? How many soldiers will keep us safe?”

“All those details will be explained to you in town. I will make sure that you have food and safety.”

Jose agreed to meet in Sinaloa and find out more. ‘Maybe.’

MISSION SAN GABRIEL

After St. Mark's Day service Father Cambon watched Nicolas Jose witnessing over a flood of new baptisms. He seemed agitated. He kept walking to the window and looking out into the fields.

"Are your supervisors doing a good job?" He asked.

"Yes, Father. No problems. We have enough help."

"How is your spirit and righteousness?" Wondering if he'd been slipping into the old ways.

"I'm considering marriage. I've found a good woman."

He had watched her from the cattle fence in the early morning. She carried buckets to the milking area. He set course toward her. She looked wary, as she often did, at his approach.

He wasn't someone she admired. He was a smug power broker and user of women. It was a only small step above being with soldiers in the degradation she saw.

The chief of her village had acquiesced to Spanish threats and brought all the women and children into the Mission saying the village food and water had been poisoned.

Juanita looked at the Mission's straight walls and angles and was puzzled why people wanted ugly shapes around them or to wear so much clothing when days were kind and warm. Those who'd been there a while seemed frightened of offending the invaders or the spirits the invaders prayed to. She kept to women as much as she could. Men from other villages no longer respected women as they had. Herbs of confusion and 'Blood of Christ' made them rude and foolish.

"A'a-heh." He said, falling into step beside her with a dialect of the Seebas or the Yavit.

"What do you want? I will not go to soldiers," more directly than any neophyte woman had spoken to him.

"I would not disrespect you in that way."

"Why am I worthy of respect? The other women. Are they worthy of your respect?" She kept her eyes on his. "I think you may have forgotten what respect is. What is this respect that you have for me? "

No woman spoke like this other than Tooypor. Anyone else would raise his anger. 'I won't walk away,' sorting the challenge. It stung. He admired her courage.

"I'm in a position that is strange for me. I see what you are saying. I've disrespected. I know that. What you say has truth. I see you differently. You have wisdom and I can't misuse you or misunderstand what you say about the other women. I'd like to speak with you more." Stopping. "But I'll think about what you say. I want to become worthy of your respect."

She turned, walking backwards to keep his eyes. "To become worthy of your people's respect. That will be good. We will talk." Turning away and walking off to the milking area with a pleased smile.

He watched, unable to see the smile, and felt better than he had in weeks, thinking, 'A good woman. I am blessed.'

CIUDAD DE MEXICO – NEW SPAIN

General de la Croix sat across from Viceroy Bucareli as additional papers were carried in and placed on the center table. They thumbed through and read aloud the more finalized plans for the new civilian settlements north of the San Diego fort and capable of holding costal positions against British and Russian invading parties.

Aide de Rochemont spoke. "Fages thinks that these two would work best because of proximity to Missions and workforces. A Pueblo de Los Angeles is next to a solid and growing San Gabriel Mission."

They huddled over the maps that were updated to show California, upper and lower as contiguous with the contenent and not as a giant island.

“The descriptions of the area in spring show it as supportive of both wheat and cattle. The natives are friendly and do the Mission’s work without complaints.”

De la Croix spoke for better costal armaments.

“The bluffs along the coast by the Pueblo support canons and long gun fire to keep any invaders in defeat. The passes to the Northeast are defensible and difficult to skirt. It would take a massive invasion to imperil the place. I don’t think that England, with their colonial war on the Atlantic side, could spare enough ships and troups to be more than a token threat. The Russans on the other hand, have footsoldiers in the North moving steadily toward our lands. We have to stop them by concentrating on Northern expansion. We can have civilian settlements where we know that no force can reach them, but the North must be where our strongest forts and settlements must be.”

Bucareli read all of the reports and said. “We will start recruiting expeditionary forces. The one to the North should be led by Rivera y Moncada, but after the San Gabriel ceremonies are held. We will stay a day or two….”

“If Serra isn’t there.” De la Croix added.

“And return to the Capitol.”

WESTERN SERRANO LANDS

Tooypor brought her entourage of six guards, four provision gatherers and four bearers of goodwill gifts. She traveled the foothill trails above Asuks-gna to the Serrano villages of the high desert. Tah-ur and her party met them at the Six Great Rocks Springs. It had been two years between meetings.

“You skinny little lizard girl!” Tah-ur laughed, poking her friend’s ribs. “You‘ve been starving yourself!”

"I'm preparing myself as a warrior. The storm will come. We'll all need to stand against it and through it. You look stronger too!" Seeing the gravity the years had brought to her.

"I've said the same to our elders." Tah-ur hugged her spirit-sister. "They are so defeated in spirit. I show them the numbers. How could it be wrong? Sometimes they agree and say, 'If the others will join us' but they make excuses and chant for food, animals or rain or forgiveness for some stupid thing. I'm so glad to see you!"

Tooypor slapped Tah-ur's shoulder and sat by the spring. "We have more contacts in the Mission. Many soldiers pass through but don't stay. They are building forces to the north beyond the Tataviam mountains in Chumash lands"

Their attendants broke in groups to eat and talk. Tooypor opened their treats of cattail pollen and honey. They dangled their feet in the water and splashed each other, laughing like girls but aware of the realities of this meeting.

Tah-ur nodded as the splashing ended. "More than half of my village is gone. The beards make promises and the weak ones believe them. The ones who return bring sickness."

Tooypor stared deep into the spring. "So many dead. Friends of mine had signs of the sickness when we left." Looking beyond the wavy bottom. "I miscarried two moons ago. I wanted him. I wanted him to live."

Tah-ur hugged her. "I'm so sorry, my heart spirit. It's the worst thing that can happen to you. You have a home and husband. You have a need. I did too! I miscarried. I liked a boy who was guarding me. We were in the hills for days. Later, I was surprised at changes in me, but then pains came and the blood" She had tears. "And the little baby. Hardly more than a mouse, but my own baby."

They held each other and rocked, looking with closed eyes at the lives that could have been.

Tooypor whispered. "You were right. The numbers tell the truth. The firesticks are the only thing that unbalances our victory. We must separate them from their weapons."

"There will be more of them soon." Tah-ur whispered. "I'll talk more to the hill people to show them how it will leave them unprotected if Seeba-gna falls to the invaders."

"The Pimo-gna Plain villages are the ones that can make the difference, but they won't talk to me because they think that Seeba-gna controls the ground meal trade. Why are they so stupid? They spend time fighting over little things and let our lives be taken away. They help them destroy our life-ways and don't even notice it.

Tah-ur pinched Tooypor's ribs and laughed. "If we knew that, we would be Gods. We see it. We can't make the others see it. Look at our guards. They travel with us. They know what the invaders are doing and how separate the villages are." Waving her hand across the hills and plains. "But my villagers see the one patch of land they've known since birth. The Mission, the Invaders, slavery, rape, disease, are only words. Even most of the chiefs and elders near me only know the village next to them. You and me, and Hachaaynar. We are the ones who can make it happen."

Tooypor leaned back to see her. "You get a few trusted helpers and work the Pimo-gna and Asuks-gna villages and eastern Serrano. I will do the same toward Pasake-gna and Yan-gna. We will build a core."

They brought their vision to the guards. They spoke their minds and saw the time coming of change. They slapped arms and returned home with relief, love and hope.

(1779) - SINALOA

Juan sat with his wife at the dinner table and announced his decision to join the recruitment for the Northern Pueblo. He had waited in line with twenty others. Most of them thought that they would be paid in advance rather than collect benefits after arrival in this new Pueblo of the Angels.

"Do you think we all will be safe?" She fretted. "There will be wild Indios who are not like us. Anza's expedition was attacked and killed up there."

Juan patiently explained that the lands above Presidio San Diego were more peaceful and that most of the Indios were Catholic like they and their friends, and anyway, Anza was in a completely different place.

“The benefits that they are promising will give us much more land and more tools than I have now. They say we will have horses, cattle and the support of soldiers and Mission Indios who will help up build a better house than we have here, with a Church almost next to us and the best families will join us.”

After a long evenings discussion of the reasons for a move Maria Eugenia saw the wisdom of it, after much work to make a new life in a new place.

They were finally agreed.

“I will go back to the recruitment center tomorrow.”

In the morning Juan returned to the recruitment center and saw five men sitting on benches before corporal Garcia. They looked unhappy.

“Good morning, Corporal Garcia.” Expecting a warm greeting.

“Good morning, Senor Castillo.” Garcia replied with an apologetic shrug. “I’m afraid I have to tell you, and these other men, that the recruitment as been postponed. I don’t know for how long, but if it’s reinstated, I’ll contact each one of you.”

Juan returned to Maria Eugenia, who had already enthused the children, that the move was probably not going to happen.

MISSION SAN GABRIEL

Two riders brought important dispatches in the same week. The first was from the north. The new capital of Monterey.

Sergeant Olivera spread the word from soldier to soldier about a civilian pueblo to be built a short distance to the west past Seeba village, near the large village of Yaanga. The plan included reducing the number of Indians there.

“We can‘t accommodate more here on Mission grounds. We have to move them west by expanding the pastures.” Verdugo explained. “The shepherds need to stake out more land each week until the villages are contained. Our orders are to increase the cattle herds to be the largest in the Empire. This new civilian settlement will enrich us all.”

The second rider brought a dispatch from Loreto in the south for Padre Cambon. “Father Serra plans to visit to inspect the Mission and adherence to Franciscan principals. He will go on to build more Missions to the north.” There was no indication of when.

Padres Cambon and Somera sat with excitement and dread for the opportunities and potential for disaster of a visit.

“We are in no shape for an inspection.” Somera sighed.

Cambon nodded. “We need to enforce more discipline than the neophytes will accept. Getting the drunken soldiers to act as good examples will never happen. We could be assigned here for the rest of our lives.” Nervously dipping his quill in the dry ink well. “Or, if God is with us, we will be reassigned to a more civilized place.”

“It starts with the soldiers. We must push them to more Christian behavior.”

Cambon pursed his lips in agreement. “Quite a task.”

<<< 0 >>>

Juanita was aware of Nicolas Jose through the next days. He would be at the periphery of her field, riding by, stopping to talk with an overseer, resting on a far hill with the field in sight. Looking in her direction more than other areas of the field. He must see that she also could watch his movements.

On the forth afternoon he and his huge horse stood in her path. He dismounted, disregarding the others on their break.

“Juanita.” In a gravely voice from nervousness or trail dust, clearing his throat. “I’ve changed my ways. It’s because of you and your anger with my womanizing.” Holding his palm up to let him finish before stopping him.

'He is nervous!' She thought. 'The big, strutting, powerful Nicolas Jose is a scared cub because I can stand up to him!'

"I won't be like that again. I won't misuse my position. I'll be loyal to one woman and respect her if she is the right woman to build a good life with." He lay his hand on his chest. "There is only one woman I respect and want to build a strong life with. To have healthy children and make a home. It is you, Juanita. Don't answer now." He took a step back. "Think about what I say and we will talk tomorrow. I think you are a good, strong woman. I will be a good and strong man for you." Stepping back to his horse as she looked at him with an amused half-smile.

'What did her smile mean?' Wondering through the humid evening. 'Was she pleased? It was a strange kind of smile, as though she didn't have any kind of answer.'

'He wants me to be a wife!" Giggling inside. 'He wants his hands all over me and to pump into me and make babies, but he is selfish and Old!, fretting her brow and wanting to tell someone. 'I'd have privileges and not have to work much but I'd be bored and I couldn't have my friends stay at my home or speak to people freely. I'd live like an elder. No. Not me.'

Her friends in the sleeping quarters laughed at her luck in attracting such a powerful man. She tried to sleep. How will he react when she tells him no? Would he forgive her and look for someone else? Would he stay the parasitic person that he was before promising to change?

Young Jose Rivera was the best new cowherd in the Mission. Fastest in training horses and best at cutting an animal out of the herd for feed or stud. Tall and lean, fresh from his Baja California town of Rosarito. He wore his shirts open and was lightning fast with both temper and jokes. He had a magnetic, charming smile and an easy way.

He rode past a flock of girls and headed into the squash and new corn patches. A slender but womanly girl, squinted up at him. Everything about her unforgettable face made him stop, block her path, and turn his brightest smile to her,

"I am Jose. I will be your servant and protector. Allow me to introduce myself at the plaza fountain at dinnertime. I will wait, even until dawn, to see you again," bowing his head and backing the horse carefully and confidently to the side, never losing his childlike grin of pleasure.

"Oh, Wiote! What tricks you play! Two crazy men in a week!" Squinting as she walked, head turned back at the painfully handsome, arrogant man who was after her womanliness. 'He is so good looking! Why would he think that I understand what he says in that Spain language?' But knowing what he wanted.

An older woman translated what he said. She felt a tingle that grew as a warm feeling, letting the rough cloth excite her as she walked. She closed her eyes and smiled, oblivious to the chatter around her.

<<< 0 >>>

Nicolas Jose heard knocking on his door after the sun rose. It was a humid night of clouds and higher than normal temperatures. His sleep was fitful with thoughts of Juanita.

Somera entered at the second knock. "I expected you to be out with the work crews by now. Are you ill?"

"No Padre, My crews are at work under proven neophytes. I need time to prepare my routes. I needed some rest to plan well."

"And a little wine?" Walking around the small room, peeking behind clay pots and folded clothes, noticing three bladder bags of wine and a bottle that could be brandy.

"There is too much wine consumed by both soldiers and trustees."

"I save some for Saint's days. To pray and to consider the suffering of our Lord."

Somera smiled at the predictable response. "You must be careful about excess these next months. We need to make the Mission clean and trouble free. The Esteemed Father Junipero Serra, The senior leader of the order, will come to inspect our Mission and to ensure that we are righteous. It is the most important moment for all of us. You must be strict with all of your supervisors and workers."

He knew that he would be rebuked about the wine, but if he nodded at the right places, he would show repentance and it would be accepted. He saw that whoever this Esteemed Father is, he could pass the speech on and any responsibility would be spread around. There wouldn't be much change for him one way or the other.

"You must not be a fornicator and must not allow fornication among your people. That is written in stone. I hold you responsible for the behavior of your people. If you fail you'll no longer be considered as Alcalde. You'll be prisoner of the soldiers and sent away if we fail an inspection by the Blessed Father. It will be good if you marry. Do you understand?"

A cold chill spread from his neck to shoulders. His mouth felt dry. "Yes Blessed Father. Yes, I understand. I will be with wife again if Juanita a good Christian woman will accept me. I'll ask her "

LORETO – NEW SPAIN

"Another dropout from the list. How will these lazy farmers be induced to go? We are offering more than we have as soldiers of Spain! They are all lazy meztisos and blacks! What do they want!" Corporal Tellez ranted.

Ramirez had more patience, having seen cancellation after cancellation of the orders from the top.

"I would drop out too if I were pushed back and forth like an idiotic child. We make offers, and then we take them back. You wouldn't put up with this shit. How can you expect them to?"

CHAPTER 14

JEALOUSY AND POWER

Juanita woke with the noise of scrambling rooster calls. She was uneasy leaving the meal quarters. She ducked behind a group of women so that either Jose or Nicolas Jose wouldn't see her.

'I don't hide, but what craziness this is.' Weighing Nicolas Jose's speaking a language close to hers, his personal power and charm against his age and reputation as a user and ally of the soldiers. She thought of Jose's arrogance, lowly position, and that he also was an ally of the invaders. 'He's so handsome!' She felt excitement being close to him. 'He only went to me. No-one else. What a good looking man! He didn't even look at anyone else! I'll have to tell Nicolas Jose that I can't be what he wants me to be. I have to keep Jose waiting for now'.

<<< 0 >>>

Jose Rivera knocked at the frame of Padre Somera's open door. The man read at his crudely hewn desk and raised his eyes.

"Come in my son." He rasped, trying to place this strong and somehow noble looking mestizo young man. "What do you need?"

Jose shifted his feet like a young boy and raised his eyes. "Padre, there is a neophyte woman that I want for a partner for life and to marry."

"Is it that Juanita from the squash field?" Seeing immediately the inevitable conflict over the child. It instantly fell in place. She would bring too much strife if she were not taken. She was much too young and pretty for Nicolas Jose to have a settled life. He saw how temptation emanated from her. It would be much better for her to be with a handsome younger man.

"She is the one I ask for to marry with your blessing, Father Somera. Please give your blessing to me. To us."

"I will consider it." Somera said, wanting to meet this somehow magnetic girl first. "I will consider it."

SINALOA

Manuel Camaro had finally found the work that he wanted on thefarms of Sinaloa. He was good with heat and an anvil. He could form small bits of metal into hinges for gates and cabinets and form larger ones for garage doors.

He was making a good living for one so young, but he also supplemented his income with occasional Monte games at weekend fairs.

The women were still fun and it was easy to find a new one to play games with, but, MariaTomas Garcia was different. She was special. She was smart and had to be respected.

He knew that if he made a life with her he couldn't be unfaithful.. He would have to change his habits, actually, change his life.

"Am I ready for this?" He asked himself often as he rode his new horse to her parent's house. "Yes. I am ready.

MISSION SAN GABRIEL

The sun rose high and heat bore down hard on the dusty valley. Nicolas Jose entered the squash field at a canter, passing rows of tilling Indians. He made waves of acknowledgement like blessings but was unaware of anyone but Juanita. The only one who seemed unaware of his approach. 'How could she not see me?' He wondered.

Juanita felt dread on seeing the horse and rider leave the Mission grounds moving toward her field. She kept her eyes averted as the shape approached. Yavit Marta on her right laughed. "Here comes your lover," as the horse came near. She resolved to face it straight on. There was nothing to gain by being weak and vague.

He feared she might be ignoring him and would refuse him as he came closer. He hid his worry as her eyes met his.

'What a smug little Spanish pretender,' she thought looking up at him. She walked across the front of the horse into an open, untilled field knowing he would follow. 'It will be bad if he's embarrassed in front of the workers.' When they were alone she stopped and looked up at him.

"You want me to be your woman. You want me to marry you but I can't be what you want. I have another. A horseman, my age, has asked me to marry him. I will be pledged to him. The Fathers have blessed it. I will be his." Lying for time"

He felt immediate anger and a hot flush and made a stone mask to hide it. He was unprepared for this coldness and lack of respect. He looked around. He was surprised at the number of people watching them. She must have been talking about him. He thought that the blood boiling within him was making him change color. They would all see it.

She watched the changes in his face and feared that he could strike her or whip her. If he did that he would be more foolish than she'd estimated. There would be trouble for him with all these witnesses.

"I respect you, Nicolas Jose. It is a hard thing to choose between a great leader and a boy of my age, but I am too young and cannot be what you want of me." Feeling untrue to herself but deflecting his anger.

Emptiness swept across him and brought the dream to the ground. He had power but didn't have youth. He could command but couldn't ask or beg. He spoke as he turned the horse casually away from her and spurred it lightly to a canter.

"As you wish."

Juanita kept her eyes on him re-entering the work field. 'He is a dangerous man.'

"What did he want?" Marta asked.

"He wanted me to be his wife. I told him I wouldn't."

"I hope he asks me." Marta sighed.

Nicolas Jose stonily ignored the greetings of Somera, riding too fast through the wood and whitewashed adobe entryway, glaring back at the hypocrite. He muttered furiously to himself walking in his room to the brandy. He put it down after two deep drafts. He knew he'd be barged in on and asked why he hadn't answered the Father.

'Why should they ask me anything? What if I came in their rooms and asked them whatever I felt like asking them about? They'd call in the soldiers and hit me. Why can't I hit them?.' He paced three steps from wall to wall knowing he'd be killed if he beat Somera or or followed his heart and threw Spaniards out of his space. It was longer than he expected when the knock came and the door was opened.

"You're wanted in the chapel." Cordero barked. "You need to come now."

Somera searched the angry face and frowned as Cordero stood at the neophyte's side and seemed wary.

"You appeared angry as you passed. Please explain." Interlocking his fingers behind his head.

As he'd expected, The Padres would use him to keep the neophytes in line. He'd control his people and they'd give him privileges until he needed support in His life! Was he supposed to not feel anything? Not have needs? to live a normal life after giving two wives and his children to them. They promise Juanita to a new man from the south because horse herders are needed for the new herds. He'd earned more support than that! He'd speak to them the way they expected him to speak. He'd hide his anger but he swore not to forget it.

"I asked the neophyte Juanita to marry me. She said she would. I went to her this morning. She said you had promised her to a young horseman."

Somera groaned. 'It's unfolding too quickly. How could a vague conversation this morning become so volatile? No promises were made. Why does he think I had?'

"I made no promises. Why do you say that I did?"

“Juanita said you promised her to the Baja man“ He knew that the Padre would lie to keep him quiet.

“I’ve never spoken to this Juanita other than her accepting the sacrament last month. She may be interested in the young man, just as he is interested in her for marriage. I‘m sure you can see that they are close to the same age.” Seeing fury poring out of Nicolas Jose’s eyes.

Nicolas Jose watched the liar’s nervous face fixed on him. ‘Yes, he feels fear, He can pray to his God who hates liars.’

“You are saying you never blessed their plans? She lied to me?” Seeing the worm squirm in his chair to avoid him. How can he keep this lie after Juanita and the Baja boy came out in the open? How many years had he shown his loyalty to him? Juanita could change his life and make children. She looked too healthy to fall into disease like his wives had.

Cordero saw expressions he’d never seen on the ‘Alcalde-to-be.’ Glaring rage isn’t smart with the man who controls your future. Nicolas Jose usually had a smirk or impatient frown when things didn’t go well. A slow worker or unwilling woman brought out irritation, but nothing like this.

Cordero kept his hand on the hilt of the saber. He wouldn’t use the blade but the hilt and fist if necessary. The Indians would be hard to control without Nicolas Jose. ‘If giving him the girl will smooth it out, Somera should give her to him.’

The Padre stood. “I’ll have Cordero find this Juanita and bring her to me. I’ll find the truth and not be called a liar. Cordero, take Nicolas Jose to his quarters.” Feeling any moment he’d would lash out. He was like a coiled snake with devilish eyes. He hadn’t seen hatred in him before.

“Let us find the truth in this. Perhaps it is a misunderstanding.”

Nicholas Jose was walked out of the building, striding through the courtyard ahead of the wary Cordero, thinking, ‘Misunderstanding! How stupid do you think I am?’

Cordero growled. “Stay in your quarters until you are called.” The man nodded sullenly and went inside. Cordero stood a moment trying to read how much of a threat he might be and realized he actually liked the strutting fool who kept the troublemakers in balance and was so charming with the women.

Nicolas Jose stared down his bed in the darkened room, biting his lip, feeling new and unwelcome emotions. His forehead hurt and his eyes itched. They were wet like a woman! He wanted to turn on his side and hold his knees, pull the blanket over his head and stay forever. He felt the wetness grow and sobbed, cursing his life.

<<< 0 >>>

Baja Jose brought two stray calves back to join the herd as they grazed on mixed hay and wild grass under mild breezes and broken puffs of clouds.

Cordero rode to the young horseman and saw instantly why any young woman would be swayed by his posture, shape and look as he sat straight in the saddle. When he saw the face and flowing black hair under the flat-brimmed Spanish hat he knew that Nicolas Jose could never compete with him unless the girl was only interested in power.

“Rivera! Come! Father Somera needs to speak to you.”

Juanita stooped, sorting the squash that was without worm holes, throwing them in her burlap bag, piling up the bad ones the beside her workmates.

“Here comes Nicolas Jose.” Carmenita said, standing to relieve her back, seeing a horseman leave the east gate, turning south-east on the path to their field. She squinted. “No, it‘s a soldier”

Juanita was fearful because of the lie. She didn’t look up as Cordero approached.

He rode through the tan and green speckled field into a group of twenty women in white burlap smocks hunched with their darker tan bags.

“Who is Juanita?” he called. Three women stood. He instantly recognized the slim pretty one that all the fuss was about. “Come with me. ”

She felt relief that however it went, it would be resolved on this day. She could face it.

Somera sighed. It all made sense when she entered with Cordero. Her youth, Rivera’s looks, Nicolas Jose’s age and desperation. The ways of the flesh are imprinted in the mortal condition and sin may be avoided by the union of these…puppies. It was all too obvious.

Juanita poured out her feelings in broken Spanish and Tongva through tears at not being able to express herself and for lying. Somera saw the only way it could be resolved is through their marriage. The sooner the better. Nicolas Jose will have to find another.

Nicola Jose stayed in his quarters for two days. He watched through the hand sized hole of a window in his adobe wall. The laborers, soldiers and occasional padres passed.

“False people. Liars!” Meaning the Spanish but including so many of the villagers and recent arrivals from the south. “You will see. You use me. You will see.” vowing to never show his anger until it was the last thing they’d ever see. He slept easily, after working out ways to kill Somera, Cordero, the Baja neophyte horseman, and the lying Juanita.

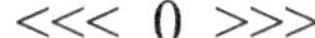

On the third morning Cordero knocked on the thick wooden door and Nicolas Jose opened it with a wide grin.

“I haven‘t bathed in four days. Please forgive the smell.” Motioning to the fields. “I need to get a woman, not Juanita, to clean my room and wash me.”

“I‘m glad you‘ve calmed down. I was worried about you. I thought Somera should have given her to you, but I guess it was the right thing. If she is so stupid to pick that boy over you, you are better off without her. Better to know now, Better than after you get married to the wench!”

<<< 0 >>>

Nicolas Jose watched coldly as the barely teenaged girl fearfully washed him from a pair of buckets and clumsily responded to his demands to handle his manhood to release. She collected his bedding and clothes and walked up the path to do his washing. He felt some of the old power of his position. He could function as if nothing had changed. On the other hand, it had changed so deeply that none of the advantages and pleasures could hide the treachery and insult that had been done to him.

He mounted for his first day's ride of the fields. Many faces turned to him. Many turned away when he held their gaze. He was pleased that he was talked about. He felt more power over his people than he'd felt at any time before. Maybe more of than he'd imagined would join him to help kill Somera and the two evil ones. He watched faces looking for potential recruits.

Some of the young men made greeting gestures. Most of the older ones were too fearful to help. He planned 'there should be no obvious assailant. Somera should go first, perhaps during a hastily scheduled confession. He'd be stabbed in the booth by an unknown neophyte.' Nicolas Jose would have long since shown forgiveness and friendship and wouldn't be suspected.

Turning through the flattened northern field he thought, 'how much of this new planting is fertilized by buried fetuses, children, runaways and victims of Rodriguez?' He guessed dozens had been shoveled over,

Juanita and the Baja horseman would have to wait a month or two to join their beloved Padre. He wanted Juanita to mourn for the horseman and to see her sorrow grow. He dropped thoughts of killing her. She might turn back to him for comfort but he would show her scorn and give her to the soldiers. He smiled at the variations of the story.

He did the work of the Mission as well or better than he ever had. Even Cordero remarked on his progress.

<<< 0 >>>

Somera and Cambon brought a carpentry crew through the chapel for repairs to the transept's water rot. A morning chill had stayed through noon. An agitated young man stood in the shadow of the archway looking shakily at the Fathers. He bowed to Somera and motioned to the booth. He looked nervous and frightened.

Cambon asked. "Have you seen him before."

Somera looked at the dirty boy, not from the inner courtyards, his clothing and hands. "He's from the fields. He looks terrified." Motioning for him to come to him. "Do you understand me?" Squinting into the boy's darting eyes.

The boy nodded.

"Have you sinned?"

"Yes. I sinned." Tears welled up. The voice quivered. "Sinned bad"

In the confessional Father Somera felt relieved to sit after hours of directing the carpenters.

The boy spoke slowly and hesitantly in broken Spanish. "I not bad man. I told man I be bad. I kill."

Somera couldn't remember any recent deaths.

"I want good. Be good man. I not bad."

"Did you kill someone?" Waiting for a response but only getting choking sighs and hard breathing. "My child. Did you kill someone?" Hearing rustling in the darkened booth, straining to identify the sounds.

The boy felt the metal dagger in his inner waistband and wiggled it out back of his tunic. He stared at it in the half-light. "Father." He half sobbed it out. "I told. Kill you."

Somera hesitated before standing slowly and backing away from the screen. He stepped out as the boy slowly left the confessional booth with a twisted face and dropped the dagger at Somera's feet.

"I not bad. I not kill."

Somera shouted. "Soldiers! Soldiers quickly!" Pico and Vargas were upon the boy and the questioning began.

<<< 0 >>>

Tooypor and Tah-ur met by the caves above Asuks-gna as they did on every season of the rising flowers and in the season of the rising clouds. Guards and runners kept watch as they compared changes forced by the invaders and the diminishing workforces of the villages and the lack of young people.

"The grains and acorns will be gone and more villagers will be pulled to the invaders camps."

They walked in slow circles, sometimes hand in hand. Tooypor listened to descriptions of the changes in life from Tah-ur's tribal lands. Tooypor knew Haapchivet could never be affected that way. No invader had set foot near the village. No intruder could survive attacks from the rocky hiding places. The supplies would be ample for any season of siege. Attacks had been tried before by Mojave and Tataviam. Haapchivet had prevailed and always would.

"You must move your people higher in the hills and use more plants like these." Pointing to seasoning grasses that helped preserve the rabbit and deer meat. "You'll become safer. It will prepare you for the battle that will come soon. It isn't far off. We have people in the invader's camp who report their strengths and weaknesses. Seeba-gna has lost so many. So much. Few young people have stayed. Some moved to the mountains and Yaanga. We are making plans. It will come."

Tah-ur nodded. “I know it will. We can‘t fight them in the desert. Hills will give us the advantage. I‘ll start working on it. I know some of the young people will want to go where there’s better hunting. They’ll help the carry older ones.”

They slapped arms in a fast and simple agreement and returned to their villages with hope for strength and time to return to the ways.

MONTEREY - CAPITOL OF ALTA CALIFORNIA

Governor Felipe de Neve looked over the final draft of Reglamento to offer potential settlers of the newly approved Pueblo de la Reina de Los Angeles.

He knew that recruitment would not be easy with a reputation of hard to cultivate desert land to fight against.

He, i.e. The Crown, was to offer:

1. A house lot and a tract of land for cultivation.

2. Each poblador will receive $116.50 per year for the first two years.

3. $60 per year for rations

4. On condition of repayment they will be granted horses and mules fit to be given and received. Payment of large and small cattle at just prices.

5. Tools and implements at cost.

6. Two mares, two stallions, two cows, one calf, two sheep, two goats, one yoke of oxen or steers, one cargo mule, one plow point, one hoe, one spade, one axe, one sickle, one wood knife, one musket and one leather shield.

To the community:

1. One forge and anvil, six crowbars, six iron spades or shovels, tools for carpentry,

For the governments assistance in these grants the pobladores will be required to sell to the Presidios the surplus products of their lands at fixed prices to be set by the government.

It looked workable. 'We'll see if they can sell it in Loreto and Sinaloa.'

MISSION SAN GABRIEL

Pico held the musket down at his side standing behind a low wall watching Cordero and Galvez waiting beside the stall where Nicolas Jose would dismount. They saw the apprehension in his eyes.

Nicolas Jose was on fire on his tour of the fields. The calmness of the mild weather with a soothing breeze, the orderliness of the field workers and neat piles of produce couldn't distract him from his thoughts of revenge and the ways it could go. He altered his route to avoid confrontation with Juanita or the Baja horseman. 'There will a time to see them pay for their arrogance.'.

He wondered why Cordero and Galvez were standing near his stall. They looked up too often. Could the boy have failed? What if Cambon was only wounded?

Galvez grabbed the reins. Cordero seized the arm and yanked Nicolas Jose to the ground. Pico stepped forward, musket raised, as Cordero brought a small club down on the back of the prisoner's head. Carrying him kicking across the courtyard. Clumps of neophytes watched, some sullen, some pleased at the fall of the man who had abused them.

"Their dog sees that he is only a dog to them now"

"All the times he sold me! I hope they rape him the same way! Over and over!"

The soldiers dragged him across the courtyard to a small cell down a brick walkway past the chapel.

Maria Regina looked up from her spinning wheel in the chapel patio. She remembered her experiences with Nahaanpar and his hypocrisy as Nicolas Jose.

‘He was never a good person.’ She thought. ‘A hypocrite and a sinner. Maybe this will make him repent.’

He saw her as a blur through grit and tear filled eyes bouncing along the dusty path and badly laid bricks. He recognized ‘Atooshe’, so betrayed by him. ‘Forgive me, wife of Sevaanga-vik. If I had known Rodriguez….’ His head bounced off a raised brick.

He woke in the night. Aches from mid-back through left shoulder into his neck, left ear and skull. He remembered the sudden pull off the horse and the impact of the hard ground. Before he could sort it out he slipped into unconsciousness.

When it was light, he woke twice and slipped back, each time with worse pain in his ear. The third time it was dark outside. He stayed awake with the pain but it diminished enough to think about the ways in which the plan went wrong. He was not close to understanding as a fitful sleep came again.

<<< 0 >>>

Cordero and Galvez were the only soldiers present when the Fathers discussed Nicolas Jose’s fate. They started before Olivera, Verdugo, Alvarado and Pico arrived.

“It’s all about those two young people.” Cambon said to Somera. “He believed you took her away to placate the cattle drivers. He believed that cattle are more important than agriculture. It‘s foolish, but he seems desperate for a wife.”

Somera continued to look at the floor. “Desperate enough to kill me? Quite insane. The boy was a blessing.”

“A blessing indeed.” Weighing the damage if the Alcalde-to-be was executed, imprisoned or exiled. He’d seen many in middle age go crazy for a younger woman. This Juanita turned heads. The soldiers would become troublesome over her. She was clear about not wanting attention other than that handsome Jose.

“Nicolas Jose has been an asset. He is the best in communicating the Church’s interests. The best translator. The model Indian in many ways.” He paused. “Brother Somera,” Meeting the uncomfortable Padre’s eyes. “What would you think about putting Nicolas Jose on trial, observed by the other trustee Indians, and imprisoned for enough time to assess the depth of his discontent.” Somera’s brow furrowed. “We’ll send the girl and the boy to San Diego. We can get horsemen anywhere, not trusted communicators.”

“How can he be trusted?” Somera waved his hands. “He conspired to have me killed! After Father Juame was killed in San Diego I’ve always been nervous, but I understood that the Diegueno Indians were more warlike, but this is too close.”

“It’s Lust! Pure and simple. Remove the girl and give him time to calm down and sanity will return.”

Cordero watched in disbelief. Furious that Cambon could look at a murder attempt like this. Why should a subject live after an assault on the Crown? Worse, He started a plot! Bringing in accomplices! It was out of place to interrupt, but these were Franciscans. ‘To Hell with it!’

“Blessed Father. If Indians start conspiring to kill us, we’ll have little protection. We are few and a sneak attack from inside will kill us all. He should be made an example and executed as soon as possible.”

“No, no, no.” Cambon said. “The one he trusted was a boy who proved loyal to us. I‘m not saying to release him. Not by any means, but our forgiveness carries the message of the Church with more weight than an execution that few neophytes would respect. We have a chance to change what made us look vulnerable into a message of greater strength. Neophytes will see the power of the Church.”

Somera considered it. “It would be a powerful message of doctrine and forgiveness, but my being a sacrifice to an experiment in conversion doesn’t appeal to me. How can we know the depth of his repentance if he is only imprisoned for a short time? ”

‘What idiots!’ Cordero said to himself, ‘What a bunch of idiots!’ knowing that Catholic thinking could carry the day over common sense and the post would be in danger.

“I need to bring The Sergeant and the other men to help decide. It may put the Mission at risk. Please excuse me.” Hiding his rage in a formality he had difficulty wearing.

He entered the mess room and saw them playing cards, laughing and gesturing, with wine stains on the tablecloth.

“Come Cordero!” Verdugo yelled. “Replace me in the next deal with these vultures.” Getting good natured laughs from Olivera and Galvez.

“The Padres and Andres are talking about forgiving Nicolas Jose for the murder plot!” Shouting. “How can you play cards now?

Olivera raised his eyebrows, surprised by Cordero’s intensity. “First you shuffle.” Pause. “Then you deal, and then you take his money.” Pointing to Verdugo.

“This is important. We can‘t let him live after trying to kill a Priest, even if he is an Italian.” His anger eased, thinking. ‘It might be better if a Priest was killed. We need more soldiers here than we need Churchmen. The land is Spain’s, not Rome’s.’

“Nicolas Jose is the best Indian we have.” Alvarado said to Cordero. “He just went crazy for that little bit of pastry. He‘ll find a new pretty one. He will be fine again.”

“Then you don‘t want a trial?”

The Sergeant shrugged, rearranging his cards. “Yes, of course a trial. We‘ll say ‘Bad Boy,’ he‘ll say ‘I’m sorry,’ and we‘ll let him wander off with a new wench.” He looked at the group. “We will all keep an eye on him and his moods, but he’ll be a good boy again.”

<<< 0 >>>

Tooypor watched the leaves swirl from the door of her Pula hut. A tiny mother with two misbehaving children walked down the wind swept trail from Haapchivet. She was on time. The boys had disobeyed parents, elders and council by stealing, breaking pots and tools, fighting and kicking elders. They'd repeated their offences past the council's patience. Tooypor saw fear in the mother's face. It was the last chance before they were sent into the arms of the coming winter with no village to go to, or else killed by council.

Tooypor watched their postures, alternately glaring and flitting about eyes, looking for things in the hut to steal or break. They hadn't learned to hide their anger or scheme for the things that they wanted. They never made eye contact with their mother. 'She beats them.' Watching the small woman's fear and rage. Fear from the boys, who could overpower her if they chose to, and her rage at her habit of hitting them since they were babies.

"Respected Mother." Seeing the woman's lined and anxious face upturned. " I want your boys to sit with me. Will you walk to the stream and wait until we come for you?"

"Yes, Pula. As you say." Hesitating until a gesture told her that it was time.

The boys sat on the mat and looked at this big tough Pula who didn't look weak enough to attack easily but wasn't as fearsome as Japchi-vik 'Aachvet or the council men. They had heard stories of her powers. They were unimpressed by her seeming gentleness. Just more phoniness.

"Has your mother always hit you? Both of you?" Seeing sudden interest on their faces.

"Father is worse.' The older one said squinting up at the only older person to ever ask.

Tooypor sat as the boys unloaded story after story of being wronged and falsely accused by their parents. "They think anything we say is a lie! If I'm banned from the village, I'll be happier than this. I can hunt for my self." The younger one rocked in agreement.

After four fingers of the sun, the mother came to the door. They talked until nightfall and slept together on the floor. At sunrise she watched the three walk up the trail to Haapchivet swearing a new life.

The sun rose, flickering through the pines. A runner from Seeba-gna entered the hut's clearing shouting "Pula."

She gave him water as he breathed deeply of the sage and chewed smoked deer strips.

"Sevaanga-vik sends respect. He'll come soon. Nicolas Jose, Nahaanpar, may be banished or put to death for trying to kill a Beard Pul. We have people inside. We will help him escape if he is ready to rejoin the Iitaxxum. We of the land." Straightening with pride at being able to say that. "Sevaanga-vik says it is the chance he has been waiting for, if Nahanpar comes back."

She gestured. "He takes trails, gets lost and admires himself because he is on whatever it was. Why trust a man like that? He is like a tumbleweed."

"Hachaaynar says it's an opportunity to fight the beards.

"That won't work." Annoyed it would be considered based on Nicolas Jose. "The ones they bring from Pemuu'nga and the coast, even from beyond Asuks-gna, only want the comfort of the beards food and huts. Their own lifeways have been destroyed along with their families and homes." Feeling the sting of distant tribes people placed on her lands by the invaders.

She continued without hearing more. "I've seen this man who was Nahaanpar. When I was a girl I had to trade with him to recover Hachaaynar's father's head" The runner nodded in recognition of the legend.

"He wants his vision of the moment. He has no ties and will never have ties. Any help will bring disaster to Seeba-gna. Tell Hachaaynar to have no contact with him. Tell him it's a mistake of Spirit."

“Hatchatynar has ideas on how to bring him in. Do you want me to bring him your message? You should come to Seeba-gna if it is a mistake. You should stop it.” It was rare for a runner to inject an opinion. She saw it was wise.

“I’ll go.”

CHAPTER 15

A SEARCH FOR ONE'S SELF

Nicolas Jose stared at the wooden ceiling supports in wonder at the precision his crew had accomplished four years ago. 'I've done so much to put this place together and make it work. They can't do as well without me.' Calculating that if they would kill him with so few who came close to his skills. He weighed approaches to explain his actions. The neophyte gave details about his tries at recruitment, even naming Juanita and Jose. No denial would be believable.

Overwork and sleeplessness weakened his ability to step back to see how foolish his anger was, but now he saw it with clarity.

Like a story, there was Juanita, looking less pretty and more frightened and childish. Jose, prancing on his horse and the whole of the Mission, Seebag-na and surrounding countryside laid out below, and there, pouting and raging, stood him, throwing away everything he had worked for in order to be something he wasn't, a younger man who was still partly Nahaanpar while trying to be the invader's main Indian. The Alcalde. He looked at it separated from it.

One of the soldiers might walk in and shoot him in his sleep. He could be dragged into the courtyard in front of a crowd and flogged or shot while they watched.

'Would they cheer? Cry? Would some run away or revolt?' He imagined reactions of some he had dealt with. Especially the ones he had whipped for theft.

If he could return to the life he'd led, he swore he'd never let anger consume him. He'd sleep. He'd give all of the Blood of Christ and brandy back to the soldiers or pour it on the ground. He wouldn't curse in their language or be disrespectful to women. He'd recall the old songs and dances and try and re-connect with the Spirits

He rocked, squatting at the edge of his straw mat, humming low so no guard or prisoner would hear him in an invocation to family, hoping his mother's spirit would forgive him. He reformed the chants of his youth and whispered them long into the night until sleep came.

He woke feeling resolved to put his ambition and anger to rest. He spoke to the rough clay wall. "I'm ready to die," and continued the prayers to Chinigchnish, Wiote and the Spirits of the Lands of the People .

Hachaaynar waited for Tooypor's arrival for three hands. The messenger's midnight report smashed his hopes and the beginnings of his plan. He walked the rounds of Seebag-na. Checking and double-checking the milling, thatching and new herding areas.

The Mission in exchange for access to Three Tree Spring traded three cattle and three sheep. Two of the cattle died after a short time. No matter how good it sounded, he wanted no more trades with the invaders. He was foolish to let this agreement come to pass. Sickness is what they trade in.

Two mothers came to him.

"Can you talk to our daughters? We miss your mother so much. She'd know what to do. They won't listen to any of us. They get crazy with boys every night. What can we do?"

"Follow me to old Anch'a'eh and Che'rah'e." Leading them to a lane near the women's kitcha. "They raised their wild squawkers to be leading men. Honorable. Hunters. They were four wild boys." He laughed at seeing how wrong his plan could go.

"Have your daughters meet with the wise women away from the village, when the boys are away."

He sat with the women until they felt good with each other. They were like old friends when he left.

He walked north to see if she was on the trail. After two fingers he saw her and her runners entering the flatlands from the foothills.

In the Greathouse they waved the guards outside.

“This is a real opportunity. If he‘ll escape, he can become a bridge for us. It can make the difference of success for us all. I know you don’t trust him but he has contacts there and more influence…..”

She was annoyed that he usually sees the same visions of the path but puts trust in a proven loyal dog to the invaders.

“He’s betrayed us over and over. He had betrayed your father. He helped to kidnap, rape and convert your mother. Why can’t you see it? What good can come from trusting him?”

“Why would he try to kill a Brownrobe? Not just a soldier but a religious leader!. That takes him out of their circle of power!” Seeing her fixed stare. “This is not their Nicolas Jose. This is our Nahaanpar!”

“It’s an illusion. Too little information. Has anyone see him since this…story of his change?”

“We have people coming tonight with news.”

“I will say no more until real witnesses come to speak to us. You shouldn‘t either.”

<<< 0 >>>

Charaana and a young Yaanga man walked in the Greathouse after dark. They only had second and third hand stories of Nicolas Jose sightings but no-one other than Spaniard soldiers had seen or spoken to him since his arrest.

Charaana’s face was a flurry of emotions. She listed rumors of Nicolas Jose’s fall.

“Some of the new ones from the coast say he tried to get them to help with his plan against one of the brown robes. If you think he was fighting our fight, no, no, no.” With a grin.

"He went crazy like a whirly beetle. One day he would ride up to our group when we were pulling up the plants. He would yell that we were lazy and the worst crew in the fields. The next day he said 'Good! Good! You are doing good!' If there was a new sexy girl, he'd stay and watch us and talk until the girl ignored him. Then he would say something to show he was boss and ride away. A pretend Spaniard! Until he met Juanita!"

She grinned again. "Now, here's what I heard happened" She described the infatuation, obsession and marriage proposal and the laughter that ran through the fields. Juanita's feeling of shame and her fear of losing respect by the other women and her meeting with Jose.

"I know this part." The smiling man added. "I was taught to ride horses. Jose was new but he was always the best rider. He helped us learn." He shook his head. "He changed one day. He'd been homesick but now he was smiling and singing, talking about this Juanita. He was going to marry her. She wanted them to escape to his family's village in the south. They got the Padre to keep Nicolas Jose away from her but he went crazy."

Hachaaynar's face sagged in disappointment. Her judgment was vindicated. It was more sadness than victory, but enough tricks had been played. When we want something badly, we trick ourselves.

The man continued. "He wanted to kill them. Juanita, Jose and the Brownrobe Somera. He asked young people and new people to do this. He didn't ask people who knew him."

Charaana spoke up. "The little brother of one of our new girls was the one who he talked into it but he's just a little cub. He said yes, but when it was the real thing, he got scared. This isn't something you should find hope in." Making a cutting motion that the story was over. "He isn't Nahaanpar."

<<< 0 >>>

Andres and Lopez found Nicolas Jose sitting crosslegged against the wall on his mat. He greeted them with a mild smile.

"I'll give you no trouble. I've made peace with my devils. They are no longer with me."

Andres looked at the man who strode about with such airs and manipulation. Something was definitely changed. It was a different man who held his hands out to him to be restrained.

Lopez fastened the cuffs and frowned. "What's happened to you? Has Christ finally entered you?"

"It could be." Willing to accept anything. There wasn't a name.

Walking in the dirt to the main Mission building, Nicolas Jose wondered if Christ could give this feeling of connectedness with life, ancestors and the world. Could the Padres show this vision of the illness he needed to shed? He saw that his need to win at games, to learn what made the metals and cloth of the Spaniards so special that he would leave his family for them, to need to have sex and control over the women and to have control over the people under him was a sickness. He had fed this sickness to control everyone. It was a part in him that grew even crazier when he was trying to please and speak for the invaders. He was surprised to use the word for himself. 'The Invaders'.

It was the chanting of the old stories for his ancestors, for the creation of the world, for the blessings of the Earth, Sun and Moon that brought him this peace. The repetition soothed and helped him to be ready to step into death.

Officers Olivera, Pico, Verdugo, Alvarado and Galvez sat in a semi-circle. Padres Cambon and Somera flanked them. Olivera presided. Cordero, the only man with a firearm, sat in the back of the room with the two new Franciscans who were being trained for Mission duty.

The prisoner and two soldiers entered. The relaxed humility of Nicolas Jose was unlike him. He seemed neither rebellious or ashamed, merely accepting. He nodded in a bow to the officers and Padres and was seated.

He listened to the charges calmly. The boy was brought in. He answered in his hesitant way about being approached and convinced to do the "evil thing" by this man who promised him extra food and protection. That no one would be in the chapel. Escape would be easy.

Next Cordero described the sullen changes in attitude and drunkenness of Nicolas Jose. His violence in words and deeds and "anti-Spanish" sentiments.

He let the facts wash over him like cooling water, eyes focused beyond the tabletop, nodding at recognition of his failed acts and foolish obsession, thinking 'I am ready to die. I can die now.'

As he was questioned, he was calm and humble. He spoke directly to Padre Somera.

"All they say is true. I was foolish. I didn't see any good in things. I only saw what I wanted. What I wanted to have. You see I was filled with evil. I tried to kill you. I only saw anger for not having what I wanted. What I thought I wanted."

He remembered words of the Padre's books and in the Masses. It came back to him.

"I was Coveting, because I wanted something I couldn't have and was crazy angry. It was Lust because I wanted a woman with a need that made me blind and made me angry more. And 'Thou shall not kill,' the worst commandment. That is where the crazy person took control."

He kept his eyes on Somera. "Please forgive my bad actions, Padre Somera. I am ready to die if you wish."

The room was silent and amazed by his command of Spanish and clarity. It wasn't the Nicolas Jose they'd known.

Lopez shuffled, unable to keep quiet. He raised his hand for recognition by Olivera.

"Sir. When I brought the prisoner, he talked this way. I asked if Christ had come to him, He told us that he had. That he had accepted Christ into his heart."

Cordero winced. "Is he crazy too!?'

Olivera weighed it. It was an opportunity to keep from losing a useful asset. If he could be rehabilitated after an imprisonment and kept under supervision, he could train the next wave of overseers and spread understanding of The Empire's goals.

"Look how good his Spanish is!" Alvarado said. "Look at his humility and the remorse in his eyes. Hearing him speak this way. This isn't the man I'd come to know. I don't really understand but……this is surprising."

"We've trusted him as a communicator. He became the best and kept order." Looking back to Cordero, squirming and rolling his eyes. "On the other hand, he had abused the trust by womanizing, being arrogant with both Indians and soldiers, and by plotting our deaths. How can we see him as other than a threat to our security?" Expecting Nicolas Jose to react, but seeing the same resigned neutrality.

"We must give this some thought."

Somera didn't want a conclusion made too early if a true conversion to the faith was shown. "I'll speak for the Church, if I may." Knowing the two new Brothers were enthralled by this seeming miraculous conversion.

"I saw the development of this situation. I worried about his drinking and especially his misuse of women. I respected his willingness to learn and to follow directions. I've felt that of all the natives, he was most suitable to be Alcalde, but for his temper. I saw how the loss of his wife and child made him desperate for a stable life and how this young Juanita became too much of a temptation for him."

"She came to me in sincerity, hoping that I could bless the union that she and the young boy wanted. To help Nicolas Jose to understand their desire to make a life together in peace." He watched the prisoner's relaxed face and calm eyes turned toward him. "The way he reacted was frightening."

Nicolas Jose couldn't dispute it. Listening to one after another describe his behavior and faults. 'That's all fair.' He nodded. 'Get it finished.'

After a long litany, Olivera signaled to Lopez and Andres. "Return the prisoner to his cell."

On the walk back Lopez said. "I remember some of the good things you had done. When Rodriguez started the war and you negotiated. That was good. You may have saved us all."

The prisoner smiled to himself. To him it was a half remembered drunken fog after many helpings of 'The Blood of Christ.'

CHAPTER 16

RECRUITMENT - 1779 - 1780

It fell upon Lt. Governor Don Fernando Rivera y Moncada to oversee the recruitment of soldiers to escort the settlers to the new civilian settlement. It wasn't at all as difficult as the previous attempts.

Families with strong children were the first priority and soldiers who had their own famiies who could follow were the most desirable.

Private Pablo Antonio de Cota was ready for any travels that would find a better place to raise his family, but the big incentive was the common knowledge that large land grants were going to be given out to soldiers who had proven service to the Crown.

He had traveled with Portola in 1769 and continued all the way to the bay of Monterey area before it was chosen as the capitol. He was with Padre Junipero Serra in founding Mission San Antonio.

Escorting poblabores to Mission San Gabriel and the new Pueblo of the Angels sounded like a good choice. He went to his wife, Juana Maria de Lugo.

"We are moving. Have our things packed by Monday."

He went to his older brother, Private Roque Jacinto de Cota, and was enthusiastic about the decision to leave.

"Go with Moncada and me. It is going to be a great town with a Presidio on the sea, away from the Franciscans and full of cattle and land to grow on."

Roque went to his wife, Maria Verdugo, and told her with a firm voice.

"We are moving. Have our things packed by Monday. "

YAANGA

Tooypor, Hachaaynar and the four runners moved through the dry weeds of the flatland to Yaanga. It spread four hundred round huts over four low rolling hills with rocky streambeds separating them. Smoke rose from morning cooking fires and hung above the valley. The haze was held steady by the ocean breezes as it was pinned against the northern mountain range.

At the outskirts they passed flattened huts being burned because of insect and rodent infestations. Two playful families with their possessions bundled in mats on their backs, headed to the opposite side of the village to build new homes.

Walking past large and old homes toward the Greathouse. They went between shapely piles of rocks to divert the rains into channels between the houses.

Yaan-vik and five elders stood at the doorway with their guards. He'd heard of Tooypor and had met Hachaaynar before he was Sevaanga-vik. The runners went aside to play with walnut dice.

The chief spoke. "Those from the coast are on their way. Runners from Puvin-gna have arrived in advance. The Chief of Pimo-gna is already here. Come in. We are eager to hear you."

They sat in a circle of twenty men, all older than Hachaaynar and Tooypor. Hachaaynar was known as a boy in the company of his father. Yaan-vik stood beside the young pair.

"This is Pula Tooypor of Haapchivet. Advisor to both her own village and to Seebag-na."

"Aren't you Serrano? Isn't Haapchivet a Serrano village in the mountains?" Asked a Yaanga elder.

Another answered. "I knew her father, Japchi-vik. He is Tongva, Iitax'um like us. There are Seranno there. I've been there. This one probably speaks both languages. They are good honest traders. I've seen her trading in Yaanga."

Yaan-vik put his hand on Hachaaynar's shoulder. "And I knew 'Ahtooshe', Hachaaynar's mother. A great Pula, worthy in every way. She taught our Pul medicines from the Mojave. She helped stop the cramps and yellow runs. She was killed by the Beard soldier who killed old Sevaanga-vik. Seeba-gna had bad luck. We need to help them. The bad luck may come to us next. We will hear them."

Hachaaynar looked sadly to Tooypor. He had to do the backtracking of the facts by himself.

"I have bad news. An opportunity came from a…rumor from the invader's camp. It was false. The Seeba-gna man who became our hope turned out to be false. I am sorry to have called you here. I will offer trading concessions in your choices of Seebag-na offerings. Our leached acorn meal is the best in the valleys, and from Tooypor's instruction and our women's crews, our medicines are among the best."

He tapped his chest with a sidewards glance, seeing Tooypor's approval. "It is with great embarrassment, but with great respect for your safety, that we say this is a wrong time to bring the villages together against the invaders." Gesturing for Tooypor to stand and speak.

"I was very honored to be chosen by Pula Ah'too'che as her pupil, Our Haapchivet Pul Tuwaru chose me to be his successor. Our location, high in the mountains, had me travel far along the coasts and deep in the deserts to trade and learn from the Pulum of other regions. I saw that many are ready to fight the invaders, but only if others would join them. We thought this was the time," pausing and making eye contact with the stronger looking of the younger men.

"This is not the time. Nothing could be worse than losing our best people through poor planning. But…" Gesturing inclusively. "Prepare! When the time is right and the right plan is in place, with help on the inside, we will call on you. You will be prepared and we will win. We will live in our lands without invaders. Our children will live in our ways. Prepare! Together we will end their terror. We will win."

<<< 0 >>>

Hachaaynar and Tooypor reached Seebag-na after dark. Tired from walking and relieved that they hadn't been mocked.

"You handled it well." She rephrased it several times but never got a reaction other than a grunt. "Do you trust me that what I told them is true?," pulling him down on the mat with her and rubbing the back of his neck. "You know the time will come don't you?" Gently biting on his shoulders until he shrugged loose and faced her. Looking down in his anguished eyes, she saw his hopes for a revolt connected with Nahaanpar's return were deeper than she'd seen.

"He was your teacher." She whispered as he pressed his brow to her shoulder and into the nape of her neck. He didn't want her to see his face. It was more emotion than he wanted to show. She rolled to the side to see him better. He touched the side of her cheek.

"He was my father's guard. He was my mother's guard. He was my teacher. He was the man that father trusted to go back and forth from the invaders to Seebag-na to help us survive and to defeat them. He was my best friend. I had friends my own age but he was the only grown-up I could ask questions and get clear answers."

"I wanted him to talk about what men and women did when we went to your ceremony." Forcing a smile to her. "I thought about you all the time. I started to feel that he didn't care about us anymore on that trip. When we returned, he had private meetings with my father. Then he was gone for many seasons, until he came with them, on a horse. He was one of them!" She saw beginnings of a tear but looked at his mouth, ignoring it 'Silly', she thought, how men think of themselves.

"He looked right at me and my mother as though we were strangers, then he spoke to my father in their words, as to an enemy. I was confused and I hated him. All the trust I had put in him, All the trust my family put in him!"

She kissed him. "It was a horrible betrayal."

"When my mother was taken and my father killed by their men, I suspected he was part of it, and when you negotiated with him, he knew they were holding my mother prisoner, but said nothing. I wanted to kill him. I wanted one of our people to kill him,...but when I heard about his arrest and organizing neophytes to kill Beards, I forgot the betrayal. It sounded like what my father wanted him to do. It made sense to me. Isn't that crazy? After all this time, this traitor, and I let stupid hopes!… I made this crazy wish!…I betrayed my father, and he could see me doing it! He could see into my heart and see that I would trust his killers!"

She kissed him again. "You didn't have information other than rumor, a good sounding rumor that gave you hope." Smoothing his brow. "We all want that."

"But you knew!" He said. "You told us to wait."

"I only trust full information. I've seen him more, and more recently than you have. The rumors didn't make sense."

"My vision was wrong. It wasn't worthy of the leader of a village. I could have led us into a trap."

"You didn't. You listened." He closed his eyes and spoke almost inaudibly. "My father didn't listen. So many died."

"You did. So many were saved."

He buried his face in her chest. She stroked his hair. His hands ran along her waist as she slid down to meet his mouth.

"You listened. You were wonderful."

"You were the wonderful one."

Nicolas Jose slept early without dreams or fear. His death would release him to the arms of his father and mother. He would walk the path of Chinigchnich and dance in the respect of his ancestors. Looking at a misused life. It was a compact joke with a beginning, a crazy middle, and finally, a happy end. A completed circle in a story of foolishness.

He woke again, admiring the ceiling beams, straightness and beauty. If there was one worthwhile thing he learned from these people it was working the wood into precise shapes. A thing his father would be proud of.

Boots echoed in the short hallway. He stretched and rose. The key moved the clumsy lock with a low click. Lopez entered with Cordero standing back, expecting trouble and wearing a look of contempt.

Nicolas Jose found it funny. “You’ll get your chance to shoot me later. I won‘t give you an excuse today.”

Lopez looked back to Cordero. “I don‘t think anybody‘s going to be shot today.” They walked to the chapel and stood him before the seated tribunal.

“Nicolas Jose.” Alvarado began. “Do you admit that you initiated and conspired in a plan to kill Padre Somera and the neophytes Juanita de Diego and Jose Rivera?”

He felt comfortable saying. “Yes sir, I did.”

“Do you understand that the penalty is death?” Looking to Somera and Cambon. “That can be death?”

“Yes sir, I do.”

“If your life were spared, Nicolas Jose. If you were imprisoned and put to hard labor, would you continue to plot against us?”

He hadn’t considered lately that he might not be killed. What would he do? Dig trenches or saw wood? Would he be kicked by the guards? What did this have to do with his view on his life and death?

“I understand my wrong to you and the young people that I wronged. I have no anger. I am ready to die.”

Alvarado again signaled to Lopez. “Take the prisoner back to his cell.”

Time passed slowly. He paced, sat and paced again. He’d seen the path, and now, it may have been a dream. A myriad of paths wove and shifted before him. ‘What a trickster life is,’ his mind churning. He started the old chants and sought unity with his ancestors. He began a dance. The dance and chant that he had last danced high up in the mountains at Tooypor’s womanhood rites.

As he quietly repeated the motions and trancelike words, he visualized his family, but also young Hachaaynar and Tooypor, the two children who were now powerful people in their world.

His consciousness slowly embraced, 'their world is also my world' and soon including 'my parent's world.' As he contemplated his place in the world of spirit and matter, he danced amid images of the invader's Jesus, a bearded man in white robes, a bleeding thin man nailed to crossed lengths of wood. A huge white bearded God who was angry in the sky. A pale and sad, quiet woman in long dark red robes who misses her son.

His eyes were closed as he shuffled, lips moving, around the cell in a giant world of spirits that stretched on forever, including every person, tree and animal. Again he said. "I am ready to die."

He flopped down on the mat in exhaustion with pain in his lower back and thought of the possibility that he would be imprisoned or exiled. He spoke slowly to the patterned ceiling thinking of the worst pain he could expect at labor.. "I am ready to live."

<<< 0 >>>

'Aachvet heard a runner from Seebag-na with a report about the invader's village and his sister's intervention to prevent an attack. He called elders and Pul Tuwaru.

Pul Turaru claimed that days before, he had a vision of many villagers running through a woods of tall pine and being trapped and killed by falling trees, until Tooypor came through a bright field, standing before the forest. The trees stopped falling.

'Aachvet was always surprised by the interest his little sister created, even when she wasn't around. 'It's a good thing they don't see what a brat she can be'. 'Falling trees' is the way the invaders' firesticks were described, although he had never heard one.

"Send a runner to Seebag-na to see if she will return to us." A respected elder said.

After a moment's thought 'Aachvet said. “I'll take four guards. I will go myself.”

<<< 0 >>>

Pico, Alvarado, and Verdugo listened. Olivera asked their opinion on the outcome of several verdicts. All except Cordero agreed his death would serve no useful purpose

“But would it be better if he were held for a while at San Diego?” Alvarado asked.

Pico shook his head. “What will be the reaction if he is held here for several months? until we know the sincerity of his conversion, if that‘s what we call it, we need to listen to the ones in construction and the fields. We need a new translator who can be accurate. We haven‘t done our job in developing a second level of supervisors. Nicolas Jose was our one and only with the skills.”

Verdugo, who had spent the most time with the cooking staff, spoke. “The next best in understanding directions and giving directions is Marco, the kitchen overseer. He speaks more Spanish than the others.”

“What tribe or village is he from?” Pico asked.

“I don‘t know. Does it matter?”

“Very much.” Pico replied. “We don't want anyone local or with the same dialect as Nicolas Jose. We want opinions from neophytes other than Seeba or Yaanga persons. That is the first thing.” He tapped the table with his index finger for emphasis. “We want a person who only has Spanish, not another language or dialect, in common with Nicolas Jose to then sit in the cell with him and draw him out. We can listen unobserved. We need to know what he really thinks. Whether he'll be safe in the future. It may be a short time if he is sincere. If he's not, we need to remove him quickly.”

Olivera wondered what made this protected-from-above Africano such a planner and plotter, usually with clear notions. He rarely spoke, but when he did, it was with an answer that was unassailable.

Alvarado spoke. "I'll call the other men together. We'll build the next level of overseers. We'll interview this Marco and learn more about the tribes and languages of the men."

Pico interjected. "None of this will be mentioned to the Padres. Control of the native population is the business of Spain, not the Church. It is important to know their dialects and tribal background to use differences among them. To find their divisions and emphasize them. I've been compiling dictionaries of their key words for my use. Language is the most important weapon the Empire has to control populations. It's proper use will neutralize dissent faster than firearms."

The soldiers nodded like they understood, but knew that only sword, musket and canon solved the questions of empire.

Hachaaynar and Tooypor walked the freshly damp land to the southwest of the village. It had been half a moon since the meeting in Yaanga. 'Aachvet stayed two days expecting excitement, but left with acorn meal and a small metal bell.

There was no news from the Mission. The few who'd made the run at night had listened and asked around, but Nicolas Jose was still in his cell and the soldiers and brownrobes showed no change in what they did and said.

After two weeks Tooypor said. "I'll leave for Haapchivet in the Morning."

He held her shoulders. "It's the right thing. You helped me see things hidden. Things that seemed real because of wishes. Not real things. I thought it was a vision. It was only a wish."

She hugged him. "I've seen visions that proved to be false. I've felt ashamed." Holding him tight. "People rely on me. On things I say. They change their lives. I don't always know if I'm right."

"You were right this time." Whispering in her ear. "Many people are alive because you made us wait."

She closed her eyes, pressed against his chest. "I'm glad we are here. We didn't die this time, but in my heart's vision, I'm not sure this wasn't the right time to call the villages. That this wasn't the time they could have been beaten. When there are less soldiers there. When their dog-man wasn't with them."

After a sleep interrupted by incomplete dreams she called her runners together. He sat on a boulder watching her leave, their hearts and eyes filled with love, sadness and hope with their world in delicate balance, knowing they were the only ones who could save or lose the future, at nineteen Autumns of age.

SEPTEMBER 1780

Private Galvez rode the southern end of the Mission holdings looking for the promised party of settlers and governmental surveyors from Baja California. He watched for horses coming down from the foothill pass trail from River Santa Ana. At noon he saw lines of wagons descending into the flatlands. He galloped to the Mission.

Father Crespi stepped out of the chapel.

"Padre Crespi." The Sergeant shouted. "They're here." Pointing. "To the left of the pepper field oaks."

Crespi said. "Tell them we've prepared a large camping space against the north wall. Take them there." Galvez rode south.

Crespi spoke to Verdugo. "It's the engineering party for the space near Yaanga. I picked that out with Portola. How long ago? Twelve years ago!"

Verdugo said. "We can't let the Russians come further down… God knows their Eastern Church isn't Christian!"

"Barely Christian." Knowing the soldier didn't care about the differences but was trying please him. Plans for new settlements were always vague and secretive.

He called the four Padres to come inside the chapel.

"Be courteous to the guests and report all conversations related to the new settlements to me. We mustn't let the godless ones control the allocation of food or control over the neophytes. This is the outpost of the Church of Rome and not of secularists of tho Crown."

OCTOBER - 1780

Eight Afro-Mexican settlers, Corporal Ramirez, two privates as well as surveyor Emilio Cervantes carried the preparatory plans for the new town from Governor Philipe De Neve. It would be the largest civilian settlement on the coast.

After an orientation by Olivera at sundown, the four mulatto men and their wives prepared huts outside the north wall. Cervantes directed them.

Crespi, Cambon and Somera invited them to evening mass. They looked confused until Olivera ordered them to attend and they complied grudgingly.

After the service and seeing only that two knew the words and what was expected in a Mass, Father Crespi left with a headache.

<<< 0 >>>

Tribespeople often came in groups to Tooypor's hut for cures and advice. Distant ones told of increased travel of invaders on the trail they called Kah'mee'noh. They described giant horses pulling carriages with old men in brightly colored uniforms or brown robes. Some carried large boxes of wood and metal. Tooypor found it important that the number returning south had increased. Runners came from the Kumeyaay and coastal Tongva telling of a large party that left the San Diego soldier's base to the south going to the Mission near Seebag-na.

Tooypor packed hurredly and left for Seebag-na. She was surprised that there were so many visitors in the village from Yaanga. She sat in the Greathouse beside Hachaaynar listening to their stories of beards with sticks and strings, making marks on white leaves. There were marked spaces only several stones throw from Yaanga.

Four villagers agreed to defect to the Mission and live as neophytes to learn the invader's plans.

Charaana reported. "New soldiers have arrived from their Diego base. They accompany nine builders to do something near Yaanga. They ride out and come back to the Mission. The Padres are angry at the new soldiers and builders because they leave food on the ground. They don't clean and we have to make their beds. They drink the sacrament wine. They smoke a crazy weed. They joke and disrespect about the Padre's gods."

Tooypor saw opportunity in access to the soldier's quarters. She thought about kitchen access. There were several poisons that could be hidden in the invader's spicy foods. The chilis could mask bitter tastes. She could plant trustworthy ones with Charaana in the kitchen. "It looks like they are making plans for an invader village next to Yaanga. She said to a visiting elder. "A village of invaders next to yours may destroy it." Tooypor saw again that with the arrival of more invaders, time was turning against a successful attack

NOVEMBER 1780

Two dust encrusted messengers arrived in the afternoon with dispatches that threw the Mission into turmoil.

One was from the Franciscan Order to Padre Cresi. The other was addressed to Sergeant Olivera from the Northern Colonial Administration. Both announced parties would soon be en-route to inspect the Mission.

The governmental dispatch was from Viceroy Bucareli and Commandant General de la Croix. Governor Filipe De Neve would arrive within two months and would need sleeping arrangements for five officials, twenty soldiers and thirty to forty new colonists with additional livestock.

Alvarado called the men to his office in two shifts.

"We've been hosting those builders on their mysterious mission near the Yaanga village." Holding up the five page document. "Now it's clear. The plan is for a civilian pueblo near Mission

San Gabriel that will be a center for cattle herding. The first colonists are builders and farmers, but the herds from the Mission will be moved closer to the new pueblo. It will be very large to produce food for the presidios. A seaport is planned. All the land north of Seeba village will be grazing land."

Pico said. "This place has been stagnating under the Franciscans. This will mean large land grants for all of you. A growing pueblo."

Alvarado agreed. "Lord knows we aren't paid half the time and food isn't always on the table."

Olivera added. "We were the first wave of the Empire. We'll be appreciated by the Crown for all this…shit. We have to make sure it's a success for De Neve. We are no longer subservient to the Franciscans. We have a clear claim to the lands. The English and Russians can no longer occupy it." All the soldiers understood that the message held visions of a wealthy future. Father Crespi walked the inner courtyard noticing things he'd passed over until he heard that Governor De Neve would stay at Mission San Gabriel Archangel.

The directive came from Mexico City and passed through Sonora. Most Reverend Father Francis Palou had signed it. Although the emphasis was on making the grounds ready for the De Neve party, it included a reference to a journey to the north by Father Junipero Serra.

"This will never pass inspection by Serra." He told Cambon and Somera. "With soldiers tearing up the fields and furniture. The loose morals of the natives will have to be changed. The Alcalde will have to drive the neophytes harder to clean up the grounds."

Somera said. "It's his job to promote discipline and cleanliness. The soldiers won't. "

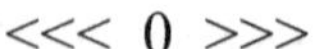

Nicolas Jose entered the expanded chapel and faced Padres Crespi, Cambon, Somera and Delacour. He'd regained their trust after two years of exemplary service. He'd learned the responses in the Latin Mass and Common Prayers. He'd witnessed and assisted marriages and christenings. He had a greater command of Spanish and understanding and willingness to accomplish the goals of the Church. After hearing the first of the two critical problems, the quartering of up to one hundred visitors, he asked.

"Can we build thatched wooden lean-tos along the courtyard walls with circles of tents in the center yard? I'm sure the soldiers have tents. Can we send a rider to see what they are bringing with them?"

Crespi acknowledged. "Good. We'll ask the military people. They aren't cooperative. This will make them more arrogant."

"I'll make a plan to make the grounds so they're clean. It will look good to any visitor." Nicolas Jose bowed.

Cambon continued. "I remember that in the past you were aware of relations between the soldiers and some of the neophyte young women." Nicolas Jose thought 'What a polite way to say that.'

"We have seen open displays and fraternization with neophytes that suggests fornication. This must be stopped."

"I will speak to both the soldiers and the women. If they consort," pausing dramatically. "It will be through the blessings of marriage,"

Nicolas Jose saw the division between the Vatican and the Crown. He'd learned from Corporal Andres that the last church group that started to convert native populations, the Jesuits, had come out of favor with the royal families, called "The Crown."

The Jesuits were expelled and, Corporal Andres said, some were killed for siding with the 'Indians,' to the far south in a fight against 'The Crown.'

That 'Crown' had been the 'Habsburg Crown,' but now it was a different 'Crown,' which was called the 'Bourbon Crown,' with a 'Carlos number three' wearing the Crown, which is a real hat made from a rare metal called 'gold'.

Andres spent time with Nicolas Jose. He read leather bound books brought with the supplies. He said his 'patron' in Sonora paid extra for them to be delivered. He was learning a language called 'French.' He was interested in the customs of the Tongva Iitaxum, The People of the Land.

Nicolas Jose thumbed through the books, squinted and ran his fingertips over the fine graining and embossed gold and black lettering on the deep red leather. 'How do they do that?' Andres explained but it seemed impossible.

Andres talked about history. About Europe and what were called 'The Americas.' He showed that the Tongva lands were only a small spot on the map. Less than a fingernail on the soldier's map. He told about the histories of the Crowns. The 'Hapsburgs' and the 'Bourbons.' In one of the stories he told about destruction of Barcelona and why Rodriguez became so crazy, but they agreed that it didn't matter what caused it. Crazy is crazy. Bad is bad.

He learned that the "Catholic Church, "Jesus Christ" and "The Word of God" were things taken very seriously by those of the religious orders, but "The Crown," "Spain" and "The Empire" saw the religion as a way to control land and the people on it. As long as religion didn't get in the way of expansion it was supported. When it became inconvenient, it was ignored or suppressed, like the Jesuits.

After the meeting with the Padres, Nicolas Jose found Andres in the stable preparing for night rounds. They compared the Church and military meetings and goals.

"You can become a top person, maybe Alcalde if they build the new Pueblo if you impress De Neve and the administrators with your work."

"I can do this. I can have the neophytes keep their lust out of sight, but, I will need your help with the soldiers."

Andres chuckled. "I'm already joked about as a celibate priest in training. If I start ordering my comrades to keep away from women they might arrange an accident for me." but Andres put up his hand. "I'm joking. The risking of the promise of large land grants will make them behave."

Nicolas Jose said. "We can work together."

<<< 0 >>>

In his quarters he burned a candle and stood in the center of the small room's carefully assembled wooden floor. He had patiently laid it as a month-long evening project. It was the smoothest and most precisely fitted floor in the compound.

As he did every evening, he started the chant for the cycles of the Moon and Mother Earth, the Blessings of Father Sun, and then an appeal to his ancestors, moving softly in circles repeating the words, thinking of his tasks in life.

Before sleep, he made a perfunctory genuflection to the crucifix in the corner and softly said. "Bless this home. Bless my People's home and Bless my People. Keep them safe" He then lay down to sleep in the Real World.

The Real World was the world of ancestors and the world that he'd envisioned at the time he'd passed out of his crazy-life and found his true-person. Where Sun, Moon and Stars rained life on Mother Earth. Where Chinigchnich had walked to land. Where the creation of the world on the backs of seven huge turtles caused chaos and Wiote brought the Humans to safety from the vicious Original Creatures.

The religion of the Padres, of Jesus Christ, walking on water, God in the Heavens creating the earth in seven days, the giant vicious Satan in Hell, even the Angels seemed a reflection of the Spirits that are part of Life and Living in the Real World.

He accepted that many in the Church and Empire believed in these things and, in their angry and fearful way, wanted all the people in 'Their Empire' to say the words, in the other language, that would make them obedient.

It made sense. The control they kept over his people didn't make him angry as long as they lived by the gentle words of their Savior. Rodriguez wasn't a Christian. Some of the soldiers were in the grip of sinfulness. Sevaanga-vik was foolish to attack the Spanish before he knew what had happened to 'Ahtooshe'. Three Hawk's attack was foolish.

There could be peace if the Spanish were wise with the tribes-people. There would be more food and protection from angry weather.

If we work well and avoid the sickness, we can be comfortable and happy, holding the old ways in our hearts, living by the rules of the Church. It could be done if he could be a good steward and Alcalde.

There had been no woman in his life for these two years. He was formal and distant to the ones he'd slept with and polite to the young attractive ones.

'A wife may or not come. It is well either way.' He'd formulated. 'I'll find ways to be of service. I'll be a servant.' A wave of peace had washed away his desire for power.

In the predicted hot spell Seebag-na had prepaired bundles of leached acorn meal, cattail pollen, herb, honey and agave paste sweeteners for Yaanga'a great winter trade fair.

The Pase'keg-nahs brought the best flat throwing sticks for rabbit hunting. Asuks-gna people brought their special herbs and large crude baskets and thatched wall panel coverings.

The bear rugs and shoulder covers that Aachvet brought would bring business for Haapchivet. It was a cold winter. Obsidian spear and arrowheads were always in demand. He wanted items from the coast. Dried fish from Pu'vung-na in the south and preserved shellfish, seashell and dentalium small cutting instruments and jewelry from Topang-na and Pemuu'nga.

Hachaaynar led carriers across the vivid summer plains to Yaanga. Kwetii' and Kyukyu carried a heavy load on a wood pallet doubling as a lean-to wall. Charaana and Sa'ar'i risked coming from the Mission at night.

Tooypor's delivery of a healthy baby boy brought joy when the babies crying and laughter brought wonder and immediacy to her home, but fear for the babies safety was always there. Hachaaynar had only seen the baby six times since birth.

Tooypor and the infant came down the long trail from her hut with two runners. She held tight to the napping boy and broke past the pines and clumps of dense brush, passing the Pase'keg-na outer huts onto the plain. To the southeast, she saw the new high tower at the Mission, and beyond, Seebag-na village in the gray-brown mist.

She looked right and saw Yaanga. On the outskirts were dozens of lean-tos, hastily built kitcha huts and a few blankets from the far eastern deserts.

Hachaaynar saw her coming down the hill. He ran with Kwetii' and held the baby, laughing at how he had grown.

“How strong and handsome he looks!” To hide his tears, he turned and buried his face in the babies stomach covering it with kisses. Tooypor saw it all, grinning at her husband's display of emotion. ‘A thing more pleasing than strength.’

“He's handsome and strong like his father.”

Tooypor and Hachaaynar carried two-year-old Ka'ari'par through the aisles.

Over thirty displays were spread on mats and blankets. Blackened sandstone bowls and jars. Tightly woven bowls and water carrying bottles made of woven seaweeds covered in the tar that bubbled above Mali-wu, treated until water wouldn't leak from them on a long desert trip.

There were new crafts influenced by the techniques of the invaders. Forearm sized squares of smoothed wood with flat bottoms to hold mud and straw to dry and become flat fitted stones for floors.

Tooypor handled a soft circle of woven strips of cloth. Discarded or stolen Mission clothes were cut into strips, died with herbal dies of many colors and woven in a circular design with a hole on the middle to put over the head and drape over the body to the waist. She heard coughing from the back of the improvised hut, the sound that ran through every village.

She put the cloak on and turned to Hachaaynar. Charaana said it was beautiful and a good choice. Tooypor removed it and draped over Charaana's shoulders.

"Would you have it?"

Charaana looked down as though ashamed to receive a gift. "It is pretty, but no."

"It is beautiful." Taking Charaana's hand. "But I couldn't wear it. I think you know why."

"I couldn't wear it in the Mission. They'd know it's their material and not Tongva."

"And we couldn't wear it in the villages because we know that it's material from the invaders." Tooypor lifted it off of and handed it to the Asuks-na woman who'd made it. "It is beautiful, but we could not wear it."

The woman looked back to her husband, who said, "We are proud of how it feels and looks, but you aren't the first to say that. I won't wear it. My wife won't wear it, even though we admire it."

Tooypor gave respectful complements to them on the quality of their work, but added. "No-one of self respect would wear or own anything of the invaders. Wear it but only in your home."

The couple said. "We understand. You said it more politely than the last men who stopped. They said that we might be killed for collaborating with the invaders. We will take your advice, Pula'pahr. Thank you."

They wandered more stalls. Displays of otter and seal furs, long flexible hut supports, flutes, drums, gourds and hollowed out wooden clacker musical instruments.

Tooypor watched children playing on the ground at the side of the display areas. Clumps played tag games. Some had to hop holding one ankle up to catch each other. Some ran backwards looking and laughing over their shoulders.

One group, making drawings on the ground, made her walk away from Hachaaynar with the baby in her arms. They were making drawings in the sand with twigs. One bent low in concentration making a large village of huts and stick men. A few feet away two sisters were beginning and wiping out each others drawings, alternately laughing and screaming at each other.

She moved to four boys kneeling at the far side with sad faces. One had light tear marks running down the dirt on his cheeks. She looked at the symbols of family, village marks and seasons. There were marks for death circling each area. They scribbled with such intensity she squatted to look into their faces. The one in front looked up and tried to smile to an older person. His teeth were pink with blood as he tried to suppress his coughs.

When they returned to the Seebag-na lean-to Sa'a'ri' was calling to them. Kwetii' was jumping in the air grinning and pointing to packets of meal on the mats and the large packs against the back wall. Less than a third was left and the day was less than half over.

Hachaaynar slapped his chest. “Now we’ll trade with your brother. Spear heads, arrowheads and blades.”

He looked at the hilltop to the north. Four horses and men were silhouetted against the distant purple mountains. “Invaders are watching us.”

Eyes turned to the hill from the trade fair.

“They are too few to attack us, but they see that we are many here.”

Hachaaynar felt alarm. “Is Seebag-na safe” Looking east.

CHAPTER 17

7 HILLS - A ROMAN DESIGN

For the fifth day Engineer Cervantes and three guards left their temporary camp pitched against the northern Mission wall. They'd camped for a week without socializing with the soldiers or the sullen and uncooperative Padres.

The flat plains to the east of Yaanga promised a classical Roman model. Symmetrical and expandable between and over the seven hills adjacent to it.

"A Rome in the making." He'd say. "Filippe chose this location well."

He rode the trail along the foothills to overlook Yaanga and mark the northern boundaries. It was tempting to continue to the pass at Cahueng-na to build in the flats below but Yaanga gave better access to the seaports to be. Below him a throng of Indians was setting up what looked like a Turkish bizarre.

"What are they doing in our field?"

"I don't think joining them will be a good idea, Sir." Said Corporal Fuentes.

"I agree, Sir." Cervantes said. "We'll observe from afar." Leading to the top of the hill and dismounting.

"Look." Fuentes pointed west and east. "More Indians coming from all over."

"Like a Moorish fair in Barcelona. Do you think they have fish?" Cervantes asked, sitting in a grassy spot, pulling out a flask of brandy and passing it around.

They watched for an hour and returned to the Mission. There would be two weeks to prepare the field and documents for the arrival of the Governor.

"They can enjoy their field for now, but very soon it will be our Pueblo of the Angels."

PRESIDIO SAN DIEGO

Gunsmith, Antonio Miranda Rodriguez sat in the Presidio infirmary with his daughter, Maria Margarita, in deep depression. She had slept fitfully with deep wheezing and fevers for the past three days, as had he. He prayed constantly for her survival.

"Sweet baby, Sweet baby girl. Kumuha rin. Huwag mamatay, Mahal.Laban!," in Tagalog, their own language from the Philippines.

Both of them were in isolation with smallpox. His wife had died on the trip from Sinaloa and they had the choice of returning or trying to reach the new pueblo.

He decided that they would press on in spite of the greater risk to them both.

The military doctor walked through the curtains with a brush of the hands and spoke softly.

"Senior Rodriguez," leaning forward to whisper. "If you continue with the Rivera party there is a good chance that both of you will die. It's more than a good chance. It's a certainty. There will be other settler parties leaving soon. Please reconsider. For both of you."

Antonio stroked Maria's hot forehead and felt her neck.

"We will stay until you tell me that it is safe, but if there is any chance.." looking imploringly, "please let us go with Governor Rivera."

<<< 0 >>>

He had heard the Fathers speak of 'Father Serra.' They sounded frightened when they spoke of him. They didn't speak of the 'Palou' person the same way, more admiration, not with fear.

Charaana moved next to him, asking. "Why have you picked us from the kitchen to be with these workers from the fields? Are there new crops to learn?"

"We're going to make the Mission shine more. We want to get the soldiers to be more respectful and not misuse our people." He said.

She squinted up. "You've become better in protecting us from the rude ones. I admire the way you have changed," stepping back to let others come closer.

A herd rider from the south came up. "The soldiers with the engineer said that more are coming. One of the soldiers is Tarahumara like me. He said important change. Do you know what he means?"

Nicolas Jose liked the man. He was a little like that Jose Rivera horseman. Looking back, he'd viewed Jose all wrong. If he were still here, he would be the best herder and his cheer and enthusiasm would help the other riders. But it was his own bad spirit time. He accepted it.

"Yes, there will be changes. I'll wait until everyone is here." The group filled out and he shouted.

"There will be more than one hundred visitors coming next week." Projecting to the standing group from a mound. "Some will be soldiers guarding the Governor of this region of the Empire of Spain. His name is De Neve. He'll bring farmers and herders to live and work near Yaanga in a new village. It won't be part of the Mission."

He made eye contact across the group. "The reason I've picked you is because you are the best people we have at the Mission. I say 'We' as the Alcalde. 'We' is the Franciscan Order. You are the ones who make everything work. Rodrigo keeps the herders organized, doing their rounds on time and keeping strays from getting away. Charaana makes sure that everyone is fed. She keeps the kitchen and eating areas clean. Over there I see Manuel, one of the groundskeepers for more than six years."

"I want you to make this better than it is. I know Manuel has seen soldiers dropping food on the ground, peeing and taking shits in the bushes and having sex. We'll tell them not to do that."

There was a stirring until Pedro Yavit spoke. “We can’t tell soldiers what to do.”

“We can we tell them what to do,” Nicolas Jose said loudly to the group, “and we can and will tell them what not to do to make this Mission respected.”

Charaana saw futility in any efforts to make the invaders respect the people of her land. All these schemes seem to work for a few days but would turn false. This plan gave a chance to work with other neophytes and talk about the soldiers actions. It was a good way to start and keep contacts with the new ones who can help when the time comes.

He continued. “We’ll keep all areas cleaner than they’ve ever been and we will not let them slip back. Anything you see you will fix. We will not have sex where it can be seen. Only with our mates in our rooms or far from the Mission in the woods. We won’t allow anyone else, including soldiers, to have sex. Only if they are married, in their own spaces.”

Those who’d known Nicolas Jose for more than two years found it hard to believe, but they’d seen no sign of his sexual or corrupt nature since his imprisonment.

“We will make this a place of Spirit. Those Spirits of the Catholic Church. And also of the Spirits of our Mother Earth.”

Murmurs of confusion rose at the two views of Spirit being interposed. The Fathers and soldiers told them that there was only one true God and that Jesus Christ was his living son on earth and that all of the old beliefs that differed were bad and sinful.

The Alcalde was saying that the old spirits were still part of this land. That the old lifeways were acceptable! The two soldiers leaning on the corral railing couldn’t understand what he was saying but felt the disturbance running through the listening crowd

“What did he say?”

The old Tongva man replied, “We will work hard. Much hard.”

Charaana planned to get Nicolas Jose alone and see what was in his mind. She saw the 'big changes' all around. She saw new European faces coming to the Mission. Nicolas Jose must know why and how and what these changes were.

"We will break into four groups. I'll appoint a leader for each. We'll assemble in the four corners of this corral and start our plans to make this place shine."

Nicolas Jose knew which overseers were the most moral and persuasive. He knew who were the most permissive and corrupted by favors or threats from the soldiers. He guessed, based on past encounters, that Cordero, Machado, Galvez and four of the new men were the main promoters of promiscuity. Andres and Pico were committed to their fiancée's in Mexico and he was confident they'd rejected infidelity.

Alvarado, Verdugo, Olivera, Lopez and the Padres were unknown. He didn't like thinking that the men of the Church might be taking advantage of the women who'd put their trust in them. He had noticed Somera in the past, looking with what might be called 'lust' at young girls on hot days, but that was far from immorality. He never saw coupling,

He mounted his horse, 'Toyeh', named for the holly plant.

"Ah'a'he." He greeted the crews of construction and fields, weighing each one as an asset or liability in making the Mission a better place.

He had heard the Fathers speak of 'Father Serra.' They sounded frightened when they spoke of him. They didn't speak of the 'Palou' person the same way, more admiration, not with fear.

He chose eight people in his first tour of the fields. The most visible problem would be the fields where men and women worked side by side. Next would be the kitchen and serving people, then groundskeepers. The grounds cleanup areas were the ideal place, as he knew well, for men and women to slip into private spaces for sexual unions.

Men only did construction, herding cattle and sheep. All he had to do with them was to have them pick up any scraps and leftovers to make the place beautiful.

The kitchen people were self-disciplined but shy about criticizing soldiers or anyone Spanish or Mexican. They'd yell at neophytes who offended them or complained about food or portions. Charaana from Seebag-na was one of the best.

He rode the Mission holdings and picked twenty men and women, feeling sure of the four overseers from each sector. He watched them arrive at the empty horse corral to the east of the Mission wall. Some were eager to have new responsibilities and showed they were happy. Others were wary of extra work.

After dark Sa'a'ri' ducked into the space between the western Mission courtyard wall and the waist-high hedge, waiting until Galvez rode past her and turned the corner. She scurried from bush to bush to Seebag-na.

Hachaaynar and Tooypor were in the greathouse with Tu'koo'par, Kiukyu and Ponu, expecting Charaana to report.

Sa'a'ri came in and sat on a straw mat completing the circle. "Charaana has responsibilities. Nicolas Jose has made her overseer of the kitchen. She can't risk coming here. I'll bring messages."

She told of the engineer and soldiers camped at the north wall and the coming of the Governor and settlers.

"Then it's true." Hachaaynar said. "This village, Yaanga and even Pasekeg-na are in danger. More than in the past. Ten firesticks can be overcome, but five or ten times that number will make us all slaves to the invaders."

Older Kyookyu spoke softly. "We could attack the Mission before the others come and then set traps for the Governor Chief on the Kah-mee-noh. I could miss his shield and hit his head." There was silence for a moment at the boldness of the idea.

"I say no to that.." Hachaaynar was looking at the mat in front of his knees with a distant look. "It sounds brave and if each part was done right, like a thing that could bring a success for a short time." He looked at the faces.

“The response would destroy us all. Every village would be burned. Every person who wasn‘t forced to work in their fields would be killed. They would bring their full force from the San Diego village and hundreds from Mexico with firesticks,” feeling chances getting slimmer and hating his indecision.

Tooypor felt each day that hopes were slipping away. The time had been best many seasons ago when there were eight firesticks at the most.

“We can‘t do it with a straight attack. Hachaaynar is right. I wish you had said that three springtimes ago, but I delayed then. I know it‘s right to delay now.”

Sa’aa’re’ nodded. “There are three hands of soldiers now. Many firesticks. Charaana says that with more contact with the grounds keepers and with the fields people, she can bring more people in and get more information.”

She signaled that she was finished and whispered to Tooypor. “She says you had ideas about the soldiers food. I’ll tell her what you want. She’s kitchen chief now.”

“I’ll tell you before you leave.”

After the people in the room agreed an attack would be ill timed, Hachaaynar spoke.

“We’ll watch the arrival of this governor and his soldiers. We’ll count them and their weapons. When they go to Yaanga we’ll look at their planned village.”

Tooypor added. “We’ll stay the night in Yaanga when the settlers come and see how they intrude in their space. Yaanga was always spread out. They aren’t used to being limited.”

<<< 0 >>>

Governor General Rivera y Moncada was following the orders of General de la Croix by taking an Eastern route to connect the Colorado River to the projected Pueblo de Los Angeles.

He led a contingent of eighty settlers with twenty mules, forty cattle and twenty-four Soldados de Cuero on leather-vested horses to make a stop at the new Mission Purisima Consepcion before traveling on. At the Mission four of the settlers were with fever. Two soldiers stayed behind to escort them later.

Rivera followed the river north until they reached the second Mission on the far side of the Alta California mapped border, San Pedro y San Pablo de Bicuner.

He called Corporal Lorca who rode to his side

“The cattle look too dehydrated and tired to keep up the pace. Send the pobladores on ahead. They need to arrive on time. As soon as the cattle seem fit for the drive I’ll catch up with six of the soldiers and about ten herders. You’ll take the rest ahead at,” pausing to calculate, “a reasonably slow pace. The cattle won’t make it if we continue without stopping for a while.”

Lorca left with seventy settlers and twelve soldiers moving across the desert toward Mission San Gabriel at a leasurely pace in increasing uncomfortable heat.

The way ahead started to become steeper. They entered a narrow rocky pass with a trail that made them go to single file in parts.

Boulders and rocks poured down the cliffs ahead of them and at the same time they heard the path behind them being closed off.

They looked up as a rain of arrows and stones crushed and pierced them and swarms of Mojave and Quechan Indians ran into the trail to finish them off with clubs and obsidian daggers.

On the next day Governor General Rivera brought the rested settlers, soldiers and cattle. As they approached the rocky pass he had a feeling that something was wrong and slowed, raising his hands for the column to halt.

An arrow whizzed by him and a dozon more bounced off his armor and his ducked-down helmet. One arrow pierced the light leather under his right armpit He gasped in pain as a hundred archers rose from the mesquite, tumbleweeds and palo verdes.

Muskets fired over and over. Arrows flew from far away from Quechan and Mojave Indians in the desert dips. After hours of battle the ammunition ran out and they found themselves surrounded by tribesmen with arrows, rocks and blades.

Rivera was hit by a rock and then a flight of arrows breaking through the leather, hitting the gaps at the arms and his face.

As he slid off his horse losing consciousness, he heard the last fading musket blast, screams of pain as well as his own, ...and ....finally, ...silence.

The news didn't reach Loreto for months.

JUNE 9TH -1781

Two advance scouts approached the Mission gate, Crespi and Ortega greeted them and sent them to the dining room for the best that could be offered.

Padres, soldiers and trustees fanned out on the southern walls watching De Neve and the settlers approach. The first scout handed Olivera a rolled leather document pouch and said. "There are many Indians down the road. No horses. No weapons that we saw."

Olivera said. "We will send four men with you. How far is the party from here? "

"Twenty kilometers. The Indians, maybe two hundred of them are less than ten away. They're standing and sitting to the sides. Just to watch we think, but do you think there is a threat?"

"We have a peaceful population here. We haven't had serious troubles in nearly ten years. It is a good place for the pueblo. I'll send four men."

<<< 0 >>>

Nicolas Jose felt both excitement for the idea of a separate space that would shift the cattle away from the Mission to the West and the slight chance that the growth of the new center might give more room for Shevaanga to re-build.

On the other hand he held the fear that if many new arrivals came they might expand to the East and destroy everything of his people's villages and lifeways.

'My people'was a constant thought as he stood in a line against the Mission front wall to the South with two hundred Tongva and Serrano Christianized neophytes to his right and four soldiers at ease to his left.

A similar group lined the wall to the North with the Spanish officers and the Padres in the center arch.

"My people," also in the far distance he could see people from Shevaanga along the road where some dust was rising from the high ranking party coming to the Mission in less than three fingers.

He wondered if there might be an attack but put it aside as unlikely.

His charges to his right side looked bored and annoyed that they had to stand in the sun dressed in their best smocks and shirts waiting for, what?

The soldiers to the left were laughing and talking about what they would do when they were rich. They knew that they would be rewarded for putting up with the natives and Franciscans.

The three Padres were more at attention than the soldiers. He knew that they didn't want a civilian settlement near the Mission. The legendary Father Serra, he'd never seen him, said that this settlement would be a secular offense to the Church and would interfere with the Catholocism of the 'natives.'

He knew that the one goal of the Padres was to insure that a large church was in the center of whatever was planned and that Franciscan control would be in place.

He squinted to the Southern approach and could begin to identify horses and wagons. He looked again to each side and wasn't proud to be going on a horse in front of all of 'his people' in this strange parade.

As he imagined how strong he would appear in the parade, some of the pride returned.

"I can do this. I should do this!"

AUGUST 18 - 1781

Filipe De Neve and Pedro Fages rode at the head of a procession flanked by eight of the best riders and marksmen in the colonial army. De Neve was trained well in planning a classic Roman designed community to work well as an asset to the empire. Fages, a Lieutenant, was a man on the rise. Viceroy Bucareli predicted that Fages would soon be Governor.

The settlers from Loreto survived five hundred kilometers of winds, fevers and cracking skin for $118 per family for five years labor in building the new town.

The wife of the Filipino died of smallpox outside San Diego, but Antonio Miranda Rodriguez stayed for her burial and watched over his sick daughter. He promised, after her recovery, to continue to the town of the Lady of the Angels in a few weeks.

Jose Antonio Navarro was forty-three and the three children small seemed eager to play at starting a little farm on their own land while dad was starting his tailoring business in town.

As their wagon in the procession had approached a large herd of cattle and a Mission surrounded be green vegetables, a soldier rode by.

Private de Cota had galloped from wagon to wagon pointing to the north-west shouting, "The new pueblo will be at the base of those two rolling hills," pointing past a dumpy looking Indian village.

"How can we make a farm there?" little Jose Ricardo asked his mother, Maria.

Maria Regina Glorea Dorotea de Soto was a prize beauty in Sinaloa and her marriage to the tailor Jose, was celibrated by the churchgoers and led to more business for the Navarros. She turned in her seat and called back to the three.

"Maybe farming will be difficult here. You can play in the dirt. It's desert." Turning to Jose, "You will do fine here but the kids have a problem," calling back, "Don't make up your minds too quickly. I'm sure this chosen for a reason."

Jose turned. "I'll do well here. The Mission alone will keep us fed until I'm established."

Jose Fernando de Valasco y Lara was a Spaniard from Cadiz. He had arrived in the first July group and was settled into Mission life on the August arrival.

"Jose Lara," he would say. "Just call me Jose. This is my wife, Maria and the three kids are off playing in the dirt somewhere."

At fifty years of age the children kept him exhausted. The place was ugly. No harbor here could match Cadiz or even the New Spain ports. The ground was parched and the hills didn't have the grace of Sinaloa.

He immediately began looking for other options.

Pablo Rodriguez had come early, in July, with his wife, Maria Roselia Noriega and his infant daughter, Maria Antonia Rodriguez, and waited impatiently on the Mission grounds until the mass arrival. It looked like a place where he could work.

He borrowed a horse to take an early look. His bit of land looked as though, with good irrigation and fertalization, it could produce good crops for the family and for the soldiers.

Jose Maria Vanegas, an Indio like Pablo, also came with an infant daughter. He and Pablo walked the Mission grounds talking about their old town of Rosario. On a slight rise, they looked west to the site of the pueblo.

Jose spoke. "This is more desert than I expected."

"This is Summer. Wait for the rains."

Jose chuckled. "We just passed Springtime. How much rain do you think fell this year?" Not wanting to sound too negative. "I'll tell you. If we can hold the water that runs off of those hills or keep ditches and divert the springs and streams, you can have some good crops here."

Negro tailor Luis Manuel Quintero expected this new land to be a true paradise but the dryness and lack of water dimmed his hopes. He started thinking of options before the ceremonies had begun.

At fifty-five years old with five surviving children and a good and strong wife, this was too primitive to have good work here. Tailoring for the soldiers and the few wives of the farmers wouldn't take the whole day and farming in his spare hours would be foolish and would lead to illness.

The children could do the hard work, but he worried about Maria Gertrudis being out in the field without an adult. She was pretty and liked to flirt with the soldiers.

"Lord, what a mess of problems this place has," He groaned.

Basilio Rosas, at sixty seven years, came with his wife, Maria Manuela, and his five children in the same July group as Quintero and his family. They ate the Mission food together and walked to rises to see the pueblo's site and Jose's view was very different.

"With the tools and materials that we're given we can make this place into a paradise!" He looked into Luis' face, a map of negativity, and tapped his arm. "I look at your children. They are little, but strong. They are smart. They can help you just like mine do. Look, we'll help each other"

After days of discussing the possibilities of a better life in the new pueblo, back and forth with laughter and more than a little overstatement of their arguments, Luis seemed to accept Jose's hopes, but only on the condition that all of the children help whoever was having problems. Even the little ones.

Antonio Villavicencio and his pregnant wife came with the July party.

"Oh, thank God we're here." She repeated it often, walking the grounds rubbing her stomach. "What a horrible bumpy ride," to anyone who would listen. "At least there are shade trees here to keep out of the Sun. The bunkroom gets so hot, I don't see how anyone can stand it."

Antonio paced with her and comforted her with fresh cups of water and soup.

"This will be a magnificent place to raise a family. The Mission will be close to us and there will be another church right near our house."

She said quietly, but often, "Look at those Indians there. See their looks? They don't look friendly. Those over there look angry. They don't look like they are Christian."

"They probably haven't seen many Spanish people out of military uniform. They look more curious than angry."

Little Maria Antonia listened quietly and became very frightened of the strange looking Indios.

Antonio Mesa had just arrived with his wife and was surprised to see that so many from the July contingent were already settled into Mission life. From the moment they saw the pueblo site and were led in their cart to San Gabriel Mission they agreed. "This sure isn't Sonora."

They walked the grounds together and saw that grape vines had started and cattle were in fields by the thousands.

"What do you think of this place?" Mesa asked Quinteros and Rosas on the front, newly cobblestoned, Courtyard.

Quinteros continued his monthlong conversation with Jose.

"We've been going around and around about it. I first thought it was….a mess. It looks so dry and rocky. Not a place for farming, but look at the Mission. It used to look the same as the pueblo. Jose is a builder. He met a French guy who's building an aqueduct. Maybe it will help."

"We had two days of rain last week," Jose pointed to the west, "There is an ocean out there. Look at the clouds out there. In two or three months this all will be muddy and turning green".

Antonio and his wife still held doubts but agreed to wait more before forming an opinion, "Well, maybe after an aqueduct."

Manuel Camero also arrived in the new group with his young wife, Maria Ana Gertrudis Lopez, with high hopes for a place to advance and build an acceptable life. He wasn't sure how to define it, but a life away from Monte games and an undefined Lust. He was sure of his commitment to Maria and swore to himself that he would never be unfaithful, but he still didn't fully trust himself in new environments.

"It certainly isn't as pretty as Rosario." Maria patted his back and grinned in her impish way. "We'll make it nice." Waving to the older Maria Rodriguez, also from Rosario. "Let's join them."

Manuel saw the Rodriguez' and the Quintero's families with quilts on the ground, eating an Indio looking gruel from clay pots.

"What is that?" Manuel asked, unaware that this wasn't the best approach after months of separation.

"It's so good to see you" Maria said loudly over his voice, wanting to poke his ribs.

"There are a lot of Rosario people coming here," Jose said, with the children waving and greeting them loudly.

"Thank God there are some other younger people here." Sixteen-year-old Christina Quintero whispered to fifteen –year-old Jose Rosas.

The three families enjoyed the goat, corn and squash stew with ample chilies.

"Great food." Echoed about the meal they shared. They spent many hours in groups talking about their plans. Corporal Jose Vicente Feliz trotted up to each of the families he had escorted and bowed his head to honor them.

"I am traveling on to make a report about Santa Barbara, but we will only only stay for a short time. Cordero, Alvitre and I will return to help you get set. Don't worry. You will be well cared for. I will be the Chief Public Official of the Pueblo. I'm not sure for how long, but when there is stability, you will have a civilian Alcalde. "

"How many soldiers will we have to protect us?" Jose Rosas asked.

Feliz pointed west. "Six for the pueblo. Six for the Mission, so there will be fifteen when the three of us return"

<<< 0 >>>

A courier rode though the Mission gate calling for Lieutenant Fages.

" Governor De Neve is on approach. Prepare for the pueblo inspection within two hours."

Fages calculated how many soldiers he could muster. 'The ones I need are gone.'

"How many are with the Governor?" seeing, and showing worry at, the first failure of his career if it were less than eight.

The courier sensed his fear and hesitated before letting a smile break through and saying.

"Governor De Neve has an escort of," shrugging and hesitating more, "a detachment of the best cavalrymen in the world, but only sixteen."

Fages laughed and shook his fist at the courier. "I'm sure you know that's a relief."

"Yes, I know. The regulars here are legendary."

Fages waved him off, remembering the Cataloon private. 'A good man' he thought, watching him speed back to the Governor's party.

He sent Olivera to ride through the Mission grounds to call all of the families together in the courtyard at sundown. Several people in the first July group had returned sick or had died from smallpox and other fevers but the mulatto and mestizo families in the second group had survived. They had all been briefed on the dangers and had all agreed to make the commitment.

He spoke from a high point on the Mission wall after making sure that none of the Padres or neophytes were present.

"El Pueblo de Nuestra Senora la Riena de Los Angeles, is central to the permanent claim of Spain to the west coast of the Northern Americas. The reputation of this Mission is a tarnished one with night attacks, murders and rapes. They have had a history of slovenly soldiers, lazy Indians and incompetent Franciscans."

Olivera and Pico listened and nodded in agreement.

"You will bring a great moment in history. Your work as the founders of this pueblo is the most important work of the empire. You and your children are the great heroes of this age."

The farmers and carpenters understood few of the big words and ideas but the families felt valued and hoped it could become a better place than the one that they had left.

Governor de Neve and Fages led a meeting in the morning including the Padres.

Engineers Flavien and Sylva rode behind, carrying more detailed plans for streets and structures than Cervantes had. Behind them rode sixteen soldiers in fours when the trail was wide, and twos where the Camino Real narrowed, as it often did.

Behind them, walking, riding horses and standing in the tailgates of three wagons filled with building and farming tools, were experienced builders to show the proper techniques. They demonstrated the tools to the forty-four settlers.

After four and a half months of working their way up from Mexico, the sturdy dark Indian mestizos from central Mexico and Afro-Spanish ex-slaves had survived.

Crespi, Cambon and Somera joined the assembly.

"The fields and Indians look better than I expected.“ De Neve called back to Fages. "That‘s a well ordered staff by the gate. I recognise Olivera to the left of the Franciscans. Clean walls. Neat rows of squash."

De Neve pointed to the right. "Well fenced cattle. That‘s a very good-looking herd. This looks better than the reports." He saw Father Crespi raising his hand in a blessing greeting. The other Franciscans did the same as the Mission soldiers saluted neatly.

After introductions to the officers and the Indian's notorious Alcalde, De Neve was led to the brightly candlelit chapel.

Engineer Cervantes' maps were laid out on a large table in the center of the chapel. He saluted and bowed to the Governor and the others. They gathered around the table.

A central plaza was marked with four radiating streets and a church adjoining the plaza.

"It looks good." De Neve said. "Engineer Silva has the plans for the first six structures. The church, judicial and civic building and three large sleeping quarters will be first, so the builders can branch out to make individual family houses. Huts actually at first".

Silva laid out his plans. "The next stage will be to convert the large sleeping buildings into hotels to promote trade along the Camino Real."

"They'll be simple wooden structures in the beginning. But as the town grows they'll be replaced with adobe and stone buildings of essentially the same design." Spreading individual plans over the street map. "This type of small family structure can be built on any of the streets radiating from the central plaza."

"We'll add additional streets outward as far as the town will support. Here is the great advantage of starting with impermanent wooden structures. As the town expands." Gesturing beyond the borders of the page. "The older residences near the center can be torn down and replaced with larger commercial buildings."

De Neve added. "Continual expansion can be achieved." Pointing to Flavien. "And our fine engineer from Paris will build our aqueduct and water distribution system for the town and farmlands."

Flavien gracefully bowed to De Neve. "From the very good design that you've created."

Cambon looked from Crespi to Somera. The church seemed an afterthought and the settlers seemed ragtag. How would spiritual needs become addressed?

Crespi spoke. "We haven't been told the plans for the church for the pueblo nor have we been informed as to who the pastor would be."

The Governor smiled and said. "A Church of our Lady of the Angels with be connected directly to the plaza. For now, the colonists will travel to your Mission on Sundays only."

Crespi asked. "When will this church be built and who will be in charge of it?"

De Neve answered. "All of this will be covered in future dispatches, both from Mexico, and I imagine, from Italy."

CHAPTER 18

THE BIRTH -SEPTEMBER 4 – 1781

Tooypor led the Seebag-na group south of the invader's settlement to a hillside view. Yaanga people spread themselves in a wide circle to watch the village being made. Most elders and Chief stayed on the highest plain. The Spanish hadn't arrived yet. The procession was coming up the trail, moving very slowly.

Nicolas Jose could see what had to be the Shebaagna villagers on a hillside to the South of the site. He had gathered up the Mission neophytes with the help of two of the new soldiers.

He rode tall on his horse feeling that this was a time for him to shine in the Mission's eyes. He had heard the word 'Alcalde' used and knew that it ment the leader of a large group. That would be his title in the new Mission life.

As the group moved forward he felt hundreds of eyes upon him from the approaching hills.

"To Hell with them," he thought, not wanting this time spoiled by their fears or anger, or hatred. 'I've worked for this time and I deserve it!'

Three Padres walked in front followed by mounted Spanish administrators in bright red and gold clothing that was unlike any that had been seen before at the Mission. They stood tall in their saddles and were talking and laughing. Next came eight soldiers on each side of three carriages with large boxes piled on them.

Following them was a large crowd of dark complexioned men, women and children dressed in loose and colorful clothes and hats unlike any of the soldiers or Brownrobes. Ten meters behind them, rode the traitor Nicolas Jose, with two soldiers and a clump of forty walking neophytes in freshly washed and hand pressed Mission clothing.

Tooypor saw Charaana and Taaherkwe' in the invader's crowd and pointed them out to Hachaaynar.

Three Padres stopped in a large rectangle marked with small mounds of earth. They held crosses to the winds and spoke words many of their Brownrobe words to bless in the Brownrobe way, the new village.

Tooypor held Hachaanar's hand and whispered, "This looks bad."

"I know," He said. "Something much larger than the Mission. Next to us and between us and Yaanga. How will we trade? How can we live on our lands after this?"

Tooypor's hand tightened. "It's the end of our Lifeways. It's the end for all of us unless we can find a way to stop them." She glared. "We must stop them!"

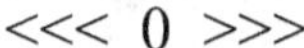

Governor Phillipe De Neve and Lieutenant Fages were the only secular men standing within the borders of the center area. They turned frequently to watch the laborers, neophytes and the throngs of natives on the surrounding hillsides.

The blessings were spoken loudly in Latin as Father Crespi walked to each side of the rectangle sprinkling liquid from a clear flask on every part.

De Neve stood in glowing contentment and said. "This was an ideal placement. A beautiful view of the mountains and sea. Look at those peaceful natives watching us.They will help make this pueblo grow and thrive. They are unarmed. They seem happy that we are here"

Fages looked back with a wrinkled brow. "There have been mixed reports as to their cooperation. There may be difficulties but comparatively minor ones ahead"

Sa'aa're' painted herself with red ochre as a disguise to hide herself from the neophytes. She pointed below. "That is the 'Holy Water' that the Padres say is magic. It will protect their place from harm and evil spirits."

Tooypor and Hachaaynar smiled, then on thinking about what she'd said, laughed. It was the same smile on the face of people who knew the area. It was time to say the obvious.

Hachaaynar whispered to Sa'aa're'. "Look. They are building it in a low place with those two hills above it." Pointing to one of the rolling mounds to the north where Yaanga had started a thousand years before. "At the first good rain, it will be under rushing water. Their 'Holy Water won't help them."

After short speeches by Governor De Neve and the Lieutenant Governor of the Californias, Don Fernando Rivera y Moncada, wine was passed to all of the troops who had traveled from Loreto and San Diego as guards and to all of the construction workers and engineers. The exhausted mulatto settler families also gratefully accepted bota bags of wine to toast the birth of the new "Pueblo de Nuestra Senora, la Reina de Los Angeles. " The new town planned to become "The Cattle Capitol of the World."

The neophytes were escorted by the Mission troops back to San Gabriel with Nicolas Jose mounted at the head of the walking column. He rode back and said to each group. "You were all wonderful and a credit to our Mission," making eye contact with each one. In spite of some confusion about the new order of things, most smiled back and admired his leadership.

The Padres walked to the site for the Church of our Lady of the Angels with Engineer Cervantes.

"It is very small." Crespi frowned. "Merely half the size of judicial center building. We need a much larger church grounds. There isn't room for a proper burial yard."

Cervantes nodded in agreement. "The population is very small, for now, but the land around the first church walls will allow unlimited expansion. We need to conserve and ration our wood, but the Church of Our Lady is central to all of the Pueblo." He patted the Padre's shoulder.

Yang-vik looked down from the hill at the men milling in the square. “Truly, Coyote is their guide.” The view from the hills of Yaanga showed the foolishness of the location. “They want to be so tricky that they trick themselves.”

The elder beside him said. “We’ll keep our tar sealed hats and mats near our door” Laughing. “When the rain starts, we’ll come to watch them swim.”

“In their me-tal clothing.” Said another.

Yang-vik shook his hand toward the invader’s village area. “The rain flooding their village will happen within three moons. Sooner!” All of the elders and the families close to the chief saw the next stage clearly. “They will move up the hill onto our land.”

They sat, pondering the inevitable.

“With their firesticks, and so many of them.” Yang-vik, a man who had lived his life in peace and was always in a protected environment, shook his head. “We will never survive, fighting against them.”

“How will we survive if we don’t fight“ The elder said. ”When even more come.”

De Neve, Fages, Rivera y Moncada and the other officials left with carriages and escort for the trip back to their offices in Monterey in the north, Capital of Alta California, or Loreto, in the south, Capital of Baja California.

It went better than expected. The natives were peaceful and easily controllable without a strong military presence. The Padres predictably fretted and wanted more power but they weren’t as annoying as most of Serra’s men with demands for control of the civilian populations. They were solicitous to Frey Crespi, praising him for choosing the location of the pueblo so many years ago.

Crespi wasn’t pleased by the servant’s door treatment given the Church and the Order. They’d taken notes on the Mission buildings, fields and herds but didn't promise more than vaguenesses about some future expansion. "A Godless lot" he mumbled often.

Vargas wrote the census of the new pueblo:

- 11 families
- 44 Pobladores. 23 children. 11 boys. 12 girls.
- 21 adults.
- 11 Men – 1 Mestizo 2 Spaniard. 2 Mullatto. 2 Negro. 4 Indio.
- 10 Women – 5 Mestizo. 5 Indio.

The families:

- Rosas, Alejandro, Indio, male, 20. Juana Maria, India, female, 21.
- Lara: Jose Fernando de, Spanish, male, 50. Maria Antonio. India, woman, 23. Maria Juana, girl, 6. Jose Julian, boy, 4. Maria Faustina, girl, 2.
- Quintero: Luis, Negro, male, 55. MariaPetera, Mulatta, female, 40. Maria Gertrudis, girl, 16. Maria Conception, girl, 9, MariaTomasa, girl, 7. Maria Rafaela, girl, 6. Jose Clemente, boy, 3.
- Navarro: Jose Antonio, male, Mestizo, 42. Maria Regina, woman, Mulatta, 47. Jose Edwardo, boy, 10. Jose Clemente, boy, 9. Mariana, girl, 4.
- Rodriguez: Pablo, Indio, male, 25. Maria Roselia, India, female, 26. Maria Antonia, girl, 1.
- Rosas: Basilio, Indio, male, 67. Maria Manuela, female, 43. Jose Maximo, boy, 15. Jose Carlos, boy, 12. Maria Josefa, girl, 8. Antonio Rosalino, boy, 7. Jose Marcelino, boy, 4. Jose Esteban, boy, 2.
- Camero: Manuel, Mulatto, male, 30. Maria Tomasa, Mulatta, female, 24.
- Mesa: Antonio, Negro, male, 38. Maria Ana, female, Mulatta, 27. Maria Paula, girl, 10. Antonio Maria, boy, 8.
- Moreno: Jose, Mulatto, male, 22. Maria Guadalupe, Mulatta, female, 19.
- Villavicencio: Antonio Clemente, Spanish, male, 30. Maria Seferina, India, female, 26. Maria Antonia, girl, 8.

- Vanegas: Jose, Indio, male, 28. Maria Bonifacia, female, 20. Cosme Damien, boy, 1

Several of the children had died on the journey but these were the survivors.

The Spanish visitors had kept an eye on the Alcalde, who had occupied so many negative dispatches in the past. He now seemed to have the respect of both the Franciscans and neophytes. The notes generally praised Nicolas Jose's devotion to the goals of Mission San Gabriel Archangel.

A large unused corral was filled with neophytes who had helped Nicolas Jose make the Mission visit a success.

"You have done more than anyone expected!" He shouted from the height of an inverted horse trough with a board nailed across it.

"The great changes weren‘t clear until this week. It means that we at the Mission are now second in importance to the new pueblo of Los Angeles. We'll produce food crops, but the herds will be moved over toward the town. We'll have more squash, grapes, peppers and corn. They will be planting a new grain that we will learn about."

"We'll have more freedom! We'll have less hard work to do and more time for our mates and children. We'll be more independent of the soldiers and I'll be open to you. If you are disrespected by soldiers, you can come to me and I'll tell the Padres to stand up for you."

The neophytes listened, many were pleased that their extra work was being appreciated and that their rations and rest might be increased, but most felt that nothing would change.

Taaherkwe' motioned for Sa'aa're' and Charaana to come to her as the meeting dispersed. When they were out of sight they shared humor at Nicolas Jose's illusion about change in the invaders' Mission.

"I'll go to Seebag-na tonight." Sa'aa're' said.

<<< 0 >>>

Cordero, Lopez and Galvez rode west below Yaanga and Cahueng-na to reach the herd of Pemuu'nga Indians being driven in from the coast. That was how it was described by Sergeant Olivera. It was an odd way to talk, but as the group came into sight it looked like a herding of animals.

There were three riders on each side of the three hundred huddled, forced march Indians. Two riders followed. There were shots.

"Look! They're shooting the ones who fall." Lopez exclaimed. "Look!" As another straggler was shot.

"It's about time!" Cordero shouted. "Get rid of the weak ones."

Lopez shook his head. "You're crazy." Just loud enough to be heard, as they slowed to a lope.

Galvez pulled closer to Lopez. "We can't keep feeding all these people if they can't work for us." At Lopez' shoulder level. "It's a pueblo now. We'll have loyal civilians coming from Mexico, Europe, Everywhere"

"I don't see how that excuses them." Lopez kept his eyes forward.

"We'll have a workforce of our own people. We won't need them."

Cordero joined in. "It's simple. More of us means less of them. We don't need to be surrounded by hostiles. They're savages. They pretend to be converts, but they'd turn around and kill us if they could."

"It's our time now." Galvez said. "We'll empty the islands and make a seaport. That's what Fages was saying."

The rider in the lead had blended in with the crowded Indians until they got closer. He sped up to meet them.

"I thought they'd send us six or eight to take over. We need to get back to San Diego." The soldier with corporal's markings said.

Cordero replied. "There aren't that many at the Mission. I see you have Indians for outriders. Ours are too untrustworthy to use like that."

”I’ve heard.” The corporal said. “Ours are Kumeyaay. We’ve had plenty of time to train them. They use firearms against their own.”

The column approached. The four soldiers watched the frightened and bedraggled mob shuffle forward. Some carried babies. Some limped desperately, their eyes either half closed to escape the real situation, or wide with panicky fear. There were none with eye contact with the Spanish troops.

The Kumeyaay horsemen rode by with wide grins and waves for the three from San Gabriel.

“They don’t dress like Indians. They look like European Gypsies ” Cordero raised his brows in amazement. “They enjoy their work.”

The Corporal agreed. “They never liked the Tongva from the coast, especially the islands. They don’t share or trade. They‘re happy to see them go.”

“How many have been shot?” Lopez asked.

“Maybe thirty. Maybe fifty.” The corporal looked as if it wasn’t a proper question. “We can‘t leave sick, or pretending to be sick people, all over the countryside. Either they‘ll work, or they won‘t”

Cordero looked at Lopez indulgently, seeing him getting softer with each season. “That‘s how it has to be, my friend.” Turning his horse to join the men at the rear.

<<< 0 >>>

Two hundred Seebag-na Tongva walked to the north edge of the village to watch the procession pass between them and the foothills. They watched for any turn toward them. The firestick sounds spread fear, but the group kept a straight line to the invaders’ mission.

“What is this?” Hachaaynar asked. ”None of the Mission people said there would be new ones. Not like this.”

Tooypor squinted. She had better vision than most. “There are more people than this village. More than Haapchivet.” Looking to the left toward Yaanga. “If they were clearing out Yaanga, a runner would have reached us.”

“They must have cleared out some villages.” Looking to the western horizon, Hachaaynar pointed. “The smoke. Blacker than the gray clouds, way out there near the coast”

“Yes.” Tooypor said. “More smoke than village fires.”

“They’ve burned a coastal village. That‘s where those are from.” Hachaaynar looked back to his villagers on all sides of him. “ There are more invaders now in the Mission and in their new village. Are we next?”

<<< 0 >>>

Crespi, Cambon and Somera watched the approaching mass from the chapel patio wall. “Our blessed neophytes.” Crespi intoned. The wind turned colder under the clouds.

“So many!.” Somera said. “Where can they sleep?” Turning to Crespi. “Do you remember the lean-tos that Nicolas Jose stored in the old corral?”

“Call him now!” Crespi snapped. “Have him assemble a crew now! What was I thinking? They never said there would be so many. Somera, have Ortega lead them around back until something can be set up.

Nicolas Jose rode the north section of old corn fields where the new crop called ‘wheat’ was poking through the cleared earth. He watched the approaching mob with twelve mounted men around them. They had to be transplants from another village. ‘This can’t be good. Too many.’ as he heard his name called.

Somera looked comical riding toward him at full speed on a burro, shouting his name. “Come quick!”

Somera described the problem. Nicolas Jose had the building overseers assemble crews to drag the posts, boards and mats into position make improvised structures. He filled with anger at the condition of the Indians arriving and the fear and degradation in their faces.

They stood in confusion outside the walls as the riders headed them off, circled them and told them to sit in the dirt. Cordero rode up to the Alcalde with an exaggerated flourish of his hat.

"They are all yours. Make them into good Christians" Turning to the front gate. Saying to himself. "Teach them to dig graves."

They lay on the ground and rolled on their sides. They slept on the dirt, forearms under cheeks, knees brought up like newborns. Mothers held babies and did what they could to clean them. All of them, men and women, were soiled. The stench reached beyond the Mission walls into the chapel.

He had crews place posts, nail boards to the sides and lash the mats until he saw Crespi watching from a distant point on the wall. He went to the priest before he could duck away to pray or find a way of avoiding the crisis.

He spoke as calmly as he could. The old feelings of anger whirled in his mind. He vowed not let it show.

"These people need water and cloth for washing. They need food, but they can't go inside shelters as dirty as they are. Let me get crews from the fields to bring buckets from the wells and clothing for them to change. It may rain soon. They will have to stay indoors. If they are this unclean, it will make their stalls unfit to stay in."

"We don't have enough water or clothing for them!" Crespi said with more force than was his habit. "Summer has left the wells low, and their body coverings," Pointing disdainfully, "are so tattered and disgusting that washing won't help them."

"They need water to drink. They need food."

"We will bring some water to drink. There may be small portions of bread and corn to share, but," Crespi gestured in uncharacteristic hopelessness, showing how out of his control it was. "they will have to stay out there. They will have to undress and wash in the rain before entering Mission grounds." Crossing himself and starting to walk away. "This is the worst bunch I've seen."

Nicolas Jose stepped in front of the Padre and stopped him. "They've been mistreated. I don't have to talk to them to see how frightened and hurt they are. They are not a 'worst bunch.' The men who forced them are a 'worst bunch.'" Almost nose to nose with Crespi.

"You are a man of Faith, as you say. The Lord of Mercy watches over you. What you decide is His Will, no? Please. Now, dear Father. Be the man of God to these people. Have all the food and water that can be found, how you say, 'Given un to Them' the ones without fortune. Any covering too." Looking up at the quick moving, darkening sky. "Maybe bathing outside is the good idea you had. I see. I see, but food, water first"

Crespi hadn't seen the calm Alcalde as agitated in years.

"I'll have Charanna prepare all the food available. We will fast tonight. Our guests will be fed tonight"

"Thank you Father. Thank you Father." Touching his forehead to the back of Crespi's hand. "Thank you Father."

<<< 0 >>>

. JANUARY 1782

The Moreno family added adobe squares around their thatched hut on the main western street of Pueblo de Los Angeles. It was all built to the administration's designs. A simple copy of the native's "kitcha," with large willow branches and the trunks of very young trees bent and lashed together in a dome shape, with a vent on top and layers of woven insulation, planned to be expanded with square rooms built in adobe the next Spring.

The families from Mexico added an outer coating of mud and straw to keep the inside temperatures even and for more protection from wind. It was a dry wind until this morning. They watched the dark clouds building from the southwest. Gray covered the sky as the day wore on. It became cold, unlike the winds before tropical storms in Mexico.

They gathered with the other settlers at the southern edge of the new pueblo to watch the procession passing four kilometers to the south of them.

“Aren‘t they coming here to help us?” Young Miguel asked his Father.

“No. To the Mission. We will not have help here. We are on our own, my son”

The Delgado girls asked Miguel if he could stay and play stick games until dinnertime.

“Miguel must make bricks today.” Father said.

It became dark as the first drops fell. The family was finishing a meal of grilled corn patties and peppers

Sleep came easily with a soothing patter on the thin mud covering the hut.

Miguel woke late in the night to urinate in the pit behind the house. There was a shovel to spread sand over the pit. The urinal would last a month before the job of hauling the dirt into the desert.

As he stepped in the street his feet slipped in the mud. He kept his balance but sloshed carefully around the side touching the sides of the hut. The adobe felt soft against his hand. He poked at it and his finger went through to the woven straw inner panel.

He peed into the flowing stream of water that covered the pit. He aimed at a rolling dirt clod and watched the stream coursing down the main street. He entered, wiping his feet on an old unwashed shirt, He pulled an extra cover on and tucked it in his mat. It was hard to sleep. The drumming got louder.

He woke again while it was dark. Splashing drops came through the roof. He put his hand down to push himself up and found a puddle around his bed.

“Mama! Papa! Wake up!

They jumped to their feet. “God! Jesus! Save us!” Putting their sandals and ponchos on and took Miguel by the hand, stepping onto the new adobe squares that were under three inches of water.

There was an oak several meters up the slope beyond the second street. The water was over six inches and running fast as they crossed the street. Four families huddled together on the drier ground under the tree.

They all turned suddenly to the left, hearing and seeing the growing river coming between the hills to the north and running through the central plaza.

“My God!” Was on each set of lips as the new wall for the church tilted and slowly collapsed into the mud.

<<< 0 >>>

Yan-vik and three elders had prepared for the rain with tar coated mats and lean-to shelters. They waited until the rain became heavy before going to the rise overlooking the invader’s village. They sat cross legged as the water rose.

They watched panicking people leave their homes. They laughed as the large stone walls collapsed. The elders shook their heads at the foolishness of the invader’s village. One spoke solemnly. “They have no connection to Spirit. They assume the Earth obeys their wants”

“Coyote-men.” Yan-vik said, pushing off the mat, carrying his shelter home. He slept easily.

In the Mission fields rain splashed down in heavy drops on the tilled farmland. Hundreds of elderly, men and women, boys, girls and babies shed their clothes on the ground and marched in a long circle in the field, herded by mounted soldiers in leather vests and hats.

There were screams and shouts. An aged couple from Topang-na, who’d walked sixty kilometers in the two days, were in the inner ring. She stubbed her toe on a root and fell toward the inside. He grabbed her arm and slipped into the mud with her. The bunch behind them jumped or stepped around them, but the ones following could not see. More than ten people had walked over them before a pack of young people pulled them to the center to lie unconscious in the mud.

A barely teen woman, holding her baby, trudged in the center, eyes barely open, following the broad back of a man in front of her. She all lost sense of where she was. Her vision blurred and the baby slipped from he arms. She screamed and was pushed forward until she fell and crawled to the inner space of the large circle of her people. When she stood, a booted foot left it's stirrup and kicked her to the ground.

Saenz looked down as he was passing, hoping, but doubting that the young girl would survive. 'The kind we need more of.' He thought, as her convulsing body slipped out of his view.

Nicolas Jose watched the construction crew, urging speed and accuracy from them. He watched the horrible scene of degradation in the flooding field.

A passing overseer whispered to him. "I heard Cordero telling Sergeant Olivera that the dead ones out there would make good fertilizer. Olivera thought than was funny!"

He didn't feel shame at the tears. He felt pride at being able to feel the sorrow and a connection to the kidnapped Tongva from the coast.

"Jesus," He said in the words of the Mission. "How much they must of suffered!" Thinking, ''Like you did, except, the ones who drive and torture them are the ones who claim you as their God and savior. Why is that? Why do you let that happen?'.

He wanted to sit with Corporal Andres to understand how the 'Empire' or the 'Catholic Church' could make people suffer so badly and continue to say, or to think, that they are 'helping' or bringing 'progress' to the widows, widowers and orphans they create. He wondered at the nice words they use to hide what the reality of what their words do.

He remembered how he'd used people over and over but ignored the damage he was doing because it gave him power over them. The things he used in order to hide what he was doing to them. How 'The Blood of Christ' or brandy made him forget. How the sexual power over strangers made them under him in his mind.

Was this how 'The Church' looked at him? At all those people in the field? Did the words in the Latin language act as a shield against pain? How can Jesus of 'The Church' excuse the sins of the soldiers? Not only Rodriguez and Cordero. All of them have either killed or kidnapped people. Even Andres, by carrying the weapons of 'The Empire' frightens them into giving up their homes and lifeways.

He covered the four work groups, pleased with their speed. He didn't see any representatives of the church out in the rain. Only mounted military men and Kumeyaay riding around. Sometimes riding down the naked new arrivals with hoofs crushing them into the mud.

He entered the chapel, seeing Olivera, Verdugo and Pico sitting across from the three Padres. Crespi turned to Nicolas Jose.

"I'm sure that the work to be done is beyond your resources. It is certainly beyond ours."

"Stop the marching." Nicolas Jose said. "and let them stand. Some spaces will hold eight at a time. We can give them our spare clothes, Let me bring them into shelter. God and Jesus would want that."

Olivera and Verdugo's faces wore contempt. Pico said.

"I'll help you. I'll get Lopez, Andres and Machado to help you." Turning to Crespi. "We will build trouble for the Mission unless we resolve this quickly. We need to have them clothed and indoors. A Mass! A Mass tomorrow morning. I'm sure that you were planning it already."

"Yes." Crespi said, seeing a way out. "It will be outdoors at the front gate. All those who can be clothed will be given our own clothes. We will take a collection from the neophytes."

<<< 0 >>>

Tooypor moved rocks and scraped away soft dirt to make gullies as the water threatened to wash the hut away. During light periods the water forked to either side into the ditches. A stronger downfall sent foaming streams leaping over the stone barrier.

Her shoulders and thighs ached as she rolled heavy rocks to the center divide to raise the height to start the split farther uphill, parting the stream earlier.

Her shins and ankles were scraped and she yelped with frustration that she couldn't foresee a stone, root or branch under the floe. "Why didn't I see that!" loudly to the wind.

As first light silhouetted Four Eagles Peak, the rain suddenly stopped. She walked into the hut and found that the mat and floor was nearly dry. She lay on the mat. Sleep was instantaneous. She woke twelve fingers later to the sound of squirrels investigating the corners of the hut.

She smiled. "It is saved." Seeing more successes ahead.

PUEBLO DE LOS ANGELES (1782)

Antonio Villavicencio and his wife Maria didn't want to weep in the church with all of their friends watching them but the more they tried to hold back, the more their grief poared out into loud sobs that they couldn't control.

Their first daughter, Maria Geronimia, was the first child born in the Pueblo and now at only five months old, she had died of what looked like the Indian's disease. Her lungs were full and her tongue was dark colored.

Every person in the church knew about how many of the natives were dying of "The Indian Disease" and they were frightened that it might spread into the town.

They were all polite after the service, but they all stood a little farther back than they normally would, looking for coughs or signs of illness.

MISSION SAN GABRIEL

Pico watched Corporal Andres enter Nicolas Jose's room in the early morning. There was something about Andres that didn't fit. He was the only soldier from Mexico who was pure Indio, His parents, and apparently on and on, were Tolteca. He read books. He was one of four soldiers who could read. He stayed away from Cordero, Machado and Saenz, the most outspoken ones about dislike of Indios. He showed respect to the Padres and the other soldiers. He showed too much respect to the Alcalde. It didn't fit.

Pico looked to all sides. The room was against the cornfield side of the Mission where crews were nearly a kilometer out of view and the sounds from the herds on the opposite side were nearly unheard. He walked around the corner of the building until he was out of sight of the chapel and quietly crawled around the back wall until he was beneath Nicolas Jose's high and small rear window. He didn't mind kneeling in the mud if it meant learning answers to a vexing puzzle, but he doubted he could hear very much.

Andres sat on a stool. Nicolas Jose flopped down on the sleeping mat and leaned, sitting with his back against the wall. Andres knew that he'd be asked again to explain the cruelty of the world through the eyes of the Spanish.

Nicolas Jose spoke about the newcomers and the bad things he had heard soldiers say and about what Saenz and Cordero were supposed to have said and how Olivera laughed.

"How can the religion of the Padres allow this to happen? These soldiers break all of the commandments! They covet the land and take it from under the people who have always lived there. They kill! They rape! They are slothful when they are here in the Mission and when they aren't doing evil things. How can the Jesus Christ and the Mother Mary and the Father God let this happen? How can the Fathers act so afraid to speak about it? "

"I am from Mexico." Andres said. "From an ancient people of the land. Tolteca. A big empire like the Spanish. Not little villages like here, but also Indio! We had wealth. We had metal and fine cloth. We had Gods and Spirits and we knew how to use the seasons to make a good world to live in. Before the time of my father's fathers, the Spanish came to my country with their soldiers. They killed so many of us with their advanced weapons that they had complete control over us. They did that all across Mexico, with every tribe. Later I learned that they did the same thing to hundreds of tribes to the south of Mexico."

He rocked gently. “I showed you the map. You remember how small the land of the Tongva was on it? All of the rest of the map is land that was Indio, Land that now belongs to their ‘Empire.’ Thousands, ten fingers ten times, then ten times more of that, then ten times more of all of that and more of that and all of that”. Gesturing until Nicolas Jose waved him off.

“That is too much. I can‘t think that many.”

“Many more than all the people you have ever seen in your life, and all the ancestors of all those people who can be remembered. All of those were killed by the soldiers. All of the curanderas, all the healers and elders. All of the chiefs and fighters. All were killed long ago.”

“But how can so few kill so many?

“Weapons. It is simple. They have the weapons, like my musket, the pistol, the sword. The first are killed and the rest follow.”

“But the Kumeyaay carry the weapons too. Why do they give weapons to them? They treat them like Spaniards.”

”They find ones from local tribes to do their work. Control is what they want. They first find people who will speak for them, in the native‘s language.”

“People like me.”

“Yes, People like you. How could we have done this without you. You made all of this possible. I understand why you started. We all did for, I’ll bet, the same reasons.” Andres met his eyes. “I‘ll bet that you wanted to learn about the animals. Horses, no?”

“No, not the animals. It was metal. The little cross they gave 'Ahtooshe', Regina Maria, when they rode by our village. And glass! I’ve never seen anything as beautiful as the polished ice in my hand. I wanted to see how it was done so we could do the same things in my village, Seebag-na,” with sadness at saying the word. The life that was slipping away from the earth.

“But now you ride horses.” Andres continued. “You have glass beads. You have all of the crucifixes you could ever want. But…..” Pausing.

“But, I don‘t have my life! My ancestors. All my friends that I grew up with. Most are dead.”

“But you have a good life here, no?”

Nicolas laughed. It sounded like choking. “Yes, I have a good life. My people are dying of black tongue all around me. My two wives and my boy died of it. These people brought to us! And now, there are all these new ones from far away villages. They won‘t survive! They will die here. I have such a good life. I am ashamed.”

“This sounds strange to you, but I’m also ashamed. I am lost from my people. From my ancestors and all of our history. What I can learn of our history comes from Europeans. Spain is a European tribe. I get books that tell about how they conquered us. How my great grand parents died. How we became Christians and renounced our pagan gods, so that I am now a Catholic Franciscan who is supposed to hate the Jesuits, Protestants, Jews and pagans like your people, but not the neophytes, who are being taught to be Christian like me. What does that make me?”

“But everything,” Nicolas Jose said. “That their Christ says is different from what they do! I can‘t stop thinking about that. Father Crespi turns the other way when people are being treated worse than animals and when soldiers do evil things.”

Andres added. “Or when Father Somera would let Regina Maria die rather than trying to help her.” Andres couldn’t forget the timidity of the Father. “They are only decorations for the Empire. Like your glass beads or the beautiful colors of the flags and uniforms. They will talk about helping the poor, the meek and the powerless, until the powerful, their bosses, not God, but their real bosses, say forget the poor. Let’s go and conquer people who will make us richer!

If the church says ‘No,’ they will throw out those priests and find priests who say what they want said. There are many versions of their Bible. They can say. ‘This is what Christ said’ or ‘This is what John, or Peter or Ezekiel, or whoever helps leaders control people’s minds.”

Andres leaned closer. “In the tribe of France, that’s the center of their empire, even more than Spain, there’s a movement of free thinkers. We who understand that the world doesn't belong to Kings."

"The Crown' is the Royals, that means the Empire. "The Catholic Church." That means the Jesuits, Franciscans and other tribes of their church, they come from Rome. That's in the country, the tribe, of Italy. The Church of Rome works for all the European tribes except for England."

"Stop!" Nicolas Jose put out his palm and shook his head. "Too many tribes. Too many countries."

Andres nodded and leaned back against the wall. "I'll go slower, but it will help you understand. There are things that are happening now. I've been saying all of these names of countries. The map will help. I'll bring it tomorrow. Look at this. He moved three shirts and two pants into five islands on the floor. He pointed to each one. "These are the countries, tribes, of Europe. This shirt is Spain. That's where the Spanish come from. This is France. That's where the King of Spain comes from. He doesn't even speak Spanish! You speak more Spanish than he does! But he runs many tribes, or countries. That is what 'The Crown' means. The Bourbons are 'The Crown.' They are French! But look!" Pointing to a third shirt. "They are both tied to Rome. That's the Catholic Church. That's their excuse for invading our lands. Their excuse for having Kings and Crowns. That's their excuse for killing the Peoples of the Land. That's why they send the Padres and start the Missions. Do you see that? The three shirts want to own the world?"

Nicolas Jose had his head down, nodding at the shirts. "Those are big places? Many people?"

"And many, many soldiers with many muskets, swords and big canons that can kill many men at one shot. Canons can even knock down buildings."

"Will they have those here?"

"They have them in San Diego and the new presidio at Santa Barbara. But look! Their empire is falling apart" Pointing at the forth shirt. "Here is one big part of why."

"Is that is a different country?" Nicolas Jose was concentrating hard on the shirts and parts of the conversations he had heard. "Is that shirt England? Or Russia?"

"Very good, Nicolas Jose." Andres smiled at the speed of his pupil. "Yes, that's England. That is why Los Angeles pueblo was built. To keep the British out. To have this of all for Spain. For the Empire." He gestured grandly and kicked the shirt to a corner of the room. "But wait! England has a King. A German king who doesn't even speak English! England has a new problem. The same problem all kings will have."

"We, in the lands of the original peoples. We are what are called 'Colonies' of the Empire. England had colonies near here. Many days past the Mojaves. The English colonies fought against them and won! England is now too weak to come to the Californias. You said Russia. I didn't put down a shirt for them, but they are too far to the north. The Spanish have strong presidios and Russia is too weak."

Andres took the fifth shirt and placed it over the first two.

"This is the shirt of the future. This the land of the free thinking people of the European kingdoms and the people of their colonies who will become independent of empires. Like the colonies that call themselves America, who defeated England. Soon the Spanish and French people will throw out their kings and empires and the hypocrisy of the churches and become free thinking people. Their colonies, like Mexico, like California, will be free! All the tribes and all the villages of the world will be free!"

Pico heard small parts, but the flow was clear. 'We have a Freethinker revolutionary among us,' crawling away before he could be discovered.

In the soldiers' quarters, he changed his clothes, sat on his bed and fished his notebook from the mat and wrote his observations. He decided he'd had enough observations to write about the way the Mission was run, he didn't need to include this part about Andres in his report.

<<< 0 >>>

Hachaaynar, Kwetii' and Kiyukyu were stopped often on their walks along the lanes of Seebag-na. The questions and worries were often about having less oak trees and acorns for meal. The northern and eastern sides of the village were fenced off for the Mission cattle herds.

One or two young men were missing. Friends of the boys said they left their families to live in the Mission. The fields where hunts had been good now had fewer rabbits.

"These are hard times." He would repeat. "I'm doing all that I can. We'll gain our lands back, but it will take time." Having less and less faith that it would ever happen.

He hadn't seen Tooypor in two moons. Her runners told him that she was well. Her guards from Haapchivet were helping her build a new Pula hut higher in the foothills.

Her messengers reported she'd seen Europeans, Mexicans and strange People of the Earth, either Chumash or Pemuu'nga People, close to her. They were riding or walking through the lower forests where she hunted and gathered. She was frightened that one might have a firestick. He sent her a message. "For your safety, you should move closer to Haapchivet. I'll miss you."

She might explain these changes to him.

"Kwetii'. Get my wife. We need help."

CHAPTER 19

MISSION SAN GABRIEL – A MODEL NEOPHYTE

Cordero and Alvarado rode the north wall at dusk. The new encampment filled the west side of the Mission. The neophytes from the coast should have been preparing to sleep by now in their tar-coated lean-tos, but they now saw shouting Mission neophytes running into the courtyard with a dozen naked coastal Indians chasing them, throwing stones and swinging clubs made from roof supports

"What in hell!" Alvarado shouted. He and Cordero dismounted and ran to the first neophyte's men's sleeping quarters.

A dozen shouting neophyte men stopped outside, blocking the door and were confronted by more than twenty of the coastal men wielding chair legs and pointed broken sticks. They shouted in different dialects.

Pico, Verdugo and Machado came around the corner with muskets. Cordero and Alvarado had sidearms. Alvarado took charge by firing his pistol in the air.

The natives turned toward the soldiers but didn't drop their weapons. For a long moment no words or motions were made.

"Get Nicolas Jose!" Alvarado shouted to Machado. Voices shouted from the neophyte ranks.

"Nicolas Jose! Nicolas Jose!"

Machado found him in a field listening to complaints about sickness in the stock of the newest cattle from Mexico. Machado rode toward him, calling his name.

"There are troubles. We need a translator."

They entered the front gate and turned right. It was surprising to Machado that the Indians and soldiers stood in the nearly the same frozen stances after so much time, simply staring at each other when a simple blast would end it.

“Stay!” Pico shouted in the Tongva language. He had told Alvarado and Verdugo that it was about the only word that he knew, but that was far from true. The word plus the leveled muskets assured obedience until the translator arrived.

Nicolas Jose dismounted and walked to the door. The coastals spoke loudly, gesturing at the neophyte doorway. He squinted, trying to understand the dialect. The coastal villages slurred in a strange way but ‘stole,’ ’not stole,’ ‘attack,’ and ‘insult’ were clear enough.

“What happened?” He asked Diego Yavit, standing forward of the doorway in a defensive stance.

“They stole blankets and our…religious strings while we were working in the fields. They don’t even work. We took them back. They came to attack us.”

Nicolas Jose saw it wasn’t unlikely that outsiders would steal blankets. It gets cold out there. The afternoon was a good time to enter the workers quarters, The soldiers were making their rounds, but, religious strings or exchange strings, were artifacts of the coastal and island people. They had lost many to the soldiers during ‘the bathing,’ but there were still some from every family.

“They stole some blankets, but to get even, you took the shell exchange strings from them. Don‘t lie! You never have shell beads!.” Turning to the newcomer men. “How many beads did they take?”

One man from the lower villages understood it and explained it to the leaders. As they were talking Diego reached into his shoulder bag and dropped a handful of beads on the ground. Three other men did the same. “Tell the thieves to stay away. Stay in the dirt where they belong.”

TONGVA LANDS

The old man hid in the brush behind the oak where the invader soldier stopped and drank his red fluid and slept. It happened nearly every day when the sun was at it's highest. He watched the horse approach and felt no fear.

His wife and two children had died. His sister was dead. Half the people of his village were either dead, stolen from their homes, or seized while they were out looking for food.

He lay flat on the ground holding the thick broken oak branch with a flat hammer-like curved end. It was perfect. He knew what it was for when he found it three days ago.

He was curious to see the movements when the soldier would dismount, when he would drink and when he would fall asleep, but patience was what the hunter needed. To wait calmly until the moment is right and not reveal yourself.

Small sounds described the invader's actions in the shade of the oak; The tethering of the animal, the stretching and groaning of the man, the spreading of the blanket and lying upon it, the sighs after the fluid was drunk, and slowly, silence, and then, snoring.

He gently raised himself up, having earlier cleared the leaves and twigs that might make sounds as he approached.

He was calm and content with his plan as he crept over the man, avoiding having his shadow pass over him. He felt as much emotion as aiming a blow at a sleeping rabbit.

The man's leather hat was at his side. His long and tangled hair of dark brown with lighter streaks had small leaf fragments in it from rolling on his side and then turning on his back. His face was pale and his trimmed beard was a dark brown, almost black.

The soldier didn't move, other than his hands twitching up, trying to reach back when the club smashed down on his forehead full force. The attacker let out loud grunts of rage, letting out years of hatred as he brought the heavy oak branch down again and again on the red pulpy face and turned the strokes to the chest and flat hands until the fingers were gone and the identity was unrecognizable.

He stood back, panting from the exertion. He felt this had been a good day. His ancestors would be proud. He would not mention this to anyone in the village. One day he would find another soldier, and learn his habits.

LOS ANGELES

The de Cota home had moved a few hundred meters North to a gentle hillside away from the center, but to a place, where with mud and straw packed into wooden boxes and dried brick by brick, it would become a comfort to the five of them in all seasons.

A promotion to corporal helped a great deal to fund their dream, but the chance of retirement was becoming real.

He met Antonio Mesa leaving the church and sat down on a Plaza bench to talk about the new plans for adobe to replace the straw walls.

Pablo de Cota's wife and the three children walked on to home after seeing that Mesa's face looked pained and that it was going to be a private conversation. She liked the family but from what she could see and heard from the neighbors, nothing was working out the way they had planned.

"What's going on, Antonio?" Pablo asked, seeing sadness and despair on his friends face.

Antonio gestured at the street with a distaining glance.

"Look at this place." Waving for a sage teacup from Rosalia, the vendor. "You remember Sinaloa. Can this place ever be the same?"

"You've been given so much. You need to use your resources to make your land grow. Look at Rosas. He's an old man but he's done so much to improve his plot. He always has a smile at the market."

"He came with more money. He's smiling because all his children and grandchildren do all the work. Look at his land! Mine is all rocks and gravel. I can never make it that rich."

"You can do it! Just you and Maria Ana start at dawn and start pileing. That's what he did.

Antonio grimaced. "We have. We have tried over and over. This place is not for us. All of our friends are in Sinaloa. It's beautiful. This place is ugly desert, This will never become a growing town, all the Indians, all the dust storms and smoke. They can give their horses and tool to someone else. We will move."

His face became calmer. "It's the first time I've said that," and made a light smile. "I'll tell Maria."

Pablo saw his demeanor change in a flash.

"What are you saying?"

Antonio grinned. "We are moving back to Sinaloa."

CHAPTER 20

FATHER SERRA - 1783

After many false starts the riders arrived. The Padres gathered around Crespi

“The Blessed Father Junipero Serra’s party is two days south of Mission San Gabriel Archangel. He had started walking from San Diego last week. He will stay and inspect our Mission and meet with Governor Fages here.”

“He’ll bless the construction of a new Mission near Presidio Santa Barbara. He’ll bring the grace and blessings of the Church to the northern savages.”

He looked from face to face with a despondent sigh.

“How do we conceal the new arrivals? Two hundred more this week! We have three thousand Indians here! We don‘t have materials for new lean-tos.”.

Cambon said. “We can offer several hundred as helpers to the Pueblo of Los Angeles through our Church of Our Lady of the Angels. They can bring tents or build their own structures.”

“We don‘t have tents to spare.” Crespi said. “I’ll request them from Olivera, but even if he helps, which I doubt, it will take weeks to arrive. We need Olivera and Nicolas Jose to organize things for us quickly!”

Lopez, Galvez and Andres gathered all of the able bodied men into a herd and walked hundreds of the newcomers to do brush clearance on the hillsides of the Pueblo de Los Angeles. The weather was mild enough for them to sleep outdoors for two days out of sight of the Blessed Padre.

<<< 0 >>>

On approaching Mission San Gabriel Archangel, Father Junipero Serra wrinkled his nose from the stench of an endless herd of cattle in the pastures to his left.

“They have five thousand head! A disgusting smell!” Padre Cerriani said, waving his hand in front of his nose. He had walked beside the limping Serra for over one hundred miles with a support wagon and a six man guard trailing by a hundred yards.

Serra had read dozens of lengthy reports and dispatches describing the conditions at this Mission. ’Deplorable conditions’ and ’Steeped in Sin’ were common phrases, although the descriptions of neophyte behavior were mixed with favorable comments.

He had confidence Crespi was doing his best, but as far as he’d seen, Cambon, Somera and the newer visiting Padres and monks hadn’t proven themselves. They’d been without proper guidance for years and the soldiers’ lustful excesses were legendary. His minimal confidence diminished on approach.

To the left and right along the Mission walls, he saw trashy improvised native-like structures with naked children and curious poorly clothed Indians peeping around corners as though they’d been ordered to stay indoors.

The array of Church and military people at the front gate was designed to be orderly and impressive but in the wider view, it was all disconnected from the overall disarray.

After florid greetings, Serra asked for private quarters to rest and wait for Governor Fages.

Lying on the narrow bed, looking up in quiet rage, he visualized the expressions and many excuses that Fages would use to deny funding and access to the planned Missions that would Christianize the entire New World from Argentina to the icy floes of the north.

The French Church would unite and the Eastern Church and the Russians would be banished from the hemisphere. All this could happen and the world would reach salvation under the true church, except for the secularists and their sabotage.

He thought through several approaches: The logical and commercial, showing the economic benefits of a tame workforce. The idealistic, appealing to the Europeanization of the Indians, bringing real music and fine art to the western Americas. He knew that Fages was an art lover and might respond to an appeal to self interest. On weighing the options, he chose guilt.

Fages was a lapsed Catholic. His appearance at Mass was an occasion to show his underlings his French clothing and entourage of sycophants. 'God only knows when he had confession, or stayed for communion.' But by being reminded that he was flirting with eternal damnation and was likely to be a mockery throughout the Christian world, he might be moved from his commercial interest in blocking the Church and it's Missions. He slept a sound and welcome sleep until late in the morning. A timid knocking awoke him.

"Blessed Father. A pair of messengers are in the hallway." The pretty Indian woman, no doubt a maid, said in a low reverent voice. He looked at her well made, probably imported from France, dark red dress. It was familiar. As she walked away, he said.

"Turn."

She stopped, facing him. He looked her over from a distance and saw that the dress, or 'costume,' was a copy from the popularly reproduced Italian painting of the Blessed Virgin Mary.

"Ummm." Waving her off with a flick of the hand, unsure if the display was actually reverent or merely a mockery of the Church's images.

Two bedraggled soldiers in the hallway snapped to attention as Serra approached them, handing him a leather pouch. Cambon and Somera stood aside as the pouch was opened, following Serra out to the courtyard, watching him reading, scowling and pacing.

"Was this given to you by the Governor or by a subordinate?" Glaring at the nearest soldier.

"By Governor Fages' assistant, but the governor handed it directly to him."

Serra whirled and shouted.

"I am not important enough to meet with the Governor!" Pointing to the horses at the trough. "Mount your horses and go directly back to Loreto. Tell him that my party is continuing to Santa Barbara to do the Lord's work." Turning to Cambon. "Bring Crespi to me. I'll inspect the Mission and leave tomorrow morning for Santa Barbara."

Crespi walked Serra around the grounds, followed by Somera, Cambon, and two soldiers carrying muskets who'd been assigned as Serra's security.

"This is filthy." he said often. "Why aren't they properly dressed?" Walking around the lean-tos. "Those are men and women working together, aren't they? Are they married? Or kept separated after work?" Stopping and turning an accusatory look to Crespi.

"They have separated sleeping quarters."

"Who watches them in the fields? I see many bushes and trees where they can partake of sinful acts."

"No, they're well monitored. Overseers watch them."

"And the soldiers? Do they watch them? Do they see them at night? Behind the buildings?" Waving his hand to indicate that he had finished with these fields.

"We are becoming the beef center of Alta California" Crespi motioned for the group to follow him past the western side of the Mission encampments, but Serra stopped him.

"I want to return to the courtyard. Is this Nicolas Jose still an overseer here?"

Crespi replied. "Yes, Blessed Father. He is now Alcalde, and doing a good job of keeping peace" Glad to change to a subject that reflected well on the Mission.

As Serra walked, he kept his head down, thinking of how to approach it. There could be no equivocating on moral issues. The corruption of this place can only be undone by clear bold actions. Our Lord wouldn't hesitate, nor would he want a man of God to turn away from his duty.

The central courtyard was clean. The older neophytes had raked the leaves away and were sitting on the brick benches around the central oak tree. They stood looking busy as the Padres entered the yard.

Serra stood beside the tree and said loudly. “Where is this Nicolas Jose. Bring him here.”

Crespi responded. “He should be with the shepherds at this hour. He will ride in before dark,”

“Have a soldier find him and bring him here.” He paced, speaking loudly to no specific person. “Bring the other soldiers and neophytes. We are going to have a spiritual awakening here. A time for rejoicing and rebirth!”, walking to the chapel. “Crespi. I am going to my room to meditate. Get me when Nicolas Jose is here.”

Somera looked at Padre Cambon. “He will probably scold him for the mess of the newcomers camps.”

“Thank goodness there are fewer than last week!” Watching Crespi sending Lopez to bring the Alcalde back.

Crespi returned to the two, saying. “I don‘t know how to interpret this. All the reports have justly praised Nicolas Jose. Possibly he will also praise him.” Sighing. “Possibly he will excommunicate him.”

Nicolas Jose was surprised at the large number of neophytes in the courtyard with the fathers and Olivera. He knew of the arrival of the Franciscan chief Padre. It would be a gathering of all the Mission to hear the Blessed Father speak and wish him a safe journey on his way north. It would be a relief after that. Back to normal life.

He dismounted. Crespi beckoned him to the central group where Serra held a steady and intense gaze on him.

Nicolas Jose bowed and kissed the ring on Serra’s hand. He looked up and the gaze was unchanged. He stepped back and saw that everyone, soldiers, priests and neophytes were looking at him.

Serra cleared his throat and spoke in a stentorian voice, so that all within thirty meters could hear clearly.

"Nicolas Jose, Alcalde of Mission San Gabriel Archangel." Waiting for a response.

"Yes, your Grace." Never having had to address someone as important as this. Was 'Blessed Father still correct? Was your Grace said only for the Pope person? Or a King?'

"You have become well known in the centers of The Church, Perhaps, even in the Vatican"

He tried to remember what a 'Vatican' was. It sounded like an important word, like 'Crown' or 'Empire.'

"Thank you Blessed Father. I am honored." Hoping it was the correct word to show humility to a superior.

Father Serra looked steadily at his eyes, then to Crespi and the Franciscans, and to Olivera and the soldiers.

"I had heard many things about you from the Fathers and officials who have passed through this Mission. I look at you and hear you. I can see why you have been so popular with some of the soldiers and some of the neophytes who have come under your influence" Looking from right to left and addressing all those within earshot.

"This man who has become your Alcalde has brought sin and dishonor into this place that was blessed with holy water and the sanction of the Church of Our Lord. This Mission is here to promote Christian values and bring morality and righteousness to the people of the world who live in darkness."

Pointing at Nicolas Jose. "This man has promoted fornication among the innocent neophyte children. He's brokered prostitution between native women and soldiers. He has been a fornicator and has even threatened to kill men of the church. His sins are incompatible with the standards of the Mission. He must renounce the title of Alcalde and confess to his sins."

Gesturing to his guard of soldiers. "Officers Moreno and Gallardo, Seize this man, strip off his shirt and have him kneel before me."

Crespi, in shock, started to speak, but Serra's stern glare and raised hand silenced him.

Nicolas Jose's thoughts raced in dizzying arcs of confusion. 'I'm Good! That was years ago in a past life! I've renounced that! I have accepted Christ!.' He started to speak as the first soldier pulled his arms back. "Father Serr…" the second soldier slapped his face and dragged him to the ground.

Charna, Sa'aa're', Taaherkwe', the field and herd overseers, who'd known and worked with him the past two years, the soldiers who'd seen him change, and Padres Crespi, Cambon and Somera, stood in fear of raising their voices as a third man, dressed nearly like a soldier, appearing to be a Kumeyaay trustee from San Diego, stepped forward with a thickly braided whip that was too short for animals, but a fearful instrument for use on humans.

Corporal Cordero was uncharacteristically slack-jawed, amazed that this person, whom he now didn't like for his prudishness, was being flogged for behavior that Cordero wished were the situation of the moment. 'What idiots.' he thought, applying it to all of them.

Corporal Andres saw the irony before him and tried to project the future effects of Nicolas Jose's sudden fall. He looked at the faces. Sergeant Olivera, Corporals Verdugo, Alvarado, Machado and Galvez seemed unconcerned spectators at an unexpected drama. The injustice made him furious, but it was consistent with the hypocrisy of the church.

Lopez was shaking his head silently mouthing "No." Then he looked at Corporal Pico, who was standing across the crowd, looking directly at him. Their eyes met for two seconds, but Pico went back to watching other expressions in the crowd, looking for traces of rebellion.

Nicolas Jose vowed to not shout or express pain. To show that this person couldn't hurt him. His people were watching him. His ancestors were watching him.

The first two strokes were heavier and more painful than anything he could have prepared for. By the third lash he dropped any pretence of stoicism. A moan couldn't be suppressed, followed by groans, outbursts of breath and whimpers of pain, until no more was heard as he slumped in unconsciousness, blood running off of his torn flesh.

Serra paced back and forth looking at the ground before his feet. When the sounds from Nicolas Jose stopped, he waved off the whipman and faced the crowd from over the body, flat and twitching on the ground.

Loudly and clearly he spoke. "When the man is ready, he will confess of his sins. He will repent and take communion, and, if he is truly sincere, he will rejoin the family of the saved."

LOS ANGELES

Pablo Rodriguez was surprised to hear that there was a letter for him to pick up at the Town Governance Building.

He was not sure if he could read a letter if it were written with a pen and not printed in clear letters.

At the desk he asked what kind of letter it was and who had sent it. The cherk read the name as Maria Teresa Velasco y Lara, the Sister of his friend, Jose. She lived in Nayarit and wrote to Jose often.

Pablo squinted at the script and couldn't understand the words.

"Could you read this to me."

The clerk didn't like having his work interrupted by one who should have learned to read. He grudgingly opened and scanned it.

"Her brother died in an accident visiting her."

Pablo left the building and walked home in anger at the way the clerk dismissed the death of his friend and flipped the letter across the desk as though it wasn't something important to him.

Three of his best friends, y Lara, private Alvitre and Luis Quintero, had both moved to the new township of Santa Barbara to help build the new Mission Buenaventura, but he thought that Jose would stay there rather than returning to Nayarit.

It was confusing. Many of his friends had left or were planning to leave soon, either back to San Diego or Sinaloa, or to Santa Barbara and the new Capitol to the North. Monterey

He decided on the spot to stay. He and his wife had put in too much work and had so many friends in the pobladores and soldiers to leave this place. It was too good after the summers to not have a great harvest.

MISSION SAN GABRIEL

Taaherkwe', then Sa'aa're' and Charaana slipped out of the mission and threaded their way through the spread out cattle sleeping on what once was the trail between the Mission and Seebag-na.

Hachaaynar slept early. He'd felt increasing waves of hopelessness as cattle fences moved closer and closer to the village and more food sources disappeared. The new invaders only depressed him more. His guards brought the three women into the greathouse. They described the events and the chief Pul who had come from far away.

"Charaana. Sa'aa're', you and Taaherkwe' will return now. I will bring Tooypor here. One of you return to us on the night after next to meet with us. Charaana, you will stay in the kitchens. You are too important to risk."

<<< 0 >>>

He had no memory of being carried to the little infirmary behind the chapel. He kept his eyes closed during the handling and washing. He let himself moan. He tried to not understand the words of the women packing a thick and soon soothing poultice on his back. It was all shame. He hated himself for trusting these people. For being blind to what he really was. Disposable as any neophyte was.

After more than a day he became aware of a person sitting over his right shoulder in the corner of the room. During and between the handlings and bathing, he kept his eyes closed to avoid any contact or conversation, but in blinks, the shape was there. He wondered if it was real. If it was the spirit of his mother or a spirit watching over him.

He spoke in the darkness of the evening. "Who are you?" And waited. "Why are you here?"

"I'm ashamed by what was done to you." The woman's voice began. "You gave so much to them. I hated you, but then I saw you becoming good." Her voice was smooth and soft. Her accent was soothing. "You became a real Christian. The kind they talk about. You sacrificed. You tried to help the powerless and ease their suffering. I don't know what changed you, but you became complete."

"'Ahtooshe'?"

"Maria Regina. That's what I am called, Nahanpar. I don't know who 'Ahtooshe' was. She died and I was born. I'd see you and I hated you. You were the reason that 'Ahtooshe' suffered and died. You were the reason that her husband and son were killed. That our world died." She rose and pushed the chair around to face him. He saw the face that was so familiar and a source of strength to him in his youth. His pain increased on turning his head, but it felt worth the pain to see the one he had betrayed. He hadn't thought of it as a betrayal. He'd seen it as a twist of fate that was out of his hands. Her pose of superiority annoyed him. Allowing her self to be called a 'Queen' and dressing as the Virgin Mary. 'Stupid posing' was what he'd called it. Her looks at him didn't seem as much hatred as looking at an inferior person, as the Spanish did.

Her eyes were soft and motherly. "I hated you, but I hated everyone. The Padres, the soldiers and the ones captured like me. The only thing I cared about was the wool they gave me and that spinning wheel. They treated me like one of their pictures. I wore their dresses. They had women wash me and make my hair the way they wanted it, but only watching the wool become yarn and making the yarn into blankets was real. I'd look at you but only think about the yarn. I would say a greeting to a Padre, but I was looking at the air in front of him, not him. I didn't really see anyone. I didn't want to see anything else, because everything was pain."

He closed his eyes half way through, remembering seeing her watching him dragged to his cell by Cordero and Lopez. "I felt your hatred"

"But two days ago…I couldn't turn away. I saw you disrespected and watched their faces. I know that you'd become a different person than their traitor. You tried to help our people to suffer less. I saw that the people who saved my life were killing our people's spirits. I cried and cried. I couldn't stop it when they did this to you. I sat at my wheel on the patio and remembered everything. The soldier Rodriguez, The times that you were like a son and a teacher to my dead son."

"Your son isn't dead." With his eyes closed.

She wasn't sure she'd heard him right.

"Did you say something about Hachaaynar? That he's not dead?"

"Did no one tell you? Hatchayar escaped. He is now Sevaanga-vik. Your husband was killed when he tried to rescue you." He told her about the severed head and Tooypor's recovery. She remembered the chants outside the shed where she was kept. Her shoulders shook and sobs rose as it flooded back.

"Why didn't you tell me! I could have healed!"

"You seemed to be too much their little obedient slave. You would never listen to me." He wanted her wails to stop before she attracted people to the room. He'd only heard the same old women enter since he had gone unconscious in the courtyard. Fear was with him every moment.

."I was told Seebag-na was destroyed. All the young men had been killed. How could my son still be chief"

He remembered slinking down on the steps, wishing to be too drunk to recognize the sound of the shooting.

"Some of the men attacked and were killed"

"But Hachaaynar wasn't with them?"

“I saw him and Tooypor watching when the Governor came here and the Pueblo was made. They were with the Yaanga people. They looked good. Did you come?”

“I spun yarn. I don‘t go where they tell me to. I stay as one of their statues. I saw women from my village but I wouldn’t speak to them”

“Seebag-na exists. Only smaller.”

“I want to escape. I want to be with my son. Will you come?”

He closed his eyes again. He might be killed or exiled when he could rise and walk. “I am too confused to think of tomorrow. Everything is false. I was ready to die. I can‘t die feeling like this. I understand what you say but I don‘t know if I trust you either. I only want to sleep.”

“I’ll come again. I am sorry for what has happened to you, Nahanpar.”

“ And I am sorry for all that has happened to you, 'Ahtooshe'. Do you forgive me?”

“Yes. Yes I do.. .Nahanpar”

<<< 0 >>>

Crespi waited for two days to approach Nicolas Jose. He had met with the other Padres, soldiers and overseers separately for a consensus on what to do with the Alcalde. He decided to not make a decision until he spoke to him and had a feeling for the depth of his anger.

Cordero had an unexpected reaction, praising the way that Nicolas Jose was silent and didn’t interrupt Serra. “I would have been yelling my head off! The information was three years old! I have problems with him but that wasn’t fair.”

Andres said. “This breeds disrespect in the neophytes who’ve known him as an upstanding man. If he remains as Alcalde there will be little disruption. If he’s able to deal with the humiliation, make him Alcalde again. It was terrible misjudgment of Serra's. It leaves doubt about the Church's ability to govern."

Olivera had a similar approach, for different reasons, the same goal. "It will pass. Let him recover slowly. The neophytes will understand. He must be furious but we'll give him special care." Thinking, 'what better a way to drive a wedge between the workforce and the Franciscans. Serra has done the damage. We can use this against him.'

Lopez came straight out. "That was the worst thing that could have happened. There isn't any way we can gain respect from them after this. He'll have to go to San Diego or Santa Barbara. He'll be too angry to work with."

Saenz said. "He has to leave. We can‘t have a troublemaker. That‘s what he‘ll be." Having enjoyed the entire humiliation. He had heard all of the stories of Nicola Jose when he had supplied women to the troops. It was funny to see Serra become so crazy.

Alvarado and Verdugo urged a long wait and see before deciding what to do with him.

Cambon and Somera prayed, asking the meaning. They and Crespi agreed that Serra hadn't read the reports that were sent to him. "How could he do that to the best man we have without talking to us first?" They all agreed that Crespi alone would see him in the morning.

Taaherkwe' told Tooypor and Hachaaynar about the flogging of Nicolas Jose. The greatest news was of 'Ahtooshe' walking into the kitchen and hugging her and the other women. They screamed with pleasure. She was alive! She told them about what had happened to her and how Nicolas Jose's flogging made her memory come back.

"I'd seen her before, but only from a distance. I never knew who she was! She sat behind a patio wall in a red dress and hair like their 'Maria' paintings. I thought she was a Padre's wife, except they aren't supposed to have wives. She was alive all the time. "

“My Mother is alive!” Tooypor hugged him tight.

“Our mother. Our teacher.”

“She thought you were dead.” Taaherkwe' said. “She wants to escape and come to you. She was excited. She was told that you were dead. That Seebag-na was destroyed!”

Tooypor looked to Hachaaynar. “I always felt she wasn‘t dead, but I had no feeling of where she was. It was as though she were very far away.”

“She was.” Taaherkwe' took both of their hands. “She told us that she was dead for three years. Seeing that happen to Nahanpar woke her.“

“Is that what she called him?” Hachaaynar still held a spark of hope.

“She wants him to escape too.”

“Will he?” He asked.

“She doesn‘t know.”

<<< 0 >>>

Jose Pico had ridden a hard sixteen hours before being led inside the building and flopping down on a bunk in the Santa Barbara Presidio prison. He slept for four hours before the new jailer woke him.

“Senor Hannibal?”

“From the fields of Carthage.” He answered.

“The first prisoner is two cells down on the right. I‘ll take you.”

Pico removed his uniform and dressed in Mission smock and pants. He pulled a stool in front of the cell where two groggy and bruised Indians slouched in the corner.

"Ah'ahey." He said, and kept his gaze fixed until they replied. He sat for a several minutes looking at their fearful faces before saying in clumsily accented Tongva

"We will talk."

Nicolas Jose knew he was in the room at the back of the chapel near the neophyte men's quarters where the fight with the coastal people had taken place at the doorway.

Nicolas Jose looked at the ceiling hearing every sound with interest. He was hand spooned five small meals each day by a young kitchen worker. He was bathed and had his dressings and poultice changed twice a day. His fever had risen. He perspired under the soft blankets 'Ahtooshe' had made for him. He expected her to come for hours and could not sleep.

The sounds from the sleeping quarters were often arguments or raucous laughter. A sound was now coming softly from more than one man. It was a slow chant of mourning. He guessed that it was the variety practiced by men in Asuks-gna. It repeated and he felt that six or more were keeping the old rites alive.

He grew sleepy trying to mouth the words for more than an hour when it changed to a blessing for good food and then a hunting chant. He grinned with the first real pleasure in four days. He had no idea the old ways were still practiced in the neophyte quarters. He wondered if the other men's and women's areas were the same. It would be wonderful if the lifeways continued here.

'Here,' he chose purposely, 'among the Invaders.'

<<< 0 >>>

Taaherkwe' and 'Ahtooshe' wore earth-stained Mission shifts waiting in the bushes until Galvez passed on his night shift riding the western range.

They darted, hunched over, zigzagging from bush to hollow to bush until they ducked through the cattle fence and threaded their way through the sleeping cows. They were followed by restless bulls but went between enough cows to leave the bulls behind.

They approached Seebag-na where Hachaaynar and twenty of the most respected villagers looked up the old northern trail for them. Tooypor, Kwetii', Kyookyu and old Kethu were there, sitting on a smooth log stool.

'Ahtooshe' ran, then danced toward them as she'd last danced at her son's wedding. Her laughter was returned as they bumped together, hugging and whirling with Hachaaynar and then with Tooypor. Friends and family who had long thought she was dead surrounded her to touch her and welcome her home.

Only the three women entered the greathouse with Hachaaynar. 'Ahtooshe' wanted Tah'her'que with her.

"I was told so many lies! I heard you were all killed. They said nothing about my husband's head or Tooypor's help. I felt I should have died, so I killed my own life. I became their little blanket making doll and sat in their patio."

She heard about the diseases that continued to kill many of the Seebag-na people. 'Ahtooshe' closed her eyes.

"I've had many happy moments in my life. This is the happiest."

Taaherkwe' said. "I have to return after eight or ten fingers. Will you come?"

"I'll never go back. I'm home."

Nicola Jose was dressed and bathed in the morning. A horrible itching and burning was replacing the pain. He twisted and rubbed against the rough sheeting the find relief when Charaana came in the room.

“’Ahtooshe’ has returned home. They want to know if you will go too.”

“Who is the ’They?”

“'Ahtooshe'. Hachaaynar.”

He considered the options and emotions that were at war in him for ten years, answering.

“I don‘t think I can stay here. I don‘t think I can stay in Seebag-na. I don‘t belong anywhere.”

“Tooypor wants to meet with you. You can be a great help to your people if you are ready to come to them.”

He looked into her almond eyes. Her round face was uncreased and youthful. She was always neutral in kitchen squabbles and well organized in her work. He’d never thought of her as still actively trying to regain the land.

“Do you report everything I say to Tooypor?” Seeing a smile before she made a motion of her hand to signify “no.”

“I was in the kitchen when a person from the village came to me and told me. He wanted me to tell you.”

Nicolas Jose tried to shrug, but laughed at how much pain a simple shrug would make. “I can‘t decide anything now. I don‘t want to leave this bed.”

“Many people here respect you. The evil done to you has made many people angry. I know it was a surprise, but more than Serra, you saw the ones who threw you away. The blessed Padres. You aren’t theirs any more. Come to your people!”

He watched the ceiling until he fell asleep. The sound of a man clearing his throat didn’t wake him. A hand on his sleeve slowly brought him to.

Father Crespi studied the face he’d seen so many times in these ten years. The deep lines appeared more so in slanted shadows. Nicolas Jose had prepared for this moment. He’d rein in his emotions and hear the Padre.

The old woman who dressed him said the whole Mission thought it was wrong. He didn't really expect to be condemned by the Padres or soldiers after all his service , but life was full of surprises. He felt ready for anything and felt far from it all at the same time.

Crespi wore an expression usually given to wounded animals with wide soft eyes and crinkly pulled together brows. "How are you healing, my son." He said.

"Slowly. The pain and the itching is very bad. The old women who help me say I'll be here for many days."

"My son." He said a low soothing voice as one might speak to a beloved child. "There are times in this mortal life when we are tried by sometimes unknowable challenges. When we ask God to help us to understand the trials of the soul. To find forgiveness in a forest of doubts and anger. When we feel that the whole world has turned against us. When we cry bitter tears at the unfairness of it all. When we, perhaps, blame ourselves for past transgressions..........."

Nicolas Jose listened as the room slowly became foggy. Some of the words were unknown to him, or ones that he had heard but was unsure of the real meaning. The thing that was clear to him was that Father Crespi was afraid to say anything bad about Father Serra or to admit a mistake. It sounded as though he was saying that Nicolas Jose should feel guilty about his past life and accept the beating as part of his 'purification.'

".....you know that you can always come to me or to any of my Brothers to talk about anything that is troubling you, and that we are always here for you. There is nothing that you can't come to us with, for comfort or forgiveness, to find balance your life."

He stroked the hand as the paw of a wounded dog, saying. "I feel the pain that you are going through, as I feel the pain of our Lord when He called out to his Father for forgiveness, He knew not what it was for, but through Him, God brought forgiveness to Mankind, to all who accept his son Jesus Christ as their savior." He bowed his head deeply to Nicolas Jose.

"Do you understand me my son? We are asking for your forgiveness."

Tiredness overwhelmed him. It would be good to fall asleep now. To not answer this question. It was insulting. He didn’t offer anything. Nothing about his work or room. He wanted something from him! A big something! He offered Nothing! Only a trade in ‘forgiveness!’. No one has offered to let themselves be whipped by me! I don’t know what I want or what will feel better, but it is not forgiveness. He felt confident the neophytes were on his side and saw the injustice.

“Blessed Father.” With eyes closed. “I’m still so confused…and tired. I’m happy that you have come to me, but…. I must sleep now.” Trailing off to a quiet, hopefully convincing, mumble.

Crespi looked at the Indian’s slack face. He’d expected fire and anger, but instead found calm acceptance. He would come around. The thought occurred that the man might need last rites if an infection became uncontrollable, but he had confidence that Nicolas Jose would return to the bosom of The Church..

“I still don‘t trust him” Tooypor argued against ‘Ahtooshe’’s proposal in the greathouse. Elders were seated in a semi-circle. Fragrant smoke hung in the air from herbs in the central flame pit. “He goes to whatever or whoever seems to offer him some shelter from his demons. He is filled with demons and Pula ‘Ahtooshe’ Pahr, you have suffered because of it.”.

“I’ve seen him change.” 'Ahtooshe' answered. “He’s not the same man that I saw when I was a prisoner.”

“You’ve seen him change many times. We all have. We can’t put our hopes in one who could betray us all. We would have NO hopes of keeping our land and our lifeways from the invaders. I want all of you to agree that we have to watch his every move for two or three moons before we even talk about approaching him. He has a way, a manner, that attracts people. He’s clever. If he had a balance to him, he would be second only to Hachaaynar as a leader, if he were ours.”

“He IS ours!“ 'Ahtooshe' interrupted.

Hachaaynar hoped she was right but he'd seen too many opportunities pass by. Looking back, it seemed Tooypor was right at every time.

"No mother." He said. "He must prove himself."

The elders nodded and showed assent.

"We are near agreement." Tooypor gestured around the room and spoke to 'Ahtooshe'.

"Respected teacher. You've been a prisoner of the Invaders for many years. You've seen him as Nahanpar and as Nicolas Jose. You haven't seen the outside life. You don't know the damage they do and what they've already done. They are destroying whole villages. The Pemuu'nga islanders, the coastal villages are being wiped out! "

"I was in the Mission when they brought them in!"

"When they brought the ones who survived in!. So many were killed before they reached the Mission." Her eyes bored into 'Ahtooshe''s. "We are inland. There are Tongva villages on all four sides of them. They don't attack us like they do the villages that are isolated because the villages that are connected could unite and overwhelm them. That is how we must plan, but in ways that cannot be revealed to them. Don't you see that one traitor can lead us into a trap? A man like Nicolas Jose could make us promises and cause us all, and all of our lifeways and children, to be crushed. Gone forever."

"At least talk with him." 'Ahtooshe' pleaded.

Hachaaynar waved his hand. "Tooypor's vision is clear. We will have him watched for two moons and then talk about it more. This is over."

Sa'aa're' nodded. "We will comfort him and listen to him. One of us will report to you every two or three days."

Hatcheynar looked to 'Ahtooshe' as Tooypor held her hand. "I hope you understand, Mother."

'Ahtooshe' smiled. 'Let them decide. I'm just glad to be home."

CHAPTER 21

A DANGEROUS PATH

Tah-ur and three hunting women from the relocated foothill village ran leaping and shouting through the high grasses leading to the flatlands. They ran on the downside of of a hillside trapping a panicking tan young deer. It hesitated and ran zigzag. They ran straight. If they could get ahead to start uphill along side of it, they could force it to the wedge of a rock drop off and have a stationary target.

The deer edged right and nearly fell into the rocky crevasse. It stopped wide eyed as the first arrow flew past it's nose. The second arrow struck it's flank and in an instant, two entered it's neck, making it stagger in a tight circle and fall twitching on it's side. There was laughter as they carved the animal into sections to carry home in their wide leather shoulder slings.

They entered the new village, tucked into a deep cut in the hillside. The hard ground slanted downhill with no pockets to catch rain. Drainage was good. The village had thrived. The ease of life, compared to the harsh desert, had energized a dying tribe. The vegetation and small animals kept them well fed.

"Two invaders." The young boy ran to them, pointing toward dust in the valley to the east.

"They're riding to the Mission." Tah-ur looked to the other three. All picked up the same thought and nodded.

"Can we?" The youngest asked.

"We'll get close, and if we're unseen and the land lets us, we'll look at each other." Tah-ur looked at each one. "We'll signal 'yes.', and if we are positioned right, we'll kill them."

The four women slapped arms and ran angling to the west to intersect the soldier's trail, snaking down gullies, hunching through the dry and dusty underbrush. They carried six arrows each. They felt no fear. They felt a thrilling shared excitement that a moment they'd dreamed about was about to happen.

They moved behind a wedge of stratified rock. The trail came into view and the approaching horses could be heard.

Tah-ur pointed at three bushes on the side from five to twelve paces from the edge of the trail. It would be shielded from the riders until they were right beside them.

"I'll shoot first" She said, squatting behind a saguaro, driving five arrows into a sandy spot and loading the bow, listening to the horses coming closer.

Two arrows struck each of the soldiers almost simultaneously. The first was hit in the right shoulder and the waist within the seam of the loosened leather. The second one was hit in the temple and wrist as he raised his hand defensively. He slumped and started sliding off of the saddle as the first soldier clumsily tried to draw a sidearm with his injured arm. The leather kept the arrows from penetrating deeply but the pain was debilitating.

Tah-ur's next arrow went into his upper lip. Two more struck his neck and knee. The pistol dropped from his hand as he slid off the saddle.

The four women walked around the two fallen invaders in amazement. It was easy! They stared at the horses pawing the side of the trail and eating the straw-like plants.

"Do you think they will come with us?" Tah-ur asked.

They walked beside the horses and took the reins in hand. The horses pulled away and stomped around in the brush. They shouted and clapped as the horses ran away and walked home joking about each other's marksmanship.

Nicolas Jose lay back with tired and suspicious eyes, watching a procession of people pass, wishing him good health and a fast recovery. The priests never made apology. They wore apologetic expressions and had a glaze of fear in their eyes. They were quiet and polite, as to a dying relative, but no honesty came from them.

The neophytes who considered themselves "Christian," showed sadness, but none said anything critical of the church hierarchy. They were usually silent other than a nod and a Spanish "Bless you, Senor." He didn't feel anger at them. Only disappointment in their fear of Serra.

The ones with the ties to the outside, who came to bring the old life back and to drive out the Spanish, came often. They asked how he felt. How he felt about what had happened. How he thought and felt about the Church and the soldiers. He knew what they wanted to hear but didn't say what they wanted to hear.

"I only want to recover." He'd tell them. "I'll try to understand this when I can walk and stand in the trees alone. I don't want to think until then."

They spoke among themselves about his condition.

"He'll make a break with them and join us." Sa'aa're' said with conviction.

"That's foolish." Taaherkwe' added. "I've seen him over the years, and he'll do what benefits himself. All Crespi has to do is say is 'You'll be Alcalde again' and he'll forgive Serra. You and 'Ahtooshe' see what you want to see but I see the damage he can do."

Charaana, as the first to report to the village, couldn't find anything that would make the trip worth the risk of being caught. After giving her view that nothing was worth reporting, the others agreed with her to wait another week.

On the fourth day Corporal Andres entered the room and sat beside him. Nicolas Jose watched his relaxed and unreadable face, wondering what took him so long.

"It was a bad thing," Andres began. "It shocked everyone. Even the Padres were lost for words. It's divided the neophytes into those who are angry and speak out, and those who are frightened and silent, but none of them feel the same as they did."

He put his feet up on the little table. “Are you in pain now? I didn‘t want you to have to talk before you were able. I hope you didn’t feel that I wasn’t always aware of you and your pain. I respect you and the troubles you are going through.”

‘That’s fair.’ Nicolas Jose thought, glad to hear he had support outside beyond the villagers.

“Many people visit me but they don’t speak. They look at me like a wounded animal, say ’Bless you’ and leave. I’m still in pain. Maybe there is another word. I itch as though ants were biting all of my back and sometimes it turns to burning like coals on my back and I can‘t move or scratch. I remember my manhood ceremonies when I dreamed I was on fire. Have you had datura?”

“No.” He laughed, “We had herbs that burned in a pipe and yage we inhaled but nothing as strong as datura. The elders and curanderas use strong roots and a mushroom that only they can use, but I was never allowed to. Some of the neophytes take herbs at night.”

Nicolas Jose put two fingers to his lips to quiet Andres.

“I keep all of that separate from the command.” He shook his head. “But the new soldiers are always with crazy herb and brandy every day!. Even ‘The Blood of Christ’ is in their botas more than water. The soldiers take so much that the priests had to cut down the portions for sacraments.”

“I used to do that. The wine, brandy. All of it. I don’t want to forget. I want to remember. I want to understand everything.”

“That’s good.” Andres said. “That’s a good way to deal with pain.” Leaning closer. “Is there anything I can bring you? Maps? Food?”

“No, my friend, but,…please come back tomorrow.”

When Pico asked the neophytes who monitored the chapel entryway to name the visitors to Nicolas Jose, Andres was mentioned three times. After reading news from Europe in the infrequent dispatches, Pico requested a transfer for a suspected Freethinker and revolutionist away from this place that he now considered a flashpoint of discontent.

<<< 0 >>>

The trip from Sinaloa was like an adventure from a Moor's tale of deserts and strange animals for Cornello Avila, wife Isabel and their six children. They made games of counting the coyotes and bears. They climbed out and chased around and made up stories to make the time pass.

The road from San Diego was becoming as good as the ones in the Baja and friendly soldiers and traders waved as they passed by.

The Pueblo of the Angeles was far more beautiful than anything they had imagined in this distant land. There were Indians by the side of the road looking like they wanted food or trinkets, but they didn't look unfriendly.

They tethered the utility carriage that they had bought for the trip in front of the modest but clean looking church on a Wednesday afternoon. The town square seemed almost adjacent to the church with an empty lot between it and the official's

Buildings.

Immediately he had to know what the plans for the lot were and if it were for sale.

"Can't you imagine how perfect it would be to live next to that church!" His eyes gleamed to Isabel. "We can afford it!"

She knew how much they had sold their land for in El Fuerte.

"If we can, I can't think of a better place to raise the family. If you can buy it. Please do. But if you can't," pointing West. "Up on that hill would be as lovely as I could ever want."

<<< 0 >>> <u>1784</u>

Cordero and Lopez rode through the red tiled circle of Plaza de Los Angeles before noon to drop off the requisition orders for Mission supplies, admiring the new brick walls of the civic building and the crisply dressed soldiers at attention by the wide doorway.

"What a change!" Cordero exclaimed, remembering the crudely stuccoed wood of nine months ago.

In the accounting office a purebred Spanish clerk wrote a receipt. Neither of them could read well, but it felt important to be handed the paper. Lopez folded it and placed it deep in his inner breast pocket. The Spaniard wore beautiful civilian clothes with lace at his cuffs. Cordero frowned at the idea of a man wearing lace like the painting of the Blessed Virgin.

There was a bright new coat of anise, thistle and poppy plants on the trail to the Mission. Ahead, they saw Alcalde Nicolas Jose pass, riding the northwestern fence of the cattle herd with two mounted trustees at his side.

The Mission's cattle, sheep and goat herds now exceeded seven thousand head. The nine hundred neophytes had a high death rate from black-tongue and new feverish diseases. Dozens of newcomers were brought each week from remote villages Many of the far villages no longer existed. Raids and disease made them unlivable. Shrinking trade turned some displaced groups to banditry. Alliances between the Spanish, some Kumeyaay and Mojave had fostered inter-tribal fighting and internal religious wars.

The nearby villages of Seebag-na, Yaanga, Asuks-gna and Pimog-na had only a third to half the population they had in 1779.

Cordero and Lopez entered the Mission walking their horses around workmen repairing the fallen entry arch. It had collapsed during the last rain with few supplies to replace the termite infested large beams. All of the strongest and healthiest wood was now being diverted to repair the fragile structures in the pueblo of Los Angeles.

New Padres Sanchez and Cruzado had replaced the happily transferred Padres Somera and Cambon. Their comments and advice on leaving was to do anything possible to undermine the secularists' plotting against the church and to keep the native population within the San Gabriel borders and working hard to increase agriculture for the Mission.

Sanchez motioned for Cordero and Lopez to enter at the main doorway. Olivera, Alvarado, Saenz and Pico were in the small room off the chapel. Pico motioned for the others to sit. The Padres and senior officers had given him the central space.

“I want you all to be vigilant in watching for heathen rites conducted in the nights in the fields or the sleeping quarters. Also, there are artifacts and charms to watch for. Within this Christian Mission a trend is present that endangers us all. Not from the outside, but from organized unconverted gentiles within.”

Cordero had heard sounds like singing at night. It was a monotonous drone that was like the sounds from the Jewish temples near home in his childhood. He mentioned it but Lopez was hard of hearing from too many muzzle blasts.

“What do we do if we hear them at night, or if we see rituals in the fields?” He asked.

Pico motioned. “You’ll investigate. You’ll go into their quarters in pairs, armed. You’ll note the names of the central people and give them to me. We’ll give rewards to trustees who report the leaders.”

Padre Cruzado spoke. “This can’t be underestimated as a threat. Resurgent paganism can destroy everything the Mission stands for. They can’t be Christian and pagan at the same time. At each mass I’ll speak on the dangers of their false and damnable ways. We’ll announce that all pagan dances, chants and icons are banned. Severe punishment will be dealt those who disobey.”

Pico added. “I want us all to keep a close watch on our Alcalde Nicolas Jose. He may be at the center of this.”

Cordero and Lopez looked at each other. It seemed now that Nicolas Jose was the best Indian ever trained and a model of conversion.

CHAPTER 22

TOOYPOR CONTACTS AGAIN

Kethu and 'Ahtooshe' helped rub coats of lime and aloe over Tooypor's face, neck and arms, temporarily lightening her dark skin. They made a paste from wildrose petal and aloe to color her lips in the style the neophytes girls had started to use. She dressed in a Mission smock Sa'aa're' had brought They stood back to admire her.

Sa'aa're' said. "No one would look twice at my kitchen helper."

"Maria." Tooypor said. "Maria, the victim. They like that. I am one of their hundreds of Marias."

They walked through the cattle herds, avoiding groups where they could become boxed in. They waited for Saenz to ride by and crawled to small gullies. They saw lean-tos along the west wall. They left the bushes and fell in with children who'd been urinating in the field. They climbed into the courtyard, crossing in front of the chapel to the kitchen. Charaana waited at the door.

"Aahe" Tooypor smiled as she entered.

"Aahe, Tooypor-pahr." Charaana whispered in her ear and patted her shoulder.

"Maria. I am one of the Marias."

Charaana gave a girlish giggle. "Maria-pahr. Try my corn cakes." Pushing a pinch to her mouth.

"Ummm! It's good! Give me more."

They sat at the crude mess table in the farthest corner and held hands.

"He's asked to see you. He could never leave unobserved. We'll sit here and Sa'aa're' will bring him."

Sa'aa're' stood. "None of the invaders come in here this late, but if one does, pretend you are falling asleep and that you are new Serrano kitchen help, Maria. You don't speak our language."

Tooypor nodded. “Serrano only. I understand.”

Nicolas Jose hadn't seen Tooypor in four years, since the founding of Pueblo Los Angeles. He'd only seen her and Hachaaynar from a distance but felt her presence strongly. Many Tongva neophytes had pointed to the Seebag-na group and kept looking over to them. It was hard not to be aware of them. The last time he spoke to her was in 1779 during the negotiations over Sevaanga-vik. He hoped that she forgave him.

Sa'aa're' knocked gently and leaned against the wall beside the door. She knew he would come with her with no conversation. She looked in all directions to see if anyone was watching. As the door opened she felt no one was near.

He opened the door and patted her shoulder looking both ways before walking straight along the wall of the trustee‘s quarters to the kitchen with Sa’aa’re’ at his side.

He was surprised by the appearance of the pale and delicate woman sitting with Charaana. He would never associate this shy looking person in the baggy smock as the wiry, dark and muscular Tongva Pula who had inspired such respect and fear in the Spanish rulers.

He lowered his eyes to her. She was surprised by how much he had aged. The arrogant and controlling stance seemed to have melted into more humility. His eyes were gentle. His smile seemed unforced as though he was not trying to win her over. She bowed her head and returned a greeting smile.

Charaana tapped on the table for him to sit. Sa’aa’re’ put a dish of cornmeal on a nearby table for him to switch to, stepping outside the door to sit at the entrance and watch for unexpected visitors.

“I’ve heard about the banning. I’ve heard that you’d returned to our ways. It must make you angry.”

“They need to do that to keep control. They see that their story of God and Obedience isn‘t controlling us, as long as we have contact with Earth, the Sun, the Moon, the natural world. Our ancestral homes.” He couldn’t look into her eyes and started to feel the burning that made tears. “I’m ashamed. I did so much that was bad.”

Charaana saw his eyes cloud. “These last few years.” Touching his hand. “You didn‘t abuse your personal power. You stopped the punishments of some weak people. You kept the trustees from doing bad things.”

“I was working for the invaders. I‘m no longer proud of what I did.”

Tooypor took his other hand in hers. He saw no contempt in her face. “It isn’t too late to come back. Your ancestors were calling you. They’ll no longer call you a traitor. We know that you keep the Lifeways in your heart. Does it hurt to hear the word ‘traitor’?”

“Yes. It’s a bad word, but.. my ancestors know, it’s a true word. I betrayed everything in our world, becoming one with the invaders. I know it. I know why, but it doesn‘t help.”

“I‘ve seen death around me for years but I felt the spirits were still around somehow. I said the words of their Holy book and thought of their Heaven and Hell where all of their dead people go, but,..it was the Christians, with their symbols and weapons and disease that were killing them all. All of us! How can a person find a place in Heaven or Hell if the Christians are killing us all? What are they bringing us other than slavery?”

“I hoped you’d have seen that twenty seasons ago.” Tooypor said. “But things are as they are. There are still the ways of our people here in the invaders‘ camp.” She squeezed his hand to emphasize her point. “You know that we have people here that are willing to fight to preserve our ways, don‘t you?.”

“Yes, I have seen many. I see many who I knew in Seebag-na. There are not enough of us to defeat them.”

“Of all the prisoners here. I’ll call all of our people here prisoners. Of all of them, how many practice the ways of Chinigchnish? Or Quo-ar, Wiote or Nakomah?”

He thought of all he’d seen and heard in the fields, outside the walls at night, near the groupings of oak trees, sounds from the sleeping quarters in the late hours. “As many as three out of every ten. The others would defend the invaders because of the steady food, or run back to their villages to continue their lives, but not fight the Spanish. I doubt if more than one hundred people would fight. The others might throw a rock or two and run to the four directions." He shrugged.

She looked pleased. "The most soldiers they'll have is ten. If they are weakened or demoralized at the beginning, we could overcome them quickly and leave in the night to free Yaanga as the sun rises."

He'd expected anger and depression, not optimism and aggression. She looked and sounded confident, but he couldn't see a reason for it.

"Why would they be weakened or demoralized?"

Charaana and Tooypor shook their heads but had a shared twinkle.

"That will be seen. They will be weakened. We will drive them from our lands." She spoke with quiet surety. "The ones here, the Iitaxxum, who do not belong on our lands, will return to their homes in the desert, mountains, the coast and the islands. Seebag-na will be restored with it's families returned and my Haapchivet will be kept safe. That's my vision. It was long in coming, but it's solid."

He saw it as unrealistic. "The villages are being torn down." She needed to see the extent the Spanish were dominating the countryside. "Some of the Mojave and Kumeyaay are their allies now. They carry firesticks to serve them as soldiers. It can't be that easy. Not like you see it. You need allies from the villages that still survive. Asuks-gna, Pimo-gna and others."

"I must ask you this first." She said, watching every movement of his face. "Will you be with us with no changes, no doubts or going back. To the death?"

He remembered Andres. The only invader who would stand beside them to fight for their freedom. He thought a long moment.

"Yes. All my ancestors are at my shoulder. To the death, and for life."

She continued looking into the eyes of the man who'd been a mystery to her for so many years. She rose to leave.

"Nahanpar. I am glad to see you again. We will meet again.. very soon."

He watched them leave. It ended too quickly. There wasn't enough of a plan.

Saenz and Verdugo stomped loudly from bed to bed in the sixty four man sleeping quarters. Pico and Lopez stood at the door holding muskets as bed after bed was inverted and searched for banned items. Saenz held up a sage bundle with a loud grunt and pushed the man at the bed to the door. The man squirmed, joking to the men at his sides. He was pushed down the aisle to stand with four others in a holding area next to Saenz.

"Tell them sage is to flavor the corn meal" The man beside him said with a grin.

"No talking!" Pico barked. "Spanish only!"

Verdugo found two more partially burnt bundles under other bedsides. Seven men were marched outside, whipped and ordered to take confession in the morning.

"If there were seven bundles in there, there were three or four chanters with each one." Pico exclaimed. Close to thirty male pagan worshipers in that one building! Eight buildings! Hundreds more sleeping in the peripheries! Can you see? We're in more danger now than we've ever been. "

Tooypor giggled in the dark, climbing into bed, wanting Hachaaynar to see her in her light skin and baggy Mission smock. She fell asleep. She woke to him poking her ribs and his laughter.

"You look cute…., funny, this way! You have to do this every day.!" Kissing her neck and wiping his mouth. "I was worried all night, I don't remember falling asleep, but it's good to see you. Even like this. I'll help you wash up."

He took water and a sponge from the coast. She stretched and purred. He scrubbed her back and turned her over. They kissed and started to make love, but she had too much to tell about her meeting.

“It was better than I expected. It was like the best part of Nahanpar, but grown wiser. He understands the errors of his past. His ancestors have returned to him and he won’t go back to being the invader‘s dog. He’s changed. Sa'aa're' and Charaana kept saying it. I didn‘t believe it but I looked in his eyes and I held his hands. He is real.”

“That’s a big change for you. I thought he’d come back. I’d given up. I heard people say he’d changed, but, you surprise me.”

She rolled onto him and pushed up on her arms to look down into his eyes. “I was wrong. I can admit it. I was wrong. I should have started this three years ago after he was whipped by the bad Pul.”

“Do you think it’s too late now?” Trying to balance her enthusiasm. He was convinced the invaders would never leave and the village would die when he did, that a son wouldn’t come in time to become Sevaanga-vik.

“He saw the same thing I did. That every village that still had fighters should be brought in to attack at a signal. I didn‘t tell him about the poisons, but he was worried about what ten soldiers could do. Well, less if they‘re dead or dying. I‘ll be traveling to villages to build an alliance.” She kissed him long and hard. “We can do it! We can finally do it!”

<<< 0 >>> (1784)

LOS ANGELES

Ambassador, Marquis De Trenet set his desktop pens and papers symmetrically with care in the long vacant room kept for councils in the Town Governance Center.

He was pleased to be sent to Alta California to see the new Pueblos, Presidios and, purely out of duty in the King, Franciscan Missions, and to make report on their progress directly to the

Crown. He was also pleased to be the barrer of good tidings to several soldiers who had served the Empire well.

He had called the meeting for three p.m., which would give the three men time to straighten up, clean up and become quite nervous about the reasons they were called from the field.

Juan Jose Dominguez, Manuel Nieto and Jose Maria Verdugo took places in the waiting room, recognizing each other and moving together, away from the fidgeting campesinos with domestic issues.

“Only the three of us?” Nieto grinned. “What did we do now?”

Verdugo looked worried. ”I had duties at the rancho of Enrique. There were stolen sheep that we had to recover. I hope this goes quickly”

They sat uncomfortably listening to hammering from the roof. The plan for a second story was being pushed ahead and was not going well because of the strong winds and sparse materials.

At the stroke of three they they were called into the small side office and were greeted by an elegantly dressed man, alone, standing behind a beautifully polished desk. He gestured for them to be seated on the three chairs that he’d placed in front of the desk.

He wore a wry smile and sat, lifting a pile of neatly trimmed pages.

They assumed that the carriage and four soldiers outside who saluted them as they arrived were his. He had to be important.

He read to them, name by name, the lands that were to be granted them by the Crown.

The breadth of the huge land grants given to them astounded them. They stretched from below the Mission to the Sea. They went west along the lower hills. They included the ghosts of small villages.

“There is a condition,” he added, pausing for drama. The soldiers now seemed too delighted for drama, so he read on.

“Many of the Indians of the area will be employed by you as labor for building, herding and farming. Many of them have had ties to the Mission San Gabriel. It is stipulated that none of the Indians in your employ will be permitted to have any contact with Mission San Gabriel of any dealings with the Franciscan holdings."

The soldiers understood perfectly.

"If they must attend services, they will only be permitted to travel to the Pueblo, here, and return. No side trips!"

They agreed with cheers and tall cups of brandy, laughing, yelling and running outside as Count de Trenet handed them the elaborately signed and wax sealed paperwork.

They mounted together and rode off to inspect their domains.

OUTSKIRTS OF LOS ANGELES

Ricardo Alvarez came with the third group of workers to arrive from Baja California. He was thirty-six with an older wife and her twelve year old son. He was a farmer. They could build a new life in the new town of the Angels, but He felt more beset by devils than by angels.

He sweated under the noonday sun working the soil removing seemingly endless buried rocks. He threw them in a pile at the side for a drainage ditch. The soil was terrible compared to the Mexican land he'd left. His plot was west of the town's outskirts and the most northerly one, against the southern boundaries of the native's Yaanga village.

Indians sat on the hillside above him., not more than fifty meters away, watching him. There was a cluster of men and boys, glaring at him and laughing when he showed exhaustion.

"Go and work your own land!" He would shout, mumbling. "You lazy bastards." They never grew anything or built anything of value. All they had to do was to copy the way buildings of Pueblo Los Angeles were made. Their bent branches were stupid ways to make a home. They never did anything except talk gibberish and watch him. As the hot afternoon came, dizziness swept around him. He'd put off taking a break for water. He sat back heavily on a boulder he'd uncovered and put his head in his hands. He felt weak, leaning his head on his knees and started to slide off of the rock.

He heard the laughing Indians on the hill and looked up, seeing a stone bouncing toward him. "Pieces of shit!" as two more rolled by his feet.

Three Yaanga men and their sons had watched the invaders building the house on the lower end of the village. The intruders had marked off a space that families used to access Little Rabbit Run Spring. When village people tried to walk to the spring, soldiers rode up and made them walk around the marked off space.

The man in the field spent day after day playing with rocks and throwing them into piles. It was crazy and insulting. The families lived for ages above where this fool stood. They couldn't get water without going a long route around him and the other invader's lands.

When the man sat, Chah'oot threw a rock, not so much to hit him as to mock him for trying to change the character of the land. Stones are there for a reason. They're part of the nature of the earth.

The man yelled in the invaders ugly language. They threw some more stones, not to hit him, but to disrespect him.

The invader-man stood, shouting. He walked to a pouch on the ground and lifted what they knew was a firestick. He pointed it at them and yelled. Chah'oot's son had never heard one and didn't believe that it could do harm. He picked up a smooth stone, and before his father could stop him, threw it hard at the invader.

"Dirty little bastard!" Ricardo swore, as the stone whizzed to the right of him, squeezing the trigger without allowing for windage or the change in elevation.

In the instant of the discharge he realized that his additional powder, leather charge disk and balls were still in the pouch on the ground and that he wasn't fast at reloading the rifle.

Chah'oot, the two men and three boys leapt to their feet at the sound. The metal balls hit the gravel several arm lengths before their feet and bounced past between them. Two of the men felt rock chips sting their legs.

“Demon!” Chah’oot screamed, running down the hill with no thought of his own safety.

The man lowered the firestick to his side, staring frozen at the six screaming Indians swarming down the hill. It was too late to reload. He put his hands up to say “Peace,” but they were on him leaping, kicking and pummeling his fallen body with fists and then larger and larger rocks until no prayers or apologies could bring him back to life.

MISSION SAN GABRIEL

Jose Maria Pico made a routine of acting drunk before the afternoon break time. He’d take a flagon of wine, sit on a bench in the courtyard slumped against a pillar or on a patch of grass, faking sleep, with an occasional snore.

He’d started to build a dictionary of Shoshonean Tongva from his visits with prisoners at Presidios San Diego and Santa Barbara. He made sure it was never one who’d return to the San Gabriel region. He’d learn bits of gossip about soldiers, attitudes toward the priests, and pagan rites.

He sat on the grass near the kitchen with his flask at his side. He leaned back against the colonnade and let his head loll to the side with an open mouth as conversations passed where he dozed for all the world to see.

<<< 0 >>>

Aachvet wasn’t called Haapchi-vik by Tooypor except as a joke. She called him brother or used insults referring to the lower orders of animals.

He sat in the Greathouse at the apex of a semi-circle of elders waiting for her arrival. Her runner sounded formal and said this would be of the greatest importance to their survival.

The council spoke about village problems until a door guard announced that her party was outside.

Tooypor, Taaherkwe', Kwetii' and three Seebag-na guards entered.

"Ah'a'he, Haapchi-vik Pahr." Bowing her head to him and greeting the elders. They saw her rarely in the past four years. She'd been a good Pula and negotiator for trade in the service of Haapchivet but now she represented her husband's village of Seebag-na.

"This is the most important time we've ever faced. It means the survival or destruction of every village. The time has come to defeat the invaders at their Mission. My vision is now complete. We can kill the Priests and soldiers in one night. We can surround their village below Yaanga and burn it to the ground. The villages and the freed slaves of the Mission can go back to the coast or wherever they were kidnapped from and take back their homes. They'll know it can be done! They'll have seen us start and succeed. That will give them courage to free their lands! It can be done!"

She looked each one in the eye and felt who the skeptics were. Some saw Haapchivet as so removed from threat from the Spanish invaders, they'd withhold any help to the flatlands. It was constant frustration when she'd visit. They held disinterest in anything beyond the village border.

"Villages of the coast and the islands have been destroyed! Their people are driven like animals to work as slaves to the invaders. Little by little the invaders have surrounded these mountains. All sides. The Chumash to the northwest. The Tataviam, Mojave and Serrano. All of them are being attacked. If they are gone, no one will defend you. All of your lives and the work of all our ancestors will be smashed to the ground."

She held enough weight to not be interrupted.

"I ask that fifteen nights after the next full moon, thirty of the best and strongest fighters of Haapchivet assemble at the Three Oaks Spring and wait for my signal. My guide will come to escort them."

"Does that sound agreeable?" Achvit looked face to face. He saw nods from the aging men. He looked at the smiling face of old Pul Tuwaru. Too infirm to travel to his cave, he was carried on a straw stretcher to stay with different elders' a few days at a time.

"She is a good girl." He said in a fading raspy voice. "Help the good Pula girl."

She had the first commitment for her vision of a United Iitaxxum. All Tongva lands finally free.

<<< 0 >>>

Hachaaynar was pleased by Tooypor's frequent visits. She spent less time at her kitcha and more in Seebag-na. He made a project of getting young people to weeding and smoothing the old playing fields. His walks of the village had more smiles and longer conversations.

They were drifting off to sleep in the Greathouse when a guard announced Sa'aa're', from the Mission.

"Nicolas Jose says that these will help in making contacts in the outlying villages." Dumping a large pile of round and faceted glass beads out of a canvas bag. They sparkled in the dim fading firelight.

"Aaaaaaaaaah!" Tooypor squealed, remembering the day with 'Ahtooshe' when 'The Sea Creatures' first came and how impressed they were with this solid ice.

"I have to wake 'Ahtooshe' and show her. She'll laugh and laugh."

Hachaaynar squinted at the beads and groaned. "Show her in the morning. Let's go back to sleep."

CHAPTER 23

OUTREACH AND ATTACK

In Jajamongna, nestled in the foothills north of Pimong-na, Aliavit was chief. He'd held Tooypor on his knee when she was a little girl, brought by her father to a trade fair at Yaanga

She'd met him three times since on trade missions for their cleverly made implements for cooking and holding roasted meats. Tah-ur had traveled with her once. She hadn't heard from Tah-ur in a while. She reached the relocated village on this trip.

"Welcome Pula Tooypor-Pahr" She sat on a finely woven pad in front of him and his wife. The woman didn't look up after the introduction.

"The village of Seebag-na brings you an offering of our respect." Spreading twenty glass beads on the space between their folded knees.

He looked wide eyed at them and carefully touched one to see what it's temperature was. When he felt that they were neither cold or hot he put one in his wife's hand. She continued to stare at it. "Why? What do you want from me?. These are amazing things. I've heard about them but I've never touched one. How are they made?"

"We don't know. They are brought from where the invaders came from. Things like these took Seebag-na's Nahanpar away to live with them. But the invaders used them to try to destroy his village. My husband's village. How many have left or been stolen from your land?"

He looked into the display of beads, thinking a while before answering.

"More than ten hands of young people. They took or killed children who played to the west. We drew a boundary and dug a trench as a reminder. Many who lost their children and went to the invader's camp never came back. We've been afraid to travel west for trade fairs. We only go to Asuks-gna or more to the east, or down south to Puvung-na, but we heard they were attacked and driven even farther south."

She'd heard similar stories from every village in the flatlands. Weakened by lack of trade and shrunken boundaries. The freedom was gone. Many children were gone.

"Have the diseases hit you hard?" Watching his face contort.

"Many dead or dying."

His wife had her eyes down in the space between them. In a quiet and elderly voice she spoke.

"What do you want?"

Aliavit turned disapprovingly but she directed a fierce glare back to him and again looked at the beads.

"I've come to renew our contacts with Jajamongna. To pledge our village's support of yours against the invaders, and, if the time comes, to ask you for Jajamongna's fighting men in a group fight to reclaim our land. Not only one village fighting alone, but many villages, fighting as one."

She tried to read their silent faces. His, a twisted mixture of doubts and fear, wanting to avoid her eyes. Hers was a granite face with glazed eyes boring through the floor.

He said in a whispery voice. "I know the elders would not allow our men to go out of our land to fight and leave us unprotected. It is good of you to come to us. We could trade more in the future. We want the leached meal from Seebag-na. We can help you in that, but, no fighting against the men with the firesticks." Shaking his head sadly.

She watched him lower his head and shift interest to the beads. She looked to his wife's stone face. The woman shook with tension. Tooypor expected her to demand that she leave with an outburst to leave her home and to never bring in the problems of the outside world.

The woman raised her face to her husband. He turned to her with a soft and loving expression. She spoke with a strong younger woman's voice.

“If you will not go yourself and send our surviving young men, I will go and kill every one of the invaders myself! If they hit me with firesticks, clubs or knives, I’ll keep walking and stab every one of them with my obsidian knife. Even after I’m dead!” She punched his arm hard. “I’ll go with her! Any time she calls! You should too if you have any sense!” She punched him again, harder. “Tell her that you will go and that we all will go!” Pushing his shoulder. “Tell her!”

“We’ll prepare.” He said. “We’ll prepare for your call.”

<<< 0 >>>

Tooypar and her guards took a hot day’s walk east along the foothills of the large purple mountains to reach what Tooypor had called ‘Tah-urvet.” Tah-ur’s village.

She watched the advance runner coming back with a tortured expression before the village’s hill was in sight.

“It is bad. It is not good.” He said. “They were attacked. There are not many people there.”

“Tah-ur? Is Tah-ur there?”

“She is there, but she is hurt. Her arm.”

Tooypor increased the pace up the barren ground in leaps until she saw a group of women watching them climb. As she came closer Tah-ur waved. Tooypor felt relief that her friend had survived the attack, but who would attack up here? She saw that Tah-ur’s right arm was missing below the elbow.

They burst into tears as they hugged, not caring about showing strength. It was a good strength to feel sorrow and share pain to purge it from their hearts and move forward. They saw it was the same between them. Strength was still in Tah-ur’s face.

“The soldiers came to us in the night and went from house to house killing the men and raping the women before they killed the older ones. We,” Motioning to the other women, “ran into the night and hid. As I ran, a soldier swung his sword at me. It cut through my arm. It was hanging and flopping around until a boy running with me tied a leather band. It stopped the bleeding. I cut the rest of my arm, my hand, right off. I had to. I became very sick but people fed me and kept my spirit strong."

"I'm so happy to see you. I love you always"

They walked to the side. Tah-ur told about the ambush of the two soldiers. "We buried the bodies and drove their horses deep into the desert, but I don't think the attack was about that. Other villages have had night attacks aimed at killing men."

Tooypor told her about the coastal villages and Pemuu'nga. How Yaanga and Seebag-na were being eaten away by the large village that the invaders had built.

"We are making alliances with villages of the great basin. Our Seebag-na and Haapchivet, Yaanga and others are coming together to attack. We'll destroy their Mission village and free their captured slaves."

Tah-ur grinned and struck Tooypor's shoulder twice with the stump of her arm. "I'll come with my fighters. There are four of us who are great with arrows and spear. I am expert with a spear now. Them with bow and arrow."

"Can you come with us to stay at Seebag-na?"

"Our village is dead now. There are a few older women and children still. Can they come too? Would they be accepted? "

Tooypor looked over the remaining villagers. They looked fit to travel. She would ask Jajamongna-vik and his wife if some could live there.

"Gather your food. We'll stop at the spring for water. We will leave together and find you new homes."

Nicolas Jose rode the bright morning fields checking work crew totals, reports from trustees on discipline problems and those who did exceptional work. There was little to report for the last three weeks. Many were intimidated by the new religious rules. Some silently waited for a promise of better time to come.

He felt under observation. Soldiers seemed too polite. The Fathers asked how his day had been and if there was anything that he needed. He looked away if Sa'aa're', Charaana, Taaherkwe' came near.

Cordero waved. It seemed forced. He returned the wave with a similar smile and rode toward the stable where Pico was slumped against a water troth, snoring like a bear with wine spilling from his leather flask. It was pathetic for a soldier to be so out of control. He considered reporting it to Olivera. 'Yes, I'll do it tomorrow morning.' It had to be done before someone else reported it to gain some credibility from it.

He stabled his horse, filled a fresh pot of water from the well and washed in his room. He sat at the crowded trustee's table at the side of the eating hall. They talked about the day's events. He didn't participate but listened, looking for slips that might be dangerous.

In his room after dinner he put some pocketed cornbread to the four directions sign and quietly chanted to his ancestors, Wiote, Chinigchnich, Quo-ar, animal spirit of Eagle and Mother Earth. As he moved his lips he kept his ears attuned to any sounds that could be an observer. He stopped twice to step outside and check the walls on all sides. When he finished he lay back in the dark in a tornado of possibilities that went long into the night.

<<< 0 >>>

Chief Tomasjaquichi fidgeted in a circle of elders and fighters waiting for Tooypor to cross the desert trail to his village at the base of the hills south of Pimog-na. He was told by runners from Jajamongna that she was close and would make a request He hoped that she had the round ice rocks that were described.

She walked in the lead side by side with a tall one armed woman with a long spear. Six men with bows followed, looking fit and strong. He doubted six from his village could match them in battle or field games

“Juyu-vik Tomasjaquichi-pahr.” She bowed her head and touched her heart walking to him. She sat in front of him on the mat. Tah-ur and the guards moved to the sides. The chief motioned them to benches outside the Greathouse.

She opened the woven bag and poured out twenty of the glass beads. The sunlight caught the facets. All nearby showed amazement at the magic.

“It was described to me, but I never could imagine the excellence of these! Did these come from the invaders?”

"From their homeland. You can see how clever they are with crafts. This material, metal and woven things.”

He looked at her with puzzlement. “Yes, I see that they are very clever. Is that why you came? To have me accept them as brothers? Should we praise them now because of their cleverness? Why do you bring these to me?”

She smiled with love for this old chief who always stood his ground to outsiders but had always shown generosity to people displaced by catastrophes or by invader’s attacks.

“No, Tomasjaquichi-pahr. I praise the crafts, but the makers need slaves to make them. They need to take other people’s land and lifeways. They need to kill histories, everything about our creation and love of our land. They kill the Earth, Sun and Moon and put their Mission and slave Marias in place on our land. They’ve been killing our villages. You’ve seen many of your people disappear and you’ve found bodies of children. I’ve seen corpses when we passed through your land.”

“We’ve lost many. We know it’s becoming worse. You have a plan, don‘t you.”

“I know many people who will drive the invaders from our lands. Some from villages near here. Some from far away. Some are in the Mission waiting for us to help them become free. I want to know if you are tired of losing your people and afraid that the future will bring the end of our lives and history. The end of our Earth.”

His eyes showed love. He took her hands. "You are an unusual woman. I've heard of you many times. I've long thought that the invaders need to be fought by more than one village. I know myself and how I used to argue with other chiefs. I have been bad at doing that. I have always hoped that one of the other chiefs, like your husband, would ask us to join him, and I would say that I'd bring my fighters for him."

"Do you say that to me?"

"Yes, I say that to you. When do we begin?"

"Tomasjaquichi. I'll send a trusted runner to you with one of these beads. You'll know that it's from me. You'll be given instructions. Prepare weapons and a fighting force ready to leave. You'll be called.

<<< 0 >>>

Tooypor and 'Ahtooshe' picked, crushed and mixed the poisons carefully. They wouldn't be ones that would act quickly. Slow eaters or late arrivals shouldn't be warned by sickness around them. The Padres and soldiers always ate their food with spices and chilies that would hide the poison's taste. They estimated a deep sleep would come after four hands had passed and that breathing would stop after one more hand had passed.

'Ahtooshe' looked hopeful and energized. "I want to see them die!."

Tooypor nodded with hope shining in her eyes. "We'll win our lives back."

<<< 0 >>>

Nicolas Jose took daytime walkthroughs to inspect the locks on the doors without being observed. The locks were simple enough to trip the tumblers with bent horseshoe nails. He tried each one three times. No soldier would be on duty in the chapel after nine o'clock. Reaching the entrance from the western wall wouldn't be difficult after eleven o‘clock. Tooypor and the guards could climb in quietly. They would find only unlocked doors.

He mounted for his rounds and waved to Verdugo and Pico by the front gate. Polite smiles all around. It was good to see Pico looking sober but the day was young.

Many fieldworkers gave nods and smiles in recognition of their now respected Alcalde, Nicolas Jose.

<<< 0 >>>

In a week of sleepy warm days in the wide valleys and plains there was a bristling expectation in the villages of Haapchivet, Pasekeg-na, Jajamongna, Juyuvit, Yaanga and others preparing for the signal from Seebag-na.

In the early morning after the dimmest moon, six runners left to the villages of the flatlands. Yaanga was not to send any people or make any unusual preparations or celebrations that could alert the Los Angeles garrison. They would be in the second stage. Asuks-gna and Pimog-na agreed to send fighters to Yaanga only after the Mission had been successfully taken.

In Juyuvit Tomasjaquichi bathed and went to the Holy sweat lodge with his elders. They chanted for victory and gathered the strong men together. They started a new victory dance in the village. Women and children joined and prayed for the defeat of the invaders and the return of their land.

In Jajamongna, Chief Alitvit walked to the highest rise behind his village and spoke to the sky. He was filled with joy at the prospect of the end of ten years of the theft of the tribal lands and the deaths and slavery of his people.

“Thank you, Thank you.” He spoke to the Father Sun. He also said thanks to the wind for Tooypor.

He returned to a shouting crowd in the village center in front of the greathouse. He waved his arms in joy.

"We will drive the invaders from our lands! We will be one people with our land and our neighbors! We will win!" They danced until nightfall.

The God Chinigchnich was a great dancer and had always exhorted his people to dance to show their connection to Spirit and to each other. They danced with swelling hopes for a good future.

In Haapchivet Achvit was amazed at his sister's plan and hard work bringing people together. He thought they'd only meet to fight over a marriage or trade negotiation.

He called a village dance. They carried old Pul Tuwaru on his stretcher to bless the dance and lead prayers for freedom of the villages of the flatlands.

Nicolas Jose rode his rounds in a trance. All the possibilities ran in circles through his head. All of the cruelties, including the ones he'd been party to, swelled like waves of cold anger.

From the far fields he took quick glances at the Mission imagining the flames and crumbling tower. He saw the cowering faces of Olivera, Verdugo, Cordero, Sanchez and Cruzado before a flood of the people they'd abused.

He boiled at how he'd helped the invaders. The self promotion and misuse of women and girls of his people. At turning his head from the whipping and killing of those who wanted to return home and no longer had homes to return to. At betraying the spirits of all those who'd come before.

Returning on the main Mission trail, approaching the adobe arch, He focused on the chapel. Tears came to his eyes. Not of pain but of hope and joy.

"I'm ready to die now. In peace with my Mother Earth."

<<< 0 >>>

Sa'aa're' carried the tightly woven packet from Seebag-na through the cattle herds, over the chest high wall, into the Mission grounds during the night.

Charaana placed it behind an earthenware pot in the corner. Their eyes met but both turned away. Charaana waited for four bells. She prepared the Padres' meal. Stew, corn, squash, roughly ground flower from the new wheat fields, chicken and chilies. She thumbed in three scoops of the powdered mixture and stirred well, watching her hopes for freedom blend into the stew.

Sa'aa're' busied herself scrubbing the floor, chopping squash, cleaning tools. She was shaking. She raised her hand flat in front of her eyes..

"Look!" Holding her quivering arms out. "How will I carry my tray without spilling it?" Charaana saw her panicked look, wondering if she were truly shaky or avoiding the risk of carrying the tray.

"Give me your hands." Walking around the grill island to hold her. Charaana felt tremors through Sa'aa're's body.

"Do you want me to carry the tray?" Looking into the doubt filled dark eyes.

"Yes, yes! I might drop it or shake the bowls off. They might see how much I'm shaking. They'll get suspicious and ask me questions. I don't know what to say. What will I do?"

Charaana stepped away from her friend and shrugged.

"I'll carry it to them. Don't worry. I won't shake."

The sun was sinking one hand above the western horizon, Tooypor, 'Ahtooshe', old Pul Tuwaru and Hachaaynar sat cross legged on mats in front of the Greathouse of Seebag-na.

Old men and women, families with children and barely walking toddlers watched a group of thirty men wearing only loincloths and ochre body rubs pumping bow and spear, chanting and dancing in the central clearing, hoping and praying to Gods, Spirits, Ancestors and each other for deliverance from fifteen years of oppression, disrespect, death and disease. ‘Ahtooshe' held Hachaaynar’s hand.

“Nothing like this has ever happened before. Coming together. I‘ve heard villages attacking one that wouldn’t trade fish, or rescuing a kidnapped girl. Recovering money stolen by gamblers, but nothing like this”

“I want to dance with them now.” He said. Tooypor was nodding at his side. She looked across to 'Ahtooshe'.

“This will be a time of legend!” As she pushed off the mat and pulled Hachaaynar up, She swung him with her into the swirling villagers, squinting across into the sun.

“Only three hands away!”

<<< 0 >>>

A crude six place table in the small room at side of the chapel as set by three old and obedient neophytes who tiptoed out as the Padres entered.

Padres Sanchez and Cruzado had dispatches about the worrisome changes happening in France. The discontent and suspicion that ordinary people were voicing was shocking. Church and monarchy were mocked. There were riots by farmers and farm workers over indenture and taxation.

Charaana carried in the tray with steaming bowls of stew. She bowed and backed quietly out of the room.

With crystal glasses from Venice and wine from France, brought by Crespi, Cruzado raised his glass.

Charaana returned to the kitchen to help Sa'aa're' dish out bowls of the stew for the soldiers mess table. She watched Cordero, Pico and Lopez take their places in argument about the quality of hides being tanned for export.

She wished them a good evening and found Taaherkwe' outside the door, She’d wait until nine o’clock before taking the route across the pastures to give Tooypor the news. The poison was in place. A sliver of moon glowed through patchy clouds in the

October sky. The timing of outriders and sentries was known by the villagers on all sides of the Mission.

Machado patroled the southwest pastures between the Mission and Seebag-na, turning right at the wire fence toward Los Angeles and north until he was even with the centerline of the Mission where the East-West divider fence sent him back to his starting point.

Nieto in the southeastern sector followed the mirror image of Machado' route, turning east at the squash field toward Jajamongna and making his arc to the north.

Their starting times were staggered and there were six fingers of time between their rounds.

Tooypor led thirteen of the strongest men in the dark fields on a careful arc following Machado's route until they branched off to the low indentation of Three Oaks Spring, the staging point for the inside the Mission group.

They lay on the grass beside the spring listening to each sound. In the anticipated six fingers of time she heard sounds of motion. Kwetii' signaled that people were approaching. His hand movements said they were friends.

Chiefs Aliyavit and Tomasjaquichi brought three guards each. The two older men panted from the long trip at night. The tension of crouching and brief runs to avoid the sentries tested their muscles and lungpower. She saw their guards lying on their backs, watching the clouds and briefly seen stars. Their chests moved quickly.

Aliyavit whispered. "Our men are camped in the hollow at Two Turtles Rocks. They have advance scouts dug into the fields with both voice and fire signals. They will attack from the north when they see your signal from the tower."

Tomasjaquichi added. "My men are in the same hollow. Even more men than his. We will free the neophytes and take them to free Yaanga from the invaders. I'm happy tonight!"

They waited for a short time. Kwetii' made a low whistle and signed a friend from the Mission was coming.

Taaherkwe' slid down the gentle grassy slope with wide eyes and a hug for Tooypor.

“It is done. The Priests and at least three of the soldiers have had the poison and should die in two hands. That leaves four soldiers.”

“We will each take three of our best men with us.” Tooypor told the chiefs and motioned to their guards. “The rest of my men will go to Seebag-na and bring our fighters to the Mission to see our flame signal from the tower. There will still be two soldiers on patrol. There may be fighting from the trustees, but Nahanpar’s men should have them captured. We’ll wait here for two hands before we enter. ”

Tooypor sent her ten man guard to report to Hachaaynar in Seebag-na that the attack was on schedule. At midnight he would bring Seebag-na‘s forces forward.

Achvit and twenty men from Haapchivet hit obstacles on the mountain trail to the flatlands. Trees fell and large boulders had rolled across the path. Hissing and growling cougars, bears and scamperings of small animals made them more cautious.

He called his fastest three runners to him.

“We’ll run ahead of the others. I have to reach my sister before she enters the Mission.”

Three scouts lay at the edge of the big hollow at Two Turtles Rocks watching the fields for Nieto to ride between their position and the Mission. They’d been watching for two and a half hands. No soldier could be seen.

One scout crept to a higher position to look ahead at a view of the whole route. There was no soldier. He ran to the hollow. The time was near.

“Advance.” Was called and forty men crept toward the Mission from the east.

Kwetii' peered at the Mission from the western position and listened to the sounds of the nocturnal animals. Machado didn’t ride toward them on schedule. “Nothing.” He signaled.

Tooypor gathered the chiefs and guards near.

"There are two possible reasons why the sentry didn't ride. One is death or illness if he ate the soldier's food, but, if he returned and found any of the others sick or dead, he may be standing guard and walking the courtyards carrying firesticks. We will send Kwetii' ahead to watch for a trap. Kiyookyu will follow and we will know if it is safe by the time we reach the wall. Nicolas Jose, Nahanpar, will meet us at the wall and lead us to the chapel."

Kwetii' ran in a crouch watching for movements or sounds. He reached a hundred yards from the wall and saw a figure standing where they planned to climb over the wall. A low whistle and wave identified the figure as Nahanpar. There must be dead or sick soldiers in their barrack. He turned and made whistles for Kyookyu.

Suddenly another strange whistle came from the field to the north. Aachvet ran, outpacing his two guards, to reach his sister. Kyookyu waved at him and pointed away from the Mission to where Tooypor waited. Aachvet turned and ran toward her hiding place. She watched him coming and made the bird sounds they'd used as children to guide him.

"Are you crazy? They could have guards out there. You could give the whole thing away!"

"We were so late. I had to be with you." As his guards slid into the hollow.

Kyookyu stopped and made the whistle series.

Tooypor, Aachvet, the two chiefs and nine guards reached the wall. Nicolas Jose helped them over and guided them to the side chapel door. They followed into the open door down a dark hallway with Tooypor close behind.

She tapped his arm to make him stop at an alcove off the hall with candles burning at the base of a statue the size of a real human with a bearded man nailed to the crossed four directions symbol.

"What is that!" She whispered, transfixed by the blood and agonized expression.

"That is their God, or one of their Gods." Motioning her to be quiet, but her head was buzzing with questions about why their god looks like they do and why they want statues of him being killed. If it makes them want to put other people in pain. If that's what their Gods wanted them to do. Kidnap, beat and kill people to make them like him?

Further down the hallway there were more candles under a realistic pictograph of a woman.

She tapped him, whispering. "Is that the Maria person?"

He nodded, touching her lips to stay quiet. 'It is strange,' He thought, 'I never thought of her as beautiful, only smart. She's wonderful. I'll keep her safe. It will be my duty.' Moving toward the door of the room where the padres slept.

Old Aliyavit was slow to get across the wall and stopped to catch his breath. Nicolas Jose waved them to come close. He used the improvised but proven key to open the lock. He peered into the room. It was darker than the hall, lit by a single candle on a low alter with a Bible. His eyes adapted to the room.

He saw five cots with two motionless men covered with blankets. The sides of the room held long and ornate tapestries. The window was covered by long black curtains.

He stepped into the room followed by Tooypor, Aliyavit, Tomasjaquichi and the nine guards. They edged close to the beds. Nicolas Jose drew his knife and came to the bed.

CHAPTER 24

SANTIAGO!

The black curtain flew open. "Santiago! Santiago!" Verdugo yelling fiercely. The tapestries were thrown aside. Three soldiers leapt from each side. The two decoy soldiers on the cots rose with sabers and muskets, swarming the frozen Indians.

Pico shouted in Tongva.

"Drop spears! Lie flat! Shut up!" Pushing Tooypor to the floor. "Shut up! Down!" Hitting Nicolas Jose across the face with the barrel of his pistol and punching Aachvet in the face.

"Shut up! Lie flat!" As the hands and feet of all the Indians were bound.

Nicolas Jose, Tooypor, Aachvet and the two chiefs were thrown against the wall by the door. They were struck, kicked and pushed on top of each other in a writhing, groaning pile. She saw Aachvet in the pile and hoped he wasn't identified as a chief.

"Are you proud? Little…" Pico searched for the word for 'Witch' and settled for. "Medicine Woman? Proud to fail? Bringing fail to your savage ….. villagers?"

She tried to control her breathing. 'How had this happened? Why is this dark man trying to speak my language? What is he? Why didn't I see this?'

Her eyes were wide and darting with confusion. He was taller than she was and a head butt wouldn't reach his nose. There were no moves that she could make with her tied arms and ankles that could injure him. Silence was her only weapon.

He watched her expressions in the clamor of the room and decided that she wouldn't answer. He slapped her hard across the mouth and said. "Our proud and stupid savage," and continued to lock his eyes into hers.

Nicolas Jose saw the slap and lurched forward to smash his body into Pico and knock him to the floor. He calculated that if he could immediately squirm up onto the soldier's chest, he could clamp his teeth into the veins of his neck and crush them before he was pulled off, but before he could make the second hop a musket butt smashed against the side of his cheek and he slumped to the floor. A flurry of kicks sent him to unconsciousness.

Aliyavit slouched down the wall, blinking and mumbling. "I'm an old man. I thought we were going to look at the big building.. I don't want to be here." Looking up with mournful eyes.

Tomasjaquichi stood tall silently and waited to to be beaten or killed, but no soldier found him worthwhile to be distracted. They looked lustfully at the near naked Tooypor.

Verdugo barked to Moreno and Garcia, on loan from the Los Angeles post, pointing to the nine on the floor. "Drag these into the larger cell." pointing to Nicola Jose and Aachvet. "Them too!". He turned away but whirled back, pointing at the bloodiest Indian on the floor.

"We'll send this one out to tell the ones lurking outside that their leaders are captured and will be killed if they attack. Corporal Pico. Can you prepare him?"

"Yes Sir." Lifting the man by the bound wrists. The Indian moaned in pain as Pico cut the ankle ties and walked him to the front gate.

Pico had him repeat "Tooypor magic is false" and that the "Soldiers and Padres alive" and "Strong." "You go far. You not die!" You be here. You die!" "You be here - We kill Tooypor. You be here - All chiefs we kill!" and "You be here - Many firesticks kill all Tongva!" He repeated it three times. He made the man repeat what he said until it sounded the same. The man looked puzzled but said the same words.

"Good." Pico said.

Olivera followed. "Lopez and I will take these three to the front gate, with Nieto, Galvez and Cordero." They carried three firearms each behind Pico and the prisoner. They hunched along the courtyard between the front chapel door and the main gate. They looked into quiet darkness and saw no sign of life.

Pico opened the front gate and told the prisoner to start walking down the trail. He fired his pistol in the air and shouted, hoping he could be heard.

"Your magic false! Your chiefs captured! Tooypor die, you fight!" as the prisoner lurched into the night toward the faceless listeners.

Pico had been learning words of the language for nearly a year, preparing for this moment. He mouthed a prayer that he hadn't used mistaken phrases and he had been understood by the unseen ones who came prepared to kill them all.

LOS ANGELES

The six sleeping troops were awakened with yells from the mounted soldier from the Mission San Gabriel.

"Up! To Stations! Rebellion! Up! To Stations! Rebellion!"

Juan leapt from bed, dressing in a panic. 'There are so many of them and so few of us!' He grabbed his musket, sidearm and sabre and lined up with the others at attention in front of Corporal Rodriguez. Jose Feliz as Private Cordero, the soldier from the Mission, stood fidgeting , constantly glancing back to the East for any signs of movement.

Rodriguez told Cordero to return to the Mission but to turn back to the Pueblo if there was any sign of savages traveling West.

"All of you mount up. You four along the East border. You two," pointing to Juan and de Cota, "Cover the South."

Cordero spoke. "The leaders seem contained but there are some hiding in ditches waiting for some kind of signal. It's unsure. I have to ride back now." Mounting and shouting as he turned. "If you hear my shots it means that there is trouble. I'll try to return," Leaving in a dustcloud.

Rodriguez swept the group with his hand. "First we will go to the doors of the Pobladores and have all with firearms to form a ring around the Pueblo, ready to defend their sectors."

"Get going!"

MISSION SAN GABRIEL

Charaana, Sa'aa're' and Ponu lay on the floor of a small cell. Charaana was the only one conscious after interrogation by Pico and Cordero.

Sa'aa're' and Ponu were hit on the head with rifle butts at the door of the cell after being beaten during the forced march from the kitchen.

Charaana fell, feigning unconsciousness when she saw Sa'ar'I being struck. Her breasts ached from being pulled along by them by the laughing soldier. Blood from her split eyebrow had caked down the side of her right eye and cheek.

"They knew everything." She wept and pawed at her eye with the back of her hand. Her fingers were too painful to use separately after the twisting and biting, to force her to confirm details.

When Ponu woke she looked at Sa'aa'ri' wondering how much she'd revealed and how much Charaana knew about how she was forced to say details about the planning. Would anyone ever forgive her? She considered taking poison as soon as she could find some.

They lay hoping for sleep. Hours passed. They woke to the sound of two gunshots.

"Tooypor!" Charaana gasped, and heard Pico's voice shouting from the gate.

Hachaaynar lay in an irrigation ditch beside twenty fighters from Seebag-na and three runners from the Yaanga, Jajamongna and Jajamovit. They watched the tower for fire or any sign that the inside force had taken control.

Too much time was passing. Hachaaynar shifted often. There should have been a sign by now.

Hachaaynar called the runners to begin the attack.

The Mission's front gate opened. Two men were silhouetted against lanterns placed within the opening. A limping tribesman, was pushed forward and a firestick made the thunder sound.

A voice called in a strange accent, but the words could be understood as Tongva. "Spirit False! Chiefs Captured! "Tooypor Killed if You Attack!"

It was an invader 'speaking in our language.' A chill ran through him, confirming his fear.

It changed to impossible choices in one moment. With the men from the other villages brought together, victory was possible, but only if twelve people could be sacrificed. He tried to separate himself from his heart.

The other choice was leaving as cowards into the night to villages that were sure to die. It seemed the worse of two courses.

The bloodied fighter from Jajamongna village was pulled off the dirt path and brought to Hachaaynar. He repeated the words of Pico and fell to his knees, head down, ready to be killed for his failure.

Three men stepped forward to give the fatal blow if Hachaaynar signaled, but he fell to his knees and buried his face in his hands.

“I can‘t kill her!” He whispered to himself, turning up with a forced stern expression to save face. “They have the chiefs. They know where we are. They knew our plans. They must have more soldiers and firesticks by now. They had time to prepare.” Memories of Three Hawks with thirty of the best fighters of Seebag-na, and the ease with which his father was killed stood foremost in his mind. He stood up and walked to the runners.

“Report this to your tribesmen and return to me quickly with their decision. I will join in the attack if that is what they decide. We don‘t know how many invaders and firesticks are in there, but they have our first wave as captives. They know about the attack. They are prepared.”

The three runners raced east through the vegetable patches. The Seebag-na contingent wore no face of bravery. Only defeat.

“They want us all to die now.” A usually aggressive boy said. “Staying here is like rabbits waiting for the hunters.” He was behind three other men and didn’t think that Hachaaynar could hear him.

Verdugo stood beside Pico at the center of the entryway to the Mission grounds.

“Would bringing those three out and have them kneel with guns to their heads. Would that dissuade or inflame them?”

“We don‘t know how many they have.” Pico answered. “Three or four villages. That could be hundreds. Even though all of the neophyte barracks are locked, if some of the doors were opened, we’d be in a hopeless position. We have an advantage in waiting. They are leaderless. If we keep silence, they may leave in disunity. If some of them attack then, it will be a small force, like ten years ago. We can handle leaderless savages”

“I‘ll keep them out of sight.”

Tooypor knelt with her eyes closed in the dirt beside the weeping Aliyavit. The blows to her face and body left strong pains but even those were drown in the numbing shame of failure. The invaders knew all of the details and she was unaware of it all. She had led her people into this trap with guidance of a vision that seemed from all of the good Spirits of the Earth. She’d be hated in all her people’s memories.

If Hachaaynar led the villagers against the beards, he would be the first killed. She saw that even the brownrobes had firesticks. There were nine invader fighters and four brownrobes with three firesticks each and four foreign Indians helping with extra weapons. Too many would be killed. ‘My fault! Killed because of me!’

The runners reached the huddled sixty men and two women under the Two Turtles Rocks. One armed Tah-ur and a woman who looked as strong as any of the men had come with the Jajamongna party.

They gathered tight. Outbursts came in waves at each revelation of the depth of the betrayal.

“Tooypor captured?” Tah-ur fought a wave of incomprehension at the possibility the one person in the world who held her total respect could have miscalculated her way into a trap.

“She must have planned to lead them into the invader‘s arms.” A Jajamongna man said. She recognized him as a loud man who lived in a kitcha near the one that was hosting her.

"Tooypor would never do anything against her people!" Tah-ur yelled in the man's face. He and two of his friends pushed her out to the side of the circle of men. Her friend stood to help her but she was also dragged by four more men to the periphery and thrown to the ground. The second in command to Tomasjaquichi stood and confronted the two women.

"Leave now! She was the one who brought you to us. We no longer welcome you. Go back to your people in the desert. She and you two have brought this misfortune on us. Go now and pack your things and be gone before we return to the village."

The two women walked away to the east but slowed and stopped with the same thought.

"We must try to free her." Tah-ur was emphatic, but her friend was ahead of her.

"We will turn north, then double back to the Mission."

"If we are to die. This is the proper time."

They slapped arms and turned toward the outline of the mountains.

At Two Turtles Rock, the crowd of Jajamovit and Juyuvit fighting men cursed Tooypor as a collaborator with the Spanish. She and Nicolas Jose planned this to kill the fighters and force the rest to be slaves.

There was no argument for an attack. Returning to the villages was the right thing to do. The three runners were sent to tell the Seebag-na men that no attack would be made.

Against the wide flatlands beneath the foothills, one Juyuvit runner looked north and recognized the two distant shapes far to his right walking west. It was the two women, and they were going to the invader's Mission! He turned back at double speed.

"Those two are going to the Mission to tell them where we are."

Tah-ur imagined how to blend into the Indian population inside the walls to find a way to reach Tooypor. She kept a walking pace to have energy to circle the Mission to find a place to climb in and hide until she could understand where things were and how to start.

The woman behind her shouted. “Look! Back there! Men running. They are going to attack the invaders!”

They stopped and waited, glad that the villagers had changed their minds and were going to join them. They stood as the group came within a stones throw and stopped.

The men stopped, loaded their bows and watched as the two offending women fell in a hail of arrows.

LOS ANGELES

Juan squinted into the darkness to the South walking up a rise and turning back every half hour to look East to the Mission trying to see any flames or activity.

There was a slight glow that looked like a campfire from that direction but there were no gunshots or signs of people moving.

The moon passed behind clouds. The glow was still there but it seemed unchanged. He thought he saw movement toward the ocean side but after staring long into the dimness he thought his imagination was tricking him into seeing fearful visions.

He walked back to the town perimeter and gave encouraging waves to the civilians sitting with muskets at their sides. Some had fallen asleep but it wasn’t worth waking them wwith no present threat. He knew that they had worked from dawn to dusk and needed whatever sleep they could get.

He walked to de Cota. They nodded.

“Nothing?”

“Nothing.”

MISSION SAN GABRIEL

Nicolas Jose lay bound on the floor of the same cell he'd occupied six years before, but now beside nine guards groaning on the floor of the next cell. He tried to find a position with less pain, but it was no better than the last position.

'Could Charaana have betrayed us?' he wondered, among a burning forest of questions. 'One of the chiefs? Remembering the sudden change in Aliyavit. Hearing his protests of innocence and ignorance. Any of the neophytes could have disclosed a small part of it but the only ones who knew about the Padres were the kitchen people. He hoped to never wake. At dawn he woke to the sound of boots and moans of the nine men being dragged into the courtyard.

At dawn the gate soldiers hadn't seen or heard Indians in the fields for over four hours.

Sergeant Verdugo paced both sides of the main trail looking south toward Seeba village, then west at Pueblo de Los Angeles, east to where the other two villages of the attack were.

"I can't do much tomorrow if I don't get sleep. Cordero and Lopez. Take three hours sleep, then Nieto and Machado for three. Pico and Dominguez. Take cots in the jail hallway. We'll flog the nine at dawn....I'll tell you what to do with them at seven." Walking to the chapel. "I'll tell the shaking Franciscans they can sleep safely, but keep them from my door. Until after eight!."

The sun rose over the purple eastern peaks. Despairing men, women and children gathered in the center clearings of three villages. The returning men told the details of the betrayal in vivid self serving pictures of their wisdom in avoiding the invaders' trap.   The effect was the same. The loss of their chief. The running from the fight. The false vision of the Pula woman from the far away mountain village. The lack of a plan to keep the invaders from destroying the villages one by one. No matter how it was said. It all was crumbling. The villages. The Earth under them.

LOS ANGELES

At dawn Cornelio Avila was told by Private Gonzales that the crisis was over. He had plans for the morning. He was exhausted from sleepless watchfulness on the eastern outskirts of the pueblo.

"What had happened? Was this only at the Mission?"

Gonzales tried to reassure the townspeople constantly that they were safe and the Indians were mainly Christianized and very few were still pagan. Only the ones with crosses on their beaded neckbands could order supplies and work for the farmers and masons. He still heard complaints about their attitudes and the way they looked at the younger women.

"It looks like it was confined to the Mission. We will keep a close watch for any savages who are out of place. I know that you are one of the most vigilant and your home is up on the hill. We will do constant ride bys. Let us know the moment you see anything unusual."

MISSION SAN GABRIEL

At eight in the morning Padres Cruzado and Sanchez entered Olivera's office after eight hours of prayer in a cramped space where they'd been locked and barricaded.

They were relieved to hear the attack hadn't happened but when did the soldiers know? How had it been stopped? Why didn't anyone tell them until after dawn?

"We had to keep you locked up in case they broke in. It was all for your protection."

Verdugo told the story with grand embellishments. The entrance of 'The Witch Tooyporina' and the awestricken savages throwing down their weapons at the cry 'Santiago!'

Somera scribbled notes about the night. By the time Verdugo had finished, the Padres were sure that a genuine miracle had occurred.

“We have flogged the warriors who accompanied the errant chiefs to within an inch of their pathetic lives and I’ve sent them back to their tribes.”

“Is that wise? Won‘t that enflame them to attack?” Somera visualized a potential cancellation of the miracle.

“They carry the message of the power of our magic. They left with fear of the Lord and our mercy. There is something that you must do today.”

“Pray, I assume.” Cruzado quipped.

“With your flock. It is important that we separate the loyal ones so that they’ll identify the instigators. We must crush every trace, but quietly and separately. You won’t be at risk. You’ll have some of the loyal Kumeyaay to protect you.”

The fathers unlocked all the doors and opened the chapel to fifty meek neophytes wearing sad expressions for the sins of their fallen brethren. Soldiers escorted more Indians as more quarters were unlocked. The ones with the right answers were released to Mass.

Tooypor hadn’t slept. She watched the sleeping Aliyavit and faced the glare of Thomasjiquichi well into the night until he rolled away and his snores echoed off the wall.

The dark face of the invader soldier haunted her. Why did he speak that way? Some of his words were wrong and pronunciations were from completely different dialects. Things she’d heard in different booths at trade fairs. He looked unlike any tribe or invader. What did he shout in a different language? Was he an evil Pul?

Her nipples ached from being pinched hard by the laughing soldiers dragging her down the hallway with the others. She saw them beat Nahanpar. He was hit hard. He bled. Could he have led them into the trap? He’d encouraged her to bring the other chiefs and given her the beads, but he didn’t know about the poison unless Charaana or Taaherkwe' had told him. If he was still their dog-man, why didn't I feel anything but confidence in him? I'd always felt truth or the lack of truth in his life as Nahanpar or as Nicolas Jose.

'Why didn't I see or feel any of this? I had a strong vision. It was the strongest vision of my life. Until that moment, I felt safe. Why had I failed?'

She was awakened and pulled to her feet as the first light filtered into the cells. A invader soldier and his neophyte helper yanked her into the hallway.

"Come Bruja!" The neophyte growled with a look of hatred.

<<< 0 >>>

By ten o'clock Verdugo had reports from all sectors of the Mission. No Indians. No sign of sabotage or missing livestock. He felt that holding the leaders and sending home the humiliated warriors had the desired effect. There would be no follow up attack from those who'd fled.

He called a noon meeting with Olivera, Pico and Machado to make decisions about the prisoners.

"There are precedents for quick execution of the ringleaders, but I want to get your opinions before I come to a decision." Pointing to Pico, who was already wearing an amused smile and spoke first to Verdugo.

"I think you know my point of view, also one with many precedents. Ringleaders like these, and I'm especially concerned about the following of the medicine woman Tooypor and our Alcalde, Nicolas Jose. They are popular, whether we like it or not, with gentiles in the villages and neophytes in our domain."

"The precedents are from the traditional Roman model of avoiding martyrs where the effect of their deaths would outweigh the benefits of their removal." He stood to emphasize his point.

"I've raised this with the Sergeant and want accord on this from the officers. I see a great victory in winning over the population if the four will renounce their plan and turn against each other for all to see. A trial in which they accuse one another of betrayal and show sorrow for their behavior will cement our control. If we show forgiveness and exile them to far away posts, we'll be shown as Christian and benevolent. Far more of a success than as executioners."

Verdugo rose and sat at the edge of his desk.

"I tended to want them all killed immediately as an example but I have come around to the idea of a trial and distant imprisonment for the four of them. I no longer think it will make a difference, but the Padres think that if we can get them to loudly convert to Chrisianity, we will completely win over the gentiles. I want to hear your opinions."

Olivera and Machado looked at each other with a shrug.

"It sounds like you want the trial." Olivera said. "I see the reasoning."

Machado agreed. "I'd like to see them renounce and convert but it will take time. Months!"

Verdugo slapped his hand on the top of the desk. "We have three cells that are next to each other. We will have to convert two rooms in order to separate them. We can keep the two old chiefs in the old outer cells."

Pico grinned, "We will have good repentant converts."

<<< 0 >>>

Hachaaynar waited until mid-afternoon at the northernmost village lands looking for a sign of a courier from the Mission, hoping that Sa'aa're' or Charaana would come with news of Tooypor. No-one came. No sign of Native people coming through or even working with the cattle. Only an occasional soldier staying far from the outer fence.

He was feverish to find someone to enter at night and find out. Who could he send? He thought to go himself if he could cover his tattoos. How could he do it without looking even more like an outsider?

Women brought him food but he couldn't eat. He looked at each one to decide if one were capable of making her way through the herds and climbing the wall undetected, but what would she do once she were inside? How would she find someone who wouldn't see her as an outsider and turn her over to the invaders?

He was no closer by nightfall. He walked the village. People looked with sadness. He didn't want that. He wanted someone else's problem that he could help solve. He needed something to think about other than the suffering and death of his wife.

<<< 0 >>>

Nicolas Jose's new room behind the chapel was the one where he'd been put to recover from Serra's flogging. Large I-bolts had been placed through the walls to hold the chains for his shackles. The heavy cot was bolted by metal straps to the wall.

He had little movement other than one meter from the bed to use the combination pot for urine and feces. He remembered his conversations with Private Andres. He was sure that if Andres had remained at the Mission he would have joined the rebellion. He'd stayed Indio in spite of being forced into their army.

He hadn't any more sense of who'd betrayed them other than suspicion of Charaana and what he'd bet was the weakest link, Sa'aa're'. She'd always seemed too childish to be involved in important things. It would be easy for her to gossip with a stranger. A stranger who might be sleeping with an invader.

The question kept coming back. Why was Corporal Pico leading the invaders? Why was he yelling in Tongva? Why did he call Tooypor a Bruja? That her plan had failed! How did he know those things?

Chiefs Alivavit and Thomasjiquichi were in two small end cells separated by a larger, empty, middle cell.

"Why are we here?" Alivavit croaked, face to the floor. "We didn't do anything bad! I only came to see what she was going to do."

Tomasjaquichi stayed on his cot with his eyes closed not wanting to listen to the whining. 'Why were your men ready to attack' he could have said, but anything he said could be overheard. He resolved to not speak in the invader's camp.

“She did it! She tricked me into following her. I could never climb that wall by myself.”

Finally Tomasjaquichi had to say.

“Shut up! Never speak to me! That’s final!”

<<< 0 >>>

A new cell was made from a storage room off the nave that had been filled with sacred statuary and bibles.

Tooypor was brought in at dawn, arms bound, then tied to the cot, She felt hands on her and heard a short angry conversation before the men left. She kept her eyes closed to not show fear. She remembered their faces and visualized smashing their heads with rocks, but no flash of anger could overcome the waves of shame and confusion at her failure.

In two hands time a knock brought her attention to the door. A voice with a Seebag-na accent spoke in a whisper.

“Tooypor…..Tooypor.”

“A‘ahe. Yes.”

“There is bad news…Sevaanga-vik, your husband…was killed in the attack.” His footsteps scurried away.

The last time she saw Hachaaynar they spoke so little. She was occupied with the preparations. In her thoughts she held his body to her in memories from their youth; when she’d conceived, when they argued and traveled, when they brought 'Ahtooshe' home, when they married as children. Her sobs were partly for her husband, but also loss of her sense of the world. Everything she’d learned was for nothing. It was all false. She’d failed the Spirits and her ancestors, and now Hachaaynar.

Miguel de Gabriel walked down the hall from Tooypor’s cell and turned the corner past Pico.

"You did well. A flagon of The Blood of Christ is in Verdugo's office for you."

She slept one and two hours at a time. Sounds drifted in of group chants in strange languages. First an invader's voice, then group voices. The language was different but it somehow sounded like voices of her people. She thought. 'Those Tongva are not my people. They never were. They are the collaborators against us. Sent from distant places to take our land.'

She closed her eyes again.

'They've succeeded. They have taken our land. They've taken Hachaaynar. They've killed our legends and spirits. I helped them do it!' Thinking of possible concoctions that could help her find death.

Nicolas Jose knew that two days had passed and this was the afternoon of the third. No food or water had been brought. The door had opened three or four times but the person was gone by the time he woke and focused.

This time a fit looking male neophyte, one who kept close to Cordero and did errands for the soldiers, entered and stood at the door while an older neophyte woman who helped in the kitchen brought a tray with a bowl of water and a smaller bowl with a corn porridge mixture.

Before she set it down the young man looked under the cot to make sure that the bolts and chains were tightly placed and the cot was secured.

"When you are finished," she said, "put both bowls on the tray and slide it to the door. If you break a bowl or do not slide it away from you, you won't be fed on the next day." She wore a stern expression like Somera.

"I understand." He watched them leave and listened to the door lock and their receding footsteps.

Near dark, the same pair entered cautiously and removedthe tray. He listened for sounds eagerly, feeling deprived of contact. There was nothing to look forward to. If he was killed, as he expected to be, it would most likely be privately, like an end of a long day. He couldn't feel a link with Spirit or ancestors. He could only move a very short distance from the cot. He rose in the dark and tried to start a low chant but the feeling of the chains and the limited movement, the lack of human sounds and the questioning of everything he'd believed made him sit in the silence.

'I am more than ready to die,' slumping back on the cot and dreading the morning.

<<< 0 >>>

Hachaaynar sat in his Greathouse sending runners to each other village for a sense of what was happening in the Mission.

Aachvet's released messenger described the trap in the chapel and that Tooypor wasn't killed but she might be at any time.

There hadn't been runaways. The neophytes were in lockdown for three days. A runner from the south brought news that eight soldiers were riding from San Diego to either the Mission or the Pueblo. It was too late for an ambush. There was nothing to do except to send more runners.

Dying Pul Tuwaru sat in the night watching the moon and stars hoping for a message, but none came.

'Ahtooshe' worried about her son more than she ever had. He'd never been secretive or bitter but now he had nothing to say to anyone. Only dismissal. His temper was outward and fierce for the last three days but a new kind of quiet had come over him that frightened her. She knew that he had found Tooypor's medicine baskets. There was something in his eyes that he wouldn't talk to her about.

"I know that you are taking some of Tooypor's medicines but you don't know how to use them. Which ones are they?"

"Mother. I am not in this world until I know about my wife's safety. I'll sleep alone in the fields until I do. You'll stay in the Greathouse. Leave my wife's things where they are."

The clouding in his eyes and the slur of his words stabbed her as he turned and walked toward the northern fields and the edge of the invaders' herds.

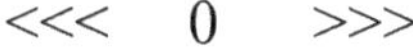

Tooypor lay facing the wall on the straw mat on the cot. She bunched straw between the chains and her aching hip and waist. She slept well. There was nothing other than more pain and shame.

After four days of inattention an Indian man and woman entered her cell. The man looked under the bed and rattled her chains to make sure they were secure. The woman left water and cornmeal on a tray and told her to slide it toward the door when she had finished.

She drank greedily and choked down the porridge breathing hard at the edge of the cot. 'How wonderful water is. The finest treasure of Mother Earth. Her love, her birth-milk' looking into the empty bowl. Even the strange ground yellow mixture tasted wonderful. She slid the tray away and lay back in a deep sleep.

The door was opened in the dark. Booted steps entered the room with a single candle. She made out the outline of a soldier wearing a hood over his face. A heavy cloth pressed over her eyes. A fist hit the side of her cheek. She was yanked onto her stomach. A cloth was tied across her mouth and her shroud pulled up above the waist.

The man hissed angry words and spit on her several times before raping her in the animal way and the human way. She tried to find ways of identifying him. She might recognize the voice if he used that tone.

She felt him slow, groan and pull out, panting like a sick dog. She felt him stand, buckle his pants and leave quickly, pulling the face cloth with him as he walked out.

She rolled on her back. There was no water to clean herself. She took a corner of her smock to remove any fluid she could squeeze out. She tried to imagine which soldier it was but there wasn't enough to put a face on him.

The next day the two brought her meal. She spoke to the woman.

“I was raped last night. By an invader soldier.”

“You must be mistaken. Maybe a bad dream.”

“It was not a dream. Send him out and look at what he did. My woman parts”

“No! Of course not. They don‘t do things like that. We are Christians here.” Walking out with the smirking man behind her.

The night came. She slept. The door opened. She tried to scream but was muffled by the cloth and hit twice as it was tied over her face. She realized it was a different soldier.

CHAPTER 25

PRE TRIAL

Aliyavit saw the soldier unlocking his cell and started speaking his own language, hoping that he'd be understood.

"I didn't do anything wrong! I only came to look at the pretty crafts. Please don't hurt me." As he was led, wrists tied, up the hall.

Tomasjaquichi listened in disgust. The old man exaggerated his limp as he passed. 'A cowardly disgrace' he thought, wondering how a chief could sink so low.

Pico had the old chief sit opposite in the chapel. Lopez moved to his side, ready to pounce if he became agitated.

"Aliyavit-Pahr." Greeting the chief with respect. A trustee helped him translate. "We are sorry you here. I know you.. not like bad people."

He smiled, happy to hear a soldier trying to speak his language. He spoke agitatedly, quivering with joy.

"They asked me to come and look at your building and it's crafts. Only when we got inside I figured out that they tricked me. I wanted to leave but.."

"Who asked you come? They promised?"

His eyes opened wider with excitement. "That woman! That Tooypor came to me with brilliant beads. She said they were from that Nicolas person in your Mission. He would give me many more for coming and seeing the Mission. I wanted to see it, but not to hurt anyone."

Pico was straining to keep up but understood that Nicolas Jose and Tooypor were the center of the plot.

"She bring beads other one? Tomasjaquichi?"

"She gave him beads. Yes, but he wanted to attack you."

After assuring Aliyavit that he'd no longer be bound and would have better portions of food in his cell, he was escorted to his cell.

Tomasjaquichi was brought to the chapel by Lopez and Cordero. He walked upright with a face of granite.

He had no intention of giving the invaders anything but his life. Others would avenge him in time.

As he hobbled into the large room with the wooden benches he was surprised to see only two men there. It was the dark man who had shouted on the night of the attack and a uniformed soldier.

They seated him in the chair and Pico watched him for more than three minutes without speaking.

"So,…You led this thing." The man was expressionless. Pico crossed his legs and waited another minute.

"You tricked Aliyavit into being a part of your plot."

Seeing no reaction. "He said you gave him beads to attack us." Seeing a twitch of the lip.

"Tooypor also said that you gave her beads to make her part of your plan." Waiting a full two minutes, observing the rock face.

"She said you and Nicolas Jose used beads to trick her and Aliyavit into attacking us and poisoning our Puls."

"You lie." He quietly whispered.

"I only repeat the words of Tooypor and Aliyavit. They will accuse you to your face."

Tomasjiquichi's eyes darted around to see if anyone else was in the shadows. He couldn't believe she would say that but he would find out in time. 'Don't let him make you speak.' He thought. He'd find out for himself later.

Pico realized the man wouldn't be moved farther. There were things that were set though that would reverberate until the next session.

<<< 0 >>>

Weeks went by for Nicolas Jose without contact other than his daily meal. No soldier entered, only the same old woman with the tray and the young man checking his chains and the wall mountings. Every three days a sour faced old man would take away the potty bowl and leave a new one.

One morning Sergeant Verdugo and Corporal Pico entered with stools in hand and sat out of reach by the open door.

“My God, you stink, Nicolas Jose.” Verdugo held a perfumed handkerchief to his nose. “How can you stand yourself?” With a chuckle. “You can see where treachery has gotten you.”

Pico watched how he reacted; The degree of anger, guilt, evasive eyes and pride. He knew Nicolas Jose’s patterns from six years of contact. This was yet a different person that the many faces he had worn in the past. Lack of confidence and mountains of guilt made this a malleable subject. One who’d condemn the witch Tooypor for all the Indians to see.

“Your plan failed. It was pathetic. Tooypor told us how you bribed her with those foolish beads. She blames you for all these troubles. Your bitterness has destroyed her people. Why did you plot this? Why did you trick her?”

“I won’t answer you. I don‘t believe anything you say. The only thing that I want is for you to die.”

Verdugo saw no point in continuing this. “You first, please,” and rose, handkerchief to nose.

“Tooypor will accuse you herself. Her hatred could knock down these walls. I pity you.” Pico said as he left.

‘Ahtooshe’ and the elders met in the greathouse for a meeting that no one wanted, the meeting to appoint a new chief.

Hachaaynar stayed in the fields and wouldn’t bathe. He returned to the greathouse to tear it apart. 'Ahtooshe' had removed the herbs but now he chewed toloache plants in the fields that could blind him.

Pula 'Ahtooshe' requested and was voted Sevaanga-vik, understanding that she'd have Hachaaynar carried into the greathouse and tied to a post, bathed daily, force-fed healthy food and drawn into conversations with villagers. Any news from the Mission about Tooypor would be given him in full detail.

'Ahtooshe' vowed to the elders she'd care for him until he was well enough to be chief.

Two weeks had passed and Tooypor hadn't bathed. She used some drinking water to wash her private parts with no material to dry with other than the bedding.

The two meal people entered with a large older woman with a pail and rags. The young man left and the older woman spoke.

"There are complaints about the way you smell. I'll wash you."

Tooypor felt rage. There hadn't been a day of freedom when she hadn't bathed each morning.

"Who complains? The soldiers who rape me? I tell her" Pointing at the tray woman "and she pretends not to hear! I want to be where people can see what is happening to me!"

"I can't do that." The woman answered, splashing water on her and lifting her leg roughly to rub with the rag.

The two women looked at each other with fearful eyes.

"Oh, dear girl!" The tray woman murmured. "I thought you were lying. I'm so sorry. I don't know who to tell! Who is doing this?"

She let loose a torrent of sobs and tears. Someone believed her! Maybe these two women could make them stop hurting her.

"The soldiers wear hoods and cover my eyes. It is more than three men. They laugh and hiss words..and hurt me."

The washing woman said. "We must tell Sergeant Verdugo. He is their chief." Looking a the prisoner with sorrow.

“He may have been one of those who raped me.” She tried to remember what his voice sounded like.

“Can you tell this to the dark man who speaks my language?” He’d hit her hard when they were trapped in the priest’s room, but she didn’t associate his voice with any of the intruders and he didn‘t look at her with sex looks like the other soldiers.

“Corporal Pico?”
“Yes, I want to tell him.”

<<< 0 >>>

Nicola Jose waddled down the hall with Lopez and new soldier Alvitre on either arm. Pico and Verdugo were seated in the chapel. He hadn’t seen a Padre in the two months since the attack. Could the poison have worked?

“Good morning, Nicolas Jose. How were your quarters and meals?” Verdugo asked, to Pico’s annoyance. ‘Why does he flaunt his superiority?’ knowing that it will anger the prisoner and make him less suggestible.

Pico added. “We’ll bring two meals a day with somewhat better food. Also, you’ll be allowed to bathe. Water, soaps and cloth will be brought to you.”

“Why?”
“We want you to be presentable for your trial. The Governor himself will attend. We’ll all hear your Tooypor testify against you. Also chiefs Aliyavit and Tomasjaquichi will tell how you bribed them through Tooypor with the beads. She told us how you made the poison and gave it to Charaana in the kitchen. Charaana told us too.”

Raising his head back to see Verdugo‘s smug face, he frowned. “Why would she say that?”

Pico leaned forward. “They all know what you did and now they’re talking about it.”

He wanted to not become involved with their accusations and conversations. He found himself slipping into it.

"It is false. I will not speak."

Pico continued to build cases against him with the other three as the accusers, stressing that Tooypor blamed him for the plan and debacle. When he saw that Nicolas Jose used self-distraction to avoid the words, Pico involved him with.

"She said she would like to spit in your face."

Verdugo added. "That would be good to watch. I may permit her to do that. You will now return to your cell."

"If this is wrong, I'm open to your side of the story. I have always thought you were too intelligent to have planned so poorly."

<<< 0 >>>

Charaana woke for the fifth time in the bouncing cart. It was barely sprung. It hit the deep ruts from the rain that had washed across the narrow King's Highway from San Gabriel to Presidio San Diego.

Only her right eye opened. Swelling on the left side and caked blood kept her squinting it shut. Her hands were tied behind her to a stake of the cart. She saw Sa'aa're''s head bobbing, tied across from her. The worst of it had been done to Sa'aa're' because she was the youngest. Their eyes met and Sa'aa're' motioned her head toward Ponu. She was alive when they were thrown into the cart. They saw that she was now dead.

Charaana thought of the life of her friend and knew that none of them would know any of the rituals to pass her into the arms of Spirit and ancestors as a Tongva woman must.

<<< 0 >>>

Olivera and Pico met with Verdugo in his office, smoking the new tobacco sent from San Diego.

“I think she is ready now.” Pico said. “Her pride should be broken enough to start blaming people other than ‘The Invaders’.”

Verdugo flicked an ash on the floor. “Maybe meeting Aliyavit will put her in the proper mood.”

“That’s a good start,” Pico agreed. “Hearing herself being accused to her face should help, but Nicolas Jose isn‘t ready to confront her and Tomajiquichi is going to be a tough one. He may have to be separated.”

“We still have three months before Governor Fages can come. They can be well coached by then.”

“Have you heard that soldiers are abusing her? ”Pico asked. “The neophytes who feed and bathe her, trusted ones, tell me that several soldiers have violated her during the night. I haven’t interviewed her yet, but that has to stop.”

Both men looked sheepish. Verdugo said. “I’ll question each one. It will stop.“

“We have a reputation to make with the Governor and the neophytes. They are doing their duties and following orders. We have good supervisors who don’t look up to Nicolas Jose. We can‘t have rumors spread about disrespect of our female prisoner. At least, not like that.”

In Verdugo’s most official voice, “I couldn‘t agree with you more.”

<<< 0 >>>

Tooypor hadn’t taken more than six steps in sequence in two months. She knew her mooncycles as surely as the sunrise. She hadn’t had one. She became sure of the baby within her and knew it couldn’t be Hatchaynars.

Keys rattled in the door latch. It was early for her meal. The cleaning woman and the young man entered. He did his inspection and left. Two soldiers stood at the door. ’Which one?’ she wondered, as the woman closed the door and told them to wait for her to finish.

"I will bathe you now. I will hold you as we walk. You are going to the chapel. You will be blessed."

Blessed was a strange word. It meant something like to have a fortunate occurrence because of the intervention of Spirit. 'Why did she say that? What could be blessing here?'

The woman bathed her gently. The chains were still on her wrists and ankles but the woman said. "The soldiers will remove these. You are going to walk today."

Tooypor looked up. She was sure the soldiers didn't understand Tongva. She hissed.

"I have a baby inside me. It is from them! There is no 'blessing!' The blessing is to die! Give me poison! Please kind mother. You are a good person. You must understand! I have to die before they hurt me more."

"No, no my child. That is 'Sin!'" looking for a Tongva word for 'sin' but coming up with a weak 'personal fault.' "You must repent and convert"

The words didn't make sense to her but it was part of the invaders' language. When they walked her in the hall she hoped that there could be a metal stick or a knife that she could put in her heart before they could stop her. There was nothing in the room that she could use.

The cleaning woman walked to the door to let the soldiers in. Tooypor watched their movements to pick up a characteristic that would identify them as the rapists. If she could grab a knife it would be better to kill one before killing herself. She imagined the actions. It would fail. They'd beat her and wouldn't kill her. The woman helped her to stand. It was unsteady. She wobbled on weak knees. Her arms were too weak to attack with.

One undid the shackles on her ankles, leaning against her knees so that she couldn't kick. The second soldier tied her wrists to the front before her wrist shackles were undone.

The woman held her arm tight during the tentative steps across the room, turning a wobbly left in the hallway toward a bright sun-filled window. Tooypor squinted, then shut her eyes against the first sun she had seen in three months. It had always been a friend, but here, with the invaders, it was a weapon.

They passed the window. She opened her eyes to see they were passing the 'Maria' painting and approaching the bearded man nailed to the four directions. They passed the door on the right where the priests slept, then turned into the large double doors to the left.

Pico, Verdugo, Alvarado, Olivera and Padre Cruzado sat awaiting the star of the trial. Tooypor was put in a chair. Two soldiers stood behind her. There was no opportunity to take a weapon. She glared at them, but from their point of view, with her droopy eyelids, she appeared meek and sullen.

"Bring in Aliyavit." Verdugo called. A door to the back of the room opened. A soldier led in the chief, hands bound behind his back.

"Trickster! Bad woman!" Screaming and walking toward her. "Witch! Bruja!" Using his new words as the soldier pulled him back. "Let me kill her! She tricked us!… Vile snake!..".

"Take him out!" Verdugo watched her face. He may be weak to her, but he's one of her own. That had to matter to her.

"You will soon hear from Tomasjaquichi and Nicolas Jose about how you tricked them into this foolish adventure."

Pico thought a minute about how to translate Verdugo's words and said. "Nicolas Jose and chief Tomasjaquichi talk same as Aliyavit."

She felt tears of betrayal. How could the ones who had supported her, who believed the invaders had to be driven from their lands, turn against everything that aimed to their survival?

"He say you trick them." In Tongva. "Nicolas Jose say you use beads. Tell beads!"

She wondered what he meant. The beads were given to her by Nahanpar, or was he always Nicolas Jose? He suggested giving them to the chiefs. Was it all a trick? Was she supposed to bring in even more chiefs so their people would be without leaders? So many questions but they all involved Nicolas Jose. Even if he was their dog-man, there was only one way to speak to the invaders.

“I know nothing about beads.” Looking away from Pico’s deep brown eyes.

“They say.. you give beads.” He wanted eye contact. She watched his boots as he moved back and forth. “Nicolas Jose say your plan. He say you poison neophytes if Padres and soldiers dead.”

A wind pulled at the back of her neck and the hair of her arms and quickly turned to heat in her chest, running up her neck into her face, thinking, ‘Lies! Lies! From Nicolas Jose? His lies killed my husband! He is killing us all. Why? He seemed sincere. Why?’

She answered. “I know nothing about beads.” Still watching his boots.

Pico turned and translated the exchange to the panel and Crespi, sanitizing the lies. “She is a tough little acorn. If she doesn‘t open up in a few more questions, I‘ll let her bake for a while and consider her sins. Would you like to ask her something, Padre?” Stepping aside.

Cruzado wanted to see the woman who tried to poison him. He’d expected a giant hag, but here sat a skinny slip who could have been a girl in her teens. She seemed full of remorse but it was more likely remorse because he was still alive.

“Yes. Ask her if she knows that to kill is to commit a Sin? Does she know what Sin is?”

Pico thought there weren’t the right words in common, or at least, that he didn’t know the right words. He walked across, noticing that she only watched his feet. ‘A device to avoid interaction.’

“Is killing bad? You know what bad?”

She didn’t hesitate, still looking down. “You invaders kill my people. You are bad.”

"She called us the sinners. That's typical of the savages to follow the injunctions of their cruel gods and ignore responsibility for their actions, but watch. She'll beg for forgiveness before long."

Verdugo turned to Cruzado saying. "We can't expect her to become a good Christian. If we're persistent, she'll confess."

Pico came close to her and said. "You stupid! Your native people kill you! We let them!"

She was escorted back to her cell. In the confusion of it, the attack by Aliyavit, the questions about the beads and uncertainty over who Nicolas Jose was, she closed her eyes and lay in the bed thinking of ways to die. There wasn't enough slack in the chains to throw herself head first on the floor or wall and the chains were too thick and short to wrap around her neck.

A knock and clank of keys made her wake. It was the woman who bathed her and had taken her to the chapel.

"Tooypor. My name is Josephina. I don't respect what you tried to do. It's wrong to hurt our Padres. They are good men, but I couldn't sleep if I didn't tell you.....That soldier, Pico...He didn't tell you the truth. He changed what the Padre said and what you said. He doesn't understand our language. My friend feeds Nicolas Jose. They tell him that you tell lies about him and the beads and that you and that yelling man, Aliyavit, want to kill him."

She knelt at the side of Tooypor's bed. "I don't like that. They treat you bad. Not Christian. I don't think Padre Crespi is bad, but that Pico man is not Christian." She watched the door with and stood to leave. "I will bring you better food if I can. I wish Christian blessing on you."

Tooypor sat straight as the woman left. It made sense that they told her lies but how much was true? She understood the rage and weakness of Aliyavit, but nothing about Tomasjaquichi or Nicolas Jose had been heard by her except through Pico. If some were lies, all of it could be a lie.

<<< 0 >>>

Late in the night, long past 'Ahtooshe''s bedtime, her guard brought the in the first escapee from the Mission in three months.

She woke and asked the plump girl to sit. She woke Hachaaynar with strong pumps to his shoulders. He was hard to wake. After depression, fevers, hallucinations and weight loss he responded more to his visitors and ate better than he had since the defeat.

“We finally have an escapee from the Mission. Come”

As he heard the news about Tooypor, he whispered “Mother!” pointing the knot tying his hands behind his waist. ‘Ahtooshe' leaned between Hachaaynar and the girl loosening the binding as he whispered. “Thank you Mother.”

The girl began with pride to be given such an important task at her age. “Some of us at the Mission haven’t given up, but many are afraid to talk to us or keep the traditions. I was sent to tell you that Tooypor is alive and Nicolas Jose is in a separate cell.”

“Can you tell their condition? Health?” 'Ahtooshe' felt a thrill and gripped Hachaaynar’s trembling hand.

“I know there are layers of trustees of the soldiers between seeing or talking to her. We’re working on it. I’ll come to you.”

“Can you get a message to her from us.” 'Ahtooshe' asked. Hachaaynar was quivering like the nervous child of his courtship.

“It will be indirect and it may take time, but we’ll try. We will find a way. She needs to hear she has family waiting.”

Tomasjaquichi preferred being tied to an anthill to having Aliyavit moaning, squawking and complaining about the fate that brought him to this place

“Shut up!” The soldier outside the hall door yelled back at the cells, sick of the jabbering of the locals. “Shut up!” Again, wanting to nap.

Tomasjaquichi shouted. “Yapping like a coyote won‘t help you. Be quiet. Stop it. I can‘t sleep with your yapping.”

Aliyavit’s tone changed to a whisper.

“When I talk that way and cry, being a foolish old man, it disarms them. Look, their plan failed. I don‘t know why, but it did. Here we are, caught in their bad plan. Look! I‘m here without being tied up like you. I walk around my cell free but you’re tied up like a deer about to be skinned.” He stood, whispering across the cell. “Listen to me. I don‘t do things for no reason. We wouldn‘t have the trade we do. We wouldn‘t be the most powerful village in the second valley if I didn‘t run it well, so, listen to me!”

Tomasjaquichi sat stunned looking at him in a new way.

“Look. They’ll have a trial, just like we do in the villages with their elders, the Brownrobes, and the ones like Pico and Verdugo. If we say ’We hate you and want to kill you,’ guess what happens to us! If we say, ’We were tricked. We didn’t know. We didn’t want to kill. Look! They didn’t even know about the men from our villages. They thought the ones outside were all from Seebag-na.”

“We’ll be killed by them.” Tomasjaquichi shrugged. “No matter what we do.”

“No. Pico told me. Because of what I said and will say at the trial, I will be set free. If I blame Tooypor and Nicolas Jose, I’ll be forgiven and released. Look! You can do the same!”

“I wouldn‘t do that. It’s wrong. You knew what you were doing!”

“What‘s wrong with surviving to fight another day. Think about it. See what kind of offer Pico can make.” He sat back on his cot and laughed. “I won‘t be as noisy anymore. Part of it was to get you talking, but I‘ll sound like a wounded coyote whenever they‘re around. You sure don‘t say much!”

Tomasjaquichi was quiet, weighing what Aliyavit had said. ‘What’s be the point of dying and leaving the village without a leader?’ He’d never have been in this mess if Tooypor hadn’t told him that poison, or her magic, had worked and the priests and soldiers were dead. She made it sound so easy.

“Aliyavit. Are you there?"

“Are you talking to me now?”

“If I tell them that she tricked me, like you did, is there a chance they will let me go back to my village.”

“You have to tell Pico and Verdugo. Ask them what they can do for you. If they say that you’ll be forgiven, don‘t hold back. Yell, but louder than feeble old me! Jump around and tear at your hair about how betrayed you were. How much you hate her! See how they react.”

“I‘ll think about it. This was a stupid plan. She needs to be the one to be responsible for it.”

“Call the soldier. Ask for Pico.”

<<< 0 >>>

Nicolas Jose stopped thinking about what might happen at the trial. He’d expected death so many times and avoided it. Not through skill but simple fate. He felt ready for anything but being hated falsely. Being hated for trying to bring back the traditional life of the Tongva against these murderers and thieves is a good clear hatred. It was one to be proud of.

Being hated by Tooypor and the other chiefs disturbed him more than thoughts of death. The question kept coming up; from Aliyavit, from Pico and no doubt from Tomasjaquichi and Tooypor. Why was that important? Why was it more important than thoughts of living or dying?

He thought not about the trial, but his relationships with Spirit and with Tooypor. In little steps he came to feel more than just a deep respect for her. It was a love that was stronger than the lustful feelings, the pride of control, or the emotional intimacy of his marriages. It was respect that he would gladly die for. She had a purity of vision that had him in awe when he first met her and negotiated with her. ‘What an impractical fierce stand from a child! And she succeeded! Her distrust and questioning when I was at Seebag-na. She was right to do that. I was so entranced by their weapons, trinkets and privilege. I'd try to please whoever was more powerful than I was. I was no-one to trust but she did, and now she thinks, or says, that I betrayed her.'

Verdugo and Pico unlocked the door, sat on stools and repeated the accusations of Tooypor, Tomasjaquichi and Aliyavit.

Nicolas Jose listened as to an often repeated children's story. He decided he would not reply matter who said what to him. After a long period of seeing no response, they left with no comments. Verdugo seemed amused. Pico scanned his face closely before leaving. He nodded solemnly.

In the night the door was unlocked to Tooypor's cell. She barely woke. The man was on her, tying a cloth around her face and entering her brutally. He left quickly without a word. She wept until dawn and fell asleep until Maria the food woman came. As she sat up, she saw the blood on her smock and the mat. Maria dropped the tray, rushing to her side to examine her.

"Oh, sweet angel!" Shaking her head in sorrow. "You've lost your baby. I'll call Josephina to help you. I'll call Father Cruzado. Oh, you poor creature!" Standing and backing out, latching the door.

Tooypor heard the girl sobbing rushing down the hall, and fell back on the mat feeling consciousness slip away mumbling "My baby."

She woke with Josephina running a cold rag over her brow.

I'll be with you here until you're well enough to see Father Cruzado."

Maria went to Verdugo after telling Josephina and the two Padres.

"I'll get to the bottom of this. Every soldier has been instructed to respect her and to never abuse her. I'll call in each one and find and punish the rapist."

Padre Cruzado met Josephina and Maria at the Chapel door. Tooypor was laid back on a pew. Two soldiers walked behind but stayed outside the door. The women would not let them assist or touch her in any way.

Padre Cruzado looked the three women over comparing the two Christians to the wild woman in the center wearing a fresh Mission smock and sullen hatred directed at him. He'd heard all the stories of her powers and how her plan was undone by Pico's hearing first the word 'poison' and then other words that gave the time and enough details to lock him away with the other Padres on that night.

Josephina spoke quietly and with reverence. "Dear blessed Father. This is the gentile, Tooypor. She lost her baby last night. It was a boy."

"Yes, I've heard about it. The remains of the poor soul was brought to me. I've blessed it to receive a proper Christian burial. It will be entered into the Mission records. Do you know if the boy has a name?"

Josephina asked Tooypor. "Have you named your boy? They need a name to remember it."

Tooypor had held her tears for hours. How can she place a name on this thing that was a part of her but produced by a horrible snake that crawled into her belly from a bearded coward of an invader? Yet, it was still part of her body, not his. If it had lived, she'd love and nourish it.

"It would have been Hachaaynar." Barely audible, but enough for Cruzado to know that it was a Tongva name.

"Hachaaynar." Josephina said. "The boys name is Hachaaynar."

"It must be a Christian name." Looking at the sincere older woman. "Your name is Josephina isn't it." She lowered her head.

"Then this baby's name will be Joseph. Like the Earthly Father of our Lord." Seeing the contemptuous face of the prisoner. "Take her back to her cell."

<<< 0 >>>

Governor Fages' detachment left Monterey with twelve cavalry troops. Six ahead and six behind his carriage were military escort. A scribe, Corporal Vargas, sat next to him preparing notes for the trial. The carriage held Christmas gifts for Viceroy Buccareli in the San Diego Presidio, for Comandante General Rengal in Sonora, and for the Comandante at Presidio Santa Barbara.

Fages looked forward to four days of civilization at the well organized fortress before facing the Franciscan chaos of the Mission and their savages. He was relieved after his posting that Baja California had gone through eighty years of developing a stable population and that Alta California was well on it's way to stability.

Fages said. "You'll be kept busy with translating, re-translating and editing of four very noisy defendants. Our dispatches will have to be tidied up quite a bit to make sense to the administration in Mexico"

"I've done enough in eight states and so many strange languages, but with men who'd grown up with it. From what I've read, we don't have what I'd call an expert translator there."

"It'll be short. We'll be out of there quickly."

Vargas settled into reading an adventure novel. "I like traveling. It will be good to see this place. I've heard so many stories about it. Pretty lurid."

<<< 0 >>>

Tomasjaquichi thought long and deeply about his situation. If he were to die now the village would be destroyed, either with one or two attacks or slowly fade from attrition.

The change in Aliyavit, seeing the hopelessness in continuing to fight after the shock of being surrounded by soldiers with firesticks, could have made it easier for all of them. There was no threat from a weeping old man, and Tomasjaquichi's own lack of resistance, for different reasons, but guided by an instinct to survive, kept them from being killed on the spot.

‘What could Tooypor gain if we defend her or keep silent for her?’ The poisoning was the biggest failure and it was purely her doing. He saw that the Spanish for that reason alone would kill her. He had nothing to do with that. All of them had dropped their weapons as soon as the invaders had yelled.

‘I only came with Aliyavit to look.’ Trying on the sound. ’She tricked us both.’ Feeling hope to move the whole village to a safer place, farther from the invaders.

‘She did trick us. She promised that everyone in the building was dead! By her magic! Instead, she led us into a trap! We were lucky not to be killed. It would be stupid to not blame it all on her.’

He spoke across the empty middle cell. “Aliyavit. Psssss. Aliyavit.”

The old man grunted. “I was sleeping.”

“Aliyavit…..You were right….Yes, tricked.”

“But don‘t forget. Loud! Angry! ”

<<< 0 >>>

“She accused you of planting the poison.”

Nicolas Jose looked disinterestedly at Verdugo‘s posturing. Cordero and Lopez stood at the door. He’d seen the expression many times before. Getting information by acting ‘friendly.’

Nicolas Jose felt that under that neutral posture there was a permanent snide smirk. He’d seen Verdugo change course to get what he wants enough to distance himself from anything he said.

“All three accuse you“ He continued. “She told Pico and the others that you tricked them into this by giving them the beads and telling them the Mission cattle and wine would be theirs if they gave you a poison to kill us." Settling into a relaxed pose.

"I didn't think you'd do that. I saw you change into a Christian man, yet, they say you wanted to kill all of us Christians. How could that be?"

Nicolas Jose took his time, fretting and scratching his head over the question.

"Maybe I was tricked. Maybe a spell was put on me." Looking into Verdugo's eyes.

"I'm not sure if you are sincere. Are you?"

"How soon is the trial?"

"Soon. Within the month."

Nicolas Jose bit at his lower lip. "I need to think…alone, alone for a while. Tell me again what she said about me. How I tricked her."

Verdugo repeated all of the accusations that were attributed to Tooypor, Tomasjaquichi and Aliyavit.

"It's hard to believe they'd turn on me that way. I never really listened to all of these bad things, especially from Corporal Pico. I always thought he was a liar, but you, you're different. I need to think about this. If I have more questions I'll ask the guard to call you. Come to me right before the trial. I'll talk with you, but not with Pico."

<<< 0 >>>

Josephina thought about whether it was the right thing in the eyes of the church. It seemed fair and moral, but she was unsure if the Padres would want to judge, and would say no to her speaking. It would be cruel to be silent, knowing she could bring comfort to a tortured soul.

'Please Jesus guide me.' She sat on a bench in the hall holding the rebel woman's tray of food. She looked up at His statue in the alcove. She stood and carried the tray to the cell.

Tooypor saw Josephina's face and guessed that Verdugo or Pico were in the hall again. It was a daily process of hearing how the others blamed the disaster on her and she should tell the court about how Nicolas Jose had bribed them into the attack. They would make another offer of forgiveness, making her a favored person at the Mission, letting her return to her village, giving her a room of her own. 'Very easy,' they said. 'Tell the truth about Nicolas Jose and accept baptism.'

She learned what baptism meant. She would kneel in front of a Brownrobe. He'd splash her with water and say words in a language, the language of The Sea Visitors, and she'd copy what he said, repeating the chant phrase by phrase like 'Ahtooshe' said they had her do. She'd wear a Mission smock, but Pico said, 'The red dress of the Virgin Mother.' What 'Ahtooshe' wore.

She could protect her brother by converting to their control, for a while. She could pretend to become their 'neefight' until she could escape. None of them could outrun her up the trail to Haapchivet, once she cleared the flats to the Eagle Rock.

Maybe Nahanpar, or Nicolas Jose, was the traitor. He could be blaming her because he planned it that way or, he had been temporarily with her but changed to please his masters. He could be with the soldiers now and laughing at the ones he tricked.

Now Josephina stood before her with her tray, lip trembling.

"Miss Tooypor, ma'am." She set down the tray and steped back to sit on a stool in the corner. Her voice was low and nervous as she kept an ear to the hallway.

"I may be wrong to tell you this, but I see you suffer. More than a person in Christian care should suffer......When I was preparing the food in the kitchen, a girl I'd never seen before came to me and told me to please listen to her. She was dressed in the smock and her hair was like a field worker."

"She told me she came from your village weeks ago but didn't know where you could be found. That she had come from your husband and….."

"My husband is dead!" Rage surged through her blood. "Who put you up the this?"

“I know you told me that he was killed, but she said his name, “Hachaaynar, and his Mother, 'Ahtooshe'. Names I’ve heard from Seebag-na people. She said they miss you and pray, in their way, for your safety and strength of heart.”

Rage subsided as quickly as it came.

“If you are a good woman, are you telling me the truth?,” looking at her face and seeing a deep sweetness.

“I never lie to you but I am scared. The Padres may disapprove. I know you think he was killed. She says he is alive. It would be bad to let you think he is dead if it’s true. I don’t know her.”

“If you see her again, could you bring her to me as your helper so that I can ask her for the truth.”

Josephina thought a moment. “That would be fair.”

Fages’ party arrived two days after the Mission’s modest Christmas celebration riding first through the nicely designed but rutted main streets of Pueblo de Los Angeles.

“It must have rained heavily again” Vargas held tightly to his notebook as the carriage bumped across a dip.

“Not quite Roman.” Fages remarked on seeing the way the East to West main road was angled off the new central circle to avoid the hills after yet another rainstorm had made it necessary to either angle it off to the Southwest or to make a clumsy curve around the low northerly hills.

As they passed the rebuilt church Vargas said, “I think this is the third location and forth rebuild, but it’s an attractive looking church.”

“Yes it is.” Looking back as they passed the crews expanding the civic center building. “This is becoming beautiful!” Waving to cheering shoppers on the neatly planked sidewalks on seeing an impressive show of power from the bright uniforms and elegant carriages.

As they turned East toward Mission San Gabriel they passed newly seeded and flourishing wheat fields. As the fields passed the herds of livestock grew to become the borders of both sides of the road.

"This place is huge!" Vargas held his head halfway out the window looking at the seemingly endless herds of cattle to the right, looking across Fages on his left at the hundreds of sheep milling on that side of the road. Up ahead, the darkly fertilized cleared fields were being readied for early spring planting. Beyond the fields new construction was expanding the Mission neophytes' quarters.

"It has improved!" Fages looked ahead. "You should have seen what a mess it was five years ago, and a funny thing about it is, much of the clean-up and discipline of the neophytes here is due to one of the rebel defendants, the fearsome Nicolas Jose."

"The rebel with a Spanish name."

"He was one of the first converts. He became Alcalde. He reverted to savagery, apparently because of a woman again." He told Vargas the story of the Baja neophyte and the fabled Juanita.

They approached the spotlessly restored open gate in a freshly tan painted stuccoed arch with low evenly peaked walls. The staff, soldiers and men of the cloth stood with good posture as though drilled loosely to 'attention,' but most were not military and seemed uncomfortable in their pose.

In the Mission a long junction of tables was set with steak, squash and wine, prepared in French ceramic ware and crystal.

Padres Crespi, Cruzado and Sanchez were seated on one side of the adjoined tables with soldiers Alvitre, Nieto and Vargas. Across from them were Dominguez, Cordero, Ortega, Verdugo, Pico and Olivera. Fages sat at the head and spoke.

"I was impressed by the progress made since my last visit. This is becoming a great adjunct to Pueblo Los Angeles." Pleasurably noticing a quick look of anger on the faces of the Franciscans. No matter how much independence and wealth they imagined they were accumulating for the Vatican, this was Spain! Spanish land

and Spanish protection, as long as they obeyed the order of things.

After dismissing request after request of Junipero Serra, all of these of his minions dreaded the further expansion of secular control. Serra's 'requests' were framed more as Orders from Above than as communications to The Crown. The commercial potential of this Pueblo would soon easily swallow up this little outpost of The Church

"Tell me about the ones who brought us together for this elegant little meal. I understand one of their leaders is a lovely bruja." Raising his eyebrows. "Will she dance for us?" Seeing fear in the Padres for a lustful reference. 'How darling! ' He thought feeling their squirming. 'They must be packed to the top of their shiny little skulls with repressed lust.'

Verdugo gave a full, if exaggerated, account of the Tongva's plan and his role in planning the trap and turning away the massed Indians in the darkness.

"They believed the temptress Tooyporina would protect them with her big magic." Shrugging. "She isn't really pretty enough for a cultivated man to take much enjoyment in her dancing. Maybe for the Indians she might be considered attractive. She has strange green eyes and isn't as round as most of them are."

"The other central conspirator is our own Alcalde, an angry man who has been in trouble many times before. I shouldn't have been surprised."

Fages smiled after having read six years worth of reports. "I know his story well." Looking over to Crespi. "Much of his anger, I believe, can be traced to the actions of the Blessed Father Serra's.....love of discipline." The Padre glared. "He may have caused all of this with his temper." Ignoring their protestations with a raised palm of dismissal.

"I have developed a series of questions, ten questions, to put to the defendants in order to get to the truth of this matter, based of reports that I have seen over the years from this Mission. I will now read them to you"

"One. When earlier the plot was discovered to kill the Padres, the soldiers and the Baja neophyte Indio, hadn't you all been warned that similar conspiracies would bring severe punishment?"

"Two. Why, with these warnings and admonishments to keep the peace, and our never having caused you any harm, did you come with weapons in hand to kill the Padres and soldiers?"

"Three. What induced you to act so foolhardy, knowing that only one shot from our Mission canon would slaughter a great many of you?"

The soldiers wondered where the canon was. The Padres looked to each other and shrugged.

"Four. Have you suffered any injury at the hands of the Padres, soldiers or any other Christians that would make you want to kill them?"

"Five. Who had conspired to plan and execute the assault, and who was the principal leader?

"Six. Who was the Christian whom you most obeyed and who was first to suggest the attack?"

Verdugo suppressed a smile at the image of old Aliyavit screaming "The Pope!" and nodded in approval.

"Seven. Were the cattle, sheep and goats that were slaughtered in the fields at night stolen from the mission corrals or taken out of the fields, and was this with or without the consent of the shepherds? Who were the guilty ones?"

"Eight. What weapons did you bear, and who furnished them?"

"Nine. How many and which rancharias or villages were convoked, and where?"

"And, ten. Do they know why they are in prison, and why the governor, lieutenant, padres and all the soldiers are so angry with them, and do they realize the just punishments they deserve?"

Verdugo led the chorus of "Excellent." and "That is a good interrogation."

Cruzado joined in. "A good set of questions." Relieved that no mention of Serra or administration was included.

Turning to each of the Padres with a satisfied grin.

“This place has quite a history of little scandals. It was a lark to read of the goings on. We will probably hear many tales of abuse and native grievances. It will be an interesting trial.”

It was a relief for the Padres when the entrée was finished and they could gracefully excuse themselves.

Other than repetitive visits by Verdugo, the defendants had no interaction for four days before the trial.

Aliyavit told Verdugo the key phrases he’d repeated from the beginning. He knew it worked well for him. He’d receive fair treatment and be released with a warning to never do it again. He didn’t think he’d have to face Tooypor or Nicolas Jose directly.

Tomasjaquichi practiced his rage to the point that any stimulus would trigger a spectacular warrior’s outburst. He told Verdugo that he would strangle the venomous snake on sight. The Sergeant moved to the Alcalde’s cell with a feeling of satisfaction. Tomorrow would be a good day.

Nicolas Jose listened to Verdugo’s reiteration of the accusations against him by the other prisoners and nodded solemnly. “I have thought about this. I was deceived. I will say no more. I am shamed.”

Tooypor realized that she couldn’t blame the words she’d heard about Hachaaynar’s death on any one person. It had been planned to hurt her. The relief at hearing that he and 'Ahtooshe' were alive and aware of her was an infusion of courage. She prepared for any lies to be thrown at her. It all would be lies.

Verdugo and Pico entered after her morning meal. Pico translated, thinking he‘d said.

“Tomorrow big day. Even brother denounce you.” Translated as. “Tomorrow large! Brother not enjoy you“. They both looked for any kind of reaction. “Nicolas Jose say he deceived……..Don’t you think you have protected him enough?” Coming across in Tongva as “Protect him Nicolas Jose? Long from you now?”

Tooypor looked at them to see any characteristics in common with any of the rapists.

"I understand there is much anger. I'll talk tomorrow."

Translated to Verdugo as, "I am angry until tomorrow." Shrugging and adding. "She may come around."

CHAPTER 26

THE TRIAL

The soldiers converted the chapel to a courtroom by moving three tables in an arc around the defendant's chair. Seven chairs were behind the tables. After a morning meal the panel filed in.

Facing the defendant, left to right, were the translator, Pico, the scribe, Vargas, Governor Fages, Sergeant Verdugo conducting the proceeding, Sergeant Olivera, Corporal Alvarado, Fathers Sanchez and Cruzado as observers. Privates Alvitre, Cordero, Dominguez and Nieto to guard and escort the prisoners.

Verdugo tapped a gavel saying. "Bring Chief Tomasjaquichi."

Tomasjaquichi didn't expect to be called first. The surprise of it sent fresh energy through him. He stood and stomped both feet as though he was about to fight. He held his wrists out to have the chain removed. Dominguez entered from behind the nervous Nieto to unlock the chain. The strength and forcefulness of the prisoner had them ready for anything.

They walked the hallway. Tomasjaquichi strode like a bear, using his broad shoulders to convey his growing anger,

He shouted in Tongva.

"Bring her to me! Show me the liar!"

Verdugo signaled to Cordero to go in the hall to help bring the chief in but he was elbowed aside as the enraged man burst in.

Sergeant Olivera moved toward him with a heavy quirt raised, as Pico shouted.

"Stop!. Sit! Sit Now! Shut up! Quiet!"

Tomasjaquichi looked around the room at all the soldiers and Brownrobes. Tooypor was not there. No Tongva were there.

"Sit! Tell truth!"

He was pushed down on a stool, listening to Pico's reading of the questions, feeling his prepared anger become diluted trying to understand what Pico was trying to say.

"You know Nicolas Jose when he bad many moons..years ago. He bad then. Did you know?"

"I didn't know him until that night. I never met him."

Pico translated. Olivera said.

"I was Corporal of the Guard then. He was never here."
Pico returned and asked. "You knew bad come to you. Why you want kill soldiers and Padres?"

He saw this as an opening to start his redemption.

"I don't have a problem with the soldiers or Brownrobes. It was her! That.. Bruja!" Using a new Spanish word. "She tricked me! She tricked us all! She used sweet words but made threats! I want to strangle that snake. I want to pull her lying tongue out!" Standing suddenly and making the table shake.

"She got me into this! She even threatened me! A Chief!" Squirming at the ropes on his wrists and shifting foot to foot. "That no-good Christian, Nicolas Jose, riled me into a blind rage to kill you Spaniards. He said you were white devils who would salt our lands and make us slaves".

He moved forward. Three soldiers sat him down. Pico knelt beside him to try to fill in the words that he hadn't understood and after a long pause signaled Verdugo to continue.

On the next questions Tomasjiquici called 'the snake Tooypor and the traitor Nicolas Jose' the ones who'd planned it and tricked them. Nicolas Jose was the only Christian. Nicolas Jose started the idea of the attack.

"I don't know anything about sheep. I heard that your shepherds gave them away."

He said the only weapons they had were ones they made with their own hands.

"How many village come attack?"

Tomasjaquichi looked down and scratched his big toe into the earthen floor four times. He looked up and moved his feet to the right and made two small scratches.

"What is that?" Pico asked.

"Small villages. Not many men. The biggest was Asuks-gna, where we met. The other small village was the witches village, Haapchivet where her brother is chief."

"I admit I came along. I was the chief. I brought some men and we brought weapons. That was very bad. I deserved to be locked in your cage. I deserved to be punished." Attempting to stand again.

"Take him back to his cell." As the soldiers led him out he had one more chance.

"It was her! The snake tongued witch made us do it!"
His shaking eased as he stepped into the cell, thinking of whether he should have underplayed his role in the village.

After a brief review they agreed that Fages' structure worked well. Verdugo called Chief Aliyavit.

The elderly Chief was helped into the room by Nieto holding his arm. The limp became more pronounced approaching the chair.

"Chief Aliyavit of Jajamovit rancheria." Pico began.

The doddering chief claimed no knowledge of Nicolas Jose's troubles or history. His face reflected only confusion. He rocked back and forth on the stool.

"I knew none of these people. I saw them walking along and I followed them. I wanted to see what they were doing. They looked like rabid animals. They had paint on their faces. I was just curious. That's why I went along."

When asked who the leaders were, he answered that when he was brought into the priest's room, it was clear that it was Tooypor and Nicolas Jose,

Olivera leaned to Alvarado and whispered. "Funny how this harmless old fellow moved to the front rank so easily."

“What weapons did you carry?” Pico asked.

Aliyavit shrugged helplessly. “Of course I carried my Chief‘s bow and arrows. All village men carry them. I’m expected to. Aren’t I the chief?” Pointing at Fages’ gold hilted sword. “Like you. You are a chief. You have to carry that bright stick.”

He answered that five villages were in the war party. His voice became shrill.

“I know why I have been locked up here. It‘s because I followed that treacherous woman. I only wanted to see what she was doing, and they were up to bad things. I wasn‘t... ”

“Stop! Be quiet!” Pico was sick of the whining and asked about the slaughtered animals.

“Yes. I had picked them out myself, but would you believe it? My men were such cowards they wouldn‘t do it. They wouldn‘t lift a finger, so my nephew and I had to do it ourselves.”

The court had a chuckle. Vargas said “Nothing like getting the job done…… yourself!”

Before calling Nicolas Jose, Olivera leaned on Vargas’ table and had him write. “ I knew him well when I did service here. I made this swaggering and boastful Gabrielino know that he must tell the truth for justice so that God would help him. I told him that if he didn’t I would punish him severely. He seems aware of the consequences. He promised to be truthful about everything he will be asked.”

Nicolas Jose was brought in looked focused and ready. Not the strutting and arrogant buffoon that Fages had expected. He sat looking at each man right to left, not recognizing two but recalling his histories with the other five.

Pico began in broken Tongva. “On the time when they.. you plot to kill Baja neophyte, Padres and soldiers, you told you be punished. You remember?”

Nicolas Jose raised his eyebrows, made a crooked smile, and answered in Spanish, exaggerating Verdugo‘s Castilian accent.

"How could I forget your jail. It wasn't the big plot that you claimed. I was angry. Very angry at the horseman neophyte and the Padres. I felt they'd betrayed me. I remember the warnings. This time was different. I followed my heart and spirit to stop you, the Padres and soldiers from destroying my people. You've banned our worship, our rites, our dances and prayers."

"Have you got that?" Back to Vargas.

"It will take a little editing. But his Spanish is understandable."

"Who were the leaders, Nicolas Jose"

He thought about the three months of incarceration and the way she was quoted telling of his bribes and bringing the other villages into the plan. 'Does she really blame me for this?' Wondering what she would say but thinking, 'If I had a painful time these months, she must have suffered far worse.'

The respect, love that he felt for her, the strength and the struggle she'd mounted her entire life, brought a choking feeling. He turned his head but Pico saw the emotions.

"A touch of remorse." He snickered to Vargas.

"Well?"

Nicolas Jose sat up straighter and cleared his throat.

"I alone planned it. I made contact and convinced Tooypor to join because she is respected. She is the best person at making medicine to fight the devilish diseases that you spread among our people. She is loved in many villages for the help and trade that she brings to them.

"It was Me, alone. I gave her beads to give to the other chiefs. I told her that I would get the neophytes at the Mission to join us. She has a reputation for wisdom. Because of her reputation she is known in other villages, and the beads that clearly were from the Mission, induced some other chiefs who also came to see the revenge that I planned for your evil deeds."

"That's quite a story." Pico wiped a mock tear.

Vargas responded. "I'll clean it up."

Nicolas Jose understood enough to know that anything he said would be twisted into the story that they would send to their masters of 'The Crown' wherever they were.

"What weapons were brought?"

"I made my own. Anyone who carried a bow, arrow or spear, made it themselves."

"Which rancherias joined attack?"

Nicolas Jose knew the invaders wanted as many villages named as possible so they could be attacked and leveled. He'd heard that powerful teams of horses had used ropes to knock down kitcha huts. He'd heard rumors that salt and poisons were poured into wells and springs and large boulders were pulled to close off water sources.

"I'm not sure if the chiefs had troops other than their guards. I sent Tooypor to many villages, but not many came."

Pico stepped to Vargas' table as Verdugo leaned across.

"He's lying. Tooyporina's brother's village and at least five others were put under the sorceresses spell."

"We'll have time to make adjustments."

Pico returned to his notes, using Spanish and not making pretenses at Tongva.

"Were the cattle, sheep and goats that were slaughtered at night stolen from the corrals or from the shepherds in the fields? Did they cooperate?"

"I told the Tongva villagers that they could have the animals. I alone took them when the shepherds were in other parts of the pastures." Staring at Verdugo.

"Single-handed. Quite a thief."

"None of it was Tooypor's idea. I induced her to go to bribe the villages. If she wanted to kill you, you'd be dead now."

Pico, Olivera and Verdugo laughed out loud.

"What a woman!" Olivera sneered.

"Take him out." Verdugo barked to Nieto and Dominguez.
"We should relax and discuss this before we face 'The Sorceress' with her magical powers." Fages said, standing and stretching.

"Vargas. What do you make of his speech?"

"Theatrical posing to let everyone else go free. Playing the martyr."

Fages humphed in agreement. "We'll have no martyrs. Only sullied reputations."

"Yes, I understand, Sir."

Tooypor sat on the edge of her cot from daylight on, listening for sounds from other prisoners. Any shout or indication of what was being said in the big room where the Brownrobes and beards gathered.

The door was unlatched and two unknown soldiers entered, unchained her and led her down the hall. She saw the seven men at the table and stood still.

The Governor and scribe were struck by how small and young the now fabled fearsome creature was.

He motioned for Dominguez to seat her. She glared at Fages and Verdugo, who seemed to be the leaders.

She stood next to the stool, and then suddenly kicked it aside. Dominguez and Nieto looked to Verdugo for direction.

"Let her stand." Looking warily, but feeling relief. The only thing she could use as a weapon was now across the room.

Her eyes burned into them. 'These liars. My husband is alive. My people will live. I will live.' She wouldn't speak with that snake Pico hissing at her but she answered as soon as the thread of his translation became clear.

"I know nothing of your Nicolas Jose and any punishment of his in the past. I know that I've spoken to him when you killed the father of my husband. We had you savages return his head."

Pico asked. "Do you tell other chiefs and rancherias attack on uo?"

"I spoke to many chiefs. None of them want you here. None of them trust the poisoned word of the Brownrobes." Pointing at Cruzado. "I told them not to trust anything these liars say. I told them that I hate you Brownrobes and Beard invaders for living here on my native soil. You are trespassing on the land of my ancestors. You are spoiling our tribal lifeways. You've plundered our lands."

Pico repeated to Vargas. "She commanded Tomsjiquichi and the chiefs to tell all the neophytes to disbelieve the hated padres and to trust only her. She commanded them because she hates the padres and all of us for, and I quote, for "trespassing on the land of my forefathers and despoiling our tribal domains."

Pico made a theatrical 'impressed' face before returning to the questioning.

"Why trick you people attacking us? One shot giant firestick kill you all! Why?"

She sneered at Pico. "We came to drive you out of our land. If I could inspire my people, though they'd been so afraid for so long, to attack and not fear your firesticks and the smell of death that you bring, I'd do anything to be done with you pale faced, bearded invaders."

Pico laughed and turned to Vargas.

"She doesn't like pale faced invaders. I guess that means she likes me. Among other things, she called her tribesmen cowards. She wants them to not be afraid of firesticks. I'll fill in the details later, but she's an angry young woman."

She stood erect. He looked at the notes again and paced before her, tempted to offer her the stool again.

"Quite a woman!" Fages shook his head. "Reminds me of my wife!"

Pico continued, asking. "You have anger on Padres and soldiers. Injure you? You want kill us?"

She glared around the room again. 'What a stupid question' she thought. 'Does he listen?.' Pausing before answering quietly with her eyes down.

"No. They haven't injured me. Not myself, other than rape, beatings and family members that you have murdered."

"Who other rancheras in attack. Nicolas Jose give beads to join?"

"I've had enough of this. I won't speak more. If you are going to kill me, do it!"

Pico motioned to Verdugo. "I don't think we'll get any farther with her."

"What about the others?"

Pico summed up. "Nicolas Jose planned it. Aviyavit, Tomasjaquichi, the brother, others. We'll work it out.

She continued staring at the comfortable looking men, who were now talking with each other. They looked her up and down like she were one of their riding animals. An uncontrollable one.

"Take her back to her cell." Verdugo said to Dominguez and Nieto. They seemed more respectful than the regular soldiers at the Mission and bowed after affixing her chains. They softly said what must have been 'goodbye' as they latched the door.

Pico, Verdugo, Fages and Vargas sat closely at the end table interpreting and preparing a manuscript to send to Comandante General Rengel in Sonora.

"Do we have her 'commanding' the other chiefs into battle?" Vargas asked.

"She did say that they were afraid of firesticks until she ordered, or commanded,...or threatened them into action." Pico went on to give interpretations to her statements and Nicolas Jose's that accepted their responsibility and implicated the others.

"She as much as called the other Indians 'cowards.' She said that she hated 'white people."

The afternoon and evening was tedious. Cruzado and the other Padres felt left out of the process.

After dinner the administrators and soldiers approved the content of the Expediente, the trial's transcript. Each signed it and had a satisfying evenings brandy.

"What a woman!" Fages repeated. "What a Christian convert she will make!"

The noises outside Tooypor's cell were louder than at any time. There were more Mission captives walking the hallways talking Tongva and Spanish after three months of being kept out. None of the talk was about anything she could understand. Mainly she heard gossip about other men or women with Spanish names. Probably Tongva neophytes.

She wasn't sure what the other prisoners had said about her. It was strange that the questioner didn't talk about anyone except Nicolas Jose. All they did was try to have her say that he was the leader. They were liars. Everything Pico said about the chiefs and Nicolas Jose was a lie. The man outside telling her about Hachaaynar's death. It was all false.

She ate with Josephina.

"I'll bring the Seebag-na girl to you when I get the tray. She is in the kitchen. Are you better after confession?"

Tooypor laughed. "Is that what you think I'm doing? Their rituals?"

"Father Cruzado told us that you would be joining us in the Faith. He said that you had renounced the old ways."

"Crazy! What liars!"

Josephina slowed and rose, stepping back from Tooypor.

"I might be improper to bring the girl then. She is a village person."

"Wait! Wait" Touching her arm. "I have been thinking seriously about converting, but want the village's approval. We will be talking about having her whole village convert. You can see how important that could be, don't you?"

“Why did you call the Padre crazy?”

“I didn‘t call him crazy, I said that it was crazy to assume that I..”

“And Liars?” No. I need to get approval from the Padres before I can allow a visitor.” Backing out and locking the door.

<<< 0 >>>

‘Ahtooshe’ had almost given up on young Ponuu’’s return. When she was announced after dawn, the tale she told wasn’t what they expected.

“She has turned away from our ways. They say that she is now a Christian. The ways of the Brownrobes. At the trial she called the other fighters cowards.”

‘Ahtooshe’ gasped and held her head. “Oh, my baby Tooypor! They must have done what they did to me! She’d never do that or say things like that.”

Hachaaynar felt his hopes drop away. He’d prepared for her imprisonment and long separation. Even her death by the invaders, but not this.

“She wouldn’t betray us!” He gasped.

“It‘s not a betrayal.” ‘Ahtooshe’ held him tightly. “Her spirit has been kidnapped. She’ll return to us.”

<<< 0 >>>

Chief Aliyavit woke early and hissed to Tomasjaquichi.

“Yes, I am awake. Do you think we‘ll hear anything today?”

“I think I did it well. You did too. They shouldn‘t take long to decide.” Alivavit stood and paced. “I‘m so nervous. Like a boy. When do you think we‘ll know?”

Tomasjaquichi lay back, “It could be moons. They are never predictable.”

They weren't to wait long.

Nicolas Jose was still asleep when Cordero and Saenz entered the cell with Dominguez and Nieto at the door to back them up.

At the same moment he felt a fist smash his right cheek and upper lip, tasting blood and seeing a blur, and hearing a shout.

“Stand up. Maricon! We‘re finally rid of you. You little piece of shit!”

Both of his arms and shoulders were seized. He was lifted and thrown against the wall, bouncing back into their arms to be smashed hard back into the wall.

He started to speak but he was punched in the mouth again and again. He blacked out.

Moments later Aliyavit stood at the sound of footsteps approaching down the hallway. He heard scuffling at Tomasjaquichi's cell.

“What's going on?” Straining to make sense of it.

Tomasjaquichi could only grunt, with the arm around his neck dragging him down the hall.

“What's going on?” The old man called and waited for the footsteps to return. Soon Saenz and Cordero were standing in front of him.

“You pathetic old fool. You brought your bow and arrow along to tickle us?

A strong backhand slap across his face let him know that this would not be the day he had anticipated. Several more slaps and then punches doubled him over.

He was lifted by the four soldiers by arms and legs, carried down the hallway into the blinding sun, across the Mission courtyard and thrown into an oxcart on top of unconscious Nicolas Jose and a doubled up in pain, moaning Tomasjaquichi. Aliyavit's eyes closed as they tied him to a stake and walked away without a word.

CHAPTER 27

"WHAT A CONVERT!"

Tooypor sat in the early morning quietly speaking chants for family and victory. 'The invaders still have me as their prisoner but they haven't won.'

Josephina opened the door and set the tray down by the side of the cot.

"I am sorry, miss. I am told not to talk to you any more. I will only bring your food."

"What about the village girl?"

"No, miss. I told to her what the soldiers told me about you. I told her that you would only talk with Christian people. I told her to go away or I would tell the soldiers. She went back to her people." and left with a look of disapproval.

Tooypor watched her leave. 'I was stupid to use words like crazy and liars to her. Of course, as a Christian, she would be angry about anything said against the Padres. She is kind, but she's with the invaders. I'll be more careful about how I react.'

At the afternoon meal she watched Josephina enter and bowed to her, saying. "Thank you. I understand."

After she'd finished her second meal, Josephina entered with the same new soldiers who'd walked her from the trial room.

"They will take you Padre Cruzado." Josephina said. They undid her ankle chain and had her follow to the chapel office.

Padres Cruzado and Sanchez sat behind a small roughhewn desk with a Tongva appearing young man standing beside them.

"Welcome Queen Tuipurina-Pahr." The young man said clearly and flatteringly in a recognizable coastal Tongva dialect. There were no usable Tongva words for queen other than in legends from the far, far southern tribes.

"Who are you. Why are you calling me Queen?"

The man was younger than she was and stood tall and confidently. His smile was easy and calm.

"My name is Francisco. I'm named after the saint who inspires this order of the Catholic Church." Motioning to the table. "This is Padre Cruzado. This is Padre Sanchez. What the word Padre means is similar to a member of the Pul caste who consults and speaks for Spirit. They are trained in the word of God. That is the word for Spirit."

She looked for a way to put the quill on the desk through his eye. She wanted to swing the four directions statue at the side through the skulls of the Brownbeards and soldiers, but stopped the thoughts in favor of a longer plan. She kept her thoughts in the background. The soldiers could stop her easily before she could use a weapon, but the main reason, the one that she'd adhere to, she mustn't appear to be an enemy. She would be polite to Josephina. She wouldn't call these people liars. She would hear their words about their 'God,' and she'd escape when there was a good chance of success.

"Tell me about this God. Is it part of our Mother Earth?" She asked, immediately wanting to stop and make it sound less confrontational.

The young man translated to the Padres. They broke into wide grins. "Keep talking to her! Let her relax a little. You are doing well."

He made a global all inclusive sweep of his arms and said that Mother Earth, the Moon, the Sun and the Stars, the Clouds and Rain, were all part of His domain.

"His? Is it a man?"

"It is all God. He is supreme and controls everything."

"Is there a woman? A wife or daughter?"

He giggled and told the Padres to their amusement.

"How innocent." Cruzado said. "Tell her that God is male, but tell her that we will explain the birth of Jesus Christ and his blessed Mother Mary. The Woman."

Tooypor listened to Francisco explain about the Virgin Birth of The Lord and then skip quickly to The Ten Commandments. It took a long time before they thought of offering her a chair. She made a kicking motion at the chair. They jumped. She smiled and sat. They laughed. She told Francisco, who didn't seem to understand.

"They're safe."

He translated it to Cruzado.

"Yes, she'll make a good convert soon."

She listened and held her thoughts. After an hour she gestured to Francisco that her head was full.

"I'm glad that you are explaining about all of this, but I have heard too much today. Please. No more. Please?"

After asking the Padres, Fernando said. You may go back to your quarters now, Queen Tuipurina. We will call you tomorrow afternoon." He told Nieto and Dominguez to take her back. Josephina was waiting.

"Did you have a good lesson miss?"

Tooypor answered gently. "It was very good."

<<< 0 >>>

The San Diego Presidio guards pushed all of the Indian's together into mixed reinforced cattle pens. All together they crowded in

Cahuila, Kumeyaay, Serrano, Tarajumara from the far south, Apache from the far east and a few Tongva from the north.

Nicolas Jose barely remembered the bouncing trip in freezing winds with droplets stinging his body. He passed out often but not enough. The pain hadn't subsided by daylight. Three prisoners were pulled from the cart onto the ground and stood up, held in place by obedient Indian helpers to the Spanish, before a line of smartly dressed soldiers. He tried to hold his balance in a daze. Aliyavit collapsed and was yanked upright by a soldier. Tomasjiquichi edged away, not looking over at them.

"Six years each for these three shits." He heard before they were pushed into the pens.

"Did he say six years for me?" Aliyavit squeeked and touched Nicolas Jose roughly on his inflamed left shoulder. Instinctively he pushed the old chief aside and walked to the least crowded corner of the human corral.

There was no room to lean against a wall. He sat on well trampled earth at a spot that was two men deep to the edge of a wall. He saw that an empty spot was fair game unless allies protected it.

He saw Tomasjaquichi trying to find a space on the other side, looking across guiltily at him. 'You were a treacherous snake. You had better keep a distance from me.'

He looked at the layer of clouds in the sky and saw that he'd be sleeping in mud if it rained.

<<< 0 >>>

Verdugo sat with Padres Cruzado and Sanchez for a private dinner.

"I'm nervous about what to do with our little sorceress Tuipurina. If we execute or send her to prison she'll be a martyr, but if she truly converts, she'll be our little Saint. What do you think her chances are?"

Cruzado looked to Sanchez with satisfaction.

"She's a bright Indian. She asked us asked good questions about God. She listened politely. At this point I'd say, let's keep working with her. She may be what we need to raise morale."

<<< 0 >>>

In the first week Tooypor was brought to Francisco and the two Padres four times. She showed steady progress. They requested Verdugo to allow supervised walks in the garden. He complied.

"But keep her away from crowds."

She stood in the cell and felt relief. The chain was removed. She walked between Josephina and the two soldiers down the hall past the Padres door and into the brilliant courtyard.

The power of the sun was overwhelming after weeks of sunlessness. She looked at the adobe bricks and mortar beneath her feet, not daring to look ahead until she'd adjusted and was able to focus on the courtyard.

When she lifted her head she saw trees, sides of the building, the whitewashed outer walls, the arch of the entryway, the tall standing horses, and many people in the courtyard staring at her and talking among themselves

She grew wary. Many of the Tongva and Serrano in Mission robes made gestures of disrespect. She heard names for bad spirits and Spanish 'diablo' words and 'bruja' words.

"They are saying bad words about me." She said to Josephina.

"They think what you did was very bad." She said, looking at the neophytes who'd stopped their work to stare at her. "It will be a long time before they accept you but when they get used to you and forgive you it will feel like home."

In her cell she thought about faces she'd seen. She tried to remember even one that seemed as though she was respected and not an oddity or an enemy. She could not.

<<< 0 >>>

After two weeks Nicolas Jose saw three guards place loose canvas covers against the wall to be spread over the pen when rain started to fall.

He moved to a solid second position against the fence by punching a lone Mojave boy who tried to move into an old man's space. The boy slunk away. The old man invited Nicolas Jose to slide back in the space next to him. Three strong Kumeyaay against the wall behind him had grown roots and it would be a long time before he'd have a chance to move back.

There were conversations in many tongues but few in Tongva. He avoided interacting with anyone near him. He knew he was stronger than most of the others. Trying to intimidate them was a quick way to be piled on, strangled or kicked to death. He'd seen it happen. You never knew how many allies they had.

He felt feces and urine caked on him. Around him the stench was ever present. The rain was a blessing. It was renewing to walk to the trough and splash with filthy water until he had the illusion of cleanliness.

He saw sickness and death all around him. He saw Aliyavit from his position, He hadn't moved in days. He was dead or dying.

<<< 0 >>>

Six mounted horsemen and a translator stopped at the edge of Seebag-na and called for the chief.

'Ahtooshe' warned Hachaaynar.

"Don't go alone. "We'll gather men together. I'm afraid for you."

Only thirty villagers could be brought to stand with Hachaaynar in front of the Spanish soldiers. The Spanish translator spoke a rehearsed speech without making eye contact.

"The Mission herds are now too big for the pasture area. New fences will be placed here alongside the huts over there. The

Mission will need this village to move to join the Yaanga village very soon. All of you will plan to move peacefully."

He turned his horse around and the soldiers followed without hearing a reply.

"We can't move." He took 'Ahtooshe''s hand and turned to the villagers. "We can't move!"

"We won't move!" came the reply.

<<< 0 >>>

"Tuipurina! Come!" Josephina called from the kitchen door.

Tooypor looked up, separating wool strands on the grass under the courtyard oak tree. "What do you want?" She replied in tentative Spanish.

"To the kitchen! We'll give you a new treat."

She stood and brushed off her red dress. It was spring and becoming too warm for clothes, They'd become angry and lock her up if she removed her dress or acted other than the way they demanded.

She was surprised at getting access to the kitchen. She entered and remembered her last meeting with Charaana and Nicolas Jose. She wondered where he was. Maybe in another cell being 'converted' as she was. Maybe he was exiled. She'd known that the invaders 'exiled' people, as the villages did.

She learned from the cell-cleaning woman that he'd said nothing bad about her. He spoke of her with respect. The woman was friendly with Padre Sanchez. He described the trial to her, including how frightened they were when she kicked the stool. She said that Nicolas Jose had only said good things about her. She asked if he was her 'boyfriend.' Tooypor smiled that these people thought of it that way.

As she tasted the chunks of spicy lamb she asked Josephina. "Can you find out where Nicolas Jose is? Is he being converted?"

Josephina looked concerned. “I‘ll try.”

<<< 0 >>>

In August the Kumeyaay rebellion prisoners were released en masse to be auctioned off to farmers in Baja California or put to work at hard labor in the fields of the southern Missions.

Nicolas Jose joyfully moved three feet back to a spot against the wall. Leaning against a wall felt more comfortable than he’d ever imagined it could be after being stuck on the flat dirt. The yard looked open with half the prisoners removed. He chuckled, realizing he was accustomed to living in dirt.

After three weeks guards divided the yard prisoners into groups, six by six, and took each group out to bathe in clean looking water.

Nicolas Jose looked over the five men with him. Three were the kind that stole and disrespected all others. Few Tongva acted that way. The other two were barely more than children and were starting to copy the ways of the bad ones. They were all given new crudely woven shirts and pants. He was glad none were Tongva. It would be best if nothing was there. It would be good if he could remove all memories and hopes. He’d be in peace if he never spoke again. Everything from his life was dead.

He was led in chains to a new adobe building with a wide hall and dozens of small cells on each side. In the first unoccupied cell, they were chained and locked up. There was a scramble of young men for the mats in the back near the small window.

Nicolas Jose and an old glaring, deeply lined desert tribesman hung back. They made ’who cares’ shrugs and sat on mats near the door. Their eyes met. Nicolas Jose saw the same sorrow as his own but with a fierce hatred alternating from the man. ‘He has the madness. Be very careful.’

<<< 0 >>>

Her walks expanded to include more space and free time. They walked to the east wall, looking at sheep to the north and the new fields of squash spreading toward Asuks-gna and the dust of the cattle beyond.

Tooypor walked beside Josephina. An old neophyte walked behind instructing her in Spanish words and grammar.

"The snow is melt on mountain." She said.

"The snow is melting on the mountains." He corrected.

She turned left at the wall to look north toward the foothills leading to Haapchivet thinking. 'Where is my brother? Where is my Mother? Who is leading our village?' Where is my husband?' Knowing that no one could give her those answers, other than about her brother.

"Josephina?"

"Yes, Miss Tuipurina." Scurrying close.

"Did you learn where Nicolas Jose is? Is he here?"

"No miss. They would not tell me."

"My brother 'Aachvet? Is he here?"

"I don't know. I don't think so."

"Please find out. I've asked you. It is important. Do you have a brother or sister? You must understand."

Josephina wore her regretful face. "I can not ask about other prisoners. They say you should not ask these things."

Tooypor walked a few steps and turned back to her cell. Josephina lagged behind. The translator took his time behind them. After Josephina had locked the door and left, Tooypor heard tapping.

"It is me, old Juan. Next time we are alone I'll tell you about Nicolas Jose and your brother. I know they are not here. They were sent away the day after the trial. They are far away."

"Thank you Juan. Thank you."

"Bless you Tuipurina lady," As his footsteps faded down the hall. It sounded right.

<<< 0 >>>

"How is she coming along?" Verdugo asked. Padres Cruzado, Sanchez and Corporal Pico looked to Josephina and Jose for a weekly update.

Josephina started with confidence. "She wants to learn. She's a well behaved young woman."

"No problems with her at all? Any small things?"

"Sometimes she asks bad questions…, about God."

Father Sanchez raised his eyebrows with a grin. "What could be a bad question about God? Does he exist? Even she talks about her God, whatever his name is."

"She asks questions about creation and reasons for things that I can't answer. And wisdom! She asks 'If he is wise and knows all things, why does he kill people, who, in his wisdom, he forgot to tell about himself?' and 'Why, in his wisdom, does he make the invaders rapists and murders of children and women?'"

Pico snorted. "Invaders. Rapist. Murderers. That doesn't sound like much progress to me."

"Those sound like questions of a difficult unbeliever." Cruzado added.

"She asks about her brother and Nicolas Jose. I said they were sent away." Jose felt some guilt about telling her that but wanted to be truthful with his superiors.

"Did you tell her where they went?"

"No, Sergeant Verdugo. I do not know, myself, sir."

"Then there is little to worry about messages sent through their devious means." turning to the neophytes. "You are both excused. You are doing well. Thank you."

Verdugo waited until they left. "Padres Cruzado and Sanchez. Let me suggest this. Do you think she's faking this conversion to escape and turn the gentiles against us?"

"That is always a possibility." Cruzado said. "It would be wrong to assume that. It is God's work. We can't try to outguess Him in these matters."

Sanchez leaned in. "Questions about the existence and wisdom of God are natural in pagans who haven't been exposed to a lifetime of obedience and the blessings of the Church. She's new and a fiery one. We need three more months to make a judgment."

Pico felt he had a better sense of what she was about and his look to Verdugo communicated it.

"We'll meet next week on this." Verdugo returned Pico's look. It wasn't wasted on the two Padres, seeing there were more agendas at work.

1786 - LOS ANGELES

For the second time Vanegas was elected after the gambling affair had led to his first term dismissal. Things were finally looking good for the town. The cattle had spread halfway to the sea and the new 'wheat' fields were taking hold to the north. It looked like good times ahead.

SAN DIEGO PRISON

Nicolas Jose was awakened for the second time that morning. A Tongva speaking trustee sat on the floor of the hall outside the cell trying to get Nicolas Jose to speak.

"I know you are Tongva. What is your name?"

"It doesn't matter."

"I am from Puvun-gna near the ocean. Where are you from?" Holding his gaze.

“Nowhere. I’m from nowhere. Go away.”

The man stayed, looking at Nicolas Jose’s callused feet. “How long will you be here?” Showing no inclination to move. “You could have sandals. You could have blankets. You could have extra water and food? Come on. What’s your name? What village are you from?”

Nicolas Jose had seen trustees speak to prisoners in their tribal language. The men would receive extras of some kind but he couldn’t understand what the trustees received in return.

He returned every day for a week before saying.

“One of the Tongva in the cells across there told me your name. You’re a top Tongva from that rebellion up in San Gabriel.” He chuckled. “No one was hurt! That‘s the only one like that I ever heard of! How did you do that?” After a long wait of mutual staredown. “Tell me about it and I’ll bring you some cornmeal with meat in it.”

After minutes of no reaction, he stood. “You’ll see. You can do good here. You can have a lot of trouble here if you want it. Just talk to me. Tell me a little about your village. About other villages, like that Aliyavit’s village. You can make your time here much better. You don’t have to be in misery. You don’t have to be an outcast. Don’t be a stupid little shit.” Strutting away with a backward look.

Nicolas Jose laid more rocks on his vow of silence.

<<< 0 >>>

Josephina and Jose walked Tuipurina around the Southwestern wall. No part of Seebag-na could be seen through the herds. No smoke. It was strange no sign of smoke was in the air.

“Isn‘t there usually smoke from over there?”

The two neophytes were ready for her question. They knew that ‘over there’ was the village where she’d been a priestess and her husband was chief.

“You mean the Seeba village of your husband?” Josephina asked.

“Yes. Seebag-na. The village of my husband.”

“There is no more Seeba village. It was in the way of the expansion. It was moved to Yaanga. Your husband lives in Yaanga.

“How can it move? The burial places. The graves. The sand paintings! They can’t move! They are sacred!” She tried to find words in Spanish. “They are holy!”

“None of those things are holy, Miss Tuipurina. They are pagan and should be forgotten.” Josephina was proud of the way she’d said it. It would have pleased Padre Cruzado.

Tooypor turned toward the chapel. A rock swished by her ear followed by another one. She gasped as they smashed against the wall. She looked in the direction they’d flown from and saw two men in Mission clothes ducking around the kitchen wall.

’Those were close to me, and fast!’ She thought as Josephina and Jose rushed up. “Who are they!” Looking to each side in panic. She ran to where they landed and inspected them. They were the smooth riverbed rocks that were the best for hunting. A hit to the head could have killed her. “They are in Mission shirts. Is the Mission trying to kill me?”

“I don‘t recognize them." Jose said rushing to follow them.

“Be careful.” Josephina shouted, hustling Tooypor in the doorway. “Dear girl. We must be careful. There are ones from the villages who blame you. I don‘t think they are from the Mission.”

They entered Verdugo’s office. He listened and shrugged.

“You know, there is a great amount of ill will toward you in the neophyte population and the gentiles outside our walls. I‘m sure you know how easy it is to enter the grounds. We‘ll look into it. We take this seriously.”

<<< 0 >>>

Six mounted soldiers and four on foot carrying long and short firesticks drove 'Ahtooshe' and wounded Hachaaynar with seventy villagers carrying their only possessions across the pastures and past the southern edge of Pueblo Los Angeles. They climbed the gentle slope to crowded Yaanga and were flanked by troops from the Santa Barbara garrison at the town's border. The slow and stumbling ones were pushed and kicked.

The chief of Yaanga and elders welcomed them in spite of a shortage of supplies. They'd lost almost all of their oaks and had one spring left. Their population had little food and were told that they would have to trade their crafts or "buy" their food from Los Angeles stores and traders.

Hachaaynar and 'Ahtooshe' entered the greathouse and sat by the central fire. In the dark room Yaanga-vik repeated a rumor that he had heard.

"One of the escaped western villagers passed through here on the way to the coast. He said that your wife is in the Mission wearing the same red dress that your mother used to wear. She doesn't seem like a prisoner."

'Ahtooshe' asked. "Is she wearing the Cross? The four directions sign?"

"He didn't say."

Hachaaynar was no longer shocked by rumors. It was usually a blur without a center or reason. This one had a clear meaning.

"She's been so mistreated, like you were, that she's lost herself. Can we get her away from them?"

'Ahtooshe' held his hand tight knowing he could ignite easily and throw himself away.

"We don't have anyone inside." and to Yaanga-vik. "Do you have reliable contacts inside?"

“No-one. We have no-one. Our land is shrinking. Our people don’t return. They work in the invaders Pueblo and sleep in their yards or sheds. We may have to move the whole village west.”

“Move Yaanga? How far?” Seeing another part of the world falling away.

“To the next hill. One hut at a time from the side near the Pueblo. I don‘t see anything I can do.”

“We will help you. We will start leveling the ground on that hill.”

Hachaaynar and 'Ahtooshe' gathered the Seebag-na villagers to start the project.

“Mother.. .I will leave Tooypor to her fate. The village must survive.”

“That is wise, my son. That is wise.”

<<< 0 >>>

Tooypor’s Spanish improved faster than Josephina and Jose had expected. Her questions were endless and less challenging to Catholic doctrine. Her weekly reports became more positive. She no longer had chains in her converted cell. She had a table and chair and a wool mat on her cot. She could eat with the trustee neophytes.

After walking and Bible lessons she sat on the mat waiting for Josephina to bring her afternoon meal to her.

Her pillow jiggled once, and jiggled again. She looked around the room. Nothing else moved. There was no earthquake. She stood and watched it for a bit until it moved again. She pulled at it.

A rattlesnake lunged at her and fell to the floor wriggling and hissing. She sprung up on the bed, tipping the table edge to crush it, slamming it down again and again until the snake’s head was crushed. She called for Josephina, sure that the Priests were behind these attempts.

Josephina screamed as she entered and dropped the tray before running for help. Tooypor ate from the remainder in the bowl until Nieto entered to carry the snake to Verdugo’s office. A young neophyte girl came in to scrub the spots on the floor.

"You are in peril from someone." Verdugo said seating her next to his desk. The Padres sat on the other side of him. "They tell me you are making great progress. You are nearing your baptism. You are making yourself a great example of a reformed person. Tell us, Tuipurina. Are you happier here than you had been?"

Tooypor wore a neutral face. It was a test. She thought of where the threats could come from. It couldn't be from the outside. It had to be people in the Mission. Someone with a key. If she went through the 'baptism' she'd earn enough freedom to reach the outer grounds and escape to Haapchivet. She learned the right responses to Bible questions, the Latin words, and the 'sins'

She saw the resemblance of the first man and woman, Adam and Eve, to the first man and woman of the Tongva, Tobohar and Pabavit. 'Maria' who had a 'Son of God' baby was like the Spirit Chukit, who gave birth to a 'Son of God' after She was impregnated by lightning. She saw that Jesus Christ had walked on water as Chinigchnich had when he walked on water from Pemuu'nga. Christ had turned water into 'wine,' the 'blood' that the soldiers drank. 'It would be better if he changed it back to water,' she thought.

How 'God' was similar to Qua-o-ar but was old and more unhappy and wanted to hurt people as much as to help them. She saw that Earth was never honored, or the Sun, Moon, animals and elements. Everything was based around obedience to what the priests and soldiers said to obey. She pledged she would obey until the right time came.

She spoke with downcast eyes at first but raised them. "I understand the lessons of the Bible more. I am not happy enough now. I am happier when there are no snakes and throwing stones trying to kill me. I'm afraid that some people want to kill me. The Padres and you have been fair and teaching me the good life. I am happy. Josephina and Jose are good friends. I am happy, but afraid of the bad people who have keys to my room."

Verdugo replied. "We are shocked that someone placed a snake in your room. We'll find the one who did it. We want you safe. We are sewing your red dress to be like new. After you are baptized we want you to come with us to the Pueblo de Los Angeles to their new church."

She remembered how they tried to use 'Ahtooshe' in the red dress. She wondered if they would re-name her a 'Maria.'

They questioned her more on the beliefs and rites. She answered as she had remembered. Cruzado watched her carefully. Sergeant Verdugo watched her hands clenching the sides of her skirt and the looks from face to face between answers. He felt satisfied. He had been watching for months. He looked to Cruzado and Sanchez. They nodded that the session was finished.

"We will keep a guard at the end of the hall. No-one will enter your room except Josephina."

She left with Josephina and Jose. The men sat quietly for a moment after she was gone.

"She's faking." Cruzado said. "She doesn't accept a word of it."

Verdugo was pleased that they saw the same things. "I totally agree. She's looking for an opportunity to escape to a tribal village. I'm trying to find a way out of this before some idiot kills our 'Little Saint'."

"Do we continue with the baptism? We would prefer it if she were baptized. It will help nail it down."

"Oh yes! As quickly as the day after tomorrow." Verdugo agreed. "Saturday Mass? "

Cruzado rolled his eyes. "That is certainly fast!"

"We can do it!" Sanchez said. "We have taken more time with her than any Indian. Let her prove her worth."

Verdugo summed up. "If she can be baptized and kept safe for a week. Kept to her room without roaming outside, I'll have Santa Barbara send a carriage and a guard and exile her far away. I'm thinking of Monterey."

"To Mission San Carlos Borremeo." Cruzado said as Sanchez nodded in agreement.

"San Carlos Borremeo would be perfect." Verdugo agreed. "No Tongva there. A large stable community where she can't cause more trouble."

<<< 0 >>>

PRESIDIO SAN DIEGO PRISON

Nicolas Jose found a niche in the cell. By keeping silence he'd won respect and a non-aggression pact with his cellmates. The Invaders' man came less and less thinking the prisoner was crazy and had little information.

The prison started a program of yard time, ten cells outside at a time. Nicolas Jose was forced to join the others outside.

He and Tomasjaquichi looked across the yard at each other and stood still. Tomasjaquichi took a step forward but stopped when Nicolas Jose took a step back and walked away to the opposite wall. When he turned back the chief stayed opposite and had slumped against the farthest wall.

Returning to his cell he saw four young men, Tongva he assumed, gathering around Tomasjaquichi and talking animatedly. They must be new arrivals.

It brought curiosity into the wall he'd created. He made a note of their faces. If there was an opportunity to talk with one alone, without Tomasjaquichi, he might make the approach.

<<< 0 >>>

PRESIDIO SANTA BARBARA

A dispatch reached Presidio Santa Barbara on the same day as the baptism of the famed rebel leader Tuipurina.

"I just received a dispatch from Los Angeles. They need one carriage and four Privates to carry gifts, records and one exile, details later, from Mission San Gabriel to Mission San Carlos Borremeo at Monterey. Three privates will return with the carriage. One will stay to carry dispatches."

Private Manuel Montero listened with interest and volunteered along with seven other soldiers who were bored with the static life at the Presidio. Four of the volunteers with behavior citations were dropped from the role. Manuel was joyous. Passing through the new town of Los Angeles, Mission San Gabriel and riding to San Carlos Borremeo in the beautiful north of Alta California, the Capital, Monterey, was more than a dream.

The four privates were brought aside and told about the new convert, Tuipurina and her dangerous background. They would be fully briefed by Sergeant Verdugo after arriving at the Mission. It was a prime assignment.

Manuel had heard about the rebellion. No lives were lost! It was amazing that a woman was a leader. He remembered rebellions of his childhood in Puebla. They were suppressed with house to house slaughter, curfews and chained Indio men shot in the town square. His grandmother had been a minor leader. People came to her for advice from all of the neighborhoods. She cured their ills with natural medicines. She was a Curendera, a healer. She was a strong woman and inspiration in his memory.

That night he assembled a carrying bag with paper lessons to help him to learn to read when the group made their rest stops. This would be an exciting week.

CHAPTER 28

RELOCATION

She felt no nervousness as Josephina and two ancient women brought pails, scrubbers and towels to bathe her and walk her to the chapel in a white smock.

Forty-five hand picked neophytes filled the pews of the church and Padre Sanchez was on the pulpit.

She responded in all the right places and was glad that the water temperature was not cold when she was dunked in the holy trough. She'd been prepared for her baptismal name. It was foolish. It sounded humorous as Sanchez intoned.

"Josepha, Regina Tuipurina."

'Queen Tooypor' made a strange image to her. She was told about kings and queens in stories from Josephina. It sounded silly to her. As a queen for the invaders?.

She was taken from the chapel to Verdugo's office.

"You are now a baptized Catholic subject of The Crown. We are concerned for your safety. There have been too many threats from the natives, both here and outside. We will transport you to a safer place. You will leave in two days to a Mission far north in Alta California. It will be a beautiful place by the ocean with big trees and better housing, both inside the Mission and in the town of Monterey."

She felt a hot wave in her blood. It was confusing and angering. What sort of place was that? It sounded farther north than Chumash lands. What kind of people and life is there? Would there be a chance to run up a slope and lose her pursuers between trees or underbrush?

"Can I stay here longer?" She asked.

"No. It is too dangerous for you here. People are trying to kill you and now that you're baptized, you are even more at risk. Look at it this way. You are leaving here as a queen. The Queen of the Tongva. You have become very important to your people." His voice had a deep sound of importance. She wanted to throw something at him or spit on him.

"I thought I was valuable here. That I was becoming a good example."

His indulgent smile spoke for him. "At this point, you are more valuable elsewhere. I am so sorry." Sure that escape was foremost in her mind. He found himself enjoying the game, knowing he had total control.

There were few opportunities left. She kept her voice low and girlish.

"It sounds like it will be a good place. I accept that. Thank you sir." Looking down at her hands. "Can I go with Josephina and Jose to look at the grounds one last time?"

"No," with certainty. "You will be led to your room and kept to quarters until the carriage comes. It is for your own protection. You must understand that everything we do is for your own good."

She saw the last door close. "Everything you do is for <u>your</u> own good." She said clearly.

"Yes, that is true." He said, signaling Alvitre to lead her back to her room/cell.

<<< 0 >>>

PRESIDIO SAN DIEGO PRISON

Nicolas Jose saw one of the men who'd been with Tomasjaquichi standing alone in the yard. He moved toward him while looking away until he was beside him.

"Are you Tongva?" he said quietly, still avoiding eye contact.

"You are Nahanpar, Nicolas Jose-Pahr." The man whispered in amazement. Yes, I'm from Yaanga. An invader said I'd attacked him. I didn't. He wanted my wife. They sent me here."

"You know Tomasjaquichi?"

"All of us know him. He talks about you. How he let you down. How you hate him enough to kill him. Do you?"

For the first time in more than a year, he laughed. It was like freezing water dumped over him. He doubled up and held his stomach, grabbing the man's shirt to keep from falling. There was nothing really funny but a wall of ice was cracking around him. He couldn't stop laughing, bordering on crying.

"No. No. No. I don't want to kill him!" Looking up to see if he could see Tomasjaquichi. "I don't want to kill anyone but myself." Unable to stop laughing.

"You are admired, Nahanpar." The man hugged his shoulder and helped him straighten up. "You are respected in all of our territories."

The man bent his neck to look into Nicolas Jose's eyes. "I have a friend from their Mission of San Gabriel. You are respected there too. You and Tooypor. You are Heroes of our people. Forever."

"I failed. We failed."

"He told me that Tooypor was raped and beaten and made with baby and the baby died."

His laughter changed to sobs and tears. He staggered against the wall with memories crushing his lungs and heart.

"Tooypor." He whispered, sliding down the wall. The Yaanga man slid with him to comfort him.

"She's safe now. They parade her around in a red dress like one of their horses, but I'm told that she is safe." He put his arm around Nicolas Jose's shuddering shoulders and saw Tomasjaquichi across the yard and waved him over.

In the dark earthquake of sorrows he felt a body slide down the wall beside him shoulder to shoulder.

“My friend. Can you ever forgive me?”

Nicolas Jose couldn’t answer. He looked up and said. “Tomorrow. We will sit tomorrow.”

When he returned to his cell he sat against the wall looking at the other prisoners in the cells across the hall. ‘That unfortunate boy!’ he thought. ‘He’s in prison because an invader wanted his wife!’

He looked at the young and old faces. Some would be outcasts in their own villages and were still predatory. He wondered if they could be contained. He’d ask if Tomasjaquichi agreed.

Looking at more faces, he saw the same isolation and shame that had locked his spirit into more than the bars. He thought of the life of Tooypor and pledged his wishes to her for Spirit to always guide her and protect her. He rocked to the remembered chant coming back to him.

<<< 0 >>>

PRESIDIO SANTA BARBARA

Manuel and the three Santa Barbara Presidio soldiers stood at attention as Sergeant Verdugo told them the history of the rebellion, the villages involved and Pico’s breaking of their code and an exaggerated tale of the “rebellious medicine woman, Regina Tuipurina.”

“Her wrist will be tied to the handrail inside the carriage until the approach to Santa Barbara. We have a feeling, based on her native character, that she will try to leap out and run into the woods to escape. If she needs to relieve herself, two of you will keep a three meter leash on her and then return her to her seat. Her Spanish is limited, but there should be no unnecessary conversation with her nor should she be disrespected in any way. Our reputation in Monterey and San Juan Borromeo must remain honorable. Is that understood?”

“Yes Sir!” They snapped. Manuel was full of curiosity about her. He took the risk of saying.

“Sir. If it is possible, I would rather ride in or on the carriage because of new saddle sores.” There was a chance he might be replaced with a local soldier or put back on his horse regardless. He held his breath.

Verdugo looked him up and down. He seemed a shy and modest Indio from somewhere deep in Mexico.

“You’ll ride inside, but you’ll be respectful at all times. Understood?”

“Yes Sir. Sergeant Verdugo, Sir!”

Tooypor was bathed and dressed with her wrists manacled by a two meter rope to the leg of the cot. Tooypor finished her afternoon meal, expecting the guards to take her to ‘the Queen’s Carriage’ as Verdugo had said with a smirk.

Josephina entered with an apologetic looking Private Alvitre to announce she wouldn’t leave today, but tomorrow morning.

“I’ll bring you special portions from the Padre’s meals. You’ll have a queenly meal tonight.”

Shortly after dawn Josephina brought a tray with eggs, spicy corn porridge and a strip of beef.

“Eat quickly my dear one.” She said. Nieto and Alvitre stood outside the door waiting to escort her to the courtyard.

Stepping into the morning daylight The carriage made her stop. She’d seen carriages like this when she and Hachaaynar stood near the ‘Kahmeeno’ to watch officials arrive to start the new Pueblo. When important people visited the Mission, but oxcarts were what she thought of as carriages.

A soldier stood at the open door. Another sat on the seat to control the horses. Two were on horses behind the carriage. All of their uniforms were brighter and fresher than the ones of the

Mission soldiers. Verdugo, Olivera, Pico, Padres Cruzado and Sanchez stood at the edge of the brick walkway and bowed their heads as she passed.

'Are they crazy?' She thought, nervously walking toward the vehicle that would take her forever from home. She had no idea how she could get from wherever they were taking her to Haapchivet. 'A horse!' she thought. 'When I get there I'll learn to ride a horse.'

The outer wall was packed with neophytes waiting for her departure. She scanned the faces for anyone she recognized. 'I'm curious now. Where is this place? I can ride a horse to the North path to Jaapchivit. Don't kill me today,' she smiled to herself, walking to the Indio looking soldier standing at the door.

Manuel latched her manacle to the rope's ring by the armrest of her seat. He whispered, "I'm sorry to do this. I know you want freedom," unsure if she understood him at all. He stepped aside to join the other soldiers by their horses. They finished with the reading of the orders. Manuel entered the carriage and sat in the rear facing seat across from her.

In spite of wanting to be frozen in anger at being sent away, she felt excited and curious about what was going to happen. After all of this time of being tied up in a room away from the Sun and the Moon and being beaten and disrespected, this was different.

Across the aisle she looked up. Both their eyes gleamed. They grinned as the carriage suddenly lurched forward.

"I've never been in a carriage!" He said, holding his palm to his forehead, looking to all sides in childlike amazement as it sped forward.

"Me too!" She laughed, knowing the idea of what he said without knowing the exact words.

As the carriage and guards turned out of the gate, a burst of laughter came as Sergeant Verdugo rolled his eyes heavenward and exclaimed. "Thank God she's gone!"

PRESIDIO SAN DIEGO PRISON

Tomasjaquichi and a group of six Tongva gathered together. They moved away from the crowd to a less inhabited section of the wall.

The young Yaanga man from yesterday walked to Nicolas Jose, patted him on the shoulder and led him to warm and respectful greetings from Tomasjaquichi‘s men.

Nicolas Jose felt some relief from his guilt and fear. He squatted as the Tongva made a circle around him and squatted or sat on the ground.

“I became weak and rejected you.” Tomasjaquichi lowered his head. “You were the one who fought for our traditions and safety. Our survival. I betrayed you by blaming you and Tooypor. Please forgive me.” The men looked on expectantly.

“We were all lied to about each other. I forgive you, but I want you to forgive me for failing you.”

“No. No.” Came a chorus from the men. “You didn‘t fail us.” The oldest added.

Tomasjaquichi‘s voice became more forceful. “No one would take leadership except Tooypor and you. No one has ever tried to bring the villages together. I should have. Aliyavit should have. We didn’t. No one did. Only you.”

The seven men murmured assent with admiration in their eyes.

Nicolas Jose changed the subject to harassment by the guards and the shakedowns by the new gangs of crazy ones who’d formed in the prison. Each of them had examples.

By the time yard time had ended and the men were dispersed, a plan was forming to make life better for the Tongva and neighbors from the north. “We’ll make a circle tomorrow.” Tomasjaquichi said with finality.

In his cell, Nicolas Jose looked forward to the next day for the first time in two years. One thought kept recurring, filling his mind. ‘Tooypor. Where is she? Is she safe? The strongest person I ever knew!’

<<< 0 >>>

The carriage rocked and bounced past Pueblo Los Angeles into the low pass near Cahueng-na and across the long valley toward the seacoast.

Tooypor saw no chance of escape with the riders so near and the rope holding her in the carriage.

Manuel was silent but they still giggled at some of the jars and twitches from the ruts in the road.

“Have you children?” He asked, daring to break protocol and try a simple kind of Spanish.

She looked at his dark Indio features and somewhat shy eyes. “Are you Spanish?” Knowing that many of the troops were native from Baja California or Mexico.

“I am Indio, from Puebla. In Mexico.”

“Why you with them?” He seemed unable to answer. “The invaders. Why you with them?”

“My tribe ..was broken..long ago. Before I born. No work.” Unable to simplify his ideas more. “I could leave and see the world if I joined the Expeditionary Force and came to the New Territories. Here I am.”

Understanding a little. “Have you killed people?” Seeing him wince at the question.

“I’ve never been in a fight. I don‘t know what I’d do. I don‘t want to fight Indios. They said English and Russians, but I don‘t want to fight our people.”

“English? Russian? Are they tribes of north?”

“I don’t know. They told us they want to fight us and take away our land.”

“You have children?” She thought of Hachaaynar and 'Ahtooshe'.

“No children. I’ve never married. I’ve never stayed in one place. Children are the best things in the world. The reason for living.

Do you have children?" Thinking he was saying more than she could understand.

"I had two. Two boys. They die from Invaders' black lung disease. Then, I raped in the Mission. Baby die. I have no children."

He looked down and was silent a while until he quietly said, "I'm sorry."

She hoped she'd understood the Spanish words he'd used and searched for ways to put them in order to continue talking.

As they rolled along with the ocean on their left in Chumash territory she told him she had to relieve herself. She remembered when she didn't have to care, but this was with invader men.

He called up to the driver to stop. Manuel unlatched a three-meter leash from the armrest. He and the driver walked her to a clump of bushes out of view of the dismounted horsemen.

She checked behind her make be sure that they were turned away and were not watching her. Even if she could yank the rope away from the soldier there would be no chance of losing them on foot before the horsemen could chase her down in the open terrain.

When she was finished she gave the rope a tug. The man turned, grinned and handed her two rags. One was wet and one was dry. He smiled widely and turned around again. Back in the carriage he said with childlike enthusiasm.

"There are these," Pointing to rags, "and much water under the seats. There are tortillas in my bag."

"Why you be nice to me? They order you?"

"Sergeant Verdugo said we shouldn't disrespect you, but it's funny the way he said it. He said 'so the reputation of the Mission stayed honorable.' He didn't say 'nice.'"

Understanding a little of it but not sure.

"Are you Catholic?" She asked.

His face contorted as though it was a hard question to answer. He took a long time of looking out the window.

“I say I am. Everybody I know says they are. You have to say that you are. Otherwise I wouldn’t get pay, whenever they are going to pay us, or even food. I’ve heard there are Jews, very bad people who aren’t Catholics, in the Capitals. There are the English, who are led by Satan. They warn or about Russians who pretend to be Catholics but are of the Devil. There are Gentiles, like you were and my parents, before baptism made them Catholic, so I say I’m Catholic.

“I don‘t understand. Are you Catholic?”

“In my center.. No.”

“And the beliefs of your people? Before the invaders came? You know those?”

“I know some of the legends. How the Earth was made. About the first people.”

“The elements? The Earth, Sun and Moon?”

“Yes.” He said. “And Fire and the Seas. Do you have special animals? And Birds?”

They never stopped talking except at breaks when they would be observed. As soon as they were alone they found words to share memories of their villages and families. They searched for Spanish words to tell about what brought them to this place in their lives.

On the evening of the third day he left her with the guards of Mission San Carlos Borremeo. She was hesitant to step into the doorway and turned back to Manuel.

“Will I see you again?

He beamed so obviously that his comrades broke into laughter. “Yes. I’ll be sure to return to see you.”

He was teased for a long time. Some of the soldiers asked about sex in the carriage, but it didn’t dissuade him. One way or another he would find ways to return to the Mission and find her again.

<<< 0 >>>

In the first rays of dawn Nicolas Jose woke with joy for the first time since the ambush in the Padres' room. He woke before any of the other prisoners in the cellblock.

There were improvements that he could make in how they were forced to live together. He felt that they could do it! The prison wouldn't change. The invaders wouldn't change, but the way the prisoners saw each other and kept the old ways would change. Cell by cell.

He lay back and looked at the ceiling. He saw Tooypor. The precocious skinny nine year old who was 'Ahtooshe''s student. The one she'd brought to see the Sea Creatures. The crazy little thirteen year old who had challenged him over the return of Sevaanga-vik's head. She'd accused him of being a potential traitor and was right. He would have been too unreliable to have been trusted. Too intrigued by Spanish trinkets and privilege to have been steady enough.

She'd tested him for the rebellion. He'd remained steady. 'If she's out there,' he thought, 'she's solid and steady. The finest daughter of the Tongva. They can parade her in their red dress, mistreat her or make her a statue of a traitor or saint, but she will be the finest women, 'No! Finest Person!' he'd known in his life. The feeling he had for her transcended 'respect.' It was more like the chest filling invaders' word. 'Love,' of both flesh and spirit combined.

He quietly spoke aloud. Sending his voice out to all the Spirits of the Universe. "I wish everything good for you, Tooypor. Forever."

Her room/cell at Mission San Carlos Borremeo was similar to the one at Mission San Gabriel. There was one thing that she could not understand, but liked. There were good women who took her to her room. White skinned invader women, but nice, like Josephina. Invader women who were respectful.

She still had manacles and was attached by a chain to the bed but the women explained, in careful Spanish, that as soon as she became adjusted and had shown herself to be trustworthy, she would have freedom of movement.

“Will I have visitors?” Hoping Manuel would return.

“If the Padres approve.”

She lay in bed through the night, unable to sleep, looking at the shadows from the patio trees and torches playing on the ceiling, thinking about the strange paths that had brought her here.

She couldn’t see the visions that had propelled her life. No person she knew. No landmarks or paths to anywhere familiar. No way to return to her life. Probably no-one who spoke her language. There were different trees and herbs. No holy places or petroglyths to tell the local history.

As she thought of her life and the things that had been important, she thought of 'Ahtooshe' and Hachaaynar and the village of Seebag-na that the invaders said no longer existed. She hoped, and ‘prayed’ in the Catholic way that they were living and safe. She vowed every day she would pray for their safety in both the Tongva and the Catholic ways.

She thought of Nahanpar. The times she’d met him as a girl. About the times when he became a dog-man for the invaders and helped return Hachaaynar‘s father‘s head. When he helped recover 'Ahtooshe' and helped to point out the evil Rodriguez soldier. She’d mistrusted him so many times, ‘with good reason,’ but he had become true and strong for her. He’d become worthy of respect.

She prayed for his well-being and safety every day and whispered aloud to the Spirits.

“I send my respect and love to you, forever.”

CHAPTER 29

1799

Tuipurina lay at twilight in soaked robes. She was exhausted in pain with her eyes closed lying under hand knit covers in the bedroom of the humble Montero Monterey hills home.

Her wild fevers had her seeing visions of creatures of the Tongva fleeing into the sky. The Golden Eagles and Condors led processions of animals and tribes-people leaving the Earth in sorrow, looking back on the remaining ones being pulled up toward the clouds.

Her ribs ached from the constant coughing as her eyes opened and she looked into the dark round loving face of her sweet nine-year-old daughter Clementina.

“Look, Mama.” Helping raise her mother’s head to look at the floor beside the bed. “We made your sand painting. I took Juana Maria and Cesario to the beach. We ground and mixed the peppers, anise and petals until it was beautiful like you. Look, look.”

She saw Juana Maria and Cesario beaming behind Clementina. Miguel was snoring, slumped in the chair against the wall sleeping after another long night of watchfulness.

“It‘s beautiful, M‘jita.” Raising her arm with difficulty to caress her cheek. “But mommy‘s not as beautiful as that. It‘s beautiful like I want to be. It will help me be better.”

“Beautiful mama. Beautiful mama” Cesario repeated, squinting at her, wondering how, like daddy said, she could be leaving them soon. “We copied your drawing. Is it good?”

“Yes, sweetness. It is better than my drawing.”

Four-year-old Juana Maria crawled up on the bed to lie with her face against Tuipurina’s chest.

“We love you mama. Do you like it?” With green eyes turned up to mama’s chin.

"More than anything in this house, baby. You are the most talented children. Never forget how good you are."

Miguel awoke and stood with a creaky back and a moan. He stood over Cesario, inspected the sand painting, smiling and rubbing the shoulders of the children, looking down at them with pride at how strong they seemed to be.

"We'll do this at the Mission over the.. Grave-place . .when we can be alone with you. The Padres will probably try to remove it but if we plant flowers all over it and around it, they might accept it as just a design."

She felt coughs starting to rise and knew that more blood would come this time. He understood her hand signals to remove the children before the attack came.

"I must sleep, my loves." Holding onto the choking and covering her mouth with her hand as Miguel led Juana Maria and Cesario and motioned Clementina to follow.

The children had seen these episodes of coughing followed by blood on her hands and sheets enough times to know when to leave so mama wouldn't cry and seem ashamed.

Miguel whispered "Sleep, my love." as he closed the door. Tuipurina closed her eyes, knowing that the end was very near. The blood increased each day, No medications, hers or theirs, worked. She'd seen this process in her people for more than twenty years. The racking pains became ever louder with deeper convulsive waves from her lungs and throat. She could see the darker wetness soaking the rags that she kept under her pillows. In exhaustion she sank back and her world submerged in a churning sea of pains.

In the night Miguel slid into bed beside her and kiss her brow. "I love you. I always love you"

"I love you and the children. I don't want to leave you."

"You are always with us, and your people. I know you think about them always. About their survival."

"Yes, I do." Closing her eyes against his shoulder. Loving the warmth of his body and his heart. His spirit.

In the same moment, five hundred miles apart, Nicolas Jose and Tuipurina formed a thought in the night.

'I will leave this world soon.' Praying in two merging disciplines in the sky. 'If my spirit can go anywhere, I will see my ancestors' spirits survive. That my spirit survives to bless our offspring. My own and those of my people. That Iitaxxum survive.'

Golden Eagles', Condors' and Butterfly's Spirits hovered above both places.

1800

Darkness spread across the newly tilled fertile Central California valley two hours before the crew's bedtime. Nicolas Jose had a troubling storm of questions in his mind. He fought off the old need for the strong red wine that the Rancho had produced for the San Jose region with great pride for the wealthy land owners.

In the year since his release and sale as an enslaved farmhand, his remaining strength had faded. He closed his eyes in remembrance of how he'd needed the dark liquid the Franciscans and soldiers called "The Blood of Christ." How it's many soothing gulps made it easier to forget the conflicts of those days and nights. How many long and deep swallows had made the unforgivable, forgivable.

There were many things in the past he wanted to forget, but tonight, forgetting was the last thing he wanted.

He slumped back on his mattress in the cramped room for six field workers that had never lost its ancient smell of sweat and urine. He squinted up at the ceiling through eyes that had lost their acuity.

His bones and muscles ached and cramped often after many agonizing days work in the fields and pastures. He left the evening meal early to have time alone in the group's room before the other workers came.

He watched his hand silhouetted against the grays of the small window. The shaking from his tremors that came and went showed strongly against the slight remaining light. He dreaded carrying his cup and plate to the mess table fearing the liquid or cornmeal would spill before he sat and the other men would notice his tremors. He'd been seen as a traitor, a hero, a hated and loved symbol, but now, only as a useless and unreliable old man. The men would joke about him even more than they already did.

'So she really died,' after having heard dozens of false rumors over the years about her fate. That she was a Grand Lady of power in Monterey or France. That she'd become a fugitive from the invaders, leading hit and run attacks in the deserts, or that she'd become a spiritual leader, either Naturist or Catholic in a distant forest or mountain hideaway.

This time it seemed confirmed. An Indio soldier who'd passed through from Los Angeles told him. There were many details that gave the story credibility.

"I was at the founding of the Town of the Angels," he mumbled to the soldier's disinterest. "I am so ashamed."

The soldier said that he was told that she'd borne three children. The disease that claimed her was the same as the one that had killed most of Nicolas' friends and acquaintances. He wondered, as he did often since his exile, if any of his children, or grandchildren, had survived. There was no way of knowing. Few from those days still lived.

He closed his eyes, remembering the winding long ago paths that he'd tried to close off. He dug back for the conversations, glances and struggles that linked him forever to her. It was the greatest loss of all to his fragile world.

'She was the greatest loss to the world of The Earth, Sky and Moon. To all of the Elements. To all the worlds of Spirits and Continuum,' he formed.

She was younger. He never expected her to pass before he did, but there was enough fact and detail to feel it was true. The brightest light in the moonlit sky and strongest force of his life was among the departed.

"Bless you, for Eternity." Whispering in Latin in the Invaders' way and quickly feeling the inadequacy of it in the history of their lives. Of the times they'd lived through. None of it was blessing. It had all been a curse on 'The People of the Earth'

He whispered aloud in Tongva, pushing his will far past the ceiling, clouds and sky.

"Tehoovko'p'a' xaa Horuura'" Sending deepest blessings to her Beloved and Respected spirit.

The Eternal Bird-Spirits heard the prayer and committed it to the memory of the land.

1825

EL PUEBLO DE LOS ANGELES

Jose Vanegas was overjoyed that the Mexican revolution had finally sent their soldiers to finally kick the Spanish out of their offices in town and get sworn statements of loyalty to the new Government of Mexico.

His eight children had produced twenty-seven grandchildren and one great-grandchild was on the way. His second wife, Maria Victoria Valdez, now had a two year old by him and he still felt like making more.

He'd had a good life, looking out over the town center and Plaza from his hillside balcony. It was expanding in all directions, particularly to the West, out of his view.

The cattle and wheatfields were spreading almost to the ocean.

As the first Mayor of Los Angeles, as it was called for short, and elected again twice, and commuting back and forth to San Diego four times in the last three years, he'd now decided and told Maria.

"I'm going to move to San Diego. The new kids are there. The church is better. The ocean views are better. It's too dry here in the October heat. My love. We're moving to San Diego!"

1826

The town's officials, without Tongva representation, sold to German investor Johann Grogegnan the last remaining parcel of land of Yaanga, hemmed in on all sides by the town's growth.

He evicts the remaining Tongva to wander homeless.

1835

In the 1835 New Census of the greater Los Angeles Pueblo Holdings, 526 'Gabrielino' Indians were counted. Over 6,000 Tongva were buried under the Los Angeles land since the Spanish Occupation.

EPILOG

San Carlos Boromeo Mission records show the marriage of Manuel Montero to Regina Tuipurina Montero, also spelled as Teipurina, and the birth of four children to them. She lived to thirty-nine years, dying in 1799. Her name and versions of her history were translated as 'Toypurina' in English language stories. Her surviving offspring use Teipurina or Tuipurina. All of the versions of her name seem like Latinizations. I used the name Tooypor because it did not seem inconsistent with the known, at this time, Tongva patterns.

Nicolas Jose is shown as deported in accounts to either prisons at Presidio San Diego or Presidio San Francisco. I've found no accounts of his later life.

Both of them are legends in the rebirth of their nation. The Tongva/Gabrielino people have a growing identity and organizations throughout Southern California.

WWW.TONGVA.COM
WWW.GABRIELINO.COM
WWW.TONGVA.GABRIELINO.COM

The village of Shevaanga lies under parts of San Gabriel and Alhambra. There are now monuments in the park outside the Mission to the "Gabrielinos"

Sprawling Yaanga's artifacts show how the village spread and contracted through the centuries, from Figueroa and Adams, up through Bunker Hill, Taylor yard and west toward Echo Park.

Haapchivet was nestled in the hills above Tujunga. Pimog-na was near Pomona, Asuks-gna was near Azusa, Cahuen-gna was against the Hollywood Hills. Every community in the Los Angeles basin has one of the more than two hundred Tongva villages buried under it.

Afro-Spanish Juan Maria Pico fathered two of the great figures of California history. Pio Pico, Governor of the State of Alta California and the independent Republic of California before the U.S. invasion. Andres Pico was one of the finest and most imaginative Generals of his time. He led the Californian cavalry to surprising victories over the superior armaments and numbers of the American invaders.

The Spanish Crown gave large land grants in Southern California to Alvarado, Verdugo, Dominguez, Nieto and many of the soldiers who did duty at Mission San Gabriel and Pueblo de Los Angeles.

In 1949 my fifth grade teacher announced that the Native Americans of the Los Angeles basin were 'extinct.' My classmate, in 1949 West Los Angeles, Socorro, was 'Gabrielino.' "We are not extinct!" She said in her shy way.

We talked at recess. I'd been reading about the Cavalry's Destruction of the Apache Nation and was angry at the teacher's statements that the Natives, the word 'Tongva' wasn't in use then, had no culture, only grunts for language and were primitive root diggers. We made little signs and picketed the teacher. A Latino boy joined us in predominately WASP West Los Angeles.

In my neighborhood prospective homeowners had to sign "restrictive covenants" attesting that no Catholics, Jews or non-whites would own property there. With a name like Boyd, my parents, with a Jewish mother, noisily broke the covenant and overturned it in court. We found ourselves picketed the next week by children of parents with resentments over the case and in support of the teacher, calling us "Commies," "Race Mixers" and "Un-American" whereas no one could be more American than Socorro.

Ten years later Thomas Workman Temple wrote an account of "The Witch, Toypurina," the rebellion and trial. Some of it echoed Engelhardt's "Catholic Footsteps in California" and Temple's translation of the "Diligencia," the transcript of the trial. It has had more accurate translation since then, notably by Professor Steven Hackle. The previous translators' points of view tended to reflect their attachment to Eurocentric 'Christian' supremacy.

My sense is that all of the trial, like so many in recent history, was doctored to give the impression of a functional administration, good and accurate translation and disunited opponents to the administration in power.

My work is a work of fiction, not of strict historical accuracy. There is no record of the true name of the Latinized "Toypurina" or "Tuipurina,", There is no record of the details of the rape and kidnap of the chief's wife, his killing and beheading, the display of the head at the Mission gate and the recovery of his head. Only that such things had happened and were documented. Several situations and characters have been combined.

Much of the original Tongva language is in process of being reconstructed by scholars such as UCLA linguist Pam Munro. I've used various sources, some contemporary and some archaic. I don't claim linguistic accuracy. There are many ' signs for glottal stops and many competing spellings of place names. There is disagreement on whether hoops were a part of Tongva games and in descriptions of some rites and customs. There is not consensus on some religious and animist details. I try to not be disrespectful.

I take the assumption that histories are told by the victors in order to make themselves look good and righteous. The collateral damage of whole cultures is minimized or ignored. It's a tale that continues in the 400+ years long process of European and, recently, American colonization and subjugation of cultures of the Americas, Africa, Asia and the Middle East. These stories are in mid-course and have not reached their end. The outcomes are becoming and will become a major change in how we see the world and ourselves in the not too distant future. There aren't infinite sources of funding and nationalities' remember us..

Special thanks to Professors: Steven Hackle, Jonathan Jackson and Paul Apodoca, Tongva Professor Cindi Alvitre and spiritual advivor Jimmy Castillo and to Anthropologist Chester King. To Linguist Pam Munro and the linguistics team. To Tongva activists; Linda Gonzales, Barbara Drake, Craig Torres, Kat High, Mark and Anthony Morales, Mark Acuna, Angie Behrn, L. Frank Manriquez, Tonantzin Carmelo, and long ago: Dee Garcia and Socorro Doremi. Also Jamie Masrtinez Wood and Ignacio Oliveros.

WGA Reg.# 1229692

CPSIA information can be obtained
at www.ICGtesting.com
Printed in the USA
LVHW080317120121
676270LV00013B/256